"It killed them all," the knight whispered, half-unconscious due to the strain of his own outburst.

"What?" Kaz froze. He looked at Darius, but the knight was nearly asleep. "What do you mean, 'it'? The goblins did this, didn't they?"

The knight's eyes flickered open, but they looked beyond the minotaur. "Not the . . . the goblins. They found me . . . after it threw me. I was lucky; it . . . it seemed anxious to leave. Paladine! Its skin was as hard as stone! The wings! They—"

"Wings?" Kaz shivered, recalling the thing that had flown over his head one night. He had been that close to it! "What sort of beast was it?"

Darius succeeded in focusing on his benefactor. "Not a beast . . . not exactly. The lords of the earth. The children of light and darkness."

The litany was familiar to Kaz, something that he had heard countless times during his life. It was how some ancient bard had described . . . *No!*

"You can't be saying"—Kaz forced the words out—"a *dragon?*"

Darius grimaced as pain shot through him. "A dragon, minotaur—or something akin to a dragon! Something with huge claws, sky-encompassing wings, and jaws big enough to swallow a whole man!" The knight's face clouded over. "But . . . but it left their bodies . . . what it hadn't torn apart. I don't understand. It *was* and it *wasn't* a dragon."

HEROES SERIES

THE LEGEND OF HUMA
Richard A. Knaak

STORMBLADE
Nancy Varian Berberick

WEASEL'S LUCK
Michael Williams

KAZ THE MINOTAUR
Richard A. Knaak

THE GATES OF THORBARDIN
Dan Parkinson

GALEN BEKNIGHTED
Michael Williams

DRAGONLANCE® HEROES
Volume Four

KAZ THE MINOTAUR

Michael Williams

Kaz the Minotaur

Cover art by Duane O. Myers
First Printing: April 1990
Library of Congress Catalog Card Number: 2004101051

9 8 7 6 5 4 3 2 1

US ISBN: 0-7869-3231-7
UK ISBN: 0-7869-3232-5
620-96551-001-EN

U.S., CANADA,
ASIA, PACIFIC, & LATIN AMERICA
Wizards of the Coast, Inc.
P.O. Box 707
Renton, WA 98057-0707
+1-800-324-6496

EUROPEAN HEADQUARTERS
Wizards of the Coast, Belgium
T Hofveld 6d
1702 Groot-Bijgaarden
Belgium
+322 467 3360

Visit our web site at **www.wizards.com**

To Jennifer Ashley King,
niece and godchild,
who wasn't yet with us
when last I dedicated a book
to the family

KAZ'S JOURNEY

High Clerist
Tower

Vingaard
Keep

Village

Solanthus

Thelgaard

Ravenshadow's
Keep

Massacre

Village

Sardal
Crystalthorn

Xak
Tsaroth

Start

Qualinost

Chapter 1

They sat huddled around a small campfire, twelve and one. The distinction was important, because, although the twelve followed the one who was their leader, they despised him as much as he despised them. Only necessity and a matter of honor threw them together and somehow held them together for so long.

The one was an ogre, a coarse, brutish figure well over six feet tall and very wide. His face was flat, ugly, with long, vicious teeth, good for tearing flesh from either a meal or a foe. His skin was pasty and mottled, and his hair was flat against his head. He wore only a dirty kilt and belt. In a scabbard strapped to his back, he carried what would have been, for a man, a two-handed sword, but for the ogre was just fine for one: a trophy of war.

Stuffed into his belt, seemingly insignificant compared to the huge blade, were two knives. The ogre's name was Molok, and as he used his huge, bloody claws to tear meat from his portion of the kill, he surreptitiously eyed the others.

Most of the others, when standing, were a full head taller than the ogre, not that the fact disturbed Molok. He tore another piece of the nearly raw meat from the bone in his hand and jammed the morsel into his mouth while he watched the dozen minotaurs eat their own meals. Unlike the ogre, the minotaurs ate more slowly, carefully, albeit still with a certain savageness that would have unnerved humans or elves. There were nine males and three females, and all were armed. A couple had spears and three others' swords, like those their unwelcome companion carried, but the remainder carried huge, double-headed battle-axes. The males had horns more than a foot long, while the females' were a bit shorter.

The minotaurs were too at ease, Molok decided. That did not suit him. He wanted them agitated and anxious to be done with this task, if only so they would not have to travel with an ogre much longer.

"It's been near a week, Scar-face, since you found any trail." Molok picked a piece of meat out from between two yellowed fangs. "Is it maybe that the coward is craftier than you? Be he your *better?*"

At the sound of his gravelly voice, all twelve of the minotaurs looked up, the fire giving their eyes a burning, haunting look. One minotaur, whose ravaged features bespoke many fierce combats, threw his meat down and started to rise. A smaller one, female, grabbed hold of one arm.

"No, Scurn," she said quietly. Her voice was deep, but for a minotaur, it would have been considered quite pleasant.

"Release me, Helati," the one called Scurn rumbled. His voice was like the low, rolling thunder before a great storm. The battle-axe he used, which lay next to him, was huge even for one of his kind. Molok had seen it wielded most effectively, but was not concerned. He knew how to manipulate this band. Had he not kept the chase alive for over four years now?

"Easy, Scurn," muttered another minotaur next to Helati. These two bore a strong resemblance to one another. Hecar was sibling, brother, to Helati. They were the weak links as far as the ogre was concerned. Over the four years, they had gone from dedicated pursuers to abject admirers of the renegade the band sought. The renegade that these minotaurs could never return home without.

The scarred minotaur settled down, but Molok saw that he had already accomplished his purpose. He had stirred things up. As always, the band began to talk about the latest setback.

"Cannot deny that Kaz is crafty."

"Even cowards have minds!"

"Coward? He survived the lands of the Silvanesti!"

"Scurn said that was just a rumor, didn't you, Scurn?"

The ravaged head tipped forward briefly. His horns, even in the light of only a single moon, Lunitari, were quite plainly worn from action. Scurn was a fighter, one who, if his mind had been as strong as his body, would have been leader of his people by now. Scurn was headstrong. He was perfect for Molok's purposes.

"Kaz never journeyed into the lands of the Silvanesti," Scurn snorted in derision. "He's a coward and dishonorable. Just another ploy to throw us off the trail."

"Which he be doing all too well," added Molok casually.

Scurn glared at him with blood-red eyes. He wanted to take the ogre by the neck and squeeze until the life was gone. He could not, however. Not, at least, until their journey was over and Kaz was either dead or captured. "You've been of little help to us, Molok. All you are good for is telling us how bad we are. What have you done to speed up this Sargas-be-damned quest? We are as sick of staring at your mongrel face for the past four years as you are of staring at ours."

Shrugging disinterestedly, the ogre bit off another chunk of meat. "I was told that you be great trackers, great hunters. I see nothing so far. I think you be losing your edge. Does your honor mean so little to you? What about Tremoc? Would you be less than him?"

The ogre liked to bring up Tremoc at times like this. It was a favorite minotaur tale. In the name of honor, Tremoc had crossed the continent of Ansalon four times in his quest to bring the murderer of his mate to justice. The pursuit had lasted more than twenty years. It was a useful story for two reasons. First, it reminded his bullheaded companions of dedication and what was most important in their lives and, second, it urged them to renewed efforts. None of them wanted to be doing this for twenty years.

He had stirred them up enough. Now it was time to get them thinking about the hunt. "If not among the elves, Scurn, where be he?"

It was Hecar who answered. "Whether or not Kaz journeyed to the lands of the Silvanesti elves—which he could have—he probably turned west."

"West?" Scurn glanced at the other minotaur. "Qualinesti? That's as foolish as entering the lands of the Silvanesti!"

Now it was Hecar who snorted. "I was meaning Thorbardin. The dwarves are more likely to leave him alone. He can go from there to the land called Ergoth."

Studying them both, the ogre said nothing. He was interested in hearing what the scarred minotaur's response would be.

Scurn rose, tore off a piece of fat and gristle from their catch, and tossed the piece into the low flames. The fire shot up, a sizzling, spitting sound erupting where the fat melted away. The disfigured minotaur laughed, an ugly sound.

"You are either growing stupid or you have come to admire Kaz so much for his ability to run and hide that you are trying steer us away!"

Hecar started to rise, and it looked as if the two creatures would come to blows. Many of the others began to grow agitated, snorting loudly in their excitement. Helati, once more trying to be peacemaker, quickly rose in front of her brother, facing him.

"No, Hecar!" she hissed quietly.

"Out of my way, female," her brother muttered through clenched teeth.

"Scurn will kill you," she whispered. "You know that!"

"My honor—"

"Your honor can take a little punishment. Remember, it is the wise minotaur who knows when to pick his battles. Another time, perhaps."

"I will not forget this. The others—"

Despite their difference in height, she somehow managed to look him straight in the eye. "The others know full well that you can defeat any of them any time."

Hecar hesitated. He glanced briefly toward the ogre, who appeared to be busy examining the bone he held on the off chance that it still held some shred of meat, and snorted quietly. Nothing is certain about that one. Finally he nodded and sat down. Helati joined him. Scurn gave him as much of a triumphant grin as a minotaur's bovine features could. What his expression mostly consisted of was a showing of sharp teeth. Hecar could barely contain his fury.

"Kaz will not go west, nor will he go east. He will stay in the south, hoping to evade us." Scurn turned toward Molok for agreement.

The ogre gazed at the minotaurs around him as if only just now remembering he was the instigator of this heated argument. It was time to settle things, Molok decided. Wiping his hairy paws on his kilt, he reached down to a pouch between his feet and pulled out a crumbled piece of parchment. With one fluid motion, he tossed it at Scurn. The startled minotaur succeeded in catching it before a sudden burst of fire scorched both paper and his own hand.

"What is this?"

Molok cracked open the bone he had been picking over and began sucking the marrow. Frustrated, the minotaur unfolded the sheet and tried to make out the markings in the dim, flickering light of the flames. His eyes widened, and he looked angrily at the ogre.

"This is a proclamation signed by the Grand Master of the Knights of Solamnia himself!"

There was renewed muttering on the parts of the assembled group. After four years of pursuing their quarry through the lands of humans, they now knew more about the Knights of Solamnia than any others of their race did, save Kaz.

"What does it say, Scurn?" one of the other minotaurs asked impatiently.

"The Grand Master offers a reward for several beings of various races. One of them is Kaz!" The last was said with total disbelief. "He is wanted, it says, for conspiring against the knighthood, specifically, the planned assassination of the Grand Master himself. There is also mention of murder here, but it does not specify whose and when." Scurn's tone indicated that he was a bit confused about what he had just read.

"Then he is wanted by the knighthood as much as he is wanted by us," someone stated.

"Where did you get that proclamation?" Hecar snapped at the ogre.

Molok shrugged. "I find it yesterday. It had . . . fallen . . . from the tree that someone had posted it on, I think."

"Why would the knights demand Kaz? He was their comrade!" one of the other females asked the group as a whole.

"As are some of these others," Scurn added. He tossed the parchment to one of the other minotaurs, who started reading it slowly. The minotaurs prided themselves on the fact that, of all races save perhaps the elves, they were the most literate. While physical strength was the final arbiter in their society, knowledge was the tool that honed that strength.

"The knights are mad!" Hecar muttered. "Have they given a reason?"

"Have they given a reason for anything we have seen in the time we have pursued Kaz?" Scurn glanced around. "They may have a reason; they may not. There are names on that proclamation that were their staunchest allies in . . . in that time."

"That time" was a war that the minotaurs were doing their best to wipe from their memories. More than one gave Molok a look of bestial hatred. The minotaurs had been slave-soldiers to the ogres and humans who had followed the dark goddess, Takhisis, in her struggle against her counterpart, the lord of light, Paladine. The Knights of Solamnia had represented that god, and in the end, it was one of their number, a Knight of the Crown named Huma, who had literally forced the goddess to capitulate. Only one other who had witnessed the costly victory had survived.

Kaz. Very few actually knew what part he had played in the final battle. Humans did not care to glorify what they tended to think of as a monster. The other minotaurs had pieced the story together over the years, though some, like Scurn, denied its plausibility.

"If the Knights of Solamnia want his head," the mutilated warrior began, "then he will surely stay in the south, where their presence is weaker."

Many of the others nodded. Molok looked at each and every one of them and then shook his head. "After four years, you know nothing. Even you who knew Kaz."

He received twelve steady glares, which he ignored, as usual. "The knights be acting strange. His friends be now his foes, even the Lord of Knights, who, if what we learned be true, called him comrade in the war."

There was a pause. He had their full attention now. "Kaz will go north—north to Vingaard, I think."

It was fortunate that the land they presently roamed was empty of settlements, for the shouts that rose among the group could no doubt have been heard for miles around. It was finally Scurn who quieted the others—Scurn and Hecar.

"The Knights of Solamnia may have become twisted, Molok," Hecar blurted, "as we have seen time and again, but do not make Kaz one with their madness. Despite all else, he is still a minotaur!"

Scurn nodded. Even he did not believe their prey was enough of a fool to head north.

Molok retrieved the proclamation and glanced at it one last time. With a toothy, predatory smile, he thrust it into the fire. After watching it burn to ash in mere seconds, he looked up once more at his companions . . . his hated companions.

"He be no fool. Never said he was." Molok reached down, gathered his few belongings, and rose. He gave the minotaurs a look full of contempt for what they were. Even now, no longer slave-soldiers, they needed an ogre to lead them around by their ugly noses. "He be Kaz, though, and that be why he will go north to Vingaard. He needs no other reason."

The ogre turned and stalked away, a disturbing look on his face, hidden from the minotaurs.

Chapter 2

I should go west, Kaz thought grimly. West or remain in the south.

He snorted as he glanced back at the path he had been following. The sun was high in the sky, making it possible to see quite some distance. *So why am I continuing north, when each day brings me nearer and nearer to Vingaard Keep and whatever madness has descended upon the Knights of Solamnia?*

His mount, the giant war-horse that Lord Oswal himself had bestowed upon the minotaur as a token of his appreciation, nickered impatiently. After five years with Kaz, the animal had picked up rebellious tendencies that would have shocked the more formal knighthood. In many ways, the horse was a reflection of its master.

Kaz quieted his mount and stared at the proclamation once more.

It was the fifth copy he had seen of this particular one, and it made no more sense to him now than it had the first time he had read it. Lord Oswal was a friend, a comrade. The elder Knight of the Rose, made Grand Master after the death of his brother, had even given Kaz a seal permitting him safe passage in any land that respected the might of the Solamnic Order. Yet now this same comrade was making unsubstantiated accusations of crimes Kaz had supposedly committed!

The notices had only recently reached the southern lands. Kaz snorted. He glanced at the other names listed as outlaws along with his. Some he recognized, such as that of Lord Guy Avondale, the Ergothian commander who had aided in the final battle against the renegade mage, Galan Dracos, and his dark mistress, the goddess Takhisis. Huma had always spoken well of the man, once going so far as to say that Avondale deserved to wear the garments of a Solamnic Knight, so admirable was his individual code.

With a snarl, the minotaur ripped the sheet from the tree. *Conspiracy and murder?* He crumpled the paper up tightly and tossed it into the underbrush.

Kaz led the war-horse by the reins to a more secluded spot to the left of the path and leaned against one of the trees to wait for someone. Patience was not a habit he had been successful in cultivating during his life so far, and what little he did have was just about used up from waiting.

"Paladine's Blade, Delbin!" he muttered under his breath. "If you don't make it back in the next hour, I'm moving on!"

He could only imagine what sort of mischief his companion was getting into in Xak Tsaroth, the city a few miles due west. Xak Tsaroth bordered southwestern Solamnia and eastern Qualinesti, the land of the elves, and was a center of commerce linking north and south. Kaz had hoped his companion might be able to purchase a few of the things they needed. He also hoped that Delbin would be able to overhear some gossip that might explain the Sargas-be-damned rumors floating in from the regions surrounding the knighthood's seat of power in Vingaard—rumors that could not—must not—be true.

But sending Delbin Knotwillow had been a risk at best. Kaz cringed each time his comrade of four months cheerfully volunteered for any task. It was that cheerfulness that unnerved the huge, powerful minotaur.

Delbin Knotwillow was a kender, and kender were born to mischief.

As if on cue, he heard the sounds of a horse. Delbin had departed three days ago, promising that he would return at the appointed time. If properly motivated, the short kender made an excellent spy. No one paid attention to a kender, except to check their personal valuables. Kender picked up a good deal of information, which they were all too willing to pass on to anyone who made their acquaintance. The kender thought this all one grand adventure, something he could brag about to his kin—and anyone else who would listen. After all, how many kender got to travel with a minotaur?

Kaz was all set to call out to his diminutive companion when he heard the second horse. He quickly reached up and took hold of his horse's muzzle. The war beast, trained for all combat situations, recognized the gesture and froze.

The trees obstructed the minotaur's view, but he thought he caught a glimpse of black. It was impossible to say whether what he saw was part of one of the riders or one of the horses. Either way, he knew by now that the newcomers were not his companion.

The riders slowed and then halted their mounts. He heard the clank of armor and the low muttering of the two men as they talked. Their words were unintelligible, but one was evidently angry at the other one. Kaz snorted quietly. This was a fine time and place to have an argument! If Delbin showed up now . . .

When he heard the third horse, Kaz was ready to look up to the heavens and curse every god. Another rider? Then he realized that this latest one was coming from the south. If this kept up, the minotaur planned to open up an inn. The location was obviously excellent, what with the heavy traffic.

The other riders grew silent. Kaz began reaching for his battle-axe, aware that at least one of the newcomers had started moving in his direction. One sharply clawed hand tightened around the lower end of the axe shaft. Only a few more yards of foliage and the rider would be upon him.

Kaz caught a glimpse of ebony armor as the rider suddenly turned his steed back toward the road. The minotaur's eyes widened. He had seen armor like that during the war against the goddess of darkness. He had served under men and ogres who had worn that armor and, near the end, had fought alongside Huma against some of the deadliest of them.

This was one of the elite, fanatical soldiers of the deceased warlord Crynus, commander of Takhisis's armies, who long ago had been dispatched to whatever dark domain his kind deserved by Huma of the Lance and the silver dragon. Kaz remembered the moment all too vividly. Crynus had refused to die; finally it had taken dragonfire to destroy him.

Regardless of the danger to himself, Kaz could not let one—no, two!—of the warlord's guardsmen roam about the countryside. It was not the first time he had come upon such marauders during the last five years. There were still a great number of the Dark Queen's servants who refused to acknowledge that their mistress had been utterly defeated. With nowhere to hide, they generally became traveling bands of thieves and murderers—all in the name of Takhisis, of course. The guardsmen were the worst; they still believed that she truly would return.

Kaz tapped the horse on the side of head, a signal that

he had learned from the knighthood. The horse would remain where it was until he summoned it. Nothing short of a dragon would make it move, and since there were no more dragons, there was no reason to worry.

Slowly, carefully, Kaz brought his axe around in front of him. Maneuvering his horse in this thick brush would have given him away. If Kaz was lucky, he might be able to bring down his opponent without a struggle, but . . .

The black figure before him abruptly stiffened, and Kaz knew he had somehow given himself away. A long, wicked blade, hidden from view prior to now, sliced a vicious arc through the air as his adversary half-turned in the saddle. Kaz brought his axe up to fend off the blow, but the guardsman had underestimated the distance between them. The blade jarred to a halt only halfway to the minotaur, its tip caught firmly in the side of a mighty oak.

Cursing, the rider tried to free his sword while simultaneously turning his mount. Kaz altered his grip on the axe and swung. The sword rose up to turn his blow from the rider, so that he struck the horse instead. Bleeding and excited, the animal fought its master for control. Kaz was forced to fall back as the huge beast reared and struck out randomly. The horse began to wobble.

The minotaur blinked. There was no longer anyone in the saddle. Now it was his turn to curse. He had forgotten how swift as well as deadly the ebony warriors could be.

A figure burst from the foliage beside him. Kaz parried the sword thrust, but lost ground in doing so. For the first time, he got a close look at his adversary. The man— he was too short to be an ogre, though possibly he was an elf—wore a face-concealing helm, but the eyes that peered out seemed to stare through the minotaur to some point well beyond. The soldier was building up to a berserker fury.

Briefly Kaz heard the sounds of a struggle coming from the path, but the other solider continued to harry him. An axe, especially a battle-axe designed for two-handed use by humans, was not a good weapon in such close quarters. Every time Kaz tried to back up, his opponent moved with equal speed and pressed yet another attack.

It was the woods that saved him. Almost unmindful of the world about him, the raging guardsman stumbled over the exposed root of a tree. It was not much of a delay—in fact, the soldier regained his balance almost immediately—but the hesitation gave Kaz the opening he needed.

He brought the axe around in one clean swing, his full strength behind it. There was no denying the power in that swing, for very few humans could approach matching a minotaur at full strength. Given the proper tool, a minotaur could chop a fair-sized tree down with one blow.

By comparison, armor was next to nothing.

The head of the axe caught the guardsman just above the elbow of his sword arm and kept going without pause. It tore into the hapless fighter's side and did not stop until its arc was complete. As Kaz stepped back, his foe, arm and trunk awash in red, toppled forward, the rage and life already gone from his eyes.

Kaz inhaled deeply. Up the path, the sounds of struggle had ceased, to be replaced by the growing clatter of several more mounted riders arriving from the south. Kaz had no way of knowing whether or not the others were friend or foe of the single rider.

No one shouted any commands, but Kaz heard a number of riders enter the woods. It wouldn't take them long to locate him. Wiping the blade of his axe, he hooked the weapon into place in his back harness. The harness was designed to allow him to carry the axe, sometimes two, at all times. Practice enabled him to unhook the battle-axe in seconds. It was a design suitable only for someone with a backside as expansive as a minotaur's, and with a reach to match.

He mounted the war-horse just as the first searcher spotted him.

"Stand where you are! In the name of the Grand Master, I order you to stay!"

Kaz twisted around and glimpsed the familiar and once respected armor of a Knight of Solamnia—a Knight of the Sword, if he read the crest right. The knight was on foot, having evidently been forced to lead his horse through the thick brush. Kaz turned away and urged his horse forward even as the knight called out something to his companions.

Long ago, Kaz would have stood and fought, likely taking a good half-dozen of the stubborn knights with him before dying from multiple wounds. Huma, however, had taught him the wisdom of avoiding conflict—and certain death—in some situations. The minotaur understood now the pointlessness of always taking a stand. Many of his own people would have thought him cowardly—not that they didn't already.

Under Kaz's guidance, the war-horse picked out a path that led deeper and deeper into the woods. That was his only hope for retreat. Kaz knew that such a path would take him closer to Xak Tsaroth, but to the north of that city, not directly east of it. Kaz realized, too, that he had probably seen the last of his kender companion. Of course, Delbin might have already forgotten him, anyway. There was also a possibility that the young kender had gotten caught in the knights' trap, for surely that was what it had been. They must have known about marauder activity in this area and had set up a trap of their own in order to catch the band by surprise. No doubt they would be disappointed in their catch: only two renegade guardsmen, at least one dead. If Delbin was a prisoner, he doubted the kender had anything to worry about. No one could possibly mistake any member of the kender race for a dangerous threat.

The knights were pursuing him in force now, though he dared not look back to see how close behind him they were. There had to be at least half a dozen, likely more, he estimated.

"Let's see how well you know this land," he muttered. He and Delbin had been scouting out this area for nearly a week. Indeed, they had crisscrossed this southern territory for nearly nine months. Always there was someone dogging their heels. Usually it was his own kind. "Be just my luck if I ran into *them* now," he added.

It was still too long until nightfall. Kaz would have to continue riding and hope that he lost his pursuers before the horse or his cover gave out. On maps, this land was not marked as heavily wooded, and the minotaur knew that in many spots the trees gave way to open fields quite abruptly. An open field would be the death of him. The knights might deliver him to Lord Oswal, but they were just as likely to deliver his body instead. The Grand Master's proclamation made it clear that Kaz was an enemy, and the Knights of Solamnia were not going to waste effort trying to capture a minotaur alive when dead was just as satisfactory.

He was putting some ground between him and his pursuers; that was evident from the slow dwindling of shouts. It was too soon to hope, however, because the order was not known for giving up easily. They might hound him for days . . . as if he needed still more following him in pursuit.

The horse stumbled over fallen limbs and depressions in the earth. The ground here was more treacherous, and a wrong step could injure both horse and rider. With a strength that brooked no argument from his mount, Kaz suddenly reined the horse to the right. The animal let loose with an irritated grunt and followed his lead. Kaz steered him around a precipitous drop, knowing that each second of delay was precious lost time. Once on level ground, he urged the war-horse on with a kick of his heels.

Kaz counted nearly up to thirty before he was rewarded by the echo of bewildered and angry cries. He heard at least two horses neigh madly and one man scream. The sounds of pursuit dropped off, but still not completely. He dared to glance briefly behind him. One knight still pursued, at some distance. His face was uncovered, and Kaz thought he looked rather young. He may have had a beard; it was impossible to say whether that was the case or whether he had merely glimpsed the knight's hair blowing in the wind. Kaz had no idea why he should care about the other's visage, save that he had almost expected it to be Huma.

An arrow shrieked past his head, embedding itself in a tree behind him. But it had come from ahead of him, not from behind.

Paladine, do you have something against me, too? What had Kaz succeeded in stumbling into now?

He was answered by the sight of several figures, some clad in green, others in black armor, moving to intercept him. These were undoubtedly the very same marauders the knights had been seeking to flush out. Kaz had unwittingly completed that part of their mission for them. Now he had to get out alive.

Desperately he turned his mount. One hapless attacker flew back against a tree, bounced there by the horse's left flank. The minotaur recalled the single knight still chasing him. He opened his mouth to warn him, but the knight's horse was already riderless; another arrow had marked the end of the determined young warrior. Kaz snorted furiously. Yet another futile death for which he would get the blame.

He fully expected a bolt in his back, but the marauders had their own problems. The other knights were catching up now, and the element of surprise was no longer on the side of the raiders. Kaz's eyes widened as he realized just how many knights had followed him. He was about to be enmeshed in the middle of a full-scale fight unless somehow he broke free.

An ugly figure dressed in ragged brown and green garments tried to pull him from the war-horse but received a skull-shattering kick from the animal instead. A few of the marauders and knights were already exchanging blows. A man with a sword was run down by a Knight of the Rose and literally trampled to death. Another knight was pulled off his horse by two black-suited guardsmen. Reinforcements from both sides were moving to join the fray.

"Paladine," Kaz hissed, "if I have done anything at all worthy of you in these last few years, would it be too much to ask to provide me with a path out of here?"

Kaz didn't expect an answer; after all, gods spoke only to clerics and heroes. Then a flash of white caught his attention. It looked like some kind of a white animal, whether a stag, bear, or wolf he could not say. Had Paladine actually heard him?

Unless Kaz departed instantly, the blood urge would overwhelm him and he would waste the last few precious seconds of his life hacking away at his adversaries, as did so many of his respected but short-lived ancestors. While he revered his ancestors, he had no intention of joining them in the land of the dead just yet.

So he turned his mount and rode madly in the direction of the white vision.

Kaz rode for a solid quarter of an hour before daring to slow down. By then, the sounds of combat had been left far behind him. He was now just northeast of Xak Tsaroth.

"I'm no coward," he suddenly whispered to himself and to whatever powers might be listening. Nevertheless, he still felt some misgivings. By rights, shouldn't he have stayed and aided the Solamnic Order in any way he could? Had he not betrayed his trust to Huma, a man he had admired as much as the greatest of his ancestors?

"My honor is my life." The phrase sounded strange now as he whispered it. It was part of the Oath and the Measure that Huma's order had sworn to follow. To a minotaur, it was one reason why the Knights of Solamnia had been held in higher esteem than any other human organization.

Maybe you could have explained honor to me, Huma.
He sighed, a very unminotaurish thing to do, and studied
his surroundings.

He was at the edge of a field of wild grass, which he
hoped would not suddenly reveal yet another dire
threat. If Kaz continued on in the same direction, he
knew that he would first come across an offshoot of the
mountain range that more or less ran the length of
Qualinesti. If he continued farther, he would find himself
in the densely packed forests of the elven land itself.
That, he knew with bitter satisfaction, was one choice he
did not have to ponder. After Silvanesti, he had no desire
to see another elf ever again. Let them stay happy in their
seclusion from the outside world. Kaz knew of a short-
cut. Delbin had told him of a river that ran north to Vingaard Keep. It meant passing through some mountains
and part of the vast forest of Qualinesti, but it would
lead him to his goal: Vingaard Keep, and a confrontation
with the Grand Master himself.

He found himself wishing the kender was with him, if
only to act as guide. Delbin knew the land well, but Kaz
could not afford to wait for the ever-cheerful little annoyance. Luckily, he carried Delbin's map.

Though he wouldn't admit it to himself, Kaz had
grown fond of the kender. Only a fool would have
pointed that out to him, however, for minotaurs are generally picky about their companions, and to admit be-
friending a pouch-picking, childish creature like Delbin
was tantamount to weakness.

With a grunt, Kaz urged his mount onward. He wasn't
going to get anywhere remaining where he was, contemplating everything under the heavens.

* * * * *

As the minotaur rode west, something stirred in the
high grass. It was pale white and hairless. The eyes had

no pupils and glowed scarlet. It remained in the tall grass as much as possible, hating, in some dim way, the light that burned in the sky. Its eyes remained fixed on the receding figures of rider and mount. When the figures were far enough away, the beast rose and began to follow. Standing, it resembled something that had once been a wolf—a wolf long dead, perhaps.

Fighting the searing pain of daylight, it began to follow the minotaur.

Chapter 3

At times, it seemed to Kaz that his life was nothing but turmoil. Following Huma's sacrifice and the war's end, he had hoped things would be different. His fellow minotaurs might have called him soft, dishonorable, but he no longer cared. The more he thought about the minotaur way of life, the less he liked it, which was not to say that the ways of humans, dwarves, elves, or even kender were any better.

The ride to the river was surprisingly without incident. If this river had a name, the mapmaker had forgotten to include it. Delbin had never said exactly where he had picked up his map, and Kaz, knowing kender, did not push the point. It served its purpose, and at least it was fairly accurate as far as landmarks.

The sun hung very low in the sky. Kaz estimated that he had perhaps a little less than an hour before it sank from sight. Lunitari was already visible above the horizon. Solinari, the pale white moon, would reveal itself later on. It would be a fairly bright night.

A river this size meant settlements and shipping along its length. That meant more people than Kaz really cared to encounter, but it was still the quickest route. For the time being, his best bet was to skirt the minor chain of mountains east of the river and just north of his present position. By the time the mountain range turned from the direction he needed to go, there would be forest, which would provide him concealment for nearly half the journey. He tried not to think about Northern Solamnia, which from what he had heard, was still a fairly desolate land. And if half the rumors were true, the knights were behaving strangely indeed.

He rode on. The mountains began to grow.

* * * * *

As the last vestiges of sunlight retreated before the night, Kaz began to wonder if he had made the right choice.

It was only a small range of mountains, and the mountains themselves were nothing in comparison to some of the giants he had crossed before. They were rather ordinary peaks. Yet he was disturbed by them in some way he could not decipher.

"Any magical weapons lying about?" he whispered half-mockingly to them. The minotaur's eyes widened as he realized that was what disturbed him—the memory of Huma, that final conflagration. Kaz could not look at a mountain without subconsciously remembering how it all started—the search for the legendary Dragonlances, the only weapons capable of defeating the hordes of dragons of the Dark Queen, Takhisis. They had found those lances, but only a couple of dozen at first. Kaz, rid-

ing along with Huma, had been one of the small band
that had first wielded them in battle. He was also one of
the few survivors of that band and the only one to see
Huma, in the last moments of his life, utterly defeat the
evil goddess, forcing her to swear an oath that she would
depart Krynn and never return. In the last five years, Kaz
had often gone out of his way to avoid getting too near
mountains. Granted, there had been times when it had
proven unavoidable, but he had always tried his best to
pass through them as quickly as possible.

Afraid of mountains! Kaz snorted in self-disgust and
urged his horse forward. Tonight he would sleep with his
head against one of these leviathans. The more Kaz
thought about it, the more determined he became. At the
very least, the minotaur would stand less of a chance of
being discovered by some other traveler. Kaz eyed the
looming peaks and tried to estimate how long it would
take him to reach the nearest one. Past nightfall, the
minotaur decided grimly. He would have preferred it
otherwise.

* * * * *

Under a tall, worn peak, Kaz made camp. At some
point, perhaps in the distant past or perhaps in the war, a
good portion of one side of the mountain had broken
away, giving it a toothy look. It reminded the minotaur
of his grandsire, a once-fierce bull who had survived to
great age despite a number of improperly healed injuries.
He dubbed the mountain Kefo, in his ancestor's honor. It
made sleeping under its shadow much easier.

After months of incessant kender chatter, it was odd to
rest with only the sounds of the night to keep him company. Kaz snorted. If he was beginning to miss Delbin,
then perhaps it would be better if he turned himself over
to his enemies!

"Paladine preserve my mind!" Kaz whispered wryly.

Delbin had come across him in the south, just after

Kaz had returned from a long, hazardous journey to the frozen lands in the extreme south. The proclamations from Vingaard were just appearing in the southern regions, but the unorthodox captain who had led the expedition and who had grown fond of Kaz gave him the benefit of the doubt despite the harsh accusations of murder and treachery that the proclamations spouted with no evidence to back them up. The seal given to Kaz by Grand Master Oswal of the knighthood only strengthened the minotaur's story of the truth. Besides, having a minotaur proved fortuitous, for the icy domains proved to be treacherous in more ways than one. A hardy explorer the human might have been, but after that one trip, when the soil of Kharolis, his home, was once more beneath his feet, he told Kaz he was looking forward to spending the rest of his days—and he was still a young man—in some nice, peaceful market haggling with customers over the price of apples or something.

A high, curious voice had asked, "Did you really come back from the ice lands? Is it true your breath freezes so hard there that you've got to melt it over a fire to hear what you said? I heard that somewhere! Are you a minotaur? I've never seen a minotaur before! Do you bite?"

At first Kaz thought the intense questioner no more than a half-grown human child with a long, thick ponytail. Only when the captain swore and reached for his gold pouch did the minotaur realize the horror that they were facing.

Delbin Knotwillow, Kaz thought in retrospect, *is probably annoying even to other kender*. Certainly they never seemed to come across any others—at least not for long. Delbin, who had stuck by the minotaur's side from that time on, plying him constantly with all sorts of inane questions about minotaurs and everything else, was a young male, handsome by his people's standards. He was slightly larger than most of his kind, perhaps an inch or two under four feet and almost ninety pounds. He considered himself studious and had taken it upon himself to write a history of present-day Krynn—a worthy goal, except that often when he reached into his pouch for his book, instead he pulled out an item that some clumsy human had apparently dropped. In the excitement of finding it, Delbin would forget all about the incident he had wanted to record.

Now the kender was likely somewhere in Xak Tsaroth or hopelessly searching for Kaz east of the city, unless something else had caught his attention. Or, for all the minotaur knew, Delbin was at this moment deep in Qualinesti looking for an elven horse, something he had always wanted to see.

Staring at the two visible moons, Kaz began to wonder if he was going to spend the entire night thinking about the kender or getting some of the rest he so badly needed. He hoped to have journeyed well into the forest before tomorrow evening.

Exhaustion finally began to overwhelm his senses. Nightmare visions of hundreds of curious and excited kender began to fade into the warm darkness of slumber. Kaz almost sighed in relief as at last he drifted away in peace.

*　*　*　*　*

He was standing before a great fortress that seemed to cling precariously to one side of the jagged peak. Creatures of all races lay dead or dying, and it was difficult to say who had been fighting whom.

"It's all over now," Huma sighed. Kaz turned to gaze at his friend and comrade. Despite his relatively young age, Huma's handsome visage was marked with lines, and his hair, including his mustache, was silver-gray. His face was pale, almost deathlike.

An inhumanly beautiful woman with gleaming tresses of silver stood at his side, her arm linked with the knight's. Kaz blinked. Every now and then, her face seemed to shift to that of a dragon.

"We won," she said sweetly.

"You have won nothing but death!" a voice cried.

The ground before the vast citadel burst open, and a fearsome creature with a multitude of heads rose before them. Huma pulled a Dragonlance from his scabbard, but the monstrosity only laughed. The woman at Huma's side melted and grew, wings bursting from her delicate back. Her slender arms and legs gave way to misshapen limbs that could only belong to a dragon. A symbol of majesty, she flew into the air and challenged the horror that Kaz realized must be Takhisis, the dark goddess.

Takhisis laughed mockingly and burned the silver dragon in midflight. A shower of ash, all that remained of Huma's love, scattered in the breeze created by the goddess's massive, leathery wings.

Takhisis laughed even harder. Kaz uttered an oath to his adopted god, Paladine. The heads of Takhisis were not the heads of dragons, as the minotaur had thought at first. Instead, most were human. One was incredibly beautiful, so that even Gwyneth, the silver dragon, was ugly by comparison. Takhisis the seductress. Turning his gaze from that visage to another did not help. The next head was the ebony-helmed visage of the mad warlord, Crynus. Spittle ran down his chin. Another was the head of the sorcerer Magius, Huma's childhood friend, who had died a prisoner of the Dark Lady's servants.

Yet another, this one the gaunt, deathly visage of a Knight of Solamnia, made both Kaz and Huma gasp. This was Rennard, he who had helped sponsor Huma to the knighthood and who, in the end, had been revealed not only as the lad's uncle, but also as a treacherous cultist serving Morgion, god of disease and decay. Rennard had died horribly after failing in his mission to kill both Lord Oswal and Huma. Morgion was not a forgiving god.

The worst was last. Towering above the other heads, even that of the temptress, was one that Kaz had never really seen, but knew without having to hazard a guess. Grinning like a death's-head, the long, narrow face swelled until it was almost as large as the rest of the abomination itself. Human was a term one could only loosely apply to it, for the skin had a slightly greenish tinge to it, and Kaz could see an elaborate network of scales, like those of a snake, covering it. The hair lay thin and flat against the head. The teeth were long, sharp, and predatory.

"Dracos," Huma muttered. "In the good graces of his queen once more." He shifted his grip on the Dragonlance, the only weapon ever to defeat Takhisis, and to Kaz's horror, held it out for the minotaur to take.

"What—what's this?"

Huma smiled at him sadly. The young-old face was drawn and white, as dead as ghostly Rennard's. "I cannot do any more. I'm dead, remember?"

As Kaz watched in horror, his comrade was caught up in the wind and scattered like ash all around. In seconds, there was not a trace left.

"Minotaurrrr. Wayward child. Time to come back to the fold."

He looked up at the leering faces and was gripped by an overwhelming panic. Despite a part of him that cried out at such cowardice, he turned and tried to flee, only to discover that no matter how hard he ran, he only seemed to be drawing closer to the five-headed beast.

The Knights of Solamnia were there, but instead of aiding him, they were jeering. Lord Oswal and his nephew Bennett, their hawklike features so identical it was uncanny, watched his struggles with as much interest as if they were studying an ant on the ground.

"I've never seen a five-headed dragon before," a familiar voice commented happily. "Will each head take a bite out of you? Does it have five stomachs? Is something wrong? Kaz? Kaz?"

The heads, maws open and grossly exaggerated in size, dove toward him.

The last thing he heard was a voice asking, "Kaz, do you want me to leave you alone?"

* * * * *

With a bellow, Kaz sat up, eyes wide with horror. Something short and wiry fell backward, landing with a loud "Ouch!" on the rocky ground.

"Are minotaurs always this excitable when they wake up? Maybe that's why nobody likes minotaurs! Well, I like minotaurs, but you know what they say about kender—well, they say something! I thought I'd never find you!"

Kaz rubbed his eyes, unsure whether the voice he was hearing was part of the nightmare from his sleep or a living nightmare instead. His eyes began to adjust to the light of the moons. Squinting, he ventured a hesitant "Delbin?"

Even in the darkness, he could still make out the kender's irreverent smile. "What're you doing here, Kaz? Did you ever see so many humans fighting each other? Was it like that during the war? I didn't get to see any of that! Grandfather said I was too young! Said I should leave serious business like that to the adults!"

"Take a breath, Delbin," Kaz replied automatically. After weeks of effort, he had finally been able to make the kender understand that there were times when it was absolutely necessary to shut his mouth, unless he wanted to chance making the acquaintance of the heavy fist of an enraged minotaur.

Delbin quieted, though it was always an effort for him to do so.

"How did you find me, Delbin?"

The kender gave him a triumphant look. "My grandpa, he could track something as small as a mouse halfway across Hylo—well, maybe not that far—and he taught me all sorts of stuff, so when I saw all those men fighting, I figured you'd either be trying to take them all on or you had gone! When I didn't find you, I remembered the river from the map, but you don't want to be seen any more than you have to, so that left the mountains, and you were easy to find after that, what with the trail you left behind! 'Course anyone but a kender like me would've never seen it, but I did!"

Kaz snorted. He had forgotten what explanations from Delbin were like, although this one was fairly straightforward for the kender. "You must have traveled nonstop."

For the first time, the cheerful look vanished from his companion's visage. "I was worried about you."

"Worried?" Kaz, unused to such sentiment from anyone, especially a happy-go-lucky soul like Delbin, grunted. Taking a deep breath, he tried to make himself look as huge as possible. "I'm a minotaur, Delbin! No reason to worry about me!"

"Well, you've been so good to me, letting me come with you even though I know I'm pretty young and maybe not as worldly-wise as some adult kender. That reminds me, I should write down what happened today, because this'll make a great addition to my book and show the others that I am smart and not a childish wastrel and—gee! This isn't my notebook, but it sure is interesting! I wonder how it got inside my pouch?" He started examining a small flat book that Kaz suspected the former owner had been searching for futilely for some time already.

The minotaur groaned and leaned back. Things were back to normal—or at least the kender variation of normal. Despite his annoyance with Delbin at times, he was forced to admit that things never looked gloomy when the effervescent kender was around. Confusing and irritating, yes, but not gloomy.

Suddenly he realized that Delbin had grown uncharacteristically quiet. Kaz raised himself up and eyed his companion. Where the bright-eyed and energetic kender had been now lay an exhausted, slumbering little form.

The day's chase had worn Delbin out completely.

Tomorrow, he decided with a yawn, he would try to say something nice to Delbin.

His eyes closed and in moments he was sleeping peacefully, the troubling dream already a distant fragment of memory.

* * * * *

Kaz woke to a chill morning and discovered himself in the shade of the mountains. An odd, brisk wind was dancing about. The minotaur stretched his stiff limbs and rose. Delbin still slept soundly.

It could not have been much later than dawn. If not for the blue of the sky, he would have assumed it was still night, so dark were the shadows of the mountain range. Kaz reached for his pack and searched for something edible. As usual, half the contents were missing. He knew that the vast majority would be located in the kender's pouch, where they had been put the evening before for "safekeeping." Hungry, he decided not to wake the kender just yet. He found some rations where he had tucked them in the lining of his pack, just as an extra precaution. The rations were tough and practically tasteless, but Kaz had gotten used to them long ago. He wondered if the kender had managed to locate any of the items the minotaur had asked him to purchase in the market. The temptation to go through his companion's pouch was powerful.

"I've got some fruit and baked sweets, Kaz," Delbin called out. There were times when the kender's ability to move so stealthily jarred the minotaur.

The kender began rummaging through his bag.

"If you happen to come across any of the things that I've lost lately, I'll take them off your hands," Kaz remarked innocently.

"Y'know, you should be more careful, Kaz. If it wasn't for me, you'd not have anything left!" The sarcasm of the

36

minotaur's statement lost on him, Delbin began tossing things to Kaz. The pile was astonishingly large and included more than one item that had never belonged to him. Half-buried in the pile were two large, ripe pieces of fruit and one somewhat battered pastry. Kaz retrieved the food and gobbled it up while he waited for his erstwhile companion to finish inventory. He was amazed to discover how much he had missed the taste of the sweet pastries that humans baked. Minotaurs scoffed at such delicacies as being for youngsters and soft races.

"My notebook!" Delbin held the battered book up for Kaz to see. Kaz wondered if there was anything written in it. Not once had he seen the kender actually scribble anything down. Delbin stuffed his prize possession back into his pouch, which somehow looked too small to have contained all of the kender's acquired treasures.

Since a seven-foot minotaur needed far more food than a not quite four-foot kender, Kaz devoured the rest of his allowance of dried rations. Somewhere along the trail today, he was going to have to hunt up some more food. Exhausted last night, he had failed to set any traps. Still, it was early enough that he might be able to catch something. Rabbits and other small animals seemed to be common in this region, more so than farther north. He suspected that the war in the north, which had dragged on for decades, had steadily pushed the wildlife either to the south or to the extreme north, where, while not untouched, the lands had suffered far less.

Kaz shook his head, scattering memories of the war. To Delbin, he said, "I'm going to try a little hunting unless you think they might be following us still."

Delbin pursed his lips in thought. The kender was trying his best to be useful. "I think—I think they won't be. Some men in Xak Tsaroth were talking about how the southern keeps are worried about Solamnia and what's going on and how they think they should send some men to speak with the Grand Master or at least his nephew, who, I guess, has a lot of say about it all and might even be Grand Master soon because some of the knights think the present one is ill and—"

All thought of hunting vanished at what the kender said. "Grand Master Oswal is ill?"

"That's what they said. It might be a rumor one old man said but a younger one thought it was true, and the nephew—I forget his name—"

"Bennett." Kaz's face grew grim, and he snorted angrily. Delbin hushed, having seen the minotaur in this mood before.

When Kaz had first met Bennett, the son of Grand Master Trake, the young, aristocratic knight had seemed little more than an arrogant tyrant. The final days of the war had seemed to change him, however, for Bennett had learned from Huma's sacrifice what a true knight should be. On the day that Kaz had finally parted company with the knighthood, Bennett had been one of those who had thanked him solemnly for his part in the final conflict.

There was an old saying among the minotaurs that warned of enemies who suddenly offered you their hand in friendship: One should always check for sharp claws first. Bennett, perhaps, had gone back to his old ways.

I should give him the benefit of the doubt, Kaz thought. *Huma would do that. But if I'm wrong. . . .* The minotaur's hands flexed as if gripping an imaginary axe.

Hunting was the farthest thing from his mind now. "Delbin, did they say anything about me?"

The kender shook his head. "They've got raider troubles, Kaz. A lot of the warlord's army came south, and I guess they thought this area would be good, though I don't know why. I always thought Hylo was much more pleasant, even though I really wouldn't want the raiders going there either. After all, they're not very well behaved, are they?"

"I find it odd that they came here at all. Why not northeastern Istar or the mountains of Thoradin?" Kaz shrugged. The marauders had no apparent leader and they had no real home. Eventually they would be weeded out.

"If they're not paying any attention to me, then we'll risk moving closer to the river. When we come to some settlement, I want you to go and buy—the key word is 'buy,' Delbin—some food for us. After we reach the woods in the north, we'll start hunting again. We should be able to gather enough to see us to Vingaard."

Eyes wide with anticipation, Delbin grinned. "You're really going all the way to Vingaard Keep? I've never seen it, but I hear it's got vaults and locks and hiding holes and—"

"Take a breath, Delbin. A deep one." As the kender clamped his mouth shut, Kaz's mind drifted to the journey ahead. He had everything planned out, and there was no word of his relentless pursuers. If nothing unexpected happened, the journey would be a safe one.

The minotaur grimaced. If he really expected it to be so easy, then there was no need for him to continue to carry the heavy axe strapped across his back. He would certainly be more comfortable if he left it behind. Kaz had other weapons better designed for any hunting they might have to do.

When the two of them rode off a few minutes later, however, the axe was still firmly in place in the harness strapped to his back. A single movement and it would be ready and waiting in his hand.

Just in case.

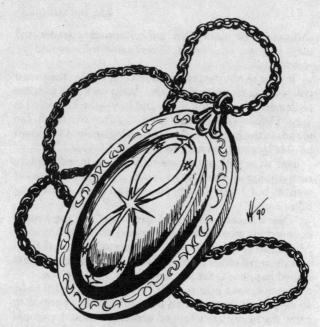

Chapter 4

"One day—" their instructor said proudly, "one day it will be the minotaurs who rule the world of Krynn. Our enemies will be crushed under our strength. They are, after all, barbarians, are they not? We are the race that shall rule. Only we can truly bring civilization to this backward land. Others have tried, but they have always lacked our determination, our discipline. We minotaurs have a destiny."

The young minotaurs huddled wide-eyed before the standing instructor. Zebak was not the best of orators, but he had the passion that counted when dealing with the young. It was his duty to spread the message to the children, so that they would begin to understand.

Another minotaur, not quite an adult, leaned through

the entranceway and signaled to Zebak. The elder nodded and dismissed the newcomer. The children knew the signal, having seen it at least half a dozen times. It meant that one of their masters was passing nearby.

Zebak began speaking of the art of war and how it should be the focus of a minotaur's life. As he progressed, another being entered the room. He was a toothy abomination, as far as the children were concerned, but then, the ogre probably cared as little for their looks. As the ogre studied the children, Kaz, sitting in the back, was not the only one who could not completely conceal his mounting hatred.

"A good class, teacher," the ogre commented, his voice rumbling. His expression was like that of one admiring a potential meal.

"I do my best."

The ogre gave him a strange look, one Kaz was too young to recognize. "So I hear."

Their visitor departed without another word, and the lesson continued.

The next day, Zebak had disappeared. An ogre trained them for the rest of the season. They were to be ready for their first combat by spring.

*　*　*　*　*

"Kaz?"

"Hmmm?"

"Is there something wrong? You keep staring off into the sky, which is pretty, I know, but the look on your face was strange, and I thought maybe—"

"I'm fine, Delbin. Just remembering." Kaz grunted. Now he was getting melancholy. Perhaps he was getting old.

"There's a place up ahead. I think it's a sort of village. There might be fishermen. Should I buy us some fish? I promise I'll be good. You'll see."

Kaz scanned the settlement. Perhaps five crude

houses—"houses" being a compliment to such ramshackle structures—sat near the river. Beyond the settlement and across the river lay the edge of the forest he had wanted to reach. High-pitched shouts made him tear his attention from the forest. A couple of human children ran in wild abandon around the houses. Kaz tried to picture young minotaurs in a similar situation but failed. Always there had been the training, even from the moment they began to walk. It was never too early to learn.

A couple of adult males were pulling a small boat in from the river. Kaz gave the boat a cursory glance; no minotaur with any pride would have bothered with such a decrepit piece of flotsam. It was a disgrace.

Someone spotted them. A cry rose up, and Kaz reined his horse to a stop. "Hold on, Delbin."

The kender looked at him curiously and, remarkably, said nothing.

Kaz waited until a fair number of people had gathered. There seemed to be three definite families and a few scattered individuals. From the fearful looks on their faces and the ragged clothing most of them wore, he suspected that they were recent arrivals from the north who had come here in the hope of starting their lives over. That raised them a notch in the minotaur's eyes. Many of the victims of the war had simply given up and were surviving, nothing more.

When no more joined the group, he urged the horse forward at a slow pace, Delbin following suit. Kaz suspected at least one or two other men were hidden somewhere nearby, watching his moves.

A graybeard with courage stepped in front of the others and said, "Come no farther, beast, unless you want to court death."

Kaz halted. Unless they had excellent archers, he knew that it would be a simple matter to wade into the villagers and disperse them. A swing or two of his axe would relieve them of any foolish souls. The urge to do just that was there, deeply embedded in the minotaur, but Kaz smothered it. Huma would have never forgiven him for attacking such people.

"I am Kaz, and this is Delbin. We come in peace, human. Perhaps to trade for some food, if you can spare it." Kaz tried to speak as softly as possible, but his deep, bellowing voice still made some of the weaker ones cringe.

Graybeard rubbed his buried chin. "You travel with a kender."

It was a statement, not a question, but Kaz responded regardless. "His name, as I mentioned, is Delbin, and he'll talk your ear off if you let him—or even if you don't. His presence alone should tell you I'm no threat, and I swear I'll keep him away from your belongings as well."

Kaz smiled slightly, aware that what he considered truly a smile would reveal far too many teeth for the humans' tastes.

"Let's kill him, Micah!" someone, a narrow, foxlike man, muttered. He had the look of an ex-soldier about him and was probably, judging by the others, the most dangerous of the bunch. Kaz's hand inched a little closer to his axe.

"There's no need of that." The voice was light and very female, as far as humans went, but one used to being obeyed, not out of fear but respect. A short, slightly robust female with long brown hair walked toward them from the direction of the river. She had large, dark eyes that reminded Kaz of those of his own kind and full lips that turned slightly downward, giving her a bit of a disapproving look, like an instructor.

Kaz found no treachery in her face and, gazing at her clothing, understood why. The gown was a simple coarse material, but that was not what attracted his attention. Rather, his eyes were fixed on the medallion hanging from her neck. The minotaur was long familiar with what was carved on the medallion, for he had seen more than a few of them during the war. A cleric of Mishakal, goddess of healing. Such a one was no threat, and her word was as good as any, probably better. Kaz moved his hand away from his axe.

"I still say we can't afford to take a chance," the ex-soldier muttered.

"If Tesela thinks we're safe," the graybeard chided. "then we're safe." He paused. "You meant what you said, didn't you, Tesela?"

She smiled, brightening an already sunlit day. "I meant it, Drew. There is no evil in this one, regardless of his race. Great confusion, yes, but nothing harmful—" the cleric paused and eyed the man who had protested— "unless someone provokes him needlessly."

The ex-soldier quickly shook his head. "I was only thinking—"

"I know, Korum."

"What about the kender?" Drew asked, frowning beneath his bush of hair. "Are you going to vouch for him as well?"

"Delbin will stay here with the horses," Kaz offered immediately. As the kender opened his mouth for what surely would have been a long-winded protest, the minotaur added, "Take a breath, Delbin."

His companion closed his mouth tightly and gave him as glowering a look as a kender was capable of. Some of the humans smiled in amusement and Drew nodded.

"Then you are welcome here for today, but I must ask you to leave by tomorrow."

"No worry there, elder. I plan to keep going as soon as possible." Kaz dismounted and handed the reins to a pouting Delbin. He turned back to the humans and found all of them, including the cleric, staring up at him in awe. They were only now just realizing how massive he was. Some of their fears were returning, and Kaz quickly tried to think of some way to set them at ease. He decided on surrendering his axe.

"You really have no need to fear me. If you like, I'll leave my axe here as a sign of good faith."

The elder was about to accept the offer when Tesela,

with a harried look suddenly on her face, spouted, "No! That—that won't be necessary."

"See here, cleric," the old man snarled. "We appreciate all your help in this past month, what with Gia and my wife becoming sick and all of us worn out, but you're a guest here as well. I wish you'd let me do what I was chosen to do."

The cleric looked downcast. "I apologize, Drew."

"Don't do that." The graybeard smiled. "When you do that, I feel as if I just cursed Mishakal herself." With a sigh, he turned to Kaz and said, "If she feels you should keep your axe, then I guess that's all right, although I can't for the life of me fathom what you might be needin' it for."

Kaz nodded his thanks. He was surprised that a cleric of Mishakal would speak on his behalf and countenance a weapon besides. A weapon was always a weapon, and to a healer like Tesela, it represented everything she worked against.

"Kaz?" Delbin was squirming in his saddle. "Can't I get off now? I promise I won't go near anything. Could I bring the horses down the river there so we can all get some water, because I don't know about them, but I could really use some. It's been a dry ride, and the sun was shining and I'd really like to—"

The minotaur looked at Tesela and the elder, and Drew nodded. "As long as he brings the horses downriver and keeps away from our things. We have little enough without a kender getting his sticky little hands on our things."

Delbin looked at his hands sulkily. "My hands aren't sticky. I even wash them on occasion, and I said I wasn't going to touch hardly anything because Kaz here doesn't like it, and—"

"Don't push your luck, Delbin. Be nice and quiet and go water the horses."

"I'll go with him," Tesela offered.

It was clear that Drew would have preferred that the cleric take charge of the minotaur, but he nodded permission nonetheless. With some hesitation, the gray-bearded man held out his hand to Kaz. "W-Welcome."

The minotaur's hand swallowed up the old man's. They shook and Kaz released him. Drew took a moment to make certain that his hand was still attached to his arm and then asked, "What will you be needing?"

Kaz rattled off a list of food and some basic goods he thought the small settlement might be able to supply him with. "I've got the gold to pay for it."

Drew nodded and began leading him toward the river-bank. "That will be greatly appreciated. We'll be able to buy a few things from the river traders and possibly even send someone down to Xak Tsaroth. We lost so much before and during our journey down here."

"You came from northern Solamnia?"

"From a place called Teal, west of Kyre."

"Kyre?" Kaz's eyes widened. "I fought near there—on the side of Paladine, of course."

The elder lowered his voice. "It would be wise not to mention anything about the war, no matter which side you fought on. There have been . . . troubles."

Grunting, Kaz said, "I hear disturbing things about Solamnia, elder, especially concerning those who dwell in Vingaard. I'd have thought the land would be on the way to recovery by now."

Drew's tone grew bitter. "It would be . . . if things had continued. At first the knighthood directed people in the rebuilding of their homes and the revival of the land. They spent their own money to buy food from those regions spared the greatest atrocities at the hands of the Dark Lady's minions, and they hunted down the scattered bands that refused to surrender. Things seemed well on their way. . . ."

"But?"

The old man's eyes grew vague, as if he were looking back into the past. "It wasn't just the knighthood, but those who lived near Vingaard as well. We can all understand bitterness and the fact that some people cannot return to a way of life the younger ones don't even remember. Did I tell you that I was once a merchant? Pfah! That's neither here nor there; my mind's going! You want to hear about the troubles. Hold on a moment."

At the elder's summons, a burly man with a bow came trotting over. "Gil, here, was our protection in case you proved dangerous. He was a master archer in Kyre, but you know what happened to that city. Now Gil is our chief procurer of meat. A better hunter you will never meet."

Despite his savage looks, the archer seemed to be a pleasant man who took Kaz in stride. "Elder Drew overstates my skill. With most of the woods to the north either dead or torn apart, the wildlife fled to these parts. I practically trip over game every step I take."

Drew shook his head in denial. "Our archer *underplays* his skill. I think Chislev, who watches over nature, or Habbakuk, who is lord over the animals, guides his hand. They know that he takes only what is necessary for food and never hunts for pure sport."

"As is only right," Kaz commented. He could see that the archer was a man of honor and fairness.

The elder explained Kaz's needs, and Gil said he would work on supplying them. With a nod to each of them, the hunter departed.

Drew watched him go. "You will find few men like him as you near Vingaard Keep, my minotaur friend. As I was saying, the aid stopped, not all at once, but so quickly that many were caught with nothing. The lands produced little food, and many of the forests were useless save as huge supplies of kindling. Then Vingaard began sending out its knights with a different mission in mind. With great efficiency, they began to gather whatever raw materials they could. They started demanding labor for the money spent. Those who could not pay, and that was most of the populace, were turned into serfs."

"Serfs?" Kaz could not believe that of Lord Oswal, or

even Bennett. The two were, in the end, believers in the Code and the Measure, and from what the minotaur had learned during his time with them, the enslavement of others was something that was forbidden. It was a law that Vinas Solamnus, founder of the knighthood, had himself created.

"I see by the look in your eyes that you disbelieve some of what I say, minotaur. Unfortunately, it's all sadly true." Drew's tone suggested that he had experienced much of this firsthand.

"I'm not denying your words, human. It's just that I have fought by the side of the Grand Master and his nephew. Whatever their faults, I can't believe they've slipped so far. You make them sound little better than the roving marauders."

"More like the greedy lords of Ergoth, I would have said, minotaur, but then I was a merchant in that land for some time. I fear, however, that the Knights of Solamnia will not stop there, as you yourself should know. I have seen the proclamation of the Grand Master, Kaz, and some of the others have as well, I'm certain."

Kaz felt his throat tighten. "And?"

Drew smiled, which did not ease the minotaur's anxiety. "A merchant learns to smell a poor investment if he wants to stay alive. I, for one, have no intention of trying to drag you back to Vingaard Keep, where I doubt they'd reward me anyway."

"How comforting," Kaz retorted. He was pleased with the former merchant's frankness, but something that he could not put his finger on still disturbed him about the human. But the elder was no magic-user, from the look of him. Kaz was wondering if his paranoia was acting up.

"I sometimes begin to wonder if it was not Paladine himself who was defeated, and that the stories of Huma of the Lance are just that . . . stories."

The minotaur shook his head. "They're true, for the most part, I suppose."

He found it hard to speak. The elder studied his inhuman visage for a moment and said quietly, "Yes . . . you were there, weren't you? I've heard one or two tales about Huma of the Lance that mention you. I get the feeling that most of the storytellers, however, dislike having a minotaur share the glory with one of their own kind."

"A lot of them cared little enough for Huma when he lived." Kaz grew somber as memories flashed by. For his part, the elder paced alongside silently, his gaze oddly anxious as he led the minotaur along.

They had reached the river. Drew hesitated, almost seeming to be torn between continuing on or turning around and returning to the others.

"I wanted to show you something and seek your opinion. Gil thinks it nothing but some animal, but I—I have seen too many things in the war."

Intrigued, Kaz allowed the human to lead him to a place perhaps a thousand paces north of the village. Trees now dotted both sides of the river. "What is the name of this river? My map did not say."

The elder shrugged. "I don't really know. We call it Chislev's Gift, but, believe me, that's strictly our name. We were so relieved to find such a wonderful location. I suspect that, if we hold out, this will someday be a fairly profitable site. It will mean some sacrifice, but we will do what we must."

"Spoken like a true merchant."

"It's in the blood. Here we are. Gil was the one who found it, but he thought it might be a good idea to show it to me, just to be safe."

"It" was a partial footprint on the damp riverbank. Kaz went down on one knee to study it better. If the footprint was made by an animal, the animal weighed at least as much as Kaz, judging by the impression. Not so much a paw as a foot, the print was obviously a couple days old, and this close to the river, it had suffered from the elements constantly. Kaz understood Drew's worry. Goblins and trolls ranged in this area at times, though there were fewer now than during the war. The front of the print indicated sharp, almost clawlike nails like those of Kaz himself, and the impression itself was facing *away* from the river.

"It crossed here."

"Crossed? It? It is an animal, then?"

"I doubt it." Kaz looked up. "You suspected a goblin or something, didn't you?"

Drew nodded nervously. "But Gil—"

"Your hunter may not have ever seen goblin or troll tracks, though I don't think it's a troll. It's too muddy to really tell." The minotaur glanced at the forest on the other side of the river. "Is there any way to cross the river?"

"We have some small boats and a pole raft."

Remembering the boats, Kaz opted for the raft. The odds were better that it could support him. The river was no monster, but it was always wise to respect the raw power of nature.

"While your people gather what I requested, I'll go take a look. It may be nothing, but I'll feel better knowing for certain."

"Gil found nothing."

Kaz snorted. "With respect to the human, I am a minotaur and a warrior from birth. I may be able to find something he . . . overlooked."

A sigh. "Very well. At the very least, it should help me to sleep a little better."

The minotaur gave him a toothy grin. "Perhaps . . . and perhaps not."

* * * * *

The river—Kaz could not bring himself to call it Chislev's Gift—proved much stronger than Kaz had imagined. Knowing his own strength in proportion to that of the humans made the minotaur admire Gil that much more. That did not mean that Kaz had changed his mind about the footprint. It belonged to no animal, although goblins and trolls, with apologies to the wildlife, were often lumped into that category based on personality alone.

He climbed aboard and cautiously pushed the raft out into the river. The pole was sturdy, for which he was thankful, and his progress was slow but steady. His thoughts turned to the possibility of goblins in the area. Kaz had a particular dislike for goblins. When he had been hunted by soldiers of the Dragonqueen for killing his sadistic ogre captain, he had fled into the wastelands, only to be captured by a band of goblins who had caught him unawares and kept him drugged.

Thinking about the past, Kaz forgot to pay close attention to his present situation and almost managed to lose the pole. The raft started heading farther downriver. Cursing, he regained control. When Kaz at last reached the other side of the river, he pulled the raft onto the bank and paused a moment to catch his breath. The current had taken him downstream a little farther than he originally planned, and he would have to hike back. Kaz wondered how the cleric was getting along with Delbin, then decided it was something he could worry about after he returned. He might find nothing, but on the other hand, he might find something.

He combed the riverbank opposite where the print had been spotted. When that proved fruitless, he moved farther north. A little more than a half a mile up the river, he found a second print. Enough of it was still visible for him to match it with the first. From there, he began the slow process of backtracking. It was simple at first. The goblin—Kaz had no reason to believe it was anything else—had made no attempt to hide its presence. The minotaur followed a trail of broken branches and crushed plant life deep into the forest, and then the trail broke off into several different directions.

Kaz grunted softly. There was more than one of them. Either the band had left this area for better hunting grounds or they were still somewhere among the trees. There were more than half a dozen, of that he was certain. If they were still somewhere nearby, Drew's people were in mortal danger.

It was at that point that Kaz realized his own jeopardy. He heard a movement to his right, little more than the shiver of a branch, but something within him, something developed over the course of his lifetime, warned him that the cause of the noise was neither the wind nor some small animal. Carefully, so as to avoid giving the watcher notice, he let his hand drift toward the handle of his axe. He cursed himself for not unhooking it sooner. His peacemaking with the village had put him off guard.

The other made a step toward him.

Kaz tugged his axe free and, without a sound, rose and whirled to the right. The battle-axe was poised, ready to strike.

"Delbin?" The glare he gave the kender should have shriveled his companion to nothing.

"Oops! I'm sorry, but I didn't want to cry out. After all, you looked so busy. What are you looking for? Tesela had to step away, so I thought that since I had been so good, you wouldn't mind if I went exploring, and when I saw that someone had left a boat lying around and you had gone off on the raft—"

The minotaur snorted angrily. "Take a breath, Del—"

At that moment, three huge forms charged from behind Kaz, taking him down before he could turn.

Someone with a deep, snarling voice cried, "The kender! Get the kender!"

There was some kind of a reply, but it was lost in the noise of the fight. Kaz, his face buried in the earth, succeeded in shoving one of his would-be captors away. Another one got an arm around his face, blocking his vision. Whatever he fought, it was as big as he was and almost as strong. It also had help, for the third one had a death grip around Kaz's legs, and despite his best efforts, the minotaur could not break it. But he would not die passively. With his free hand, he raked a face, then paused in startlement. His discovery proved costly, for the attacker secured his free limb and pinned Kaz to the ground.

"Your honorable surrender is offered. Will you give in freely?"

Kaz could not reply at first, since his snout was still pressed against the ground. Someone realized this and pulled his head up.

Reluctantly he answered by rote. "I submit to honorable surrender. Will you accept?"

"Accepted." Strong, clawed hands with firm grips pulled him to his feet.

He had been mistaken. He had assumed the footprints had belonged to goblins, but he had forgotten how many races left similar tracks. So much for his vaunted tracking superiority. Kaz had done no better than the archer, and to make matters worse, he had been captured.

By minotaurs.

Chapter 5

OF COURSE KAZ KNEW WHO THE MINOTAURS WERE:
They were the stubborn posse that had been pursuing
him for months over many miles.

Not one of the band of minotaurs was familiar to him,
though one eyed him as if they had met before. Kaz studied him but could not recall. The one who had demanded
his surrender, broad and a bit shorter than the others,
laughed harshly.

"He was right. He predicted that this one would go
north and that this was a likely spot!"

"A week of waiting around here," the one who was
binding his arms said gruffly, "and we finally capture the
coward."

"He did not fight like a coward," retorted the first

minotaur, the one Kaz felt he ought to recognize.

"It matters not, Hecar," argued the short male. "We know his crimes, and he'll have his chance to speak his case."

"Such as it is," completed the one behind Kaz.

Hecar snorted. "If I read the ogre right, Greel, Kaz will not have the chance to defend himself."

Ogre? Kaz jerked straight. "An ogre? You trust the word of an ogre?"

"Not just an ogre, criminal." Greel reached into a pouch at his side, then halted. "But we have no time for that now. It will take a good week's journey to reach the others, and we must be away before one of the humans discovers the duplicity of their elder and the archer."

"They *knew?*" Kaz fairly spat the words out. *Of course they knew! What a fool I've been!*

"An easy trap, coward. The war has made many folk pliable. Gold is still valuable, after all." Greel reached forward and pulled Kaz's pouch away. He studied the contents, pulling out a few items such as the Solamnic seal, and tossed the pouch on the ground. "We also have a proclamation of our own, like the one the Grand Master has issued, condemning you for murder and cowardice. But really, how many humans care about matters of minotaur justice? To them, only gold counts."

"The footprint . . ." Kaz muttered. *A trap!*

"Other settlements, other traders, have been made similar offers. You have run for far too long."

Kaz strained at the bonds.

"The bonds are tight," said the minotaur behind him. Huge hands, even for one of his kind, looped a noose over Kaz's head. It was lowered around his neck and tightened. "Struggle too hard and you'll choke yourself."

His eyes blood red, Kaz snorted, "Listen to yourselves! You pay off humans and take the word of ogres! You are bounty hunters, not servants of justice!"

He saw the fist of the short minotaur coming, but did not flinch. It caught him below the jaw and set his head ringing. He could taste blood in his mouth. Greel stared at him coldly.

"If the other races lack honor so much that they are willing to trade it for a few pieces of gold, it only proves their inferiority to our kind!"

"Even if you are the ones offering them enough gold to make them willing to betray their honor?"

Instead of answering, Greel whirled on Hecar. "Where is Helati? Where is your sister? Is one kender too much for her?"

"One kender is not," a new voice, strong and pleasing to Kaz, added disdainfully. "But a cleric of Mishakal is."

"The cleric? That—that—"

"Was it perhaps 'human' or 'female' you were about to say, Greel?" The minotaur who stepped into Kaz's range of vision was slightly shorter than Greel and had horns only half the size of any of the males. Muscular beyond the norms of most races, she was well formed for a minotaur. Kaz realized how long it had been since he had last seen a female of his own race. There had been none in the army he had fought with. Ogres believed in separating the minotaurs by gender as much as possible.

"I am no human, Helati, to be bothered by the fact that you are female. I have fought beside many valiant warriors of either sex."

Helati glanced Kaz's way and gave him a brief, sour smile. "Then do not underestimate the females of other races. Small she may be, but the cleric is gifted. I tracked the kender to the river, but I could not find him. I only barely escaped her notice. She senses something amiss."

"Clerics!" The leader snorted. "Weak, useless, simpering creatures—"

"You will see how useless they truly are *not* if we don't start back now. The farther we are from here the better."

Greel pointed at Hecar. "Help Tinos with the prisoner. Helati, you guard the rear. I will scout up ahead."

In this fashion, they began to move north, following the general weave of the river. Whenever Kaz tried to look over his shoulder, Tinos delivered a swat on the side of his head. Hecar gave Kaz odd glances every now and then.

Kaz wondered where the other minotaurs were camped. His captors had spoken of at least one other small group. That group was probably waiting on the other side of the mountain range. In some ways, Kaz had to admire his own people for their determination and thoroughness—and the human, Drew, as well, for his pretense of reluctance to have Kaz enter the settlement. The elder, Kaz suspected, had been shrewd and successful as a merchant at one time and was able to put on a convincing false face even to the discerning. It was difficult to both admire and despise someone, but the minotaur did nevertheless.

Tinos gave him another swat. "Dragging your feet will not save you, coward. We will drag your carcass along if we need to."

"I was only thinking of my comrade. Have the minotaurs grown so base that they must kill uselessly? He was only a kender."

"A kender! That a minotaur, even one lacking honor and the courage to face judgment, would demean himself to call one of *those* a comrade. You *are* weak, Kaz."

"It took three of you to subdue me," Kaz retorted.

That earned him yet another swat. "The high ones want you alive. You will be proof that honor and justice are still paramount to the minotaur race, despite the few who must always be weeded out."

Kaz snorted.

Hecar spoke, his tone much more civil, more calm than the fanatical Tinos. "Bad enough to stand accused of murder, Kaz, but to flee instead of facing judgment as you should have . . ."

The prisoner's reply was cut off by the reemergence of Greel from the forest. "All clear for some distance. Push him if you have to, but make him move!" The short minotaur smiled toothily. "I want to see the homeland.

After all this time . . ."

The other minotaurs, even Kaz, could not help feeling twinges of longing themselves. Kaz had not been home since the day he was deemed a warrior and sent out to fight for the glory of the Dark Queen, something he had really not believed in. Though the race of minotaurs counted her consort, mysterious Sargas, as their chief god, they had little love for the ways of Takhisis.

At that point, Greel growled at the others. "What are you standing around for? The sooner we meet up with the others, the sooner we return home."

He turned and began stalking off into the forest once more. Tinos and Hecar each took one arm and began to pull Kaz forward, almost causing him to lose his footing.

* * * * *

At nightfall, Kaz was deposited against a tree and tied to it. Both he and his captors were exhausted, but he was pleased to note that they were in worse shape. The hope that Delbin had reached the human cleric and convinced her to help Kaz had slowly dwindled away over the hours. What could a servant of Mishakal, the gentle goddess of healing, do against four heavily armed minotaur fighters? Would she even care?

Greel had snared an animal for food, and now the minotaurs were cooking it over a small fire. As Greel began to divide up the meat, a brief argument developed between the four. Listening closely, Kaz discovered that he was the cause. They were arguing over whether or not he should be fed. Greel finally gave in and handed something round to Helati, who had apparently appointed herself the prisoner's keeper.

Helati was a grumbling shadow as she stalked over to Kaz. "May Sargas take Greel's damned hide, and Scurn's for good measure!"

"Scurn?" Kaz asked quietly.

"He and the ogre lead this farce we call a mission of

honor and justice."

She dropped whatever it was that Greel had given her and fed him a few strips of meat. "I'm sorry that I cannot untie you. Hecar and I argued on your behalf, and even Tinos seemed willing, but Greel wants to take no chances. You are his prize. I daresay that by the time we reach Scurn, the short one will have us believing that he caught you alone, without our aid. Such honorable people we are. These past few years of chasing after you have changed us—much to the worse, I'd say."

"You and Hecar are siblings?" Helati's face was deep in shadow. He wished she would move so that he could see her better, be able to read her reactions better. It was always wise to know the enemy, he told himself.

"You *don't* remember us, then. Hecar was certain of that. You were a tutor for the younger classes. . . ."

Kaz grimaced at the memory. "The year before they deemed me ready to give my life for the ogres and humans. You and your brother were in one of the classes? Those were for the young just entering adulthood. You cannot be that young."

She laughed quietly. "Poor teacher. You fail to realize that eight years have passed since then. We have changed, my brother and I. We always felt you picked on us especially. Apparently it was not that important to you."

"Helati, I *had* to run after I killed the ogre leader. If I had stayed, they would have tied me to a stake and flayed me alive. I would have joined Braag's victims."

It was impossible to see the reaction on her face, but Kaz could hear her breathing catch briefly and noticed that her hand, still holding a piece of meat, had paused halfway to his mouth. He regretted causing the latter action most of all, having eaten almost nothing all day.

The female minotaur snorted quietly and continued with the feeding, occasionally taking a small scrap of meat for herself. As she fed Kaz, she spoke. "I could believe you—certainly the stories I've heard prove you are no coward and have dealt with others honorably—but Molok has his own proof. Proof that the high ones found convincing."

This time Kaz snorted, his anger flaring. "If they are the same ones who ruled when we were slave-soldiers to the other races, then small wonder! They are lackeys to the ogres and those who followed Takhisis's pet, the renegade sorcerer Galan Dracos!"

Greel rose from the fire. "If he cannot keep quiet, he does not get fed, Helati! If that fails to calm him, I can silence him personally!"

"I can handle him, Greel!" To Kaz, she said quietly, "Greel would be only too glad to silence you. He thinks your running away is judgment enough, and that you have forfeited any right to speak on your own behalf. Only his fear of Scurn keeps him from you."

Kaz swore under his breath. "You and your brother seem levelheaded. How can you be a part of this?"

"We were given a duty, and as minotaurs we will see that duty through to the end."

It all seemed so futile. This was what he had feared would happen if he allowed himself to be captured.

"Greel wanted me to show you this." Helati put down the meat and reached for the object the leader had given her. To the prisoner's eyes, it appeared to be a dark sphere, perhaps the size of an apple.

"What is it?"

"Watch. Stare into it."

As Kaz stared at it, the sphere began to glisten. Kaz shuddered without thinking. "Magic? Have we weakened so much we have turned to magic?"

Helati quieted him. "It is something the ogres use that they buy from mages. Scurn has one like it, and a proclamation from the emperor claiming the honorable intentions of our mission: the capture of an accused murderer. Now watch."

Kaz did as he was told, his eyes widening as the dark, opaque sphere suddenly became transparent. Within the sphere, he watched a landscape begin to grow from nothing. Tiny mountains rose in the background, and skeletal trees burst from the earth like mad, undead horrors. Figures began to blur into being, one on the right, the other in the center.

Kaz knew what land this was, though not the name of it. He knew it because he had served there, still blindly obedient to dark-robed mages and ebony-armored warlords. It came as no surprise that the figure at the right was him, and that the one in the center was the ogre who had commanded this army. There was something wrong with the scene, however, something that did not reveal itself to his eye at first.

The humans. The victims. The living toys of his captain, a loyal servant of the Queen of Evil. Where were the old one and the children that Braag's axe had played with? Instead, the ogre seemed intent on something in the distance and did not even notice the minotaur's presence. Kaz could predict what was going to happen next.

The Kaz figure raised a club. As the club rose behind the unsuspecting ogre, the real Kaz shook his head and denied the falsity of the scene. The club came crashing down. The ogre collapsed into a lifeless heap. The Kaz figure looked around once and fled. Other forms—ogres, minotaurs, and such—rushed forward even as the scene faded away.

It was another inaccuracy. It had taken only a single blow from his fist, struck while they stood face-to-face, to crack the skull of the ogre and send him to his reward. Not some dishonorable ambush!

"A lie!" Kaz no longer cared whether he remained quiet or not. "That's a lie! I am no base murderer! He cruelly killed the helpless, the defenseless! His action was without any honor! It was the work of a butcher, not a warrior, and he did it far too many times to be reprieved from death! I gave him a warrior's death!"

The sturdy ropes designed by the minotaurs to hold anything less than a dragon began to strain under his anger. Helati fell back, dropping the sphere. Greel and the others were already on their feet. One of the ropes snapped, and Kaz, still in a rage, roared as he felt the hold on him loosen. For a brief moment, the knowledge that he was a step closer to freedom urged him on. Then Greel and Tinos were on him.

They struck him relentlessly, Greel laughing out loud at one point. The short minotaur was enjoying every second of it. As Kaz's mind began to swim, he wondered if Greel had any ogre blood in him.

Greel's rage burned out under the endless blows, and Kaz blacked out mercifully.

*　　*　　*　　*　　*

Kaz stood before judgment, but it was not minotaurs who would decide his case. Black, mad Crynus sat on one side of the triumvirate, his head, which had been severed in life, lolling on his neck at an awkward angle. He seemed not to care.

Bennett, proud, arrogant Bennett, hawklike features glowing with the fire of his own magnificence, sat on the opposite side. He appeared less interested in the trial than he was in giving commands to the knights who rushed in an endless stream to and from him. They knelt, heard some whispered order, and each departed in haste, only to be replaced instantly by another knight.

The central figure, seated high above the rest, seemed to have trouble deciding who he was. One second he was Greel; the next he was Rennard. He became one of the goblins who had captured Kaz after the latter had killed the ogre captain. At last the central figure settled on a shape. It was, of course, the ogre captain himself. A portion of his head was missing, but there seemed to be no blood—nothing, in fact.

"A court of your peers," a mocking voice said.

Kaz looked around and found himself staring into the sightless eyes of a dreadwolf. The bone-white beast, *looking like nothing less than a month-dead, skinned animal, winked at him. It was sitting no more than two yards away, on top of a ledge.*

"The dead have no right to judge the living," Kaz shouted.

"The dead have every right," retorted the dreadwolf. "But you still have a chance to forego a trial."

"How?" A storm seemed to be brewing. For the first time, Kaz realized that, aside from the seated figures, the dreadwolf, and himself, there was nothing else, not even a landscape.

"Tell me what you know!" the dreadwolf cried.

"Know?" The minotaur's head was pounding.

"Do you know anything?"

"About—about what?"

"The citadel! When you joined with the knights in the battle against Galan Dracos!"

Kaz was sick of being pushed, beaten, and judged by others. With a roar, he raised a huge axe, one he could not recall having a moment before, and charged the dreadwolf. To his everlasting pleasure, the beast gave a very human scream and fled.

The other figures faded away. Only the storm still raged, but for some reason, the minotaur did not feel threatened by it.

As thunder shook him, Kaz realized that it was calling his name. He tried to answer, but his words came out as a groan. Then he felt himself vanish, even as the others had vanished. He felt no shock, only relief. . . .

* * * * *

"Great gods, what have they done to you?" a feminine voice whispered at the edge of his dreams. It was a softer, higher voice than Helati's, and the only one he could compare it to was that of Gwyneth, Huma's love. She had died, as in his dream, defending the knight from death by the claws of the Dark Queen. Had Paladine al-

lowed her to come back? Was she here to take him to Huma so that they could fight side by side again?

"Minotaur," the voice whispered, "you must awake. There is little time. I do not know how strong their resistance is."

Kaz tried to open his eyes. The memories of his beating came back to him, and with it the anger. He started to breathe fast, his blood boiling.

"No!" the unseen one hissed. Delicate hands turned his head until he could see the newcomer. In the dark, it took him time to place the young human face. Only when he saw the medallion hanging over her robe did he remember her name.

"Tesela?" The minotaur's words came out as little more than a croak. The cleric quickly shushed him.

"I'm sorry I could get here no sooner, minotaur. The people in the village were no help. They sided with Drew when Delbin and I forced the truth from him." She took her medallion and leaned toward the ropes. Kaz felt them fall away. With a helpless grunt, he slid to one side, landing on an already sore shoulder.

"I'm sorry!" Tesela whispered hastily. The composure she had worn during their first encounter had slipped away, revealing a frightened young woman.

"No time," Kaz managed to hiss. "Can you heal me?"

"It would take too long here. I've put a sleeping spell on the others, but I have no experience with minotaurs. I don't know how strong they are."

"Very. Undo the—the bonds around my wrists."

She touched the medallion to the ropes. Kaz felt them loosen and whispered thanks to Paladine as the circulation returned to his arms. Tesela helped him to his feet. "We have horses waiting."

"Horses?" he muttered.

The cleric pointed toward the river.

"Let's go." Despite his great pride, Kaz was forced to accept the human female's assistance. He stumbled several times but did not stop. Each grunt of pain sounded

as loud as the thunder in his dream, and he expected the
minotaurs to come rushing after them at any moment.

The horses became a shadowy mass ahead of them. Tesela, still helping to support him, was looking down, trying to avoid tripping. With the powers given to her, she
could have used the medallion to light their way, but she
feared to risk sending up a glow. For now, the darkness
was not only a hindrance, but it was also an ally.

The horses were there, but so was something else. For
an instant, Kaz thought he saw one of the nightmares of
his dream, the dreadwolf. The white, ghostly form
seemed to pause only long enough to acknowledge him.
When Kaz blinked again, it was gone.

"Is something wrong?" Tesela asked nervously.

"I—I thought I saw something by the horses."

"That would be Delbin. He was the one who told me
everything, only he couldn't understand how he had escaped. The minotaur who followed him had him
trapped, even he knew that, but then she—it was a
female—turned away in the wrong direction. It was fortunate for both of you that he was so lucky."

Kaz made no reply. Instead he asked, "How did you
find me?"

"Delbin picked up the trail. I understand kender are
good at that sometimes. He's very surprising."

"So I keep discovering."

As the horses became distinctive shapes, Kaz could see
that sitting on a pony nearly hidden by the two larger
mounts was Delbin himself. The kender succeeded in restraining himself to a simple, "Kaz!" and a wave. From
the way he squirmed in the saddle, the minotaur knew
that his kender companion had much more he wanted to
say. For a kender, Delbin was showing remarkable for-
bearance.

"We should be safe now. With the horses, we'll easily
be able to outrun the others," Tesela was saying. "And
once we cross the river, I can take the time to heal you
properly."

Kaz felt his head swim. "I . . . think you . . . had better . . . help . . ."

He went to his knees.

"Delbin, help me!" Tesela cried.

The kender leaped from the saddle and landed feetfirst no more than a yard from the others. He helped Tesela lift Kaz to a standing position.

The minotaur was breathing hard. "Get me . . . onto the horse. I'll be . . . able to manage . . . from there."

It took some doing. At last, seated on his horse, Kaz gazed blurry-eyed at the human. "You sound . . . so uncertain. I thought . . . you had done this before."

Despite the darkness, he imagined her face reddening. "I've only been a cleric for a short time—two, maybe three months. Another healer had passed through only recently. I saw him heal the bones of a man who had fallen. When my father heard about the cleric—he wanted to marry me off to the son of one of the town officials—he made certain I was never able to speak to him." Tesela mounted. "I cried bitterly. Helping people seemed like such a wonderful thing to do. I fell asleep crying, only to wake with a weight on my chest."

"The medallion?" Delbin asked eagerly.

"I found it useful that very night. It can unbind things like ropes and locks. Healing someone takes longer, since it's more delicate."

"Then we'd best move on." Kaz paused, then added, "It would be best if we crossed the river now, while they still sleep."

"That could be dangerous."

He did not even look at her. "So is remaining here."

Kaz urged his horse forward. The riverbank was bright in comparison to the forest, and Kaz glanced up at the two moons. Tonight he would have been happier with no moon at all. He was about to look away when he realized that something was amiss with Solinari, the luminous moon that represented the waxing of white magic. A small portion near the bottom was missing, almost as if a bite had been taken out of it.

"What's wrong?" Tesela asked.

Kaz blinked, and the moon was restored. He turned his attention to the river before them. "Nothing. I was debating where the best place to cross might be."

The river raged as he had never seen it. Kaz began to have second thoughts about crossing immediately. He turned to his companions. "How was it where you crossed?"

Tesela glanced at the kender. Delbin shrugged. "No worse, no better. It's not that deep, though, Kaz, because I was able to get across, and even in the dark, Surefoot should have no trouble. He's a good pony, and if he can make it, then that huge animal you have should be able to walk across with no problems because he's so much bigger and stronger than Surefoot."

"Meaning we should be able to cross. Delbin, you stand the most danger; I want you to go second so that someone is on either side of you. Tesela, you had better go first." When she started to argue, he stared her down as only a seven-foot minotaur could. "These are my people, human. Even as injured as I am, I stand a better chance of fighting them than you do. I doubt if they will let you catch them unaware twice. Besides"—Kaz reached down and patted the faithful war-horse affectionately—"I have a good comrade here."

"Why don't we cross together?"

"I would prefer that we always have someone to watch out for the others. Just in case."

Tesela gave in. Wasting no more time, she led her animal to the river. It was reluctant at first, but she spoke quietly to it, one of her hands touching the medallion. Under her guidance, the animal had little trouble crossing, despite the swift current. When she was halfway across, Kaz sent Delbin. He watched carefully, afraid that Delbin's small pony might get swept away. He hoped that would not be the case, for his mind and body were exhausted. Minotaur pride had gotten the better of him, however, and he refused to show any weakness to his companions.

The cleric was safe on the other side, and Delbin, despite the fact that his pony had to swim instead of walk, seemed assured of equal success. Kaz urged his own mount into the river.

The wild water battered his legs, and he was sprayed from head to toe. He was thankful for the bitter cold of the river, for it kept him alert. When his horse was fully into the river, the minotaur saw that the water level came only to his own shinbone. The war-horse moved forward, making slow but steady progress. Delbin's pony was just stepping onto the opposite riverbank.

All thought of his companions vanished as Kaz paid strict attention to the river. There was always the chance that his animal might step into a depression the others had missed, or that the current might change for some unknown reason. More than one overconfident rider had been lost in such a fashion.

Over the roar of the river, he suddenly realized that both Tesela and Delbin were calling to him. He looked up just as the war-horse shook violently beneath him. Kaz struggled for control with the animal, which suddenly seemed crazed. The war-horse was stumbling, and the minotaur was in danger of losing his balance. At any other time, he would probably have had no trouble overcoming his mount. The strain of weariness, however, left him in a weakened state.

His leg, slipping back, struck something hard and long. Kaz dared to turn in the saddle. To his horror, he discovered a spear buried in the animal's flank. No human or elf could have thrown such a huge spear with such perfect accuracy. Suddenly Kaz knew it must have been Greel's hand that had guided the missile.

Pain and loss of blood, combined with the struggle against the strong current, proved too much for the great war-horse. The animal began to turn in a circle as the river took control. Kaz had a spinning image of at least three minotaurs on the other riverbank and wondered if he was mistaken when he thought he saw one of them strike another down. He never had a second look, however, for with a last defiant cry, the war-horse tumbled helplessly into the uncaring embrace of the river.

Kaz was thrown back, and his head went underwater before he even had a chance to consider holding his breath. His lungs screamed as they filled with water. He struggled to find the surface, only to be pulled down once again.

Unable to cope any longer, Kaz let the river current take him where it wanted. He asked himself, as he did so often, what it was that the gods had against him.

If there was an answer, he did not remain conscious long enough to hear it.

Chapter 6

A lone drop of water struck the side of his muzzle.
Kaz, already on the verge of waking, shivered uncontrollably in the grip of memories of tumbling and drowning. There had been another dream, too—a bad one, like so many he had had of late, but all he could remember of it was that it, too, concerned water.

When he was certain that he was neither asleep nor drowned, the minotaur carefully opened his eyes just enough to get some glimpse of his surroundings. When the world around him finally registered in his waterlogged mind, his eyes widened.

"Now what?" Kaz succeeded in muttering, though someone would have had to put his ear to his mouth to hear him.

He was alone in a room, staring directly at the top of a tree just outside. It registered almost immediately that the reason he could see the top, even gaze downward at it, was that he was *in* the tree. It was a very high tree, too, because even from the mat he was lying on, he could see that beyond the treetop were countless more trees, nearly all shorter than the one he now occupied.

His surroundings were as simple as they were astonishing. This home, this one room, had not been carved into the trunk of the tree. Instead, it was almost as if the tree had obliged whoever had decided to make his home here by splitting apart at this juncture and then coming together higher up. There were natural depressions where the occupant stored a few unidentifiable objects. The floor was covered with mats, obviously woven from plants, and there was no furniture.

Kaz rose slowly from the mat. With each movement, he expected the return of pain. When the pain did not come, the minotaur began to touch his head and arms. All the wounds—and there had been quite a few—were healed!

Kaz snorted. Like most minotaurs, he was distrustful of magic tricks. Under other circumstances, he would have shied away even from the healing powers of Tesela's goddess. Minotaurs believed that the more one succumbed to the simplicity of magical solutions, the weaker one became. Whether that was true or not, Kaz pondered, it was too late to change what already had happened. Someone had healed him, and by rights the minotaur owed that person a debt of gratitude.

Cautiously he stepped toward the open entrance. He looked around for a weapon and noticed a small round pot made of clay that sat in a natural shelf near the entrance. Kaz hesitated. It was a beautiful piece of work and looked incredibly ancient. Intricate patterns and pictures had been painted all around its circumference. Most of the pictures dealt with nature, though one revealed a group of beings dancing in a circle. Kaz studied that picture more carefully. The dancers were elves.

Who else, he argued with himself, *would live high up in a tree but an elf?*

"The pot will not bite, my friend. It never has."

Kaz whirled and reached for a weapon he had already told himself was not there. Behind him, sitting in a spot the minotaur knew he could not possibly have overlooked earlier, was a tall, handsome elf with long silver hair. If judged by human standards, the elf looked young—until one looked at the emerald eyes. This tree-dweller, Kaz knew, had seen more years pass than several generations of minotaurs.

The elf was clad in a brown and green outfit that made him look like a prince of the forest. There was even a long cloak. Kaz snorted angrily when he saw that the elf was smiling at his inspection.

"Who are you?" he snarled.

"I am Sardal Crystalthorn, my friend. I think this is perhaps the twelfth time I've told you that." Sardal seemed amused by something.

"How long have I been here?" Anger began to give way to surprise.

"Just over two weeks. You were nearly dead when I found you. I am impressed. Everything I have heard about minotaur stamina was evidently true, and then some."

"Two weeks?" A sudden, fierce desire to be away from this place, away from everywhere, shook Kaz. He turned and bolted toward the entrance of Sardal's home. A hand, impossibly strong for being so slender and pale, held him back. Kaz swallowed as he stared down into yet more treetops. He had assumed there would be a ladder or steps, but there was nothing. Evidently elves did not need ladders or steps.

"Come back inside before you do something foolish."

"Two weeks!" the minotaur muttered again.

"You were injured worse in spirit than in body," the elf said gently. He led Kaz away from the opening.

"How did you find me?"

Sardal's face was empty of emotion. "I did not. Others found you. They wanted nothing to do with you, but they knew that I have a fondness for meddling. It is why I live here and not with them. It is also their excuse to interfere while pretending not to."

Kaz began to pace. He could not say what bothered him more, the two lost weeks or the thought that he was so very high above the ground in the company of an elf. "Am I in Qualinesti, then? Did the river drag me that far south?"

The elf gave him the slightest glimmer of a smile. "Hardly. It always amazes me that other races are so boundary conscious. Do you think that we stop and turn back the moment the 'accepted' border comes into sight? Only races like minotaurs and humans would think like that. When we elves—and those in Silvanesti—created borders, it was only for the peace of mind of others. We do not believe in such things, although we do have our general territories and places no other race travels through. But actual borders we definitely do not have."

Sardal, Kaz decided, was as convoluted as Delbin when it came to explanations. "So, where *am* I?"

"Almost directly north of the human city of Xak Tsaroth. If you had looked in any other direction than the way you did, you would have seen the mountains that border this part of the forest on each side."

Kaz nodded. He recalled vaguely from the map where he was now. If he was correct, the settlement controlled by the elder, Drew, was almost directly east.

"If I may ask you a question," continued the elf as he reached for a jug containing some liquid, "how did you come to be attempting to swallow the entire river?"

After the aid Sardal had given him, Kaz more than willingly told the elf the entire story. He began with the murder he had supposedly committed, which had actually been a fair combat against an ogre captain who had been needlessly torturing old and young prisoners. The minotaurs did not care about that, however. He had also broken several blood oaths in turning on the ogre and then running off rather that facing the so-called "justice" of his masters. He concluded the distasteful subject with, "I suspect that *that* is of more concern to my people. Killing or executing to preserve honor is common among us."

After that, Kaz unconsciously turned to other matters, as if to avoid thinking about his situation. News of the north especially interested the elf, and the more Kaz talked about it, the more questions Sardal brought up. By the time the minotaur concluded, the elf had extracted nearly every bit of information Kaz could think of.

"You must be greatly skilled to have avoided those other minotaurs all this time," Sardal commented.

"I survived twice as long as most during the war. Wasn't just that, though. Me, I've dealt with humans; I know better than my pursuers what to expect in this territory—the past few days excluded. Besides, while one minotaur might be able to sneak through a land, a group of a dozen or so is about as inconspicuous as an advancing army. Someone always knows, and I generally find out soon enough."

"Yet they almost caught you this time."

Kaz grunted. "They're getting better. Or maybe I'm getting tired. Still, I think I've got one edge. There's dissension in their ranks. I always wondered and now I know. Some of them just want to go home. The only thing holding them back is their oaths, and those are to leaders with no honor of their own, lackeys left over from the days when ogres and humans really ruled. I think a few of them *might*—and I may only be hoping—actually be slowing the group down purposely because they believe in me."

The minotaur put his face in his hands and sighed.

"You have a dark shadow over you, minotaur. I think perhaps that the gods have something planned for you."

He gave a brief smile. "Or you may just attract trouble as a flower attracts bees."

Kaz began to scoff, then recalled his dreams and visions. They might be merely that, visions and dreams, but there was always the chance they were not, that they were actually omens. Could he dare ignore them?

Sardal, his eyes never leaving the minotaur, continued. "Of your companions or your people, I have no word. Most elves like to avoid the affairs of other races. I have long known the folly of such acts. There were things that occurred during the war against the Dragonqueen that should shame any elf, but still, most would rather continue to ignore the outside world."

"Delbin knows that I planned to travel to Vingaard Keep and confront Oswal, the Grand Master. He may go there, and it is possible that the human cleric, Tesela, will go there also. If not, I still have to go there myself. I *have* to discover why my former comrades have turned against me."

"Not just you. From your words and the stories of others that I have heard, the Knights of Solamnia have turned away from E'li, he who you know as Paladine. If so, we may yet again see the evil of the Dragonqueen."

"She cannot return. Huma made her swear by something called the Highgod, I think."

The elf's eyebrows rose. "Did he, now? A pity, my friend, that you cannot remember the oath. I suspect there are holes in it big enough to fly a dragon through— if there were still dragons, that is."

Kaz recalled some of the images from his dreams. "She would need the help of another fiend like Galan Dracos."

"There are other ways. We have no idea what precautions she might have made. What will you do about your countrymen who pursue you?" Sardal asked.

"Like Delbin, no doubt they think I am dead."

"Yet you might still encounter them."

The minotaur snorted angrily. "I will deal with them if I have to. It is Vingaard that concerns me. To honor the memory of Huma of the Lance, I will settle with the knighthood one way or the other." Kaz rose. "Enough prattle. Show me how to reach the ground, and I will be on my way."

Sardal rose to his feet in one fluid motion. "It occurs to me that I may yet be of some substantial aid to you, minotaur, if you have no objections."

"What do you intend?" Kaz's tone indicated he was hesitant to accept yet more assistance.

"Nothing complicated." Sardal began to gather a few items he thought might come in handy for his guest. His mind briefly flickered to what his fellows would say when they discovered that, not only had he healed the beastman, but he had also given him supplies and even spoke to him like an equal. Smiling, he dropped the thought and continued with the discussion.

"When you get to Vingaard—and I have no doubt that you will—ask for an elf named Argaen Ravenshadow. He is like me and has worked among humans for generations. The elders call him a maverick, but as with me, they never fail to make use of him when it proves necessary to deal with outsiders. Let all who are there know that Sardal Crystalthorn wishes him to place his protection over you." At Kaz's expression, the elf added, "Do not be a fool, minotaur. The knighthood respects him greatly, else—but that is unimportant. You will be doing me a favor as well." Sardal held up a small scroll. "I want you to give him this. He will have need of it. I would have joined him in another month, but now I may turn my mind to other interests."

Kaz took the scroll and then the rest of the items the elf had gathered for him. One very important object was missing. "Where is my axe?"

"Lost somewhere at the bottom of the river, I suppose. Never fear. I will find you a replacement. Come." Sardal walked to the entrance of his home and then turned when he realized Kaz was not following him. "I thought you wished to depart."

The minotaur took a step forward and froze. "But how? You have no ladder, no rope. . . ."

Sardal smiled. "None that you can see. It is only a matter, however, of changing one's perceptions."

Kaz shook his head. "I don't understand."

A sigh. The elf reached out his left hand. "Take my hand. I'll lead you. I can see that you have dealt with elves before, and also that you have never been to Qualinesti. I know how the arrogant ones in Silvanesti would treat you as an ogrespawn. My people are not much better, but they *are* better."

Kaz hesitated. To be led blindly by the elf was bad enough; to remain here, untrusting of one who had saved his life, was worse. Sardal Crystalthorn was indeed far different than the uncaring, haughty elves of Silvanesti, whom Kaz had had the misfortune of encountering once during his wanderings, much to his regret.

He took Sardal's hand and closed his eyes tight.

"Just keep walking. When I stop, you stop."

The sensation Kaz felt was akin to walking down a flight of spiraling stairs. With great effort, he defeated the urge to open his eyes and see what he was really walking on. Kaz was no coward, but sorcery always left him feeling defenseless. What if he should open his eyes only to find that there was nothing but empty space beneath him?

"You said you used a battle-axe, did you not?" Sardal's voice broke into his thoughts. It seemed as if they had walked miles already.

Kaz found he was sweating—and standing still as well. "Why have we stopped?"

"We are at the bottom, of course."

The minotaur opened his eyes. They were indeed standing at the base of the tree. Kaz turned to face the leviathan, and his eyes followed its growth upward. The true height of the tree became clear to him. His stomach began to churn. "How— No! I have no wish to learn! Your tricks can remain your secrets." He recalled the question Sardal had asked him. "Yes, I use an axe."

"I had thought as much when I first saw you." The elf was suddenly holding a massive, gleaming double-edged axe. The side of the axe head had an amazing mirrorlike finish, and in spite of its tremendous size, Sardal was having no trouble with its weight.

Kaz studied the weapon with admiration. The axe was perfect, from head to handle. The blades could well cut through stone. The minotaur noted some runes on the handle. "What is that?"

"Dwarven. A gift from an old friend, sadly dead in the war. This was his finest work, and he entrusted it to me rather than to his squabbling apprentices. The runes are its name; every good weapon should be named. This one, translated to Common, is Honor's Face."

"Honor's Face? What sort of name is that for a battle-axe?"

"Never try to understand a dwarven mind." Sardal turned the axe over to his guest. "I think, though, that you have both the strength and the proper spirit to yield a weapon with such a name."

"Is it magic?" Kaz wanted to keep the blade, but a magical weapon. . . .

"I think the magic lies more in the skill of the artisan who created it than the warrior who wields it, although I cannot promise that it has no magical abilities. I've noticed none. But you will not be disappointed with it, I am certain."

Kaz tested the axe, swinging it this way and that, performing maneuvers with it that would have left many another fighter without at least one leg and several fingers. At the end of the short exercise, he hooked it into his harness with one graceful motion. His eyes were bright with pleasure, though he tried to conceal his enthusiasm. "Excellent balance."

Sardal nodded, impressed in spite of himself with the minotaur's skill. "May you need it as little as possible. I am sorry that I have no horse to lend you, but I can lead you along a path that will make up some of the time you have lost."

"Lead me? You're going with me?"

"Only to the edge of the forest." Sardal pointed in a northerly direction. "Beyond that, you will be in the desolation of northern Solamnia. Since you have been kind enough to take that scroll to Argaen, I see no reason to enter that unclean land myself."

"Is it that bad?"

The elf gave him a curious look. "How long has it been since you were last there?"

"After the death ceremony for my companion, Huma, I rode south and have not since ridden back. I have visited the lands east, west, and south of Solamnia, save that part of Istar my people call home, but never have I come within a hundred miles of that region again."

"You respected Huma greatly."

"Do you know the Solamnic phrase *'Est Sularus oth Mithas'*?"

" 'My honor is my life.' Yes, I have heard it before. It generally precedes the Oath and Measure of the knighthood."

A somber look crossed the minotaur's bullish visage. "Huma of the Lance embodied that phrase; he *was* that phrase. I've tried to live up to his memory since his death. I don't know how well I've succeeded, if at all."

"You've been unwilling to return to Vingaard solely because of that." There was no mockery in Sardal's voice.

Kaz gathered up his things. "I have. If you'd ever met Huma, you'd understand. We met when he rescued me from a band of goblins who had trapped me by surprise. To say that he was shocked at what he'd rescued would not be far from the truth, but that didn't deter him. Minotaur, human, or even goblin, Huma always sought the best in a being." Kaz paused. "I think he cried inside for nearly every foe slain. I rode beside him long enough to see that. From our first encounter with the silver dragon to the final confrontation with Takhisis, he was a human who embodied the good of the world. He dared the unthinkable, too, whether that meant defending a minotaur against his fellow knights or seeking out the Dragonlances, which were our only hope."

Crystalthorn remained silent as Kaz paused again briefly to organize his thoughts, but his eyes glittered as he listened.

"We were separated time and again, but each time I met a Huma who, despite the adversities fate had placed before him, refused to give in. He was the first to make use of the Dragonlances, and he led the attack when there were but a couple dozen of us, mounted on dragons of our own, to face the dragon hordes of the dark goddess. I say *us*, elf, because he allowed me to be one of the select, an honor like none I shall ever know again. Most of the riders and their dragon companions died before it was over, and a braver group I've never met, but the greatest was Huma. He faced Takhisis with only the silver dragon, whose human form he loved dearly, at his side and *defeated* Takhisis, though it cost him his life." Kaz shivered. "I arrived as he completed the pact with the Dragonqueen, her freedom for Krynn's. By then, Huma was almost dead. He asked me to pull the Dragonlance from the goddess's thrashing body—she wore the form of the five-headed dragon then—and despite my overwhelming fear—fear I still recall to this day—I performed that horrible task because Huma had asked it of me. I don't think I could have done it for anyone else."

Sardal waited, but after Kaz had not spoken for several seconds, he prompted, "And?"

The minotaur looked at Sardal with reddened eyes. "And he died, elf! Died before I could get back to him, find help for him! I'd sworn my life to protect his, and I failed him!"

Kaz busied himself with rearranging his equipment. Crystalthorn hesitated and finally, quietly, commented,

"I think you find it harder to face your companion's spirit than you do your own people."

The minotaur, his things in hand, was already walking in the direction the elf had indicated. His response was low, almost muffled, but Sardal's sharp ears still made out the single word as the elf moved to catch up.

"Yes."

* * * * *

They had come to a blighted section of the forest. Some of the trees ahead of them were dead, and it reminded the minotaur of the war.

"When I was with Huma," Kaz was saying, "we thought that all Ansalon must be like this—dead or dying forests and little, if any, wildlife other than carrion crows and other scavengers. It seemed amazing that so many areas had not suffered nearly the damage we thought they had during the war."

Sardal agreed grimly. "The northern portion of the continent suffered most, but there are areas in every corner of Ansalon that will not be normal for years to come—even in Qualinesti or Silvanesti. Our much vaunted solitude gave us nothing. Men won the war for us, though some remember only that men also fought for the forces of darkness."

They camped in the forest overnight. Kaz had, at one point, assumed that Sardal was going to lead him along some magic path, but the only magic lay in the fact that only an elf could have ever found this obscure trail.

The night passed without incident—Kaz could scarcely believe it—and the two continued on. They were beyond the point where the minotaur had been thrown into the river, but Kaz paused this day to stare at the rushing water anyway.

"I lost a good comrade here as well."

"I see no reason why you might not meet up with the kender once more."

Kaz laughed. "It was not Delbin I was thinking of, though, horrible as it is to admit, I grew used to him. No, elf, I was referring to a strong, loyal horse I'd ridden for five years and never even given a name." He touched the axe handle. "If some give weapons names, a good steed certainly deserves one."

"Give him one now." Sardal smiled. He had never met a minotaur like this!

The minotaur nodded. "When I think of a worthy one."

They continued on, and early the next day they finally reached the last of the trees. Beyond, the ghost forest began.

"Astra's Harp!" cursed Sardal. The elf was visibly shaken.

Kaz, meanwhile, found himself caught in the past. Before him stood a nearly dead land, seemingly untouched since the war. He remembered the goblins and the dragons, the piles of dead, and the curses of the ogre and human commanders as they drove the minotaurs forward. The battles gave him a moment of pride, until he recalled that it was Huma's comrades he had fought much of the time. There had been other battles, this time alongside the Knights of Solamnia, and about those he felt better.

Five years. By now he would have expected to see at least a few tender shoots, a blade of wild grass or two— not this barren deathscape before them.

He heard what sounded like thunder and looked up into the sky, only to understand belatedly what it was he was actually listening to.

"Riders!" Kaz pulled Sardal back.

Some distance away and riding as if the Dragonqueen was on their tail, could be seen a band of knights, twenty, perhaps. As the two watched, the party rode unhesitatingly through the dead forest. They could have only one destination in mind, Kaz knew: Vingaard Keep.

"Those knights come from different outposts and keeps," the elf commented.

Kaz wondered how he knew and then recalled the tales of how superior the vision of elves was. "They come from different places?"

Sardal nodded. "I was able to glimpse some markings. Each knight has an insignia that represents the keep or outpost he is attached to. Most of the southern forts are represented in that group. It is curious. I am almost tempted to go with you, if I did not have other important matters. . . ."

The elf quieted, as if he had said too much. Kaz pretended his attention was still totally focused on the vanishing riders. "They should get there days ahead of me. Perhaps the Knights of Solamnia prepare for yet another war."

"Against whom?"

"I can't say," Kaz muttered. "But it would explain in part why they seem to have turned their backs on their people. It may be that the remnants of Takhisis's armies are gathering together. I could have misjudged them."

"Do you think so?"

"I won't know until I get there." Even to Kaz, the words sounded lacking.

Sardal straightened. "I will leave you, then." He held out a hand, palm toward the minotaur. "May E'li and Astra guide you—also Kiri-Jolith, who I think would particularly care what happens to you."

Kiri-Jolith was the god of honorable battle and resembled a man with a bison's head. Typical of some of the contrary ways of the minotaur race, he was held by some in as high regard as Sargas, Takhisis's consort, despite the fact that, if they met, the two gods would have fought a battle royal. Kiri-Jolith was E'li's—Paladine's—son.

The minotaur returned Sardal's hand sign, then turned his eyes briefly to the ghostly forest he was about to enter. "I think my easiest route would be to follow the knights. They've left me a fairly obvious trail. What do you say, Sardal Crystalthorn?"

When Sardal did not answer, Kaz turned back to where he had last seen the elf. There was no sign of his benefactor, not even a footprint. Kaz knelt down and studied the ground. He could follow his own footprints for as far as he could see, but of Sardal's, there was no trace. It was if he had never been there.

Kaz grunted and rose. "Elves."

He turned back to the bleak lands of northern Solamnia, and shouldering his pack so that it would not interfere should he need the services of Honor's Face, he started walking. Before he was a hundred paces into the wasteland, he became aware of the sudden absence of all the normal sounds of the forest save one—a familiar one from the war.

Somewhere a carrion crow was calling to its brethren. Kaz knew that the only time they cried like that was when a feast was imminent. Somehow the birds were always there when warriors were about to die; then they would perch and wait for the feast.

The minotaur hoped it was not the crows they were expecting.

Chapter 7

Though there were few clouds in the sky, the sun did not shine as brightly in this bleak region. Kaz could not come up with any suitable explanation. Perhaps the entire land suffered under some affliction, or perhaps it would take years for the Dragonqueen's curse to fade. He only knew that he would be very happy to be away from this land.

Occasionally there were signs of life. The minotaur's first glimpse of a wild green plant brought him more pleasure than he would have thought possible. Northern Solamnia was not quite a corpse, then. A struggle for existence was going on.

Night came swiftly and, with it, a relief of sorts. In the darkness, most every land looked the same. The dead trees might have been live ones merely waiting for spring to come, although Kaz knew otherwise. The only things missing in the night were the sounds of the forest. Once he did hear a scavenger cry out to the moons. Somehow those creatures always managed to survive in the desolate areas. A few insects made their presence known, but compared to the usual cacophony of night, the forest seemed empty.

Almost empty. As he was bedding down, something huge and incredibly swift flew over him but vanished before he could even look up. Kaz had only the impression of a massive creature with long, wide wings. His first thought was that it was a dragon, until he recalled in irritation that the dragons—*all* of the dragons—had vanished at the war's end. The dragons of darkness had been cast out by Huma. The dragons of light had departed voluntarily, so some said, in order to preserve the balance. No one really knew for certain. Whatever the night flier was, it did not return. Unnerved, Kaz ate a modest meal and settled down.

The minotaur slept uneasily that first night. It was not a feeling he could put his finger on. During the night, he tossed and turned. By morning, Kaz had awakened at least seven times, each and every such moment vivid with the expectation that some goblin was about to cut his throat or some ghoulish horror was rising from the dry earth to claim him. Once Kaz dreamed that the dreadwolf was back, its burning, dead eyes staring at him, demanding answers to questions he could not recall, mocking his ideals.

He continued to follow the trail left by the party of knights. Vingaard Keep was their destination; of that, there was no doubt. Judging by the tracks left by their horses, they were continuing at as fast a pace as they could manage. They would arrive in Vingaard several days before Kaz, which suited him perfectly. Kaz wanted no more confrontations before he reached the keep.

The second day gave way to the third, which gave way

to the fourth and fifth. Kaz was slowing down. The trail
left by the knights avoided any villages, which possibly
indicated that the riders were going out of their way to
avoid other people. The minotaur dared draw no conclusion just yet.

Just after midday, he saw the birds again. Carrion
crows.

By his estimate, there had to be several dozen. He
could only make out the ones in flight at first, but as he
continued on, Kaz spotted them perched in trees as well.
Carrion crows were scavengers, and it was likely that
they were feeding on the refuse left by the knights.

Somehow, though, Kaz felt otherwise. His pace quickened. A scent long familiar to him wafted past his widened nostrils. He snorted in open disgust.

Soon the number of birds had grown so great that Kaz
began to wonder if they were preparing to attack a living
creature such as himself. When he saw the extent of the
carnage, however, Kaz knew that they need not be concerned with him.

As far as he could see, no one had been spared. The
bodies lay spread out for some distance, as if whatever
had killed them had heaved them into the air in every direction. Some of the riders had been torn apart, others
crushed. There was blood everywhere, so much blood
that even Kaz, who had fought in many violent battles,
grew nauseous. Here indeed was a vision out of his worst
memories, his worst nightmares. The carnage here was
comparable to anything he had ever witnessed or heard
tales about. The group hadn't had a chance against whatever had attacked. From the looks of things, the knights
had been caught unaware after bedding down for the
night. One victim was mangled in his bedroll.

These were the selfsame knights who had ridden past
Kaz and Sardal only days before. Twenty or so men, all
dead. Not cut down in battle, but torn apart as if by
some huge, ravaging beast, though how could that be
possible? What still existed in this region—or any

region—that could destroy so many trained warriors with so little difficulty?

Kaz reached back and pulled his battle-axe free. Cautiously he approached the first of the dead. This one had been crushed to death by the body of a horse as it fell. He was a young knight, a Knight of the Crown, as Huma had been. His sword lay just beyond his twisted hand. The minotaur glanced momentarily at the weapon and then returned his gaze to it when he noticed peculiar marks and abrasions. He reached down and, with his free hand, picked it up.

The sword was chipped, dented, and scratched beyond belief. Kaz had never met a knight who did not pay careful attention to the condition of his equipment. Soldiers in general learned early to take care of their personal possessions, especially their weapons. This sword, however, looked as if the knight had been beating it against a stone wall. And the stone wall had won.

He returned the sword to its rightful owner and moved on. The next knight had fared no better; half of his body lay elsewhere. Kaz snarled and quickly walked past. In the main group, he counted the corpses of sixteen men and eighteen horses. There was some indication that at least a couple of horses had ridden off, but whether there were riders as well as horses that escaped was a question with no foreseeable answer. Kaz found two more bodies beyond the camp, one with his head and helmet squeezed into a single mass and the other wrapped around a tree. All had been dead for at least a day, probably more.

Under other circumstances, the minotaur might have tried to give the knights proper burial. However, that would take far too much time, and it would be just his luck if another band of knights came along while he was in the midst of things. Kaz swore that, at the very worst, he would tell Lord Oswal what he had found. The knighthood would avenge its own, wouldn't it?

He found another horse and two more bodies half a mile beyond the last ones, plus brand-new sets of prints in the dry, dusty soil. These he did not recognize. They were neither human nor horse, but too vague to be identified as anything else.

There were several sets of prints, and it appeared that these intruders had dragged two heavy objects. Kaz had a dawning suspicion of what he might find and quickened his pace, hoping he was not too late already.

In this area, there was little cover save the trees themselves. The minotaur, being as large as he was, had a difficult time concealing himself. Kaz suspected that there was a phalanx of guards around somewhere. Axe in hand, he was forced to crawl through rotting underbrush as he searched. Judging by the prints, there were at least seven or eight members in the group he was following.

A breeze brought the smell of burned meat to his nostrils, causing Kaz to snort in disgust. The smell he recognized as that of horseflesh, a disgusting odor for an even more disgusting meat. The minotaur had survived on such flesh several times during the war, and he had never learned to accept the taste.

With the scent of burning meat came the first snatches of conversation. The group was both amused and wary. They were goblins.

"Stick him again, Krynge!"

"Got nothing to say, shellhead?"

"Feed him to the flames, Krynge, and let us listen to his screams!"

"Naaa. Not till we know there ain't more coming," the one known as Krynge called back.

Kaz froze momentarily, feeling an awful sense of displacement. This was beginning to sound too much like his own life, only that time it was the minotaur who had been a prisoner of the goblins. Huma had risked his own life to save his, and Kaz knew he could do no less now.

The memory fled as footsteps warned him of a sentry.

The ugly, squat green creature was dragging a long, slightly bent spear. He was fat, even for a goblin, and probably had been stuck with sentry duty because he was at the bottom of the ranks. He looked ready to take a nap. Kaz began to rise slowly, only too happy to help him on his way.

Obligingly, the goblin sat down on a rock and, with a dark look toward the direction of the camp, began to chew on a piece of old meat, probably from the slaughtered horse. So indifferent to his duty was the lazy creature that Kaz was able to sneak up from behind and, with the flat of his axe, lay him low with one blow. The axe struck with a hard thud, and the goblin's head snapped forward, burying his six or so chins into his fat chest. The minotaur leaned over and checked the still form, grunting in mild surprise that the blow had broken the creature's neck, killing him instantly. Kaz had no qualms about it. Under the same circumstances, the goblin would have run him through without hesitation.

The others were still getting their amusement out of the leader's question-and-answer session with the prisoner. So far, Kaz had heard nothing from the prisoner, and it was possible that the goblin chief had already pushed his prey over the limit. The minotaur's grip on the axe handle tightened until his knuckles turned white.

Cautiously Kaz circled around the general area of the camp, hoping that he would not crawl right into the scabby arms of another overly zealous guard. But knowing the race as he did, he suspected there would be only one or two at most.

Kaz need not have worried, for the second sentry was no more diligent than the first; this one was asleep. Kaz debated using the axe, but instead he punched him in the jaw. With a surprised but stifled grunt, the goblin rolled over with his face buried in the parched soil. Kaz felt an odd stirring of satisfaction. It was like paying one of his own captors back.

Now came the difficult part. He hazarded a guess, based on the mocking voices, that there were five more. There might be a way to separate them, but would it be too much of a risk?

His decision was made for him.

"I told you not to do that, Skullcracker! You so jumpy, go out and take Mule's place on guard!"

"But, Krynge . . ."

"Get going!"

Kaz quietly cursed several gods. He could make out a brutish figure slowly picking his way toward the spot where the minotaur had slain the first guard. Judging by the goblin's turtlelike speed, Kaz had a few minutes, but no more. Right now, the goblins were relaxed, off guard. . . .

Off guard?

There might have been better ways, and had the situation been different, he might have thought of a better plan. Still, in his opinion, it was always the simple plan that was best.

Kaz continued on in the same direction. The path would take him farther around the camp and almost opposite where the first guard had been killed. In one thing, the minotaur had been correct; the goblins, not really expecting any trouble, had posted only two guards. Had there been a third, there might have been more trouble.

His movements brought him very, very near the goblins themselves. He also managed to get his first glimpse of the prisoner.

The prisoner was, of course, a Knight of Solamnia. He was staked to the ground, and some of his armor had been torn away and tossed to one side, but there was no doubting that he was a knight. His condition was questionable. Kaz tightened his grip on the axe and raised himself up into a crouch.

"Krynge!" Skullcracker shouted from the opposite side of the camp.

The *five* goblins—Kaz cursed his miscount—turned as one. The leader, Krynge, a bulky goblin carrying a barbed spear, took a few steps in the direction the other had gone. The rest began to follow.

Kaz burst from his hiding place. He gave no war cry,

merely shouting "Goblins!" just as he reached the first of them.

His opponent had only enough time to stare goggle-eyed before the minotaur's axe sliced through his sword arm. The creature shrieked and dropped to his knees in a bizarre attempt to catch the falling limb. Kaz turned from him and took on the next. This one was slightly better prepared and met him with a heavy club. Unfortunately for the goblin, his eagerness proved a great mistake, and Kaz brought the axe down into his chest, splitting him open. His adversary fell backward, dead before he touched the ground.

Now the minotaur found himself confronting three goblins, one of whom had a spear.

Krynge poked at Kaz with his spear. The other two goblins carried different weapons. Reach was on the side of Kaz, however.

The lead goblin seemed to realize this, for he waved at the other two, indicating that they should encircle their attacker.

The one called Skullcracker appeared in the distance. Kaz knew that he would not survive four-against-one, especially since Skullcracker carried an axe almost as large as his. The minotaur glanced around. The weak point in the trio before him was the goblin who carried the club. This one seemed to be more hesitant.

Kaz feinted toward Krynge, who stumbled back a few steps. The other two moved in, thinking to take advantage of his nearness, but Kaz twisted out of the reach of the sword and turned the downward arc of his swing into an attack to his opponent's left side. Completely caught by surprise, the goblin could only manage a feeble defense with his club and was felled by a slice that almost cut him in two.

However, Kaz had underestimated the leader, Krynge. After backing up, the goblin immediately moved in again. Before the minotaur could dodge, the tip of the barbed spear caught him in the shoulder. The upper barbs hooked his flesh, and for a brief moment, Kaz was certain his arm was going to be pulled off. His hold on the dwarven battle-axe nearly slipped, but he knew that would be the death of him. Ignoring the agony, he rolled to his left.

The chieftain tore the spear away, taking a good portion of the minotaur's shoulder with it. By now, Skullcracker was near enough to be a threat, and Kaz surmised that his odds had gotten no better and perhaps worse. The pain of the wound coursed through his entire body. But he gritted his teeth and managed to hold the goblins off with a mad swing that nearly knocked the axe from Skullcracker's hands.

It was the spear that was proving the stumbling block. Kaz had a reach advantage over the other two attackers, but Krynge's spear was at least as long as the minotaur, and the goblin knew how to wield it. Even if the chieftain did not make a direct strike, the barbs on that weapon would still catch and tear. . . .

They were slowly forcing him back, and the pain in his shoulder was breaking his concentration. The goblin with the sword almost got under his guard, but a quick twist of the axe sent him scurrying back. Unfortunately, Kaz lost more ground. Eventually, he knew, they would run him into a tree and ring him tightly until he tired. It was what he would have done in their position.

With time running out, Kaz suddenly raised the gleaming battle-axe over his head and, with a Solamnic war cry that startled his foes, charged forward.

The goblins with the axe and the sword instinctively stepped back, fully aware that in both strength and reach they were at a disadvantage. Krynge, however, moved to meet Kaz, secure in the belief that his spear would enable him to blunt the mad assault. He would have been correct if, as he assumed, Kaz was trying to strike *him*.

The axe came down in a long arc. One edge hooked on the barbs of the spear. Krynge realized what was happening, but it was too late. Summoning strength that no goblin could hope to match, the minotaur used his weapon to rip the spear from the hapless goblin's claws. The spear went clattering to the ground behind Kaz.

Krynge, now unarmed, did the intelligent thing and backed away, desperately seeking some other weapon. The goblin with the sword, knowing full well the inevitable outcome of a duel with a minotaur—sword against an expertly wielded axe—turned and fled. Krynge shouted something venomous at his retreating form, then decided to follow. Skullcracker, out of either sheer stubbornness or madness, lunged at Kaz. His reach was shorter than the minotaur's, and he swung wildly. While the goblin was still following through with his attack, Kaz swung at his unprotected torso.

Skullcracker spun around once from the momentum of his own swing and then collapsed on the soil, a deep hole in his chest releasing his life's fluids.

Kaz wiped the axe blades clean and, confident that neither of the two survivors would return to bother him, turned his attention to the prisoner.

Huma stared back at him.

The minotaur blinked and found himself meeting the worn gaze of a face that now looked nothing like his legendary comrade. This one was older, in years if not experience, with a slightly rounded nose and one of the great mustaches common among the knighthood. His hair was light and not quite blond, something that might change if the dirt and blood were washed out of it.

The man's lips were cracked, and Kaz knew that he had not had a drop of water to drink for some time. He undid his water sack and brought it to the mouth of the knight. Despite a look of distrust that flashed over the human's features, the knight drank steadily.

Kaz pulled a knife from his belt and freed the knight's hands and feet.

"I . . . will tell . . . nothing, monster!" the man gasped.

Kaz snorted. "You have nothing to worry about from

me, Knight of Solamnia. I am no friend of goblins, as you can plainly see. I follow Paladine and Kiri-Jolith, not Sargas or his dark mistress."

The man's eyes revealed that he was not quite convinced, but he understood that, at least in Kaz's hands, he would be treated better.

The knight could barely move at the moment. Kneeling, Kaz did what he could to make him more comfortable. From his cursory examination, he saw that there were bruises aplenty, and the armor on the human's right leg looked bent and twisted, indicating a broken leg. He wished the healer, Tesela, was accompanying him still.

As he did his best to soothe and bind the injuries, Kaz tried to convince the knight of his safety.

"I am called Kaz. You are a Knight of the Crown, I see." He pointed at the battered remains of the human's helmet and breastplate. There were odd marks, like those made by giant talons, across the breastplate. "You are also from an outpost near southern Ergoth, I see. I briefly knew someone from another outpost in Ergoth itself. Buoron?"

The knight shook his head carefully. Kaz shrugged. Buoron had been a good knight, in some ways like Huma, who had died in the first battle utilizing the Dragonlances. The minotaur had known Buoron only briefly but had found him trustworthy and brave.

Kaz shifted, aware that his new companion was speaking. The man's voice was a hoarse whisper. "Darius. My name is Darius. You said . . . Kaz?"

"I did."

Darius pointed a feeble finger at the minotaur. "You are . . . the one wanted by . . . the Grand Master."

The minotaur laughed bitterly. "And do you plan to capture me for him?"

The knight shook his head weakly from side to side. "Not . . . after what . . . we have heard. All commands are . . . suspect."

"Suspect?"

"We were coming to . . . present our grievances. Our first messenger . . . did not return. His name appeared on a . . . proclamation. The same as you."

"Indeed. And now your companions have been conveniently massacred by goblins." Kaz shook his head. "I've come not to believe in coincidence."

Darius somehow succeeded in looking even more pale than before. "All dead?"

The minotaur nodded. "I believe so. I'm sorry, human. I have counted some good knights among my friends in the past. . . ."

"All dead . . ." The injured knight was babbling. He tried to rise.

Kaz held him down. "You'll kill *yourself* if you don't rest! I'm no healer, knight, and your injuries are going to be a part of you for some time, so relax!"

Even well, Darius would have been no match for Kaz. He settled back down, and the minotaur quickly checked him over again. It was always difficult to tell. There might be internal damage. . . .

"It killed them all," the knight whispered, half-unconscious due to the strain of his own outburst.

"What?" Kaz froze. He looked at Darius, but the knight was nearly asleep. "What do you mean, 'it'? The goblins did this, didn't they?"

The knight's eyes flickered open, but they looked beyond the minotaur. "Not the . . . the goblins. They found me . . . after it threw me. I was lucky; it . . . it seemed anxious to leave. Paladine! Its skin was as hard as stone! The wings! They—"

"Wings?" Kaz shivered, recalling the thing that had flown over his head one night. He had been that close to it! "What sort of beast was it?"

Darius succeeded in focusing on his benefactor. "Not a beast . . . not exactly. The lords of the earth. The children of light and darkness."

The litany was familiar to Kaz, something that he had heard countless times during his life. It was how some ancient bard had described . . . *No!*

"You can't be saying"—Kaz forced the words out—"a *dragon?*"

Darius grimaced as pain shot through him. "A dragon, minotaur—or something akin to a dragon! Something with huge claws, sky-encompassing wings, and jaws big enough to swallow a whole man!" The knight's face clouded over. "But . . . but it left their bodies . . . what it hadn't torn apart. I don't understand. It *was* and it *wasn't* a dragon."

Chapter 8

Feeling the lancing pain in his shoulder, Kaz lifted the gruesome burden he was carrying. With the utmost care, he placed the body of the last of Darius's dead comrades in the makeshift funeral pyre. The injured knight watched from a distance, his back against a gnarled tree. Darius lacked any strength for the task he kept insisting must be done. It was unthinkable to leave the bodies of so many brave men to scavengers like the carrion crows or, worse, goblins. Kaz had used up an entire day for this business, but he knew that Darius would not have moved on without giving his comrades a proper burial, even if he could.

There had been no further signs of the goblins. Kaz doubted they would be back, but he kept careful watch nonetheless.

The knight, more coherent than yesterday, still insisted that his band had been attacked by a dragon or something very similar. Kaz could not get the thought out of his mind. Everyone knew that all the dragons had disappeared.

"Your wound needs binding again, Kaz," the knight pointed out. "You don't want dust getting into the wound."

Grunting, Kaz squatted down next to his companion and let Darius do what he could for the binding. It was the only thing the knight could do in his present condition, and the minotaur knew that he desperately wanted to be useful.

"I thank you."

Kaz grunted. "I doubt I would've left your companions' bodies after all. I would've never forgiven myself, I think."

Though it was past noon, as well as one could tell in the overcast sky, there was a chill in the air uncommon for this time of year. The fire was to prove doubly useful. The knight needed the warmth, and Kaz needed something with which to light the pyre.

The minotaur rose and reached for the dry branch he had set aside for this purpose.

"Are there any words you wish to say?" he asked as he lit the branch.

Darius shook his head. "I said what needed to be said as you gathered the dead."

Kaz nodded and grimly stepped toward the pyre.

*   *   *   *   *

It started to rain just at the point when it became apparent that the fire had served its purpose. Kaz had calculated that the fire would burn itself out, but the rain allowed him to forego keeping an eye on it. By the time the last flame had perished, the rain had ceased.

"Praise be to Paladine," a somewhat damp Darius said quietly. He held out his hand to Kaz, an indication that he wanted to stand, and the minotaur helped him to his feet. "We should go now," the knight said.

"Don't you think we should wait until tomorrow? The rest can only help you."

A look of pain crossed the knight's pale face. "I fear that I have some wounds that only a cleric of Paladine or Mishakal can cure properly. I don't know about the latter, but Vingaard Keep's lords have always included the former."

Kaz disliked the thought of depending on anyone in Vingaard Keep for such aid, but he could not think of any better plan. Perhaps they would come across another cleric of Mishakal on their way to the stronghold of the knighthood. There certainly had to be some call for clerics in this desolate region. Someone had to be helping the villagers if the keep was not.

"We don't know what goes on at the keep now."

"But we will," Darius said with the imperious tone that Kaz recalled as being typical of many knights. Even Huma had adopted it now and then. It was the expression of someone who believes his cause is just and, therefore, one that will prevail.

With the crude, wooden staff that Kaz had made for him in one hand, the knight leaned against the minotaur. Kaz put an arm around his companion, and in this way, they started their journey together. It was awkward going, but they made progress.

The first village that Kaz had seen in some time peeked over the horizon near evening. Neither the minotaur nor the knight were familiar with this region, though both knew that Vingaard could only be two or three days ahead. Whether or not they should continue on to the village this very evening was a question.

Darius wanted to avoid the village entirely. He reminded Kaz that they were well within the range of Vingaard's patrols, and that there was still a bounty on the minotaur. "One sword stroke and you will never live to tell your side."

"I don't think I have to remind you, Darius of the Crown, that you are badly injured. We can feel fortunate that you haven't collapsed by now."

"I will do no such thing."

Kaz snorted wryly. "Even noble Solamnic knights have their physical limits. There may be a healer in the village, and I have yet to see a sign of a Solamnic patrol."

That bothered Kaz. When he had been in the general area last, the knighthood had patrolled the land with consistency. They ranged for miles around, far beyond the location where Darius and his fellows from the south had been mauled by the supposed dragon. Yet not only had that massacre gone unnoticed, but also goblins seemed to be wandering freely about in fair-sized bands.

What was happening at the keep? What was happening to Grand Master Oswal and his ambitious nephew, Bennett?

Darius was talking. "The decision is yours, minotaur. I do not claim a clear mind at the moment."

Studying the young knight's sickly visage, Kaz knew that Darius was understating his condition. That settled the situation as far as he was concerned.

"A few minutes of rest and then we move on. If there's a healer in that village, Darius, or even someone with more skill than I at cleaning and rebinding wounds, you will be taken care of immediately, or they'll learn how angry a minotaur can become." At the knight's anxious expression, Kaz smiled widely, displaying all of his teeth. "Rest easy, Darius. I'll only frighten them."

Though not entirely reassured, the human let himself be led along. The village proved to be nearer than they first thought. It was only a little after dark before they reached it. Most of the buildings were in sore need of repair, and refuse lay rotting in the streets. The place stank of unwashed bodies, yet mysteriously there seemed to be no one about. Kaz would have been of the opinion that the village was abandoned had he not noticed a dim light down the path. Their route, which ran through the center of the settlement, led directly to it.

"I see an inn," Kaz whispered. Darius nodded wearily.

As they followed the path, the minotaur became aware of the fact that, though the village seemed deserted, unseen eyes watched from virtually every building. With his free hand, he began to softly stroke the handle of his battle-axe. Next to him, he felt the knight tense. As injured and beaten as he was, Darius, too, felt the presence of watchers.

Whatever name the inn once bore, it had faded away so badly that the sign was unreadable in the torchlight. Kaz hesitated only long enough to assure himself of his grip on his companion, then pushed the door open. Without waiting for any reaction from those who might be inside, he stepped through, Darius practically dragged along by his momentum.

"I come in peace," he announced in a stentorian voice—and immediately thereafter blinked, noticing that there were only three figures in the room, and one of them was lying on a nearby table in a position indicative of death. The other two figures were known to him, which provoked a surprised expression on his face.

"Kaz!" A nimble little figure rushed forward and hugged the minotaur.

"I'm very much alive, Delbin, but you won't be for very long if you don't let go!"

The kender leaped back, that omnipresent grin aimed at the huge figure he had thought was dead and gone. "It's good to see you, Kaz! How did you survive? The minotaurs abandoned us when they saw you get washed down the river, and I guess they went to claim your body, but Tesela thought that they would never find it because the river becomes really deep and wild a little farther south. In fact, if we ever get down that way I wouldn't mind—"

"Take a breath, Delbin," the little one's companion said

in amusement. Tesela, a beatific smile across her face, moved away from the prone figure and greeted the minotaur. "We searched for you ourselves for a few days, then the kender said that he had to journey to Vingaard to speak for you, since if you were dead, then you would never be able to complete your quest."

Kaz, brow creased in puzzlement, glanced at Delbin. The kender, suddenly shy and speechless, mumbled, "You're my friend, Kaz."

Despite himself, the minotaur gave his small companion a short, encouraging smile. Delbin beamed.

"I was traveling in this direction anyway, so I stayed with him." Tesela eyed the kender. "Aside from a few occasions where people's belongings somehow ended up in his pouch, things went without incident, praise to Mishakal." For the first time, her glance fell directly on Darius, who tried in vain to bow. Tesela's expression turned to one of great concern.

"Get him over there," she said, pointing at another table. "Forgive me, knight, for being so preoccupied that I did not notice the extent of your wounds."

"I take . . . n-no offense, cleric, but what about . . . that other?" Darius gasped as they helped him onto the table. "Milady, continue with him, please. I can wait."

Tesela looked sadly at the other man, a haggard old beggar. His hands were clasped across his chest. "He is beyond my powers, Knight of Solamnia. He was beyond my powers when he came to me, the poor, frightened man."

"Frightened?" Kaz asked, his eyes on the corpse.

"Frightened." Tesela began removing the battered remnants of Darius's armor. "You actually walked around in this pile of scrap?"

The knight looked both embarrassed and insulted. "This suit is almost all I have in the world and the only remembrance of my family. Our estate is now as barren as these lands, and I am the only one to survive the war." He swallowed hard. "Until my companions and I were attacked, it served me quite well."

The cleric inspected some of the wounds. She touched her patient near the lower left ribs, and Darius cried out. "By the Three, woman! Do you intend that I join the old beggar in the beyond?"

"I have to know a bit about what is hurting you before I pray to Mishakal," she snapped. "Mishakal trusts her clerics to know what they are doing, so you had better let me continue. Depending on your injuries, I may have to pray over you for as much as a full day, although I doubt you are that badly off. And Mishakal also does not give something for nothing. She is not to be taken for granted, knight."

"I apologize, milady."

Kaz leaned over and looked at Tesela. "Is there anything that I can do?"

She glanced up at him. "You might get something to drink for yourself, and then take a rest. I don't doubt you've taken most of the burden today."

The minotaur looked around. "Where is the innkeeper?"

"Gone. At least a week. I doubt he'll ever come back. People do that here, I'm told. Just walk off and leave everything. I guess even these souls have a breaking point."

"What do you mean?"

She took her medallion in her hands. "I'll tell you later. If both you and Delbin wouldn't mind stepping into another room, it should make my task easier."

Kaz grunted assent and walked over to the counter, Delbin trailing behind. The kender had remained silent for too long. Now he was brimming over with questions.

"What happened to the knight, Kaz? Did you meet any other people? It seems that everyone fears strangers, especially knights. No one's gone near the keep for weeks, they say. Why d'ya suppose that is?"

The kender quieted momentarily as Kaz handed him a mug of something drawn from a barrel under the counter. They both drank a deep draft, then grimaced at the sour taste.

"Bad," Kaz muttered and put the mug down. He pulled out his water pouch and drank from it. The water, which came from a stream he and Darius had passed earlier in the day, was brackish, but it still tasted better than the unidentifiable liquid from the barrel.

"The people, Delbin—I sense their presence. They watched as we walked by. I *felt* it. They *are* frightened of something."

"Tesela says they are, and she oughta know, because they're surely afraid of her. That old man was only the third one to come to her since we arrived here five days ago. Death was ready to claim him, Tesela said. He was afraid she would demand payment or hard labor from him before doing any healing. He was also afraid she might send him away or beat him like—" Delbin hesitated and looked over toward the room where Darius lay—"like one of the knights had already done."

"*What?*" Kaz cursed silently. "Come in here with me," he added, indicating a door that probably led to a back room for storage.

Such was the case. Kaz found a box that smelled slightly of rotting oak and sat on it. It creaked but held. Delbin found a small stool and planted himself with great eagerness.

"Go on," Kaz said grimly.

Delbin's story confirmed the rumors the minotaur had been hearing. In this territory, the knighthood's actions had grown to resemble the very cruelties that had led its founder, Vinas Solamnus, to turn on his master, the emperor of Ergoth. Solamnia now faced ruin and panic. The knights of Vingaard Keep, heart of the Orders, no longer even pretended to patrol the land, and now goblins and other vultures were stealing into the area to raid those too weak or too listless to defend themselves.

"This is madness; this is evil," Kaz whispered angrily. Delbin cocked his head. "Are you still going to Vingaard Keep? It could be dangerous, but if you go, I'm going, too, because I was worried about you, and when I thought you'd died, it was awful. Don't you dare die for a while, promise? Say, I should write down what happened to you!"

The kender reached into his pouch and pulled out something out that in no way resembled his cherished book, although it was made of paper. It was a scroll, to be precise.

"Hmmph! Look at this! It's got funny writing on it, Kaz—and it mentions you!"

"Let me see!" Kaz tore the paper from the kender's hands and read the scroll. "My name's on it. '. . . has been found guilty of the dishonorable and heinous crime of murder, and thus, by order of the emperor's council, this oath breaker is proclaimed criminal in all lands. Those who bear this document are servants of the emperor of the minotaur race and have been granted whatever power necessary to obtain the capture or execution, if necessary, of the murderer. Cooperation with the bearers of this proclamation is requested.' Very polite and formal." The minotaur crumpled up the paper in a sudden rush of fury and threw it at his companion. " 'Emperor'! An ogre toadie still clinging to power! How did you get this, Delbin?"

The kender's eyes grew wide. "That's what I wanted to tell you! The short minotaur, the leader—remember how he threw the spear?"

"I could hardly forget, Delbin." Kaz frowned. "Only, I remember something else. They seemed to be fighting amongst themselves. . . ."

Nodding in excitement, Delbin cut him off. "That's right, Kaz! One of the other ones came up behind him, and when he saw what the shorter one had done, he hit him hard. They fought, and another of your people, I guess it was a female, stood nearby watching. The shorter one had a knife, and he tried to cut the bigger one's throat with it, but the bigger one finally got his arm around the shorter one's neck and twisted his head. I guess he broke his neck. The female, she came over and helped him throw the body into the river, and then they ran off together into the woods. A little later, I found a nifty-looking pack on the riverbank, and I thought it was yours, only there was nothing in it but some food and that scroll. I guess I forgot all about it till now."

A fight among his relentless pursuers? A fight that left Greel dead? Curious.

A loud crash from the front of the inn brought Kaz to his feet. He burst into the main room and saw Tesela moving toward the door. One of the windows, which previously had been shuttered, had been broken open by a large and very heavy rock.

"What happened here?" the minotaur demanded.

"I think that the townspeople want your companion," the cleric said quietly, indicating the unconscious Darius. "The knights are not loved here."

"We have to stay the night, healer."

"I know." She glanced outside, but there was no one there. Closing the door again, Tesela walked over to the window and managed to fix the shutters. "I need more time with him. Why don't you two get some sleep? We're safe. I don't think these terrified villagers can cause much trouble, other than throwing a few stones and running away." She glanced at Kaz. "All the same, I think we should be away from here before sunrise."

"Agreed." Kaz watched her return to her meditations. Grabbing a curious Delbin by the scruff of his collar, he retired to the far end of the room. Kaz deposited the kender on one bench and, after removing his axe from its harness, stretched out on another bench nearby. He closed his eyes just as the kender decided he could remain silent no longer.

"Where'd you get that neat axe?" Delbin whispered. "Is it of dwarven make? How come it shines so brightly? I bet it's magic! Who gave it to you? Or did you win it in a fight?"

The prattle went on and on until the kender looked more closely at his friend and decided that Kaz had fallen asleep. Delbin itched to see what Tesela was doing or to explore the village outside, but he had promised the human that he would behave himself, and now Kaz was here and he would expect only the best of his small companion. . . . The kender fell asleep only seconds later, snoring lightly.

Kaz opened his eyes a fraction. Delbin could be predictable at times, and the minotaur knew the kender must have been exhausted. Carefully Kaz's fingers stroked the handle of the battle-axe. Tesela might think they need fear little from the locals, but Kaz had learned that even the most apathetic group could be turned into an angry mob in an instant if given an excuse to vent their frustrations.

Closing his eyes slowly, Kaz allowed himself to fall into a half-sleep. All around, he could sense something happening, but at the same time, he could not discern what it was. It was a respite of sorts, therefore, but not a restful sleep. There would be time for real sleep when the matters of Solamnia, Vingaard, and his own dilemma were settled.

* * * * *

Kaz woke with a start as he detected the sounds of a pair of feet moving lightly across the inn floor. Kaz gripped the axe and raised his eyelids a crack. The healer was standing by the inn's entrance. She seemed to be looking for someone or something outside. Kaz rose slowly and, without disturbing Delbin, joined her. In one huge, clawed hand he held the axe.

"Did you hear something?" he asked quietly.

"I don't . . . know. It might have been just the wind, but . . ." Tesela had lost her mask of confidence, and once more she seemed to be an ordinary, frightened person. She had probably heard nothing more than one of the locals daring to spy on them. Probably . . .

Something heavy bounced off the roof of the inn, shaking it to its foundation. Delbin rose, blinking. Outside, a violent wind tore objects loose. There was another sound, but the howl of the wind rose to smother it.

"What's happening out there?" Kaz snarled.

"What is it, Kaz? Is some kind of tornado? Do you think it'll tear the inn down, and if it does, shouldn't we get out of here before—"

"Take a breath, Delbin," Kaz muttered automatically. He nudged Tesela aside and peered out into the gloom. It was still not yet dawn, but the moons were not visible, either.

Somewhere nearby, Kaz heard the crash of wood and a very human scream. Tightening his grip on his battle-axe, he tore out of the inn and followed the dying arc of the noise. Around him, he could hear the inhabitants of the village as they scurried to cower in their homes.

"Fools! Cowards! One of your own is dying!" His words had no effect. These people had little spirit.

Kaz stumbled. A building that had suffered a mysterious disaster was suddenly before him . . . as was something else, something very large, very powerful, and very vicious.

The thing that was in the process of reducing the building to splinters rose, revealing itself to be more than twice the minotaur's height. As Kaz retreated hastily, he heard a beating noise, identical to the flapping that had passed over him days earlier—the beast, he had no reason to doubt, that had killed an entire band of knights save one.

The beating of the wings was in his ears, and Kaz knew the creature was practically right on top of him. If he was to die a victim of a dragon, if a dragon was what it truly was, then the minotaur wouldn't die without striking at least one great blow.

Even as Kaz whirled, his dwarven axe swinging in a vicious arc, massive talons passed over his head, missing by mere inches. The skillfully crafted battle-axe struck harshly against the flank of the behemoth and bounced off with a loud ringing sound. Kaz stumbled around, waiting for the next attack, but it never came. The creature was flying away as if Kaz were nothing but a momentary obstacle.

Kaz felt the edge of the axe head. It was chipped.

"Come back here, dragon . . . or whatever pit-spawned creature you are! Face me!" What the inhabitants of the village might think, he did not care. He only knew that he wanted that thing.

It did not return, but Kaz realized that the monster, dragon, or whatever it was had come from the north and now was returning in that direction. If it kept to its present path, it would fly over Vingaard Keep itself. . . .

Kaz cursed and swung the damaged axe into its harness. Ignoring the whispers and whimpers rising from within the various houses and huts, he rushed back toward the inn. Whether alone or not, he knew that he had to reach Vingaard as soon as possible. Vingaard Keep was the key to everything. There he would find the answers he was seeking . . .

. . . and possibly a dragon as well.

Chapter 9

Kaz burst through the doorway of the inn, looking much like a demon from the Abyss. Delbin gave a squeak, and Tesela's hands clutched tightly around the medallion she wore. Darius still slept, but he seemed to twitch momentarily as the minotaur strode over to the human cleric.

"You have a horse, Tesela. Can it carry me?"

"Carry you? Why?"

If Kaz could have seen himself, he might have hesitated, for the cleric and the kender gazed upon the frenzied eyes of a berserker. His eyes said he would accept only one answer, regardless of the consequences.

"Can . . . it . . . carry . . . me?" he repeated through clenched teeth.

Tesela nodded, pale. "I—I think she should be strong enough, but—"

"Where is it?"

"Around back! Kaz . . ."

He was through the inn and out the back door in seconds. Tesela's horse was tied up next to Delbin's pony. Both animals were nervous, and it took a little doing to get the cleric's mount to hold still long enough for him to mount. Kaz climbed into the saddle—and abruptly fell off as the horse sat down.

"Sargas take you, you blasted beast! Stand up!"

The horse refused to do so. Kaz tried to pull it to its feet, but the animal's front hooves dug into the ground, and the minotaur only succeeded in losing his grip and slipping to one knee.

"Kaz!" Tesela came rushing out. "Stop that!"

"Is this thing part mule?" Kaz grumbled. He was certain the horse was mocking him.

Tesela laughed nervously. "I tried to tell you, but you wouldn't listen. She only lets me ride her."

Kaz muttered something and rose to his feet. "Is there a stable? Where can I find another horse?"

"You won't find anything here. These people don't have any horses."

"Kiri-Jolith's horns, human! I have to get to Vingaard Keep!"

Folding her arms, Tesela said with authority, "Then you will wait until we are ready to go. You cannot go alone, Kaz, and we will not let you. Give me a chance to see if the knight is healed, and then we will prepare to depart this place together. It will mean a much slower pace, I'm afraid, but you can put that time to good use thinking about what you intend to do once we arrive. I mean *really* think about it."

He let out a great breath. "You confuse me, cleric. You are so contradictory at times."

She smiled slowly and moved to take the horse's reins from him. "You should try dealing with a minotaur."

Kaz nodded slowly, thinking to himself that she might have a point.

* * * * *

Darius was awake and feeling much, much better. He stared at his hands, flexed his arms and legs, and stood. "Praise Paladine!"

"And Mishakal," Tesela reminded him.

"And Mishakal, of course. My thanks, cleric." He bowed nervously to her and she reddened a bit.

"Does this mean we can go?" Kaz asked impatiently. He was happy for the knight—no warrior likes to be helpless—but each second of delay tore at him, especially since he knew that they only had two mounts for four people and would have to travel at a slow pace.

The knight forced his eyes away from Tesela. "Go where?"

"To Vingaard Keep, of course. Your dragon was here only a short time ago, and now I think it flies in the direction of the keep itself."

"The dragon?" exclaimed Darius. "Attacking Vingaard! We have to leave!"

"What can you possibly do that all the knights in Vingaard could not do?" Tesela asked.

"That is not the point, milady! I am a knight—"

"Who should know better than to go rushing into battle—" she glanced at Kaz—"like a minotaur. You might try putting on whatever still remains of your armor. The sword would come in handy as well."

It didn't take long for the group to ready itself. Only Darius really had any difficulty, and that was due to some of the dents and bends in his armor. Kaz helped there, taking some of the pieces and utilizing his astounding strength to straighten them out as best as possible. The knight, who had never fought a minotaur, automatically uttered an oath to Paladine. Tesela shook her head in amazement. Delbin, who had seen Kaz do similar things in the past, tried to tell everyone about each and every such incident. By unanimous consent, he was told to take a deep breath and get the horses ready.

They departed the village—none of them had ever discovered its name—just as the first sunlight spilled over the horizon. Kaz had little hope that they would actually have a sunlit day. Beyond a certain point in the morning, the orb would find itself hidden behind a thick mass of clouds. This weather was not right, the minotaur knew. It reminded him too much of the war and of the lands about to fall to the servants of Takhisis. Where evil ruled, the sun rarely shone, it was said, and evil could not prevail in Solamnia. Not in the homeland of Paladine's earthly champions.

Could it?

Kaz buried the thought deep in his mind as they traveled. Vingaard Keep would be visible before day's end. He would have his answers soon enough.

The trek was hardest on Darius, though not because of his injuries. Those the power of Mishakal had healed completely. Rather, it was the land itself that seemed to affect the knight. Like so many others, he had expected Solamnia to be well on its way to recovery by now. This—this was a wasteland.

"How do so many survive here?" he asked Kaz in horror. "How do they survive?"

"The land's not completely dead, human, but I agree it must be near impossible."

No goblins harried them; no dragon or other beast swooped down to throw them about like toys. The day would have actually been pleasant, if not for the specter of the land itself. Kaz noted that Tesela constantly fingered her medallion. Thinking of Delbin, Kaz glanced at the small figure perched atop the pony next to him. Delbin was growing very moody, an odd reaction for one of his kind. Kender were habitually cheerful. Kaz thought of asking his companion what was worrying him. The thought of a kender trying to explain such a complicated emotion made him hesitate, however, and the matter slipped away.

With the early evening came a distant, mist-enshrouded surprise.

Darius was the first to recognize it as more than just another indistinct speck on the horizon. Only he made the connection between where they were and the relative size of the thing.

The one word he uttered was barely more than a whisper. "Vingaard!"

Kaz narrowed his eyes and tried to make out anything more than a blur. "Are you certain?"

"What else could it be?"

"True." Even though they had made far better time than Kaz would have thought possible, the citadel of the Knights of Solamnia was still a goal they would not reach until tomorrow. Kaz hated the thought of stopping when they were so close, but reminded himself that this land had both goblins and some great unnamed beast wandering about. Let the enemy come to them. Better that than walking into an ambush. Besides, although they had not as yet seen any Solamnic patrols, who was to say there was not one nearby even now?

It was an uneasy group that made camp that night. Both Kaz and Darius searched the skies continuously. Delbin, as moody as before, fell asleep almost immediately after finishing his meal. Tesela, having slept the least the night before, soon joined him.

Darius offered to take first watch. Kaz argued with him briefly, but gave in. It turned out not to matter very much. Neither one could sleep well that night, and each spent the other's watch period waiting impatiently for the dawn.

The night was so uneventful that Kaz had to wonder if he, too, should carry a blank book, much like Delbin's, to record such rare nights. Yet despite the calm of the evening, the minotaur rose at dawn with such anxiety that his hands were quivering in anticipation of . . . what? He could not say for certain. It was the same feeling that had been growing inside him for days. He both needed and loathed the impending confrontation with Lord Oswal.

They passed a few more poor settlements where ragged people lived phantom existences. One or two hardy souls cursed at them, but no one attempted to do them any harm. Kaz could not say what disturbed them more, his presence or that of the knight, Darius. It was apparently evident to Darius as well that some of the folk were glaring at him. He gave Kaz an agonized look. For one who had decided to devote his existence to the glory of Paladine, this was a slap in the face. The Knights of Solamnia were supposed to be the benefactors of the people, not their cursed enemies.

Vingaard Keep grew ever larger on the horizon, seeming to take on a slightly different form as they neared. There was something ominous about its appearance, not to mention the fact that they still had not been intercepted by a single patrol. Such a thing was unheard of. Kaz began to fiddle with his axe, eventually pulling it out of the harness completely. He noted that Darius had his hand on his sword, and even Delbin stroked one of the daggers he wore. Tesela, weaponless, was muttering prayers under her breath.

"The banners are missing," Darius pointed out.

Kaz shrugged. "Perhaps they only lie limp because of the lack of wind."

It was true. There was no wind, no sound. Even the chatter of the carrion crows would have been preferable to the oppressive silence overhanging the land.

They passed more buildings, some of which showed signs of needing repair, but all were empty. It was as if the people had simply abandoned them.

"No one wants to live too near Vingaard Keep, it seems," Kaz grumbled.

In some places, attempts at farming caught their eyes. Sad-looking cornstalks, no higher than Delbin, and wild patches of oats dotted the landscape. Being so close to the knighthood, this area had gone the farthest toward recuperation. Had something not occurred to bring that revitalization to a halt, there might have been tall fields by now.

"Will we have any trouble gaining entrance at the gates?" Tesela asked Darius.

Kaz, who had been wondering the same thing, stared at the gates. He blinked, thinking that his eyes played tricks. The vision did not change. He snorted in puzzlement. "I don't think we need worry about being barred from entering."

"Why is that?"

They were now close enough that Vingaard could be given more scrutiny. Kaz pointed at the gates. "Unless I miss my guess, the gates are already partially open."

Darius froze in his tracks and squinted. It was true; even from here, it was possible to tell that the gates stood wide open.

"Impossible!" the knight muttered. "This is a dereliction of duty!"

"It may be more than that," Kaz grunted. "It may be much more than that."

Their pace had been as swift as possible, considering that two of their members had to walk. Now, however, the group slowed, uneasy about the odd signs. Tesela brought up another observation, one that they had all noticed, but feared to mention.

"Where are the sentries, Darius? Where are all the knights? Shouldn't this place be brimming with activity?"

The knight nodded uneasily. "It should, but it may be that they are in a war situation somewhere, or perhaps they are at prayer."

Neither of his suggestions satisfied anyone in the least. Vingaard continued to loom. Its walls seemed impossibly high and long. There were slits for archers, but little else marked the walls. The two massive doors, more than twice the height of Kaz, were the only decorated parts that they could see. They were each emblazoned with the symbol of the knighthood, the majestic kingfisher that stood, wings outstretched, holding a sword in its talons. A rose was centered on the sword, and a great crown seemed to float above the kingfisher's head.

"I see someone!" Delbin suddenly cried, lifting himself up and down in his saddle and pointing in the direction of the battlements of the keep, much to the annoyance of his tired pony.

The other three all looked up but saw no one. Kaz turned and glared at the kender. Delbin shook his head in protest. "I *did* see someone, Kaz. I think it was a knight; that is, he wore armor, and who else but a knight would be in Vingaard Keep?"

Kaz waved him silent. "Don't explain. If you think you saw someone, then you saw someone."

"Then the keep is not abandoned," Darius said with some relief.

"Which doesn't mean it's the knighthood that now controls it," Kaz added darkly.

"True."

As they drew closer and closer, the vast, silent keep grew, like some patiently waiting predator. Despite their utmost vigilance, they spotted no other inhabitants. Nevertheless, Delbin insisted that there had been someone.

Gazing down at the ground, Darius studied the tracks of the many animals that had traveled to and from the keep. There was something amiss with the prints in the dust, and he asked Kaz about them. The minotaur stared at them briefly, recognizing what was disturbing the knight.

Kaz kicked at some of the prints. The dust scattered, obliterating several prints. He put one foot down so that his toe touched the front of one of the unburied hoofmarks. "This horse—all these horses—are riding *from* Vingaard Keep. With this dust, these prints should not have lasted if they had returned. We should see signs of horses *entering*. I only see a couple."

"And there are so many departing." Darius said nothing more, but his eyes swept across the plain before them. It was covered with tracks, nearly all leading away from the keep. Kaz could see that the knight was trying to convince himself that his fellows had entered from some other direction, or that the tracks meant nothing whatsoever. That was always possible.

When at last they stood at the gate, they were somewhat confused as to what to do. No one had hailed them, and there was an open gate. The space was wide enough for the horses to pass through with ease.

"We will announce ourselves," Darius said stiffly. He stepped in front of the others and looked upward.

"Darius of Trebbel, Knight of the Crown, assigned to the keep in lower Wystia, requests entrance into Vingaard Keep, most noble home of the fighting arm of Paladine and residence of the Grand Master—"

Kaz snorted in frustration, leaned his battle-axe on his shoulder, and stalked toward the open gate. After a moment's hesitation, Delbin urged his pony after the minotaur. Behind them, they heard Darius break off as he realized what the two were doing.

Feeling somewhat like an offering to a quiet, cold god, Kaz led the way through the gates and into the keep itself.

* * * * *

South of Vingaard Keep, near where Kaz had rescued Darius, a group of riders paused while one of them climbed off his horse to investigate something on the ground. After several moments, he looked back toward the others.

"Two sets of footprints . . . this way, milord."

A visored figure clad in the armor of a Knight of the Rose joined the ranger. The ranger, a man preferring the woodland regions to the southwest, shivered. Like many, he had come to distrust any who followed the Solamnic Order, especially here in the war-torn north. Worse yet, the knight kneeling beside him was a lord of the Order of the Rose, and at his beck and call were nearly two hundred other knights—two hundred knights and one nervous ranger.

"A survivor of the massacre and his rescuer." The knight's helm gave his voice an echoing quality. "At least, that seems likely, considering someone went to the trouble of destroying this filth." He indicated what remained of the goblin whose arm Kaz had completely severed. The goblin had crawled away and eventually died.

The knight rose and the ranger quickly followed suit. Gauntleted hands removed the helmet, revealing a handsome, somewhat arrogant man with fine, hawklike features. As was the custom of the knighthood, he wore a tremendous mustache. Dark hair flowed loosely now that the helm was gone. Despite an air of command and experience, he was young for one in his position.

"Young but getting older by the second," Bennett, Lord Knight of the Order of the Rose, would have replied. He noted that the pair of tracks moved northward, the same direction his band was even now headed. Vingaard Keep lay that way. Vingaard Keep, home to the knighthood itself. A place where he had virtually grown up, being the son of one Grand Master and the nephew of another.

He shivered at the thought of returning to that place now that the curse had been lifted from his mind.

"Two days," he muttered. The ranger looked at him blankly. Bennett explained. "In two days, I want us in sight of the keep. Not there, but in sight of it." *What is the range of that . . . whatever it was?* he wondered. *Will we fall prey to it immediately? Will it strike us in stages, one by one, until we are mad once more?*

The memory of one knight, a good knight, turning mad without warning and running himself through with his own sword made Bennett almost reconsider. They could not turn back now, however. Not while Vingaard

Keep was becoming warped and twisted, a mockery of its own tradition.

Not while his uncle, the Grand Master, a victim of the spell of madness that seemed to linger over Vingaard, sat in his chambers and fought a war against enemies who likely existed only in his own mind.

Great Paladine, is this a test of our faith? Of mine?

A flash of white in the distance caught his attention. He wiped the dust of a long journey from his eyes and looked again. *Has the madness returned so soon?*

"What is it, milord? Did you see something?"

"No." Bennett disliked the lie, but he liked the truth even less. *An albino wolf? Am I seeing memories?*

He quickly replaced the helm, the better to hide his uncertainties, and turned toward those who had put their lives in his hands. Not all were of the Order of the Rose, but all were his to command as senior knight in this crisis situation. Six years ago, he would have accepted that fact with no anxieties. Likely, he would have also led these men to their deaths—if indeed they were that fortunate. Times changed. Outlooks changed.

May I have your strength, Huma of the Lance.

At Bennett's signal, they mounted up. Nearly all of them had suffered through the same madness as he had. There was the elf, too. He wondered what had become of him.

Mounted, he turned to the ranger, who was staring uneasily around them. "What ails you?"

"The goblins did not attack the party from the southern keeps, milord. Whatever it was, it was *huge.*"

"The days of dragons are long past us, man, and I know of no creature so large and vicious in this part of the country. Rest assured, our danger lies in Vingaard Keep, not in the skies or in this desolation around us." Bennett believed that wholeheartedly. Goblins and raiders were incidental compared to what lay in—under?—Vingaard Keep.

As the column began to move, his thoughts drifted to

the two who had taken the time to give the dead knights a decent pyre. At least one, he was certain, was a knight. The other? The footprints looked inhuman, more like an ogre or goblin, but neither of those races would have any respect for human dead. It was not an elf, either. Could it be . . . Hardly. Only a fool would dare journey into the heart of a land that had named him villain. Even a minotaur was not that simpleminded.

Whoever they were, Bennett hoped they would somehow have the good sense to avoid Vingaard Keep.

Chapter 10

Stepping into Vingaard Keep reminded Kaz of stepping into one of own his nightmares. There was an unreal quality to the place, encouraged by the lengthening shadows as the day slowly died. Every second, Kaz expected some ghastly figure to leap out from a hiding place.

"Where is everyone?" Tesela whispered. There was no real need to whisper. Darius's shouts should have alerted any within these walls that the party was there. On the other hand, it still seemed somehow proper to whisper.

"Paladine preserve us," the knight muttered. He was staring at the refuse scattered about the courtyard. Several great piles, taller than Kaz, were spread about the open areas of the keep. They appeared to be lined up in some sort of pattern, but for what purpose no one could say. Everything seemed to have been included: chairs, armor, tools, and much more.

Kaz narrowed his eyes as he scanned the interior of the keep. Lack of maintenance had taken its toll on the buildings. Moss and ivy grew unchecked. Everything had a thin layer of grime and dirt.

Darius took the reins of Tesela's mount—and Delbin's, as an afterthought—and led both animals to the stable. After peering inside, he tied the horses to a post rather than leading them into the stable itself. When he returned to the others, he explained. "As near as I can see, no one has cleaned that place in months. There are no horses in there, and I would never forgive myself if I put ours in that sty. It's a breeding ground for disease."

"Evidently it's seen recent use, then," Kaz commented.

"A month, perhaps two months ago. The cleaning stopped long before that, though."

The minotaur leaned lightly on his battle-axe. "Delbin saw someone—or something—while we were riding up to the gate. A knight, possibly? I say we continue to look around."

"I don't think I'd like to separate, if it's all the same to you," Tesela said quietly. Her right hand had not left her medallion. No matter the powers bequeathed to her as a cleric of Mishakal, Kaz knew that she was no trained fighter. Bravery counted only so much against what they might find lurking in the keep.

"We'll stay together."

"It will take longer to search," Darius pointed out.

"And if one of us falls into trouble, it'll take forever to find that one. Better to stay together. Vingaard Keep is no longer what I would consider a safe haven. Goblins might have very well set up camp in some part of it."

"Perhaps you would rather we depart."

Kaz shook his head. "I've come all the way here to confront the Grand Master, and I won't leave until I know for certain whether he's here or not. If he is, I have business with him." He looked at Delbin and Tesela. "You two might be better off waiting for us outside."

He already knew Delbin's answer and was not surprised when the cleric also refused. "You yourself said we should stay together."

Necessity made for strange companions, Kaz thought wryly.

It seemed likely that Lord Oswal, if he still ruled here, would be found in his quarters, which were situated in the middle of the keep. Vingaard, however, could be a great maze to the uninitiated. Darius, who had not been back to Vingaard in more than two years, found his memories oddly vague, to the point where in fact Kaz, who had not been there in five years, was able to recall some things in more detail. Kaz ended up leading the tiny group as they made their way deeper into Vingaard. Even he, however, found his mind go almost blank at times. The minotaur grew even more unsettled, for he was certain that the lapse was not entirely his fault. There was a feeling about the place that ate at his nerves.

Shadows lengthened and swelled, enshrouding complete sections of the massive fortress. The only one seeming to enjoy their trek was the kender. Delbin's earlier gloom had given way to curiosity. It was hard to keep him from rushing off to investigate some little interesting nook. The last thing Kaz wanted to do—and he reminded Delbin of that—was to go searching for the kender in a structure as large as Vingaard. Nevertheless, Delbin continued to range farther and farther afield.

Kaz caught the flicker of a torch as what little sun there was vanished over one of the outer walls. "Look there!"

It was gone after only a moment, not as if someone had tried to hide it, but rather as if the bearer had simply walked away. Kaz suddenly had the vague feeling that the party was not so much alone as being ignored by whoever still inhabited Vingaard.

"It leads away from where you wished to go, Kaz," Darius pointed out.

"Makes no difference. If someone else is in here, I want to know who it is.

Wordlessly, they weaved through the alleys and paths as best they could, hoping to catch some glimpse of the elusive torchbearer or some other inhabitant, yet they well knew that they could be walking into a trap.

A quarter of an hour passed, and Kaz called a halt. Tesela and Darius, lacking the incredible stamina of a minotaur, were only too happy to oblige. The minotaur took a deep breath. The torchbearer was gone, to only Paladine knew where.

Cursing quietly, Kaz was about to inform the others that they should turn back when he discovered another problem. Delbin was missing. In fact, he could not recall when last he had seen the kender. Neither could the two humans.

"Sargas take that runt!" Kaz swore. He was beginning to have a terrible dream in which they all became separated and spent the rest of eternity wandering through the mazelike alleys of this keep. "I warned him!"

A huge shape flitted overhead. It was gone before any of them even had a chance to look up.

"Perhaps the kender did not leave of his own free will," Darius suggested grimly. He turned in a circle, as if expecting enemies from all sides.

"I think that we'd have noticed if a dragon—or whatever it is—swooped down and made off with Delbin. Let's backtrack."

"Do you think that is a wise idea?" Tesela asked.

Kaz shrugged. "I don't really know. I just suddenly don't like the thought of standing around here."

They had not even taken a step when a bell began to ring. Kaz and Tesela peered through the gloom at Darius, who was listening intently.

The bell stopped tolling.

"Odd. Unless I am totally mistaken, that is the bell for evening prayer. I suppose it would be the proper hour."

"We passed the bell tower some time back," Kaz reminded them. "It could be Delbin, I suppose. . . ."

"Delbin is hardly that foolish," Tesela stated resolutely. The minotaur could not argue. Kender were adventurous, not stupid.

It was difficult going now. Darkness had almost entirely claimed the keep. The trio stumbled around, vaguely nearing the bell tower.

Darius, momentarily in the lead, nearly ran into a tall object suddenly blocking their path. It took several seconds for them to realize that this particular object was a Knight of Solamnia, fully clad in mail and carrying a sturdy longsword. The knight wore a face-concealing helm. Despite the near accident, he had not budged one step.

"Did you not hear the bell?" the newcomer rumbled within his helm. "All save the dragonwatch are to be in prayer, as the Grand Master commands."

Sheathing his sword, Darius began, "We've only just arrived in Vingaard Keep, friend, and we—"

The other knight leaned forward, as if seeing his counterpart's companions for the first time. "Demonspawn!"

Without explanation, Darius suddenly found himself backing up before a sword strike intended to lop his head off. Kaz, seeing that his comrade would not be able to free his sword in time, charged forward, battle-axe thrust out before him. The longsword's blade bounced off the side of the axe head with a sharp *ting!* and the attacking knight lost his grip on the weapon. It fell to the ground even as Kaz continued his charge, barreling into his adversary before the man could recover. As the two of them collided, the minotaur was nearly overwhelmed by an odd stench emitted by the knight. The two of them fell to the ground, Kaz on top.

Kaz had always considered his strength far superior to that of most humans. Even among his own kind, Kaz's strength had won him renown in the arenas where he had vied for rank among his fellows. Now, though, he found himself struggling to maintain his advantage. The knight not only matched his power, but he also began to overcome the minotaur.

"Darius!" he succeeded in grunting. His companion hesitated, caught between loyalty to the order and his growing friendship with the minotaur. At last he moved to aid Kaz.

"Take . . . off . . . his helm!"

The unknown knight struggled in vain as Darius worked the helm off. Darius almost dropped it when he saw the face of the knight.

"Hit him!"

Gritting his teeth and praying to Paladine for forgiveness, Darius struck his brother knight hard across the jaw, and then struck him again when the other did not flinch. This time the man was stunned. The trapped knight continued to struggle mindlessly, however, and Kaz was forced to administer a final punch to the jaw.

"The first soul we run into in Vingaard, and it turns out to be a berserker," Kaz muttered, rubbing his own throat. There was some bleeding, he could tell, and no doubt there would be marks of the struggle for the next few days.

Thinking of the cleric, Kaz whirled around, almost expecting to discover that she, like Delbin, had vanished. Instead, he found her watching them with some relief.

"I'm sorry, Kaz, Darius. I tried my best, but he wouldn't react."

"React?"

"I was trying to put him to sleep. His resistance was incredible."

"Not surprising," Darius replied softly. He was kneeling next to his counterpart, examining his armor and face. "He is a Knight of the Rose. They have some power of their own in matters of faith."

Kaz stood and sniffed in disgust. "Evidently he does not have much of a sense of cleanliness."

The minotaur had confronted many knights in his time, and unlike some orders, the Knights of Solamnia believed in the virtues of fastidiousness. Not so, apparently, this knight. His armor was old, dented, and covered with grime. His mustache was unkempt, almost wild, and his hair was a tangle that had not seen a brush or any care in quite some time. He also stank like someone who had not bathed for over a month.

"What do we do with him?" Tesela asked.

"He is a Knight of Solamnia," Darius reminded them needlessly. He looked up at the others. "As such, he should be treated with respect. If he is ill, then perhaps you could help, Tesela."

"I'll try my best."

The bell sounded again. Darius rose, and all three looked toward the tower.

"Mishakal!"

Kaz and Darius glanced at the cleric, who pointed to where the other knight lay—or, rather, *had* lain. There was no sign of him, not even the helm that Darius had removed. Kaz sniffed the air. There was a strong odor, but it seemed a general smell and nothing like what he had noticed emanating from the fallen knight.

"I don't like this."

The bell had ceased ringing after only one strike, but now another sound replaced it—the sound of great wings beating slowly.

"If only we had a torch," Darius muttered.

"I can create an aura if you think it would be helpful," Tesela offered.

The minotaur shook his head. "Right now light would only make us a better target for whatever that is."

The noise grew. Pieces of roof and clouds of dust descended upon them.

"It's directly above us!" Darius whispered. Quietly he unsheathed his sword.

"That won't do us much good. I chipped my axe on that thing back in the village."

"What do you suggest, then?"

It was Tesela who supplied an answer. "There!"

The other two turned but saw nothing. Then Kaz caught a glimpse of a familiar, childlike face peering around a corner. It did not strike him as odd that he could see Delbin so clearly in the dark. The kender had a finger to his lips and was smiling broadly. With a wave, he indicated that they should come to him.

"He must have found something," Tesela suggested.

"A place of safety, I hope."

With Darius first and Kaz guarding their rear against a creature he already knew to be invulnerable to his axe, they followed the walls to where they had seen Delbin. Around them, they began to hear sounds. They were not the movements of the unknown beast above them, but the sounds one might expect in Vingaard Keep: knights marching closer and closer, the cries of war-horses as their riders brought them to rein, the ring of steel against steel.

The unnerving part was that there was still no one to be seen in the deserted keep.

"Vingaard is cursed!" Darius muttered bleakly. "The specters of the dead have risen!"

"If noise is all they can make, we've little to worry about. If they become solid, like that one back there, then we have a problem." Kaz wished his voice carried more confidence.

"Where's Delbin?" Tesela asked abruptly.

"Sargas—no! If we've been following another spook. . . ." He cut off as Delbin reappeared.

"He says you have to hurry!" the kender whispered as loudly as he thought safe. Delbin no longer seemed interested in exploring the citadel.

"Who is *he?*" asked Kaz as they reached the kender.

"No time for that now, because there're knights here, not to mention other things that he said we'd be better off not running into because the whole place has gone mad, and unless we get to the library—"

At least some things stay the same, the minotaur thought sarcastically. "Take a breath, Delbin."

The bell rang again. Only once.

Darius bent down by the kender. "Delbin, are there actually knights at the bell tower? Do you know where the Grand Master is? Is he—"

"He's waiting!" Delbin scurried a few paces. "He said it would really be bad to be caught out here. The knights are likely to kill anything that moves. He says they can't help themselves."

Kaz grunted. "If someone has answers, I'm all for meeting him."

"It could be a trap," Darius countered.

"Then we'll have to break out of it." The minotaur hefted the massive battle-axe.

In retrospect, Kaz would come to realize that Vingaard Keep was not half the maze it seemed. There were not even many separate buildings. Tonight, though, it was different, as if not all of the keep existed in the same confusing world. He was certain at one point that Delbin was leading them in circles, until it became obvious that the route was chosen to avoid certain "other things" wandering Vingaard.

Now and then they spotted ghostly armored figures moving through the center region of the keep, where the Grand Master's quarters were situated. Each carried a torch and moved at a slow pace. Not once did the unknown others, who were possibly Knights of Solamnia, seem to notice them. Still, the kender never led them too close to those dark forms.

Delbin came to a dead stop. "There it is," he whispered. "He's in the library. Follow me!"

The library stood out from the rest of the keep by being the only building in this area lit by torchlight. A massive set of steps led up to a tall, wooden door. On each side of the steps was a pedestal, on which sat a huge bird of some sort. Kaz finally identified it as a kingfisher, which was only logical. Undoubtedly a closer examination would reveal that it not only wore a crown, but also held a sword and rose in its talons.

Dawdle awhile, minotaur. Come and speak with me. It has been soooo long.

The hair rose along Kaz's backside. His blood grew cold, and his knuckles whitened as he tried to grip the dwarven battle-axe even harder. What was he hearing?

What do you know, minotaur? What secrets do you know?

Tesela was the first to notice his strange behavior. She touched him lightly on one arm. "Do you see something? Is something wrong?"

It was as if some great compulsion were upon him, and the only way to free himself was to follow it through to the end. Slowly, his head turned and his eyes sought out—what?—in the darkness.

Shall we let the chase go on a little longer?

A blurry patch of white coalesced into a partially distinct form with four legs and a long, narrow muzzle. Kaz knew that if he could see it up close, it would have eyes of a killing shade of red and that there would not be one patch of fur on its pale, cold body.

"Dreadwolf!" Kaz spat the word out.

"A what?"

"There . . ." The minotaur blinked as he found himself pointing toward nothing. The murky form had vanished. If it had ever been there . . .

The bell tolled again. Only once.

"Paladine preserve us, may they cease doing that!" The bell had a mournful sound to it, and lacking any purpose that they knew of, the tolling of the bell disturbed them more each time.

Delbin finally seemed to have lost his patience, an unusual thing for a kender, but then Delbin was proving most unusual for one of his kind. He grabbed Tesela by the hand and started pulling her out into the open. Darius started to reach for the cleric, but she shook her head and began running with the kender. The knight, not wanting Tesela to move without some sort of protection, went charging after them.

Only Kaz hesitated, not because of any fear, but because he still heard the voice of the dreadwolf.

I am wherever you go, minotaur!

"You're dead," Kaz grumbled unconvincingly. "You're dead!"

Kaz was alone. Whatever it was—ghost, illusion, a phantasm of his own mind—it was gone. Kaz turned toward the library. The others stood near the door, anxiously awaiting him. Gritting his teeth and holding his battle-axe ready, the minotaur raced across the open area.

No storm of arrows came streaming down on him, no horde of mad knights charged him. Despite the light of the torches and the relative quiet that made each of his steps sound like thunder, he went unhindered. He nearly slipped in his haste to be up the steps. Darius covered his back as he completed the last few yards of his run.

Kaz huffed and snorted. "Well? Where is this all-knowing benefactor that you've supposedly led us to—or are we supposed to wait out here all night?"

"I am standing in the doorway, minotaur, and I would suggest that you and your companions enter immediately. The night is young, and you have seen only the first signs of the madness."

The voice was very calm, almost matter-of-fact in its tone. How he had come to open the door and be there, none of them could say. In the glare of torchlight, their benefactor looked like little more than dark, swirling cloth and a long head of hair. There was something else in his voice that Kaz felt he should recognize, but what it was he could not say.

Delbin obeyed the suggestion almost instantly. Not to be outdone by a kender, Darius followed, one arm protectively guarding Tesela. Kaz reluctantly followed, pausing only when he thought he heard laughter coming from the darkness out beyond the library. When it did not recur, he tried to convince himself that it was just the wind.

The door was bolted behind them, and they got their first good look at Delbin's friend and their rescuer. He was tall, almost as tall as Kaz, and he wore robes of silver and gray. Strangely, his hair, stretching long past his shoulders, was silver, with a patch of gray in the center, as if the clothing had been designed to match. The face was inhumanly handsome, with slightly delicate features. It was a young face, until one studied the eyes, green eyes that burned with an age almost unbelievable. Then one realized that this was no human, but an elf.

The elf folded his hands, almost as a cleric would do. His expression held only a hint of emotion, a slight, upward curling of the mouth, which Kaz gathered must indicate a smile.

"Welcome, my friends, to a haven in the midst of insanity. My name is—"

"Argaen Ravenshadow!" the minotaur finished abruptly.

Looking a bit amused, the elf nodded and said, "I think I would recall meeting a minotaur. We have not met before."

"No, but I did meet one of your kind who knew you well. His name's Sardal Crystalthorn."

A stream of emotions flashed quickly across the elf's visage. "Sardal. How odd to hear his name—to hear any name—after these past three years here."

"What is going on here?" Kaz almost bellowed. "What's happened to Vingaard Keep and the Knights of Solamnia?"

Argaen's face was once more an emotionless mask, but his tone hinted of dark things. "Minotaur, you cannot imagine what you and your companions have walked into, and the odds are against you ever walking out again—at least sane."

Chapter 11

ONCE, IT APPEARED, THIS ROOM HAD BEEN A PLACE where knights could come and pore over the records of their own past. There was still a wall of shelves containing specially preserved scrolls. The rest of the room, though, had been taken over by the elf and his work.

"There. Do you see it?"

Kaz followed Argaen Ravenshadow's gaze. They stood on the upper floor of the library at a window that faced into the center of Vingaard.

"I see it. That's where the Grand Master lives and commands from, isn't it?" Over five years might have gone by, but Kaz doubted his memory was that hazy.

"It is where he now sits in a world of distorted visions, commanding an ever-decreasing band of men, each as mad as himself, and unconsciously protecting what I suspect is responsible for the insanity and the sorcery you have witnessed so far."

The elf stepped abruptly away from the window. Kaz remained for the moment, staring out at the circle of torches now surrounding the sanctum of the Grand Master. Darius, who, along with Tesela, had been watching from another window, followed the elf. "What is it? What has the power to turn the Grand Master himself from the path of Paladine?"

Argaen walked over to the single table in the room, where a number of unusual and malevolent objects rested. He picked up the most ordinary, a stick that curled inward at the end, and seemed to contemplate it. He seemed to have forgotten the knight's question. "Did Sardal mention why I was here, minotaur?"

"With all that's happened, I can't really say. I don't think so." Kaz looked at the objects on the table. "I'm not sure I want to know."

"You may not want to, but you have to now that you are here." The elf held up the stick, still examining it. "Harmless-looking?"

"Since you ask, I doubt it."

"You would be correct. I will not go into detail, but I can tell you that this tiny item was used by some to distort the weather during the war."

"That thing?" Kaz recalled the unpredictable weather during his early days in the war and the terrible storm traps created by the dark mages in the final months. He recalled the one great storm that had preceded the darkness, in which the dragons of Takhisis and the monsters of Galan Dracos had passed the tattered remains of a vast Solamnic campsite. The knights themselves had been in full retreat, in what some termed the worst disaster in the history of the orders.

"Galan Dracos either created or stole the spell to make this. It is far stronger than any I have heard of. Fortunately—or perhaps unfortunately—the only one in existence—this one—was sealed inside one of three vaults."

The elf was playing games, Kaz knew. It was a trait of the elder race.

"Tell us of these vaults, Argaen Ravenshadow, and what they have to do with Galan Dracos."

The bell tolled again, but the elf ignored it. "The citadel of Galan Dracos, the master renegade who planned to turn even those sorcerers who followed the dark path into slaves of his ambition, was originally situated on the side of a peak in the mountains between Hylo and Solamnia."

"Really?" Delbin, who had remained unusually silent, perked up. "There're ruins of a sorcerer's castle in Hylo? Can we go there sometime? I wonder if any of my family's been there. I should write this down!" The kender reached into his pouch for his book and instead pulled out a tiny figurine. "Where do you suppose this came from? Isn't it neat?"

"*Give me that!*" With a ferocity that stunned Delbin into silence and made the others stare wide-eyed, Argaen stalked over to the kender and tore the figurine from his hand. While the party continued to look on in shock, the elf thrust the tiny item into a pocket of his robe and glared down at Delbin. "Never touch another thing in this room! You have no idea what you might accidentally unleash! I promise you, even a kender would regret it!"

Delbin seemed to shrivel up before Argaen's burning eyes. Argaen took a deep breath, and for the first time, he seemed to notice the effect his tirade had had on the others. The elf put a hand to his head and frowned.

"My . . . apologies to all of you! For over three years have I labored here, and while three years is not much in the physical life of an elf, it can be an eternity in other ways. Over three years of struggling to maintain sanity while those around me, already mad, have sunk ever deeper. Over three years of knowing how close the possible solution lay but being unable to do anything about it.

Each day I wait for the madness to overwhelm me while I seek in vain for some way to reach the vaults and solve the secrets of the locks. Each day . . ." Ravenshadow closed his eyes.

"I was telling you of the citadel of Galan Dracos," he suddenly commented. His eyes opened, and the pain that had racked his visage was no more. The mask was back in place.

Tesela walked over to the elf and put a hand on his shoulder. "You don't have to tell us now. Perhaps later, and perhaps you might let me see what I can do."

"You can do nothing. This is a spell, not a wound. Trust me. I know."

"Are you sure—"

He waved her away. "I am. Now if you will let me continue . . ." The elf purposefully stepped away from her and nearer to Kaz. "As I was saying—"

"I'm familiar with the citadel," Kaz replied quietly. Images still overwhelmed him. "I was there. I rode a dragon, a fighter after my own soul. His name was Bolt. With a Dragonlance, we, along with a few others, followed Huma of the Lance to the battlements. At first we all feared we would never find the place—there was a spell of invisibility or something on it—but Dracos was betrayed by the Black Robe sorcerers, who knew that they, too, would be slaves if he triumphed."

Ravenshadow's eyes lit up, but he said nothing, merely indicating with a gesture that the minotaur should go on.

Kaz grimaced as the memories dredged up unwanted emotions. "Huma was the only one to succeed in penetrating the lair of Dracos, and it was he who fought the mage by himself, somehow winning out and shattering the renegade's schemes." He smiled grimly. "It seems Dracos intended even to betray his mistress, Takhisis. When he realized, though, that he'd lost, he destroyed himself rather than face the wrath of the goddess."

"And the stronghold?" Argaen asked.

"Without the power of Dracos to support it," Kaz concluded to a suddenly intent elf, "the citadel could not maintain its hold on the side of the mountain. It crashed to the earth, and that was the end of it."

"And there I must take over, although your story fills some gaps and is quite entertaining in itself." Argaen picked up another object, which looked like a polished black rock. He began tossing it from one hand to the other. "You see, that was *not* the end of it. Despite the height from which the structure fell, much of it remained intact—a tribute, again, to the powers of Dracos."

"Dracos deserves no tributes . . . only curses."

Argaen gave Kaz a quick look. "As you say, minotaur. Be that as it may, not only did his citadel remain partially intact, but countless items he had either gathered from those under his control or had devised himself survived as well. They were ignored at first as the Knights of Solamnia began the process of systematically crushing the now leaderless armies of the Dragonqueen. Only when news filtered into Vingaard that mysterious happenings were taking place near the site of the ruins did the Grand Master realize the danger."

"The summoning," Darius interrupted. "Five years ago the Grand Master requested aid from the southern keeps. He wanted them to help maintain the peace while those from Vingaard and some of the other northern keeps worked on some important project! Dracos's stronghold!"

"The stronghold," Ravenshadow concurred. He continued to toss the smooth rock back and forth. "Lord Oswal had men scour the area. More than fourscore clerics of Paladine aided in the search, utilizing their lord's power to seek out small yet exceedingly deadly instruments that had been buried. They gathered fragments of the more powerful items that had been shattered. I do not doubt that, as thorough as they were, a few pieces escaped their notice."

Kaz glanced at Delbin, whose eyes were bright. The

thought of the kender returning to his people and telling them about the possible treasures in the ruins made the minotaur shiver. Dark sorcery in the hands of *kender?*

"When the clerics were satisfied that they had done all they could, the gathered remnants of the relics were brought to Vingaard Keep under an armed guard so great in number that one would have thought the knights were marching on their own keep. The caravan arrived during the night, the better to avoid the close scrutiny of any spies, and the artifacts were carried down to the vaults, locked inside, and purposefully forgotten by the Grand Master and the Knightly Council."

What they overlooked, the elf went on to say, was that the Conclave of Wizards had its own sources of information. The mages were aghast at the thought of so many potentially dangerous objects in the care of an organization that knew so little about the balances of sorcery. In this, all three Orders of Wizardry were in agreement. It was only reasonable, though, that the Knights of Solamnia would be a bit leery about letting any magic-user touch the cursed toys of the renegade. Argument followed argument until the elven members of the conclave proposed that one of their own, a neutral who lived solely for research, study the relics.

Argaen Ravenshadow had jumped at the opportunity.

"More the fool, I," the elf muttered. "Rather would I trust myself than most of my stiff-necked brethren. They would have passed into madness long ago."

Argaen said he had been greeted by the Grand Master upon his arrival. Lord Oswal proved to be a formidable man and one that even an elf could admire with ease. The first few weeks seemed to pass easily. While the knights would not give Argaen immediate access to the vaults, they were willing to remove the objects one by one for his inspection. As time passed, however, the elf began to notice a couple of things. The pieces he was given tended to be of lesser power than he would have expected, and it soon became obvious that someone was carefully picking and choosing what he was to study. Also, there was a growing attitude of distrust on the part of the knighthood. Not merely distrust for Argaen, but for anyone. Projects designed to rehabilitate the lands of northern Solamnia were abandoned as the Knightly Council began to see turncoats and raiders everywhere. The locals were pressed and then punished for imaginary wrongs. Most of what little the land provided was snatched up by Vingaard as the knighthood began gearing up for a return to war with a new, imagined enemy.

All the while, the elf worked on, feeling that there was something amiss here.

"They refused to allow me access to the lower chambers where the vaults lie, and my sole attempt to steal past the sentries and safeguards proved for naught. I learned then how well the Knights of Solamnia guarded their prizes." Argaen had finally stopped tossing the black rock back and forth and now began to squeeze it with his left hand. Kaz, his gaze briefly moving to Ravenshadow's hand, watched in growing amazement as the rock began to crumble under the surprising strength of the elf. "Yet, I learned one other thing in that attempt—something was alive in those vaults. Not alive in the same sense that you and I are alive, but alive in the sense of being active . . . as a lingering spell."

Darius had returned to the window as Ravenshadow spoke, his eyes fixed on the center of the keep, and specifically the building housing the Grand Master, but he turned at this final pronouncement. "Why did you not warn them, elf? The Grand Master surely would have listened carefully to a warning concerning a threat beneath his very feet!"

"Your Grand Master was beyond reason by then, knight. He came very close to accusing me of being a spy for his enemies." The elf glared at Darius coldly, and it was the knight who finally backed down. Argaen's expression softened. "I know it is difficult for you to comprehend, human, but such was the case."

Kaz chose that moment to yawn. "I have one question for you, elf, and then I, at least, must eat and rest."

"How remiss of me!" Argaen Ravenshadow boomed. He looked over the others. "You all need something! I shall return in a moment." With an abruptness that caught all of them unprepared, the elf stuffed the remains of the black rock into one of his pockets and departed the room.

For several seconds, the party simply stared at the doorway Argaen had scurried through. Then Kaz spoke quietly. "Tesela, what do you make of our benefactor? Is he as mad as he claims the others are?"

She thought about it and replied, "I think he still clings to sanity, but the longer he's here, the worse it will become."

"He seems reluctant for your help."

"I am a cleric of Mishakal, and I've healed people's minds. Sometimes they refuse help because they don't want to admit their own failures. Sometimes I must do it without their knowledge." She looked down at the medallion.

"We are in danger ourselves, Kaz," Darius pointed out. "If we take what Argaen Ravenshadow says as truth, then each day we are here our own minds are at risk."

"I know." The minotaur snorted irritably.

"Kaz?" Darius was staring out the window once more.

"What is it?"

"I must do what I can to save my brothers."

The minotaur grimaced. He knew that tone well, for Huma had used it many a time. It meant danger. It meant trying to take on the stronghold of the knighthood and possibly dying on a Solamnic blade. "You have only Argaen's word as to what is going on."

Darius shook his head. "I have eyes as well, and other senses as sharp as any elf's. You merely have to look out the window again. You can feel the threat."

Kaz refused to be moved. "I feel nothing but hunger and exhaustion."

"Kaz, in the name of the Grand Master, who is your comrade . . ." The knight turned to him, his eyes burning much as the minotaur's did at times.

Kaz would not have refused a certain other knight, and the realization made him feel guilty. "Let's see what the daylight brings."

The bell tolled . . . once.

*   *   *   *   *

The minotaurs sat around a campfire whose embers were dying. They were on their way home after years of chasing what some had begun to believe was a phantom. A search of the river area had revealed neither Greel's body nor that of the fugitive. Hecar and Helati had described in detail the battle between the two, which, in their version, ended in the drowning of both combatants as they struggled in the raging current.

Scurn was not happy, and neither was the ogre, Molok. In different ways, their lives had totally revolved around the eventual capture and death of Kaz. Their reasons varied greatly, but their obsessions were virtually identical—and now both felt betrayed by the disappearance of their longtime adversary.

Molok rubbed a scar on his forehead, his mind afire. Kaz was supposed to have been *his*, regardless of the piece of paper the minotaur leaders had given the party. Kaz would have never made the return trek east if it was up to him.

As for Scurn, he couldn't have cared less whether Kaz died or not, as long as it was he who had bested the coward. Even branded as he was, Kaz was still known for his strength and ability in the arenas, and it galled the disfigured minotaur to think that one like the fugitive was praised still. Scurn wanted the praise, the status, of defeating one of the former champions, a fighter who could have risen high in the ranks if he had not believed those in control to be mere puppets of Takhisis's warlords.

They were camped on the edge of what one of the others had termed the Solamnic Wastes. A vast military unit had passed near here only recently. The tracks of an estimated two hundred horses cut a path through the wasteland. Knights of Solamnia, Helati had suggested, either returning to or moving on Vingaard Keep. A situation was brewing there that, at one time, might have drawn their interest. Now, however, they only wanted to go home.

A squeal alerted the group to a possible attack. Axes, massive swords, and other weapons were flourished as the minotaurs rose. The squeal had not been torn from the throat of one of their kind; no minotaur would squeal like a pig. But there was a sentry out in that direction.

Even as the first of the minotaurs started to move, the sentry stepped into the dim light of the campfire. In one hand, he held an axe that dripped with fresh blood. In the other hand, he held a quivering, cowardly goblin.

"Two of these tried to jump me."

The minotaurs grunted, growled, and snorted in disdain. The goblin tried to look as small as possible. No one cared for goblins. Even Molok looked at the sorry sight in disgust.

"Kill it," was all he said.

"Only in combat." The sentry spat. "Executing this one would be a loss of honor."

The other minotaurs nodded. There was no glory in killing unarmed opponents. Outnumbered as he was, Molok knew better than to question the minotaur code of honor.

"Besides," the sentry went on, "this bag of shaking bones and fat spouted something that sounded of great interest."

"What was that?" Scurn asked impatiently. He would have killed the goblin there and then. Goblins were not deserving of a combat of honor. They were vermin, like rats.

"Tell them. Repeat what you said to me, goblin!"

"My . . . name is . . . Krynge, honorable, wonderful masters—"

Scurn kicked the goblin in the side. "Quit drooling on our feet and get to the point! We *might* let you live."

The goblin seemed to take Scurn's word to heart and began to babble. "My band—it were much bigger then— we found . . . knights. All dead but one. We have fun and then . . . and then a minotaur attacks, killing all but three!" Krynge smiled up at the group, revealing jagged, yellow fangs. "Three goblins against one minotaur not good odds, especially since one goblin knocked out. We retreat."

The minotaur on watch added, "I found the three of them skulking about like dogs. Two of the fools attacked me in panic, and I killed them. They died from one swing." The sentry, smiling proudly, hefted his axe. The others nodded their appreciation for his skill. "This coward started babbling about 'another minotaur,' so I brought him back here for everyone to listen to."

"Another minotaur? So near?" Molok stepped up to the goblin and took the creature's ugly head in his massive hands. "What direction came he from?"

"South! Came from south!"

"Kaz!" The ogre turned on Hecar and Helati. "It's got to be Kaz!"

Scurn stalked up to Helati. To her, his ravaged face was even more disgusting so close. "You said Kaz was dead! So did your brother! Only you two saw them fight, and I wonder about that. Explain!"

Hecar stepped between his sister and the other. "Do you question my honor? Do you call me a liar?"

The other minotaurs were working themselves up for a combat of honor. Many looked sympathetically at Hecar, knowing what he faced. More than a few of them had questioned their own honor in this quest. Hecar was standing up for much more than his sister and himself.

Molok realized this, too, as he scanned the group, noting the reactions of each. Like Scurn, he no longer believed Hecar's story, but unlike the disfigured one, he knew that every minotaur would be needed if Kaz was truly alive. The ogre was no fool; he had no intention of taking on Kaz by himself.

"Hecar, he be thinking no such thing." Molok put a hand on Scurn's shoulder. The minotaur glared at him but did not interrupt. "Kaz's body was never found. Why? Because he survived and hid—like a coward!"

There was renewed muttering from the other minotaurs. They had reacted as the ogre wanted them to. Speak of honor and cowardice, and they would believe anything he said.

The two minotaurs were still facing one another. Scurn still wanted Hecar, and the other still wanted to protect his sister. Helati was caught between bringing dishonor to her brother by speaking the truth or dishonoring herself even more by remaining silent. She chose the latter.

"What about Greel?" Scurn asked. He was beginning to realize that he would gain nothing by fighting and killing Hecar at this time. The other minotaurs still favored Hecar, and Scurn, like the ogre, knew he could not hunt Kaz alone. Yet he could not bring himself to quit the argument altogether. He would lose some face if he backed down now.

"Greel was not a swimmer," one of the other minotaurs called out. "His clan is in mountains, where there are only streams. He never learned."

If not for the muttering this new fact brought forth, the surrounding minotaurs might have heard four simultaneous sighs of relief. Molok quickly took control. "You see? Greel drowned. He be no swimmer. True courage, that Greel. True honor."

Hecar and Helati exchanged quick glances. Greel had ended up in the river only because they had thrown his body into it after Hecar had killed him. As for honor, Greel had had none. It had been his intention from the first to strike Kaz square in the back with the spear. Only a shout from Helati had saved Kaz. Startled, Greel had succeeded only in mortally wounding Kaz's horse. As far as Hecar and Helati were concerned, both minotaurs had died there. No trace of Kaz had been found—that much was true. Though their faces did not show it, the news of his survival both relieved and frustrated them.

"Kaz lives. If he heads north, then he heads for the keep at Vingaard," Scurn decided.

"The knighthood would make him a prisoner," Hecar protested. "He would not go there."

"He will." Scurn looked at the others, his eyes lingering on Molok. "We will go to Vingaard. If Kaz is there, we will demand our right to him." Some of the other minotaurs looked a bit uneasy at the thought of walking up to the keep of the knighthood and demanding a prisoner. Scurn snarled at them. "Are there cowards among us? Does anyone wish to return home without fulfilling his oath?"

There was no answer. To turn back now would be a great loss of honor and an outright act of cowardice. Better death than that.

"It is settled, then."

"What about this one?" the minotaur sentry asked. He pulled Krynge to his feet by the back of the goblin's neck.

Scurn bared his teeth.

"Give him a sword. He will have the honor of fighting bravely for his life. A rare thing for a goblin."

Chapter 12

He was standing in the center of the arena, unarmed. *The crowd of minotaurs roared their respect and
approval. Kaz acknowledged them by raising his fists
high in the air and turning in a slow circle.*

*His prowess was such that no one thought him a fool
to take on an armed opponent with only his bare hands.
Rather, they saw it as the champion's way of evening the
odds. If the challenger did defeat him, however, there
would be no lack of honor in the victory. That he had
challenged the champion, rather than working his way
up in status first, indicated the challenger was either very
brave or very foolish. That question would soon be settled.*

The overlords—the "outsiders," as they were called—

watched with mild amusement from their special seats on the northern walls. They were ogre and human commanders, one of the latter an aide to the warlord Crynus, leader of the armies of Takhisis. The arena was only a pastime for them; they were here to inspect the new companies of "volunteers"—slave-soldiers, in reality. The ogres and humans were not officers so much as guards. Oaths bound the minotaurs to those who led them into battle, regardless of consequence. A minotaur who had given his oath would die for his ogre captain, or should, if he was a proper representative of his race.

Kaz and the crowd grew anxious as the moments passed. The champion was eager to claim yet another victory, one that would increase his standing. How long before the outsiders' influence made him one of the ruling minotaurs? Not much longer, surely!

The gate opposite Kaz slowly creaked open. The minotaur readied himself. He wondered if he would know his challenger. Perhaps it was one of the younger ones, fresh from the training session that Kaz himself taught. No, none of them would be so foolish. Each had already been tested and found wanting. They needed some experience before they could hope to defeat their instructor.

Slowly a figure stepped into the arena. A hush fell over the crowd. The overlords leaned forward with interest.

A Knight of Solamnia stood before the crowd. A human against a minotaur. True, the knight had a long-sword, but he wore no armor and therefore had little protection against Kaz's blows. The long mustache, characteristic of his kind, and the experienced manner in which the human carried himself spoke of a training as fierce in its own way as that of the minotaurs. Most definitely a Solamnic Knight.

The man walked toward Kaz. His face slowly came into focus. It seemed to press right up to the minotaur's own. Kaz felt panic rush over him. Not this human! Not this knight!

Not Huma!

"It has to be this way, Kaz," Huma explained calmly. He raised the sword, but instead of striking, he tossed it before the minotaur. "You carry no weapon; I will do the same." The knight's gray-streaked hair, an odd sight in one so young, fluttered in the wind.

Abruptly the face before Kaz was no longer Huma's but that of the one whom he knew to be Galan Dracos. The long, almost reptilian face leered at him.

"Tell me your secrets, minotaur. What do you know of my power? What do you know of my sorcery?"

"No!" Without thinking, the minotaur lashed out with his left hand, striking the sorcerer's face and twisting his neck at a sudden and improbable angle. Kaz's adversary collapsed to the ground. "Sargas take you!" He cried out the name of the dark god of his youth. "I don't know anything! Leave me be and haunt another!"

In horror, Kaz watched as the head of the corpse turned slowly to stare up at him. The face of Galan Dracos broke into a malevolent smile. "It is true. You do know nothing."

The face had slowly dissolved back into Huma's. There was a bitter look on the knight's face, as if the minotaur had betrayed him.

Somehow that frightened Kaz as nothing else could. The world swam around and around, until he vaguely realized that this was a dream. A nightmare. As the dream ended, darkness began to seep in. Kaz tried to escape from the coming darkness, but could not. It clung to him, wrapping him as a cocoon wraps a caterpillar. He prayed desperately for day to come, fearing for some reason that he would otherwise never awaken. . . .

* * * * *

Daylight provided no relief from the nightmare. If anything, the utter emptiness of the keep proved even more overwhelming than the shadows or the nightmare.

In the darkness, there had been the comfort that one might be able to hide. In the dull light of yet another murky day, there was the reality that whatever waited for them did not fear the day, and in fact was no more visible in the light than it had been in the dark. A bodiless, omnipresent thing.

The bell had sounded twice so far this day. There was no set time; the bell ringer apparently acted whenever it suited his fancy—or perhaps it was the fancy of the Grand Master, if Argaen Ravenshadow's tale was true.

The elf was nowhere in sight when Kaz rose reluctantly. Kaz moved slowly, his muscles sore. The floor of the room proved most uncomfortable for sleeping, but Argaen had said it was the best of bad choices. The library had not been designed for personal quarters. Kaz wondered where the elf was and what he was planning now.

Kaz jumped to his feet. Darius, already awake and performing some exercise ritual, paused as the minotaur turned to him. "Where's Delbin?"

"I thought—" The knight glanced at the kender's abandoned bedroll. "He was here when last I looked."

"He's a quiet one," Kaz snarled. "I can't say how many times he's done this to me. I should be used to it by now, but I thought he'd exercise some common sense after what Ravenshadow told us last night."

Tesela sat up, awakened by the talk. "Perhaps he's with Argaen."

"Maybe, but I very much doubt it."

Darius glanced out the window, as if he expected to see the kender perched outside somewhere. He stared off toward the center of the keep. "Do you think that he would dare go to the Grand Master's quarters? It would appeal to a kender to do something like that."

"More likely the vaults below!" Kaz roared in anger, causing both humans to eye him with trepidation. He forced the anger down. "Just to be certain, we'll make a quick search of the library."

"For what?" Argaen's calm voice floated from the hall. The elf entered, carrying a basket filled with bread, fruit, and drink. He deposited the basket on the table and faced Kaz. "What seems to be the difficulty, my friend?"

"Delbin. The kender. Have you seen him? Is he in the library?"

"Not that I know of. Kender are troublesome to keep track of. . . ." Argaen's voice trailed off. "Astra take me for a fool! I should have known better than to tell all in the presence of a kender, but I thought you had him under control."

"No one controls a kender completely," Kaz retorted sourly. "And no one would want to. The problem now is what we should do. He may have sneaked off to investigate the vaults of the Grand Master!"

"Vingaard has other places that would interest a kender," Darius suggested.

"I've—Paladine forgive me!—ridden with that kender for several months. He's gone to the vaults!"

"This is most distressing," Ravenshadow muttered. His mind seemed to be concentrating on some calculation. "Do you think he could actually break into those vaults?"

"Whether he can or not isn't the point, elf! What is the point is that he could just as easily wind up on the end of a sword, if what you told us is true. Sane or mad, I doubt that the Knights of Solamnia have forgotten all their training."

"True. If anything, they have become even more fanatical. All in preparation for their imaginary foe, of course."

"Master Ravenshadow," interrupted Tesela, "how is it that you remain here? Why do the knights not disturb you?"

Argaen seemed annoyed and answered sharply, "I was an honored guest once. That thought seems to have remained with them all this time, although I have also done my best to remain unobtrusive. That is hardly a concern right at this moment. Gather your things and follow me! We must save your companion!"

The elf moved with such impatience that the others barely had the time to react. Darius was forced to leave his armor behind, taking only his shield and his sword. Kaz removed his battle-axe from its harness. As one, they followed after the swift-moving Argaen.

To their surprise, the elf did not leave the library immediately. Instead, he stood in the front hall and removed a blue crystal from his robes. While the others waited, he stared at it intently.

Something blurry formed in the center of the tiny sphere, but no one could make out what it was. Ravenshadow held the crystal before Kaz. "You know the kender better than anyone else. Think of him, concentrate on his location."

"I dislike sorcery, elf," Kaz snorted disdainfully. "It tends to be a treacherous, unpredictable path."

"This is hardly any such thing. Do you want to find your friend, or would you rather we searched the entire keep blindly?"

With a black look, Kaz took hold of the crystal and concentrated on his diminutive companion as best as he could. He recalled the nearly perpetual smile on the kender's face, contrasted with the odd expression that had been haunting his companion of late. Delbin's book came to mind and Kaz pictured him writing his latest adventure in it, an adventure that presently had the kender situated . . .

"There! You see?" Argaen cried.

Sure enough, the blurry image had been replaced by the crisp picture of Delbin. The kender was in a dark room lit only by a small candle. It did not appear to be the vaults, nor did it seem like part of the personal chambers of the Grand Master. The room was narrow and dusty, as if it had been unused for years.

"Where *is* he?" Kaz could hazard no guess from what he observed.

An unelflike laugh burst from the mouth of Argaen Ravenshadow. It was a laugh tinged with shock, relief, and something Kaz could not put his finger on.

"Do you know where he is?" Darius, anxious, finally demanded.

"He—he is in the library after all!" There was more animation in Ravenshadow's visage than any of them had noticed so far. He was genuinely thrilled by his discovery. "Follow me!"

As seemed typical of the elf, Argaen turned and rushed off without giving the others a chance to collect their wits.

"Are all elves so quick?" Tesela asked testily. There were limits, apparently, to her kind, cleric soul.

Kaz refrained from replying, choosing instead to hurry after the rapidly diminishing figure of their benefactor.

*   *   *   *   *

They found the elf in a study room of the library, sprawled over a long, yellowed parchment that Kaz guessed was at least a century old. Argaen was nodding and chuckling, a wild sort of chuckle that disturbed the minotaur. Again he wondered how sane Ravenshadow truly was.

"Come see," Argaen called out as they entered. Without looking up, he pointed at the center of the parchment. "This is a copy of the original design for this library. Your founder"—the elf glanced up briefly at Darius—"designed more than half of this . . . the secret half."

"What?" The knight was completely at a loss to understand what Argaen meant.

"I do not know how your smaller southern keeps are diagrammed, but Vinas Solamnus wanted every building here to have one use other than the obvious one. He knew that Vingaard itself might come under siege and possibly even be broken into someday. Therefore, he had passages built inside the walls, wide enough for two men if they rubbed shoulders. Your kender friend has uncovered some of the passages in this building."

"I've never heard of passages such as you speak of," Darius argued.

"Most of them seem to have been forgotten. These parchments were located during the war, supposedly after one of your own turned out to be a traitor."

Darius turned white at the suggestion and would have drawn his sword if Kaz had not grabbed his arm. "He's right, Darius. I'll fill you in later."

The knight let his arm drop. Kaz could see the despair growing in the man again. The minotaur could not blame him. He recalled Huma's face when told of Rennard. Rennard, despite his pale-white face and lack of humor, had always treated Huma well, and indeed was one of those who had trained him. The knight's career had proven a mockery, however, for long before Rennard had joined the order, he had surrendered himself to the cult of Morgion, god of disease and decay. The gaunt knight was found to be responsible for the death of Grand Master Trake and the serious illness of Oswal. Worse yet, Huma had discovered that the fiend was his own uncle.

"Here, here, and here," Argaen said calmly, pointing at the map as if unaware of Darius. "These are the most likely entrances your kender friend will be near. If we each cut him off and converge, one of us is bound to catch him."

"He better pray it's not me!" Kaz rumbled. "I'll hang him from the top floor of this building by his shirt collar!"

*   *   *   *   *

Delbin was having the time of his life. Secret passages and locks were the things a kender lived for. He thought about how jealous some of his friends back home would be. *Serves 'em right*, he decided.

In some ways, Delbin was a bit odd for his kind. Most kender cared for little more than fun, although there were the occasional serious ones, "oddballs," as they were called by some of the young. Delbin liked adventures, but although he had never told anyone, especially Kaz, he also yearned for some purpose in his life, some grand scheme. Listening to the stories of heroes, both kender and otherwise, his ambition grew. Unfortunately, Delbin had been too young to participate in the great war, and by the time he was old enough to sneak away on his own, word had reached Hylo that She of the Many Faces, as the kender called Takhisis, had been banished to the beyond.

Delbin returned to the business at hand. A great web blocked his path upward. So far, this grand adventure had brought him nothing more than a few old coins, a rusty knife, and one amusing secret door. The web was kind of fascinating, Delbin thought, and he briefly imagined some great spider, as big as himself, spinning it. The image he conjured up was so real, the kender could almost see its eight red eyes. . . .

Suddenly the eight red eyes flashed, and Delbin found himself facing the very spider of his imagination. The thing was incredibly ugly, what he could see of it, and barely able to fit in the passageway. Nevertheless, it was making headway. Imagining a huge spider was one thing, but actually being attacked by one was . . . was . . . *icky*, Delbin decided. The little candle he had shone too weakly to scare the monster, and the knife, which was useful for picking locks on secret doors, was too dull for a confrontation. Actually, a longsword, if he could have lifted one, would probably have been just as useless. The spider was awfully large.

Its eight long legs, each as thick as the kender's arm, scraped against the passage walls as the huge creature slowly burst its way through the web. Delbin found himself paralyzed, not with fear, which he had experienced only occasionally, but with a trancelike fascination for what was happening. The multiple eyes of the spider seemed to entice him to a warm, safe place where he could sleep snugly, wrapped in his blanket.

He dropped the candle.

The spider scurried back, and Delbin's mind cleared. The horror was only a few feet away from him. He tried to turn, but to his amazement, his feet were bound together—*By webbing, of course*, he thought, as he went crashing down on the steps. Recovering from its fright, the spider once again scuttled forward toward its helpless victim.

A roar—a war cry—ripped through the musty passage, and suddenly a huge figure bathed in light stood behind the giant arachnid. In one hand, nearly scraping the ceiling, was a magnificent battle-axe that no man could have wielded with such ease.

The spider hesitated, caught between desire and confusion. Delbin watched in open-mouthed awe as the axe rang down and bit into the monster. Ichor spilled out, splattering the kender and the walls, as the great weapon fairly cleaved the spider in two. It refused to die immediately, its tiny brain lagging behind reality. The light in its eight eyes slowly dimmed as it wobbled in the direction of Delbin. The axe came down once more.

The monstrosity finally collapsed at the kender's bound feet.

"Delbin!" His axe dripping with the spider's life fluids, Kaz stepped over the creature's remains and kneeled down beside his companion. Behind him, carrying a torch, hurried Tesela. There were other sounds in the passage, running feet that undoubtedly belonged to Darius and Argaen.

"Delbin, you little fool!" Kaz muttered. He looked down at the kender's feet. "What is that stuff?"

"It's webbing," Tesela remarked. "What else would a spider use?" She handed the torch to Kaz and brought her medallion in contact with the webbing. The sticky, ropelike substance melted away.

"That thing's pretty handy."

"Yes, isn't it." She leaned back and spoke to the kender. "Do you feel any dizziness or have bruises? You must've fallen."

"How'd you do that?" Delbin was touching the remains of the webbing. "Could I do that, too? Does it just work for spiders? Well, at least I don't think I'm hurt. You should've seen it, Kaz, though I guess you did, but it just seemed to come right out of nowhere, and all I was doing was thinking that the web looked like a giant spider, and—"

Kaz briefly put a hand over the kender's mouth and looked at Tesela. "I think he's all right."

"Paladine's Sword! What happened here?" Darius, blade in one hand and a candle in the other, came running up the stairs behind Delbin. "Is that a—a—"

"A spider, yes." Argaen joined them from the steps above. While both he and Darius had obviously run, only the knight seemed at all winded. "I cannot say I've come across one that big before. Not in a place like Vingaard Keep."

Kaz wiped his axe blade off on the spider. The stench from the bodily fluids of the monster was becoming noticeable. "Have you ever been in these passages?" he asked the elf.

"When I first found those parchments—and, believe me, that was purely accidental, for they were extremely well hidden—I decided to traverse the entire library system. I came across many spiders, of course, but nothing like that."

"Delbin says that it seemed to come out of nowhere, that he was just thinking how the web looked like one spun by a giant spider."

The elf frowned. "I do not like the sound of that. Things grow ever worse. I fear that the kender himself may have somehow created that monster—by magic."

The kender was silent, but there was a gleam in his eyes that Kaz did not like.

"What do you mean?" the minotaur asked Argaen, "when you say that Delbin 'created' it?"

"That may be a poor choice of words. What I meant applies to us all, including what happened to you when you first entered Vingaard Keep. You recall the knight you told me of, or the sound of men and animals, yet there were none?"

"The knight was real," Darius stated flatly.

"Perhaps. Your knight vanished, real or not. This spider of the kender's imagination did not, however." Argaen studied Delbin intently in the torchlight. Kaz noticed his companion shiver.

"Let this be a lesson to you, Delbin," the minotaur chided the kender kindly. "Don't go running off on any adventures without me."

"Exactly how did you find the entrance you used, kender?" the elf asked with great interest. "Even I would have trouble finding them without help, and knowing how to open them. . . ."

Delbin grinned. "It's easy. All you have to do is know where to look, and the locks weren't really hidden all that great. They were kind of fun, but my uncle Kebble showed me lots of tricks. A lot of the other kender think he's the greatest, which he is, but—"

"Delbin's a kender," Kaz interrupted quickly. "That should be sufficient answer. He could go on for hours. I for one, however, would like to leave this place. This overgrown bug-eater stinks to high heaven, and I've seen less dust in a desert."

The elf nodded rather absently. "Surely. The nearest exit is the one you came through."

Kaz stepped back over the remains of the spider. Tesela helped Delbin rise to his feet. The kender seemed a bit unsteady. The cleric made a move to help him, but Argaen was suddenly there. He took hold of one of Delbin's arms.

"Allow me, human." Argaen smiled politely at her. Tesela automatically stepped away. The elf helped the kender over the spider. Tesela blinked and followed hastily after them, not wanting to be left alone with the horrid remains. Spiders had always scared her as a small child.

* * * * *

The day, like all other days he could remember, dwindled away. Nothing changed . . . ever. No end seemed in sight.

Lord Oswal sat in the central chamber, where he and his numerous predecessors, including his late brother, had held court. The throne room was a place of power, designed to accentuate the Grand Master's status as supreme commander and voice of Paladine. The chair on which the Grand Master sat was a level higher than the next closest. Anyone seeking an audience would be forced to look upward. Behind the high-backed throne, further emphasizing who ruled here, was a great representation of the Solamnic symbol. The kingfisher was larger than a man.

Once guards would have stood on both sides of the throne. More would have lined the hall, and there would have been still more at the great doors. Now, as Oswal slowly raised his head, he saw but a handful of knights, little more than a dozen, he supposed, and it was questionable how much he could rely on them. These men were filthy, unbathed, hardly typical of the knighthood as once he had cherished it. They were mad, of course, and it was a madness forced on them by *him*. He was lucky that he himself had not fallen victim to the tremendous power of *that one*, though each day it grew a little harder to resist. Each hour it grew so much easier to just let one's mind drift . . . to . . .

The bell sounded, snapping him from his reverie. His eyes widened, and a smile played across his cracked lips. Perhaps his men had thought it part of his madness when the Grand Master had ordered at least one man stationed at the bell at all times. Certainly his command that the bell be rung at random hours had been met with looks of pity from men who had once respected him. Lord Oswal knew what he was doing, however. The loud ringing of the bell stirred his mind whenever he was sinking too deep into madness. The ringing—and his own power as a cleric of Paladine, something that even most of his fellow knights did not know.

What was going on outside? he wondered. Where was Bennett? Where was Arak Hawkeye, head of the Order of the Crown? Where was Huma? Rennard? Where . . .

He cursed the one who traveled in the darkness as he realized with a jolt that some of the men he was waiting for were long dead. There were others, though. . . .

"Contemplating your mortality, Grand Master?" a voice like a hiss asked him suddenly.

Oswal was well beyond the point of being startled when *he* manifested himself. "Come out from behind me, coward."

A blur of darkness formed before the throne of the Grand Master, but none of the guards noticed. "Are you blind?" he wanted to scream at them. "The enemy is before you!"

The other knights continued to stare without reaction. They were caught in a bizarre world of fanaticism in which the performance of their duties was all they existed for. They were being the best, most alert sentries that they could possibly be, yet they could not see the figure cloaked in shadows.

Oswal refused to consider the possibility that it might be himself who was mad, and that the one before him did not, in truth, exist anywhere but in the Grand Master's mind.

"Shall I tell you what this day will bring?" the shadow mocked him. "Would you like to know what new atrocities are being performed in the name of Paladine and the Knights of Solamnia?"

It was a game he played each day at some point. Lord Oswal trembled in growing rage and uncertainty. Solamnia was in ruins. The knights were plundering the very people they were supposed to protect. Former allies were now hunted enemies.

All at the Grand Master's command.

"You can tell me nothing new, mage, and I will tell you nothing new, either." He said the last with some satisfaction. He could no longer summon up the strength to fully utilize the gifts of Paladine with which he, as a cleric and a Lord Knight, was endowed. How had that come about?

"I can save your people from your madnesssssss." Oswal had struck a nerve. "You merely have to tell me a few simple things. The longer you delay, the worse you make your own position. Do you know that your keep lies open, defenseless, and that other than the few men you have here, there are only two or three dozen remaining in all of Vingaard?" The shadow chuckled. "Soon the Knights of Solamnia will cease to exist, and all for naught."

"To the Abyss with you!" the Grand Master shouted as he rose from his throne. The knights guarding the chamber turned to look at him fleetingly, but noting that nothing was apparently wrong, they turned back to their "duties." "If you could take what you wanted, you would have taken it long ago! I have seen it in a vision! Paladine has guided me from the first! It is only a matter of outlasting you, specter! Your own time is limited! I will prevail!"

"You will do nothing. You are impotent, Grand Master. Shall I tell you a secret? Sssssoon, very sssssoon, what I want will be mine."

"Takhisis take your murky hide!" Oswal slumped back onto the throne.

"She already hasss, asss you can sseee. . . ." The shadow began to fade into nothing, but not before the Grand Master was allowed a glimpse of a face. It was a human face, but only barely, for the hair lay flat against the skull and the face was overly elongated, like that of some reptile. The skin added to the effect, showing a layer of scale or scab. It was hard to tell which.

Long after the shade had vanished, if indeed it had ever been there, he finally succeeded in whispering the name that accompanied that horrid, less-than-human visage.

"Dracos!"

Chapter 13

The light of day was fading swiftly. Around the Grand Master's stronghold, Kaz and the others saw the few remaining knights of Vingaard Keep begin what seemed to be automatic rituals. With slow deliberation, a group of some three or four passed among the others, lighting and distributing torches to each. Their pace never faltered, yet never varied, either. Kaz was reminded of folktales about the undead shambling out of their graves. Beside him, Darius watched, his hands clutching the base of the window, his knuckles white. The knights, once all were equipped with burning torches, shifted into a protective shield around the entrance of the building, each man facing the darkness without. Neither the minotaur nor Darius had seen any visible threat. It was almost as if the knights were seeking to hold back the coming darkness. The bell rang its single note for at least the thirteenth time today, though Kaz had lost count.

"How long can this go on?" he muttered.

Vingaard Keep, Kaz mused, was like a limbo of some sort, an unreal place, where everything seemed to slow down, seemed never really to change. There were no conclusions here, just one perpetual emptiness. The knights changed guard several times during the day, but they did nothing else. A few wandered briefly along the walls of the keep, supposedly on sentry duty, but Kaz knew that an enemy horde could stroll in undetected.

"What are we waiting for?" he groused at his companions. Darius nodded agreement with that sentiment. He was all for making some grand plan. The minotaur grimaced slightly. Darius was a good, brave soul, as humans went, but like many of his fellow knights, he seemed to think that what was called for was a glorious attack straight into the teeth of danger. Kaz knew that he himself was guilty of overzealousness at times, but experience had mellowed him somewhat.

Tesela was quiet. She sat on the floor, legs crossed, eyes closed. Kaz could not say for certain whether she was performing some ritual or was just plain bored, like he was. He suspected that she herself was not quite certain what to do.

Sensing his eyes on her, she opened her own and met his gaze. Something was troubling her, the minotaur felt instinctively. "What's wrong?"

The cleric shook her head. "I can't really say. I've been trying to clear my mind and have been asking Mishakal for guidance all day, but I still can't determine what it is that disturbs me . . . only that it concerns Argaen."

"The elf?" Darius grumbled.

"I've prayed to Mishakal for guidance, but where the elf is concerned, I feel nothing. It's as if there is a—a blockage."

"And your goddess is not strong enough to remove the obstacles?"

Her glare burned holes into the knight's eyes, making him turn red. "I don't snap my fingers and have every request taken care of instantly, Knight of Solamnia! Mishakal, like all the other gods, has concerns that go beyond mortal ken. I am not her sole concern, though I feel her love. There may be a hundred different reasons why I can't see what I want to see. For that matter, where is your Paladine? Why has he not helped his own people?"

Kaz, perhaps the only one of the party who had ever actually met a god—unfortunately, it had been Takhisis—smiled slightly. Gods, in his opinion, had more limitations than people imagined.

Rising from the chair where he had sat polishing his axe and trying to figure out some way to repair the one chipped edge, the minotaur stalked slowly toward the window. Other than the wind and an occasional sounding by the bell, things had been too quiet. On the night they had come here, dark, otherworldly things had been manifest. Now, save for the emptiness and the perpetual cloud cover, things were almost . . . ordinary.

Kaz did not like that one bit. In his experience, when things turned calm and ordinary, something unusual was about to happen.

"It's almost as if we're waiting for a signal," the minotaur whispered to himself.

"What's that?" Tesela called.

"Nothing. A whole lot of nothing, it seems."

"Ah! There you are!" Argaen came stomping in as if he had been searching the entire library for them. The elf always seemed to be at least a little astonished that they were still here, which made Kaz uneasy. It was as if they were temporary diversions from his normal scheme of things and one day would simply cease to exist. No doubt, then Argaen Ravenshadow would probably forget they had ever been here.

"I've brought you food!" The elf carried a plate of bread and a pot of thick vegetable soup to the table.

"Most kind of you, Master Ravenshadow," Darius said politely.

"Where do you get your supplies?" Tesela asked, sniffing the soup. Delbin was trying desperately to pull the pot from her hands. Argaen reached over and pried the kender away with a shake of his head. Delbin smiled and kept his hands at his sides, but his eyes kept drifting to the food.

"There are wells in the keep, and one of them nearby serves as one of the knighthood's storage areas. Because it is partly underground, it helps to preserve the food. I am afraid that the meat spoiled long ago, but plants can last for months. As for the preparation of the food, you can thank what little sorcery I have. I've grown fond of human foods. Elven dishes are too ethereal for my tastes these days." Argaen gave another broad smile.

"The supplies in Vingaard could help some of those villages to the south," Tesela said rather harshly.

"You are welcome to try, cleric. I am only one person and the immediate need, if you will pardon me for saying so, is here."

Tesela's expression indicated that she did not share the elf's view. For the past few years, the elf had been working here uselessly while other people were barely surviving. But what could she expect from an elf?

"How do your studies go, Argaen?" the minotaur asked. "Have you discovered something?"

The elf gave him a crooked smile. "I may have learned something that will change the entire situation. You will know before long, I promise you that. Please, eat."

The smell of the soup was mouth-watering. Kaz, used to rations and living off the land, forgot all his worries and took the pot from Tesela, who was beginning to look as if she was never going to get around to eating. Darius took out a knife and cut the bread into equal pieces. Delbin hopped up and down with anxiousness.

Argaen looked down at the kender. "Delbin, before you eat, could I ask a favor of you?"

Delbin looked at the food, then at the elf, then at the food again.

"It involves an interesting lock."

The kender's eyes gleamed. "Where is it?"

"This way." Elf and kender swept out of the room. Kaz snorted in amusement. Trust Argaen to come up with the one thing more important to a kender than food.

They each took a share of the soup and the bread. The bread was still warm and had that delicious taste only a fresh-baked loaf could have. Kaz decided there and then that sorcery had its useful aspect after all. Perhaps there was some way that Argaen could teach him the minimum spells for whipping up a stew.

"Truly, this is excellent," Darius succeeded in saying between mouthfuls.

Tesela, on the other hand, was not so enthusiastic. "It *smells* good, but there's a funny taste to it."

"Tastes fine to me." Kaz was just finishing the contents of his bowl and trying to calculate exactly how much they had to leave for Delbin.

"I'm not saying it's not delicious, but the taste just doesn't seem quite right."

"Would you trade some bread for your soup? I'll eat it if you don't want it." Kaz hoped she would take his offer.

She gave him a smile but declined. "The bread is good, but the soup is healthier. Maybe it's just me."

Kaz, disappointed, watched her take a couple more swallows. As she took the second one, he noticed something.

"Human . . . Tesela . . . why does your medallion glow?"

"What?" The cleric put her bowl down with a clatter and stared at the artifact hanging from the chain around her neck. "I've never seen it do that before!"

"Does it have to pulse like that, Milady Tesela?" Darius asked. He was sweating. "It makes my head spin."

"I don't know what it's supposed to do, because I don't know why it's doing it!"

"It must be . . . must be . . ." Kaz could not recall what it was he had wanted to say. Like Darius, he was sweating profusely now. "I . . ."

A groan from Darius prompted him to turn his head, though the action took an eternity as far as the minotaur was concerned. He watched helplessly as the knight fell to the floor. Tesela moved to aid him, but she herself was having trouble standing straight. Kaz felt his mind begin to separate from his body. With what little of his wits remained, he put one clawed hand against his leg and sank his nails into his leg. The pain washed over him, reviving him somewhat.

Tesela, he could see, was no longer trying to reach Darius. Instead, she was on her knees and holding the medallion above her head. The strain was obvious on her face.

Half-delirious, Kaz rose to his full height and stumbled toward the hall. *Delbin*, his mind repeated. *Delbin had to be in danger!* He made it halfway before his legs gave out and he fell onto the floor. *Delbin in danger . . . and Argaen?*

Kaz could no longer move. Even breath seemed a laborious thing, almost a waste of time. *Argaen*. The minotaur's mind slowly made the connection. It had to be. It simply had to be.

* * * * *

"Mishakal! I plead with you! These two are needed! I know I'm not the best of your clerics and my skills are few, but give me the strength to bring them back!"

The harsh voice broke through the sweet, warm darkness that had enveloped Kaz like a fur. He wanted to tell the voice to leave him in the quiet solitude of his slumber. What right did the voice have to disturb him? He was tired and needed rest, a *long* rest.

"Kaz! Hear me!"

He wanted to tell the human to go away. The human named Tesela. The human named Tesela who was a cleric. The human cleric named Tesela who was trying to pull him from his sleep.

Not sleep! a part of him whispered.

His mind, which seemed to have fragmented, began to coalesce again. Tesela was a cleric of Mishakal. She would not disturb him without a reason. The human was trying to help him. The thought of a feeble, human female helping a full-grown male minotaur amused him for some reason, and he started to laugh. It came out as a gurgle.

Tesela must have heard it, for her voice became excited. "Thank you, Mishakal! Thank you!"

"Stop . . ." Kaz forced his mouth and tongue to work. "Stop shouting . . . in my ears."

"Kaz!" He felt the warmth of another body on his. The minotaur began to feel other things as well, especially a nauseating sensation swelling in his stomach.

"Move!" He bellowed in a voice loud enough to make his own ears ring. Tesela moved away from him, and Kaz rolled over just in time to keep from drenching his own body with vomit. It seemed for some time that every meal he had ever eaten was departing his body in haste. Gradually, however, he finished. Disgusted, he rolled away.

It was some time before Kaz felt up to facing the others. Tesela gave him water and a cloth. Wiping his snout dry, the minotaur glanced at the two humans. Both were pale, especially Darius, who looked at least as bad as Kaz felt.

"What . . . what happened?"

"We all became ill," Tesela said gravely. "We were poisoned, I think."

"I had a wild notion about that before I—" Kaz's eyes widened. "Tesela, how close was I to death?"

"As close as Darius. You're bigger, but you finished

your bowl. He was only halfway through." The cleric beamed. "Mishakal guided my hand. Through the medallion, she could protect me, but not you. I had to act as her channel. That was what the medallion's glow meant. It was warning us of the danger."

Kaz stumbled to his feet. The selfsame pot of soup still sat on the table. Kaz sent the pot and its contents flying. "Sargas take that elf! Where is he?" The minotaur turned his gaze toward the window. "It's dark. How long has it been?"

"Midnight is upon us," Darius offered. "We owe a great deal to the lady here, and to her mistress."

Tesela shook her head in wonder. "I didn't think it was possible to heal someone so quickly. Not someone as near death as you. I think, given practice—Mishakal forbid!—and the will, I might be able to do it as quickly most every time! If only I'd known! The lives I could have saved!"

Kaz felt his legs grow steadily stronger. Try as he might, though, he could not yet lift his battle-axe properly. "Where is Argaen Ravenshadow? For that matter," Kaz suddenly recalled, "where's Delbin?"

"Mishakal forgive me!" Tesela leaped to her feet. "He could be dying of poison at this very moment!"

The trio searched the main room of the library as quickly as possible. It became apparent that neither Delbin nor Argaen were in the immediate vicinity. With a sinking feeling, Kaz knew where they should look.

"The vaults!" he muttered.

That Delbin could get past the much-vaunted safeguards of the Knights of Solamnia was a certainty in the minotaur's mind. Why Ravenshadow would try to poison them was another question.

"What can we do?" a pale-faced Darius asked.

Kaz shook his head, trying to clear it. He lifted his axe and knew that he still lacked the strength to use the weapon properly. Battling against crazed knights was not something he wanted to do, anyway. And Kaz did not doubt the abilities of Argaen Ravenshadow. Somehow he had gotten Delbin to agree to try to enter the vaults, perhaps by holding as incentive the lives of the two humans and Kaz.

"We've no choice," the minotaur said reluctantly. "I can't leave Delbin, and I can't fight. I think we should demand an audience with the Grand Master. Sane or not, I think that any warning I give will be enough to stir Oswal's interest. You two had better remain here in case I'm wrong."

"Would you call me a coward, minotaur?" Darius demanded. "And yourself a fool? You have more of a chance of succeeding if you are accompanied by a member of the knighthood as your guard."

"They might run both of you through without a second thought," Tesela reminded them. "Argaen said—"

Kaz snorted angrily. "Argaen said a lot of things that I find suspect now."

* * * * *

The column slowed. Bennett had no desire to call a halt now, but advice from his uncle rang in his head.

"Making good time in the day is no reason to go blindly in the night, lad," the elder knight would say. *"Many's the time a patrol rode straight into an ambush. Go slow . . . steady but slow."*

"Steady but slow," he muttered.

"What was that, milord?" the ranger next to him asked.

"I want you to go scout up ahead. Be careful. We'll be following at a slower pace."

The man looked at him critically. "You intend to travel during the night?"

"We must. Can't you feel it?"

"Feel *what?*"

"The—" *How can I put it?* Bennett wondered. "The—*presence*—has withdrawn! We should have felt it by now, tearing at our minds, threatening our sanity. . . ." The knight let his voice fade away as he recalled some of the things he had done under the sway of that power, that spell. He cursed silently.

The ranger was happy his face was hidden by the darkness. His nervousness always grew worse when Bennett talked like this. There was always the fear that the madness had left a permanent mark on those he rode with. The ranger sighed.

Bennett was still insistent. "We *will* move on! You have your orders, man!"

"Yes, milord." The ranger urged his horse forward and rode off.

Staring off into the darkness, Bennett tried to make out Vingaard Keep. He knew that, on a sunny day, the outline would have been visible near the horizon. Sunlit days were a rare commodity in recent months, however. It was almost as if the war were beginning all over again.

A bad feeling was developing, a feeling that something was going to happen very soon, and that Bennett was going to arrive too late to do anything about it. A disquieting feeling.

With a wave of his hand, he summoned one of his aides. The knight saluted his lord. "Sir?"

"How are the men holding up, Grissom?"

"We are Knights of Solamnia, milord!"

At one time, that would have been all the answer Bennett needed to go charging pell-mell through the dark toward Vingaard Keep. Not now. Another knight, these five years dead, had taught him otherwise.

"How are they *really* holding up, Grissom?"

The broad-faced knight shrugged. "They could use rest, but none of them are unfit. We could ride three more days before the first would begin to keel over. I think some of the horses would go first."

The hint of a smile touched Bennett's lips. "If we ride through the night, we can be at Vingaard before morning. Have you felt anything at all, Grissom?"

"Nothing, milord." The aide sounded hopeful. "Could that mean the threat has been crushed? That the spell has been broken by our brethren who remained behind?"

"Unlikely, if you recall our own minds as we rode off to—what was it, anyway?—to crush our nonexistent enemies to the south or something?"

"I . . . forget."

Bennett nodded. "I force myself to remember. We have much to answer for, spell or no spell."

"What do you think is happening at Vingaard, then, milord?"

Gauntleted hands tightened their grip on the reins. "I cannot say for certain, Sir Grissom, save that I think our final destination will be a true trial of our strength, in mind as well as in body." Bennett muttered a small oath to Paladine, then added, "It's time we moved on. Send word down the column. Slow but steady, Sir Grissom."

"Milord." The other knight turned his horse around and departed.

Bennett continued to stare in the direction he knew Vingaard Keep had to be, trying not to think too much about what he would do once the column made it there. He wondered whether they would be, as he feared, too late really to do anything.

Chapter 14

"You realize," Darius whispered, "that this plan of yours might be the product of the same sorcerous madness that has affected Vingaard and the lands surrounding it."

Kaz nodded almost imperceptibly. "Very much so, but then, everyone we've been dealing with suffers from the same affliction, so that means what we're doing is practically normal, doesn't it?"

The silence of the empty keep was at least as eerie in its own way as that first night when they had been stalked by the winged thing and attacked by the wild knight. Time almost seemed to be holding its breath, waiting. The hair on the minotaur's back began to rise.

"Look!" Tesela whispered.

Blinking, Kaz joined Darius and Tesela in staring at the scene unfolding before them.

The amassed figures did not resemble the phantom knights, though distance and the flickering light of the torches made it impossible to say for certain. Kaz estimated maybe four dozen. The thought occurred to him that maybe these were phantoms, too, but he discarded that idea almost immediately. These were flesh-and-blood Knights of Solamnia, and they looked ready to defend the stronghold of the Grand Master at any cost.

"They still haven't seen us," Darius whispered quickly. "You two could remain in the shadows. I am one of them."

In lieu of a reply, Kaz straightened and stepped into sight.

Not one of the knights so much as turned a head. They remained where they were, resolutely guarding against . . . what?

Darius, accompanied by Tesela, quickly stepped up behind the minotaur. One knight slowly turned his helm toward them. Then another. And another. Like some bizarre puppet show, ten or twelve of the figures turned to stare in the direction of the trio. They stared—and did nothing else.

"I like this not," Darius muttered.

"Really?"

At Kaz's whispered suggestion, the three walked toward a knight whose armor indicated he was of some rank in the Order of the Crown. Acting as if he were the minotaur's captor, Darius ordered Kaz to come to a halt. With great uneasiness, he steeled himself and stepped forward to speak with his fellow knight.

"Knight Darius, late of the keep in the province of Westia."

With his helm completely obscuring his face, it was impossible to tell whether the other knight even took any notice of Darius.

"I have with me the minotaur named Kaz, brought

176

here at the command of the Grand Master himself."

A mournful howl filled the air of the keep. It was answered by other howls from all about the citadel.

"They're coming!" the knight Darius had been speaking to shouted suddenly. All around them, the forms were beginning to move with a determination that amazed the trio. Lances were made ready. A few knights secured their torches and reached for bows. The arrows they fitted had tiny bits of moist cloth tied to them. Kaz realized the men were making fire arrows.

In the shadows all around, they could hear the padding of feet, the harsh breathing of several large creatures, and the occasional repetition of the mournful wail.

Kaz glanced at the knights. "They're ignoring us. . . ."

The howling was replaced by growls.

"Interesting timing," Kaz commented sourly.

"What do you mean?"

"After the day's quiet and Argaen's betrayal, I just think that this attack is too well timed."

"A diversion!" Darius blurted.

"Here they come!" someone cried.

White shapes began to burst from the shadows, long, sinewy white shapes so very familiar to Kaz. Baleful blind eyes, burning red, contrasted greatly with the dead flesh of the hairless beasts.

"Dreadwolves!"

The others looked at him. From him they knew of dreadwolves, but actually to *see* one was quite another matter. The repulsive dreadwolves charged toward the thin line of valiant knights.

Darius could not stand it. "Kaz, we cannot abandon my brothers! Mad or not, they fight for their lives!"

"Our mission is just as important! Whatever Argaen plans, I want to make certain that he doesn't end up bringing Vingaard Keep down around us!"

A fiery arrow caught a dreadwolf in midleap. The creature tumbled to the side, then rose again. When it realized it was on fire, it began to roll on the ground. The arrow snapped and the head buried itself deeper in the creature, but it didn't concern the dreadwolf. It was not alive but was merely a parody of life.

Kaz, frustrated, took Darius by the collar. "Listen, human," he snorted madly. "In times past, the dreadwolves were controlled by the sorcerer, Dracos! Dracos should be dead, but someone or something is controlling those monsters! I think the key lies in the vaults! Someone should go down there and investigate!"

Another dreadwolf became skewered on the end of a long lance. Somehow the defenders were succeeding in keeping the battle a stalemate.

As Kaz released his grip on Darius, the truth of the situation dawned on him.

"You've nothing to worry about, Darius," he said quickly. "They're like the knight we fought—illusions!"

They watched another dreadwolf, pinned to the ground, vanish. The knight who had pinned him down with his lance seemed to take this in stride, calmly awaiting the next one.

"Come on!" cried Kaz. "I doubt we have too much time!"

Though they had half-expected it, it was still a bit of a shock to discover that the building was empty. Their footsteps echoed loudly in the halls. Kaz, the only one of the three who had ever been in the Grand Master's citadel, led the way.

Kaz only hoped that Oswal had no intention of hanging him from the point of a lance. It would certainly spoil the reunion, not to mention any chances of catching Argaen before it was too late. Kaz wondered what the elf's plan was. What did he intend to do with whatever artifact or power lurked down in the vault?

They turned down the hallway and found two elaborately decorated doors blocking their path. Kaz tried the doors and, when they proved to be locked, clasped both hands together, raising them high in the air and bringing them down hard where the two doors joined.

The doors burst open with a loud crash. Splinters flew everywhere.

Beyond the entrance, seated in a throne atop a dais and guarded by a dozen stern figures, was the still-majestic form of the Grand Master of the Knights of Solamnia. Even from where he stood, Kaz could see the strain that Lord Oswal was under. Despite that, Oswal continued to radiate a power of majesty.

The aquiline features, so much like those of his nephew though tempered by age, came into view as the Grand Master looked up at those who had dared invade his inner sanctum. The eyes seemed to pierce the trio.

"So!" Oswal suddenly raged. He stood up and pointed a condemning finger at the three. "You think to twist my mind with still more of your masks, your illusions? I feel your weakness! The knighthood will triumph!"

With odd dreamlike movements, the guards on the steps of the platform began to draw toward the newcomers. The Grand Master fairly wept with delight. "They see you! I've survived your spell of madness, then!"

"How is it things keep getting worse and worse?" snarled Kaz. He stepped in front of Darius and Tesela and raised both hands high in the air, palms toward the guards so that they could see he was unarmed. "Lord Oswal!"

The figure standing before the throne stiffened. "A good ploy, but not good enough!"

"What does he mean?" Darius whispered.

"Quiet!" Kaz hissed. To the Grand Master, he called, "Lord Oswal, you know me! I am the minotaur, Kaz, friend of Huma and the knighthood!"

"Kaz?" A peculiar expression moved slowly over the elder knight's face. "Kaz is dead! I ordered his capture and execution on nonexistent charges before I realized that there was a spell of madness enveloping the keep and that I had been affected along with the rest of the men. I ordered *all* their executions—Arak Hawkeye,

179

Lord Guy Avondale, Taggin. . . . So many died before my eyes."

The guards were nearly upon them. Darius stepped up next to Kaz, his sword committed in the minotaur's defense. "Milord, I am Darius of the Order of the Crown, from a keep in the south. I know not the whereabouts of Lord Hawkeye or the one you called Avondale, but I do know that we only recently had word from Taggin, ruling knight of one of the southernmost keeps in Ergoth. He is alive and well."

"Taggin? Alive?" As the Grand Master momentarily faltered, so too did the movement of the guards. It was as if they were extensions of his will.

Kaz suddenly eyed them more closely. *Extensions of his will?*

"Lord Oswal," Kaz began, his eyes still on the other knights, "when we—when we buried Huma, you said the world needed heroes, which was why you had such an elaborate tomb built for him."

The Grand Master seemed to slump a little. "I recall that."

"I thought it more appropriate to honor him the way *he* would have wanted it, by a simple burial and a marker noting only his name."

"The knighthood needed a standard. They, too, needed a hero." The guards seemed frozen in stride as the Grand Master spoke of that time. "He was a cleric of Paladine in the end, you know. A just reward. He deserved it more than I ever did."

"He truly lived up to the Oath and Measure, Grand Master."

"Kaz." The Grand Master took a step toward them.

Suddenly the loyal guards simply ceased to be. They were, as Kaz had surmised, phantoms. He wondered whether or not the knights combating the dreadwolves had been phantoms as well. Phantoms fighting phantoms.

Kaz bowed his head as the Grand Master approached.

His two companions had already done the same. "My Lord Oswal."

The Lord of Knights came down the steps and walked over to the minotaur. He clasped Kaz on the shoulders. "It *is* you. I'm certain of it! More lies! All he ever spoke were lies!"

Kaz cocked an eyebrow. "Argaen Ravenshadow?"

A puzzled look crossed the elder knight's face. "The elf? Is he still here? I ordered him ousted from the libraries shortly after he came here. No, friend Kaz, I fear the one I speak of is none other than the mortal consort of Takhisis herself, that scaly-faced renegade mage, Galan Dracos!"

"Dracos!" Kaz shook his head, remembering the dreadwolves outside.

"Dracos indeed! Who are your companions, Kaz the Minotaur?"

"I am Tesela," the healer said.

"A brave friend," Kaz added.

"Milord." Darius was down on one knee. "Darius, from a keep in Westia."

"The province that Kharolis claims but leaves to the knighthood to defend? Where are your brethren? I was told to expect emissaries from most of the southern keeps."

"They . . . milord, I'm afraid they are dead. A dragon, so I believe."

"A dragon?" Oswal looked at the three. "Surely another of the renegade's lies! He could not have the power to enslave a dragon, let alone drag one from Paladine knows where! All the dragons are gone!"

"None of us have seen the dragon in good light, Grand Master," Kaz replied hastily. "It may be something else— a rare griffon, perhaps. Be that as it may, I think that you have been duped in yet another manner." He paused at the brief annoyed look on Lord Oswal's face. Kaz forced himself to be more delicate with his choice of words. "Argaen Ravenshadow never departed Vingaard Keep.

In fact, he's about the only one left in Vingaard besides yourself and—and a few of your most loyal men."

"All this time, I thought I was keeping a clear head," Oswal muttered. "Instead, I've been living a delusion. What more?"

"Why was Ravenshadow to be sent away?"

"His interest in the works of Galan Dracos was too intense. I saw in him one who treaded a thin line between red and black robes." The Grand Master's eyes lit up with partial understanding. "But if Ravenshadow has been here all this time— Paladine! No wonder he pressed for the secrets of the vaults! The elf does not have the magical skills necessary to ferret them out, but that is something Dracos would not need to worry about!"

Kaz sighed in relief. "You understand the situation now. Good, because we fear that this attack, an illusion like all the rest, is a diversion created by Ravenshadow. He may even now down be in the vaults, working his way through your safeguards at last."

"Impossible! Argaen might be able to bypass the magical safeguards, which I doubt, but he could never weave through the networks of traps and false locks." The elder knight tapped the side of his head. "Only I know those secrets, and I have not faltered there."

The minotaur grimaced. "Lord Oswal, I fear that I've brought a kender with me. Another companion, if you can believe that."

"A kender?" Oswal asked, a quizzical look on his face. "A kender?" The Grand Master shook his head. "A kender!"

"His name's Delbin, and I think, judging by Argaen's ability to manipulate people's minds, he's helping the elf break open the vaults."

"By the Triumvirate!"

"How do we reach the vaults, milord?" asked Darius quickly, for Oswal was simply staring out into space, dumbfounded, no doubt picturing the elf plundering armloads of magical treasures—evil treasures.

"What? . . . Yes, of course. This way!" The Grand Master led them up the dais to the throne. He touched something on one of the arms, and the chair and the floor below it slid to one side. There was a stairway leading down into the earth.

"Get a torch, Darius, will you?"

"At once, Grand Master."

"I could light the way with this." Tesela held up her medallion.

Oswal shook his head. "I would not risk that yet. Argaen might feel our presence if we make use of the gifts the gods have bestowed upon us. I want to surprise the elf before he even realizes we are coming."

As Darius returned with the torch, Kaz looked around for some weapon. He wished now that he had not left his own axe behind. To have it in his hands now . . .

"I thought you left that behind," Tesela commented in mild surprise.

Kaz gazed down at his hands. His visage was reflected back by the mirrorlike finish of the head of Honor's Face. He almost dropped it, thinking it just another illusion. It felt real, however. Somehow, it had materialized in his hands just when he needed it. Was it some minor miracle performed by Paladine, or had Sardal Crystalthorn given him a magical weapon?

"Are you coming, minotaur?" Lord Oswal called from the steps.

Kaz hefted the axe once and, feeling the good, solid weight of the weapon, shrugged. All that really mattered at the moment, he decided, was that now he had the axe. "Coming."

They descended into the cool earth.

"Lord Oswal," Darius whispered, "is there more than one entrance to the vaults?"

"There is. There is one in the chamber where he who commands the Order of the Rose—my nephew, Bennett, holds that position—speaks before his men."

"Where is Bennett now?" Kaz asked sourly. He still

was not certain just what to think about Huma's former rival.

The Grand Master paused, trying to collect his thoughts. "I seem to recall . . . to recall sending him off to fight . . . to fight Paladine! But what else have I done these past few years that I do not recall? What have I done to beloved Solamnia?"

The minotaur put a hand on the elder's shoulder. "The elf is responsible—the elf and something left behind by Dracos. You've got a lot of wounds to heal, Grand Master, but none of them are really your fault."

"You say that even though I almost had you killed?"

"Whose doing was that?"

Lord Oswal shook his head dazedly. "I seem to recall asking, or being asked, who might have knowledge concerning Galan Dracos. Ravenshadow asked me to list those who had been there!"

Kaz snorted. "Perhaps the elf thought to eliminate any who knew about the renegade's magic. We can ask him if we get the chance."

They moved in silence now, not so much out of a fear that someone might hear but because each of them wondered what they might soon face. Through the trek down the long, winding steps, they battled their own imaginations.

A sound from below caught their attention. Lord Oswal signaled for a halt. A voice, barely recognizable as the elf's, echoed upward. What he was saying, they could not understand, except that Argaen was tense, excited.

The Grand Master turned to Darius and indicated that he should give the torch to Tesela and that she should stay to the rear. The cleric wanted to say something, slightly annoyed at being relegated to a "safe" position, but decided against it. This was, after all, Oswal's domain.

Ever so slowly, they continued their descent. They stopped for a second time when they heard a new, higher-pitched voice. Kaz could not help smiling, for the voice was that of his kender companion. Delbin was not only alive, but he was also his usual self, much to Argaen's dismay, no doubt.

"How did you first get inside? How long did it take you to learn? The knights must really not want people to get in here, because I never saw such complicated locks! My uncle would've loved this place. He's the best, you know, though he taught me a lot, and I bet he would've gotten inside by this time, though maybe this one darn screwy lock would've given him some trouble. . . ."

"Be silent, kender!" Argaen Ravenshadow hissed. "I have to concentrate, or I might miss something! If I do, we may both wind up dead! What would your minotaur friend do without you then?"

"I wish Kaz was here. He's always so much fun. You know, I'm getting kind of hungry. Do you have any more of that bread? I like bread, especially with lots of honey on—"

"How can you concentrate on that lock and babble so?" Obviously the elf was reaching the limit of his patience, but he needed Delbin badly. Had the circumstances been different, Kaz would have found the conversation quite amusing.

"I think I've got it!"

"At last! The strain is becoming unbearable!"

Lord Oswal stiffened. The Grand Master reached behind his breastplate and pulled out a chain, at the end of which was a familiar medallion. The elderly knight turned back to Tesela and, with a gesture, indicated her medallion. She nodded and held it tightly with her free hand.

They crept down the remaining steps, Oswal and Kaz in the forefront. A glittering light emanated from the bottom, where the stairs ended in the entrance to what could only be the chamber of the vaults. Kaz leaned down and peered inside, axe at the ready.

At first glance, the chamber of the vaults seemed surprisingly large. The ceiling was almost three times the minotaur's own height, with enough ground space for a company of mounted knights. Another set of stairs stood opposite those used by the foursome. From the marks on the walls and various odd artifacts lying on the floor or sticking out from the walls, Kaz received a good impression of some of the nastier safeguards the Knights of Solamnia had installed. Those were only the physical traps. Argaen Ravenshadow had evidently dealt success-fully with all of the sorcerous traps—at least so far.

In the center of the room, poised beneath the shimmer-ing crystal that was the source of the light, stood the elf, Argaen Ravenshadow. His robe was of the blackest black, leaving no doubt now as to his loyalty. The dark elf held something in his hands, hands that were raised as if he sought to grasp the illuminating crystal, and he stared straight ahead, as if the Dragonqueen herself were about to burst through the vaults. *Not something to be ruled out,* Kaz thought pessimistically. Argaen's hair fluttered outward.

The vault doors themselves reached nearly to the ceil-ing. There were three of them, each with a massive relief of one of the three symbols of the knighthood sculpted into it. Argaen's attention was focused on the one that bore a single massive rose. Delbin was fiddling with something near the handle. He could barely reach it on his tiptoes.

The Grand Master's hand touched Kaz. The two looked at one another. Lord Oswal smiled grimly and whispered, "The time is upon us! Be ready to strike when I do!"

Clutching tight the symbol of his belief in the power of Paladine, the elder knight closed his eyes and whispered something.

The effect on Argaen Ravenshadow was immediate. His eyes lit up and he turned to where the four had been concealed. *"No! No!"* he screamed.

Kaz had already covered half the distance between

him and the dark mage. Darius was only a step or two behind. Bellowing like a beast, the minotaur swung the massive axe high over his head. One sweep would send his adversary to the floor. . . .

It was like striking a stone wall, only he struck nothing. Instead, he went flying backward, bowling over the hapless Darius as he did so, soon ending his flight with a heavy thud against the wall near the stairway. Kaz hit the floor like a sack of rocks, still conscious but too stunned to do anything.

Oddly unperturbed by the chaos around him, Delbin shouted out, "I got it! I should write this down, you know, because this is the best adventure I've had y—"

"Be silent, you fool!"

"Argaen Ravenshadow!" The Grand Master stepped out into the open, the symbol of Paladine gleaming brilliantly on his chest. "Your tricks have proven insufficient! Now face me directly, and let us see if your power can save you from judgment!" Behind him, Tesela crouched, clutching her own medallion.

The elf's expression became even more desperate. He stuffed the object he had been holding into one pocket of his robe, while with his other hand, he pulled something from another pocket. With amazing speed, he threw a handful of tiny spheres at the elder knight.

As Ravenshadow had done with Kaz, so, too, did the Grand Master do with the spheres. The tiny projectiles bounced off an invisible shield and rebounded to various portions of the chamber.

"Is that the best you can do? You are no mage, elf! As I suspected when first you came, you are nothing more than a thief of magic, with little actual power to call your own—"

The tiny spheres began bursting, filling the chamber of the vaults with shock waves of sound and blinding flashes. Caught unaware by the dark elf's ploy, Lord Oswal stumbled back, his eyesight blinded and his senses, already weak from his long ordeal, in disarray.

Through watery eyes, Kaz saw Argaen rush to the vault door where Delbin stood. The elf shoved the hesitant kender aside. Kaz forced himself to his feet and stumbled forward.

Argaen Ravenshadow tugged the massive vault door open. Despite his slim appearance, his strength apparently was considerable. The door began to swing outward, and the illumination of the chamber was suddenly transformed into a hellish green glow that sent chills down the minotaur's spine. There was no warmth in the glow, but rather a malevolent presence that was somehow familiar.

"Aaaah!" The shriek was Argaen's, and it was not one of triumph.

The intensity of the emerald glow was like a physical force, buffeting the members of the party. The Grand Master fell back, his body too weak, his mind too worn. No one could have done more.

Kaz stumbled to one knee. Two hands helped him up and Tesela, her face aglow with the strength of Mishakal, smiled bravely at him. She, too, was under a great strain.

"I'm not a warrior, Kaz! Let Mishakal watch over you, give you strength! It's the only help I can give!" Though there was no other sound, it was difficult to make out her voice, almost as if she were speaking from a distance.

The minotaur nodded. He thought about turning around and retrieving his battle-axe, only to discover, as before, that it was already in his hands. A grim smile played over his animal features. This was the sort of magic he could learn to like.

"See to Darius and the others!" he shouted, then stalked defiantly toward the open vault.

Even before he reached the doorway, Kaz had a good idea what it was he faced. It was the same tremendous power he had felt from a distance when the surviving dragonriders had swooped down on the citadel of the mad mage. . . .

He stepped in front of the open vault and confirmed

his own fears. With the sorcerous staff of his childhood friend, the slain wizard, Magius, Huma had attacked Galan Dracos. Dracos's power had been shattered, so had Huma said, and this thing that radiated it should have been nothing more than a thousand glass fragments. Yet this evil thing had evidently reformed itself, albeit incompletely, judging by the cracks and gaps, and now it rested solidly on a pile of broken artifacts gathered from the ruins of the magic-user's citadel.

Like a dragon atop its horde, the great emerald sphere of Galan Dracos, the same sphere that had almost made the renegade sorcerer victorious, glistened malevolently at the minotaur.

Chapter 15

FRAGMENTS. THAT WAS ALL THAT HAD REMAINED OF THE emerald sphere, according to Huma. The sphere had been the channel for the power Galan Dracos had craved . . . power he had drawn from beyond even the Abyss, power that would have allowed his mistress her full dark glory in the mortal realm of Krynn. Without the sphere, the Dark Queen would have been weakened, as are all gods who enter this plane of existence. Dracos had found a way, though, through his unorthodox manner of experimentation, to cheat this basic law. He had also planned to cheat Takhisis as well and to add her power to his own. However, in a moment of desperation, Huma had thrown the Staff of Magius like a well-aimed lance at the emerald sphere. Where the finest steel could not even scratch the artifact's surface, the magical staff had driven through virtually unimpeded, shattering both the emerald sphere and its creator's dream.

Somehow the sphere, over a period of time, had drawn itself back together. It was imperfect, though, and even from where he stood, half-blinded by its evil glory, Kaz could see the many cracks and gaps. Not all of the sphere had been gathered back together; some pieces had no doubt been buried or thrown far from the wreckage of the citadel. It was amazing that the knights had located so many.

Half-draped over the flickering artifact, blood staining his right side, was Argaen Ravenshadow. More and more, it appeared that the true Argaen Ravenshadow was a mad thief of sorcery. The dark elf smiled as he looked up and noticed the minotaur, as if for the first time.

"I never imagined it could be so . . . wonderful," he whispered. The glow made him look positively ghoulish. "This is what comes from being unfettered by the Conclave's stodgy rules! This is true magic!"

"It's death, elf. Likely yours." Kaz hefted the axe.

Argaen rose from the sphere, strain evident in every move. Blood was still dripping from a massive wound below his left shoulder. Had it been a little farther to the right, the elf would have been a walking corpse. "The knighthood . . . is very thorough. I did not expect a . . . a further safety measure within the vault itself. It . . . it almost succeeded in its task."

"It may still succeed. You look about done, thief."

The elf's smile grew broader. "A small matter now. I have access to more power than any other mage alive. Not only can I heal myself, but in time, I can become nearly a god!"

Kaz laughed mockingly. "Galan Dracos thought the same thing."

"He was in the midst of a war."

"And you have only me. I think I might be enough for

you, though." Kaz took a step toward the elf and his prize.

"Are you?"

This time it was not as if the minotaur had hit a stone wall. Rather, it was more like walking into soft cheese. Kaz struggled forward, feeling each step more and more of an effort.

The distance that separated the two was diminishing slowly, when Kaz saw the elf reach into a pocket in his robes and pull out a tiny figurine. It was, Kaz noted, the same figurine that Delbin had "accidentally" picked up once before. With that realization, the minotaur was abruptly released by whatever spell held him in thrall. His advantage was short-lived, however, because even as he ran, he saw the tiny figurine in Ravenshadow's outstretched hand swell in size and fly off. The figurine landed in front of him, effectively cutting him off from the elf. It continued to grow and grow.

The nightflyer! Darius had been slightly amiss in his assumption that he had been attacked by a dragon, for, though the thing that Kaz was now desperately backing away from had the wings, body, and jaws of a dragon, it was not that legendary beast. It was not even alive, at least by normal standards.

It was a stone dragon, perfect in every detail—a statue, a figurine, animated by some sorcery. Still it continued to grow. Already its head nearly brushed the ceiling of the vault. Kaz watched in horrified wonder as seemingly immobile wings flapped lightly. He wondered how the thing, so much heavier than a true dragon, could fly.

The stone behemoth opened its great maw wide and roared a silent challenge. Whereas it had been given a mouth with huge, sharp-chiseled teeth, fangs, and a forked tongue longer than the minotaur's arm, the creator could not endow the strange creature with a throat. The back of the mouth ended in solid rock. It could not make a sound.

Still the creature continued to grow, and Kaz wondered whether it would keep swelling until it filled all the space in the huge vault.

The dragon lashed its long, wicked tail at the nearest wall of the vault. The wall failed to shatter, but cracks ran all along it.

"Cease!" The elf glared up at the creature. "You will bring everything down upon us!"

In reply, the unliving creature glanced down at its master and gave a silent hiss. It began to shift around, as if seeking some escape from the confinement of the vault. A wing struck the weakened wall, spreading the vein of cracks farther and loosening bits of the ceiling. The dragon moved forward.

"Stop!" Argaen stumbled a short distance from the sphere, which was glowing more intensely than ever. "I command you!"

"Your toy doesn't seem to be listening!" Kaz shouted, and regretted it a moment later when the dragon suddenly swiveled its head and studied him thoughtfully with its blank eyes. It began to change direction. The tail struck the base of the wall. There was an ominous rumbling from above.

Argaen Ravenshadow was down on one knee, every movement requiring a greater and greater effort on his part. "Minotaur!"

Kaz paid him no mind at first, intent on saving his own skin. He swung the dwarven battle-axe in his left hand, cutting an arc of death that he was certain would not impress a creature that had already proven itself impervious to such weaponry. To his surprise, however, the stone beast actually backed up a step or two. It leaned forward and opened its mouth wide, eerily remaining in that stance for several seconds. The action seemed peculiar until Kaz recognized the pose as that of a true dragon unleashing a deadly stream of flame. The animated dragon obviously thought itself every bit as real as the vast leviathan it had been carved to resemble.

"Minotaur! Listen to—to me!"

"What is it?" Kaz watched in dismay as the monster tried to rise in the air. It was no sooner off the ground, however, than the top of its head smashed into the ceiling like a battering ram. Both elf and minotaur were showered by large fragments.

"By the Oath and Measure!" Whatever Argaen sought to say was again cut off, this time by the intrusion of the Grand Master and Darius. They had come in expecting a battle, but nothing like this. The stone behemoth turned to regard them.

"The Abyss take you, foul fiend! I owe you for many lives!" shouted Darius. He started for the monster in what Kaz thought was typical Solamnic fashion, a head-on charge with only a sword against a creature more than twenty times his size. Kaz was never sure whether such an action ought to be considered bravery or stupidity.

Darius was already upon the dragon before anyone could prevent him. With a loud battle cry, he struck at the nearest leg, only to have his sword rebound off the limb and go flying from his hand. The dragon raised its front paw high.

"No!" Lord Oswal reacted instinctively, rushing to pull the stunned and still angered Darius away from a danger that seemed obvious to everyone except the young knight.

The massive paw came down, smashing a vast hole in the floor and causing the entire vault to shake. More ceiling rained down, but this time it did not cease after a few seconds. The structure had not been designed to combat something so huge trying to get out.

The Grand Master managed to save Darius, but not without risk to his own safety. Several large fragments of rock struck him, knocking him to the ground. Kaz tried to reach him, but Ravenshadow's uncontrollable stone dragon now blocked his path completely. It was determined to extinguish the two knights. The minotaur steadied his axe, mentally readying himself for a suicide charge.

"There . . . is a way . . . minotaur! Listen . . . to me!"

Argaen Ravenshadow clutched at the ugly hole in his upper torso. The wound had stopped bleeding, but the elf was as white as a dreadwolf. With his other arm, Argaen forced himself to remain in a sitting position. Kaz could see that it wouldn't take much to shift the arm a little and send the dark one falling facedown into the earth, where he would be too weak to rise again. The temptation was there, but Kaz checked the thought. He looked over his shoulder and saw that Darius was trying to drag his liege lord to safety. He was not making much headway, for the younger knight's right leg seemed unsteady, as if he had sprained his ankle. Another figure darted into the vault, Tesela, with a look of grim desperation on her visage. Her eyes avoiding the monstrous threat before her, she rushed over to Darius and helped him drag Lord Oswal toward the entrance of the vault. The stone dragon trailed closely behind. Of Delbin, there was still no sign, and Kaz hoped the kender had enough sense to stay out of danger this time.

Argaen's renewed plea made him turn back to the elf. "Help . . . me to . . . bind the sphere . . . the sphere to my will. . . ."

"Hah! You're even madder than I thought! *Me* help *you?*"

The elf spat blood. "I . . . cannot control the animate . . . for very long! You can . . . see that I . . . am dying, minotaur! If I do, that thing will rampage until . . . all of Vingaard is destroyed . . . and then it . . . will start on Solamnia!"

"Another sorcerer will stop it!"

"True"—Argaen tried to smile—"but we will be long dead . . . and who knows . . . how many others will die!"

Kaz looked back and saw that Darius and Tesela had succeeded in nearly gaining the entrance. As the dragon struggled against Argaen's control, it was slamming against the walls again. The network of cracks now extended from one end of the vault to the other, and Kaz wondered if the outer chamber was in danger of collapsing as well.

"You've precious little time left, minotaur! I've . . . precious little time also!"

"What do you want of me?"

"In . . . a pouch . . . a pouch on my belt . . ."

"Gods, Argaen, not another of your little trinkets!"

"A . . . very *old* one, minotaur. This pouch . . ." The elf nodded to the left side of his body.

Kaz eyed the emerald sphere. Somehow, he could not help feeling that *it* watched him in return—with amusement. He found its sporadic surges of power unsettling, as if it were playing a game of sorts. The minotaur wondered how well Ravenshadow truly understood what it was he was trying to bind to his mind. The elf's death would be no great loss to Kaz, but there would still be the emerald sphere itself to deal with.

Kaz reluctantly stepped over to Ravenshadow and began to search the pouch. "What am I looking for? This flat, leathery thing?"

"No . . . and release it immediately!" Argaen coughed up more blood. "A tiny cube . . . a box."

Kaz found what he assumed was the cube. Carefully he pulled it out and showed it to the elf. "Is this what you wanted?"

"Yes. Now . . . help me to move . . . a few feet from the sphere."

Behind them, there was a tremendous noise, and suddenly portions of the ceiling began to cave in. Kaz nearly released his grip on Argaen as he turned to see what was happening. "Pay it no mind!" Argaen shouted madly. "This vault and . . . likely the entire chamber . . . is collapsing! Help me!"

The minotaur cursed in the name of every god he could think of as he dragged the dark elf away. When they were a good dozen paces from the sphere, Argaen had Kaz help him into a sitting position.

"Now . . ." Ravenshadow's breath was very ragged. "Place the cube on the top of the sphere."

"Raven—"

"Don't argue!" The elf nearly toppled. The other walls were showing signs of weakening. Kaz could hear the stone dragon pounding away at something and realized it was trying to get out of the vault, despite the fact that its present girth was too vast to fit through the entrance.

Axe in one hand and cube in the other, Kaz took a deep breath and made his way back to the malevolent globe. Oddly, this time he felt no surge of power, no blinding glare. Rather, there was an aura of impatience.

It's only an object, he told himself. *It's an Abyss-spawned, cursed object, but only an object.*

Though he was not able to completely convince himself, he did succeed in reaching his goal. Steeling himself, Kaz carefully placed the tiny black cube on the very top of Dracos's pride and joy, then ran.

Argaen Ravenshadow was laughing, or at least attempting to, when Kaz rejoined him. "Were—were you expecting something?"

The minotaur looked at the cube. "It's growing! Elf, if you've unleashed another pet—"

"Keep watching!"

The black cube continued to swell in size, but it also took on a new quality. The larger it became, the less substantial it seemed to become. When it was nearly half the volume of the sphere, it appeared to sink down into the artifact, as if its bottom were melting.

At the battered vault entrance, the stone dragon paused in its rampage, seemingly confused about what it was supposed to do next. Kaz's companions were nowhere in sight, and he hoped they had departed the outer chamber in quick order.

"It's swallowing up the emerald sphere, minotaur. Once inside, the power of the sphere will be muted and

197

controllable, transportable." Argaen arose, very unsteadily, but obviously without as much pain as he had been suffering moments before. "I *knew* it would work!"

"You knew it would work?" The minotaur's eyes narrowed.

"You've witnessed my pride and joy, minotaur. I designed the shadow box, as I call it, strictly for such a purpose . . . and it worked! The emerald sphere, the path of power, is mine at last!"

Kaz's huge, clawed hand pulled the elf off his feet and brought him to a minotaur's eye level. "You sound much better, magic thief!"

"Remember your friends!" Wild-eyed, Argaen Ravenshadow tore himself from Kaz's grasp and fell to the ground. He looked up at the minotaur and smiled broadly. "Especially your talkative little lockpicker!"

A huge section of the ceiling collapsed, sending tons of earth falling around the shadow box but strangely leaving it untouched and accessible. Kaz was caught between his hatred for the elf and his desire to leave before the rest of the ceiling and the earth above came crashing down around him.

"I should let the animate kill you all, though I fear that my playacting was not far from the actual truth, minotaur! Elves are a bit stronger than you think, but there are limits." Argaen stared past Kaz at the stone dragon, which still paused by the vault entrance. The creature suddenly spread its wings as best it could in the cramped space and turned, shrieking silently, toward the two. The mighty jaws opened wide, and the stone beast began to move slowly in their direction. Its movements were graceful, and Kaz could almost imagine its stone muscles rippling. The tail lashed out and struck one of the walls, sending large pieces of the wall flying and raising a cloud of dust.

Kaz stepped back swiftly as the monster, ignoring the destruction raining down, stopped just before its master. The dark elf laughed at Kaz. "I would not recommend remaining down here, minotaur! If you leave now, you might just make it before everything crumbles!"

"You can't be serious!"

Argaen's unliving pet, its eyes focused on Kaz, lowered itself to the ground so that the elf could climb aboard. "I am so very serious!"

A Knight of Solamnia might have stayed and fought. Most minotaurs might have stayed and fought. Kaz knew better. He started running.

A small figure chose that moment to come crawling over the wreckage of the vault doorway. It was Delbin. Behind the kender, Kaz could see Lord Oswal. He cursed, knowing Darius and Tesela could not be far behind them. So much for his vague hope that they would do the intelligent thing and flee while they could. The Grand Master, haggard, spotted the minotaur first and started to speak.

Kaz waved them back. "Run!"

The elder knight took one look and, sizing up the situation, obeyed reluctantly, but Delbin, caught up in typical kender curiosity, remained where he was, trying to see what was going on beyond the minotaur. Snarling, Kaz tucked his battle-axe under one arm and, with the other, scooped up the small figure. Behind them, Argaen shouted something incomprehensible.

Lord Oswal and Tesela were already helping Darius up the steps. No one paused or even looked back. The walls and the steps vibrated as the party ascended. Kaz, in the rear, felt the step beneath his feet begin to give way. He said nothing, knowing that the others were moving as fast as they could. Tesela hadn't had time to do anything for Darius's sprain.

When the steps finally ended, the party's relief at reaching the surface died quickly. The exit was barely passable; there was extensive damage.

"We must go outside," the Grand Master decided for them. "We may have to abandon Vingaard entirely until the danger is over."

Lord Oswal led them through crumbling halls. Darius was in definite pain but said nothing. Kaz, in his excitement, had forgotten to put Delbin down, likely a good idea, in retrospect. There was no way of telling whether the kender would stick by them or wander into further danger somehow.

The darkness of night welcomed them once more. Kaz, with a start, realized that only a short period of time had passed since he and the two humans had gone in search of Delbin and the elf. His encounter with Argaen Ravenshadow had seemed to last an eternity.

A few bewildered figures darted out of the darkness, the knights who were standing guard around the Grand Master's stronghold. It was a bit of a surprise to discover that those knights were indeed real and not illusions. By now it wouldn't surprise Kaz to discover that Oswal had been alone all this time.

The Grand Master instantly took charge of his meager force. As much as he admired the human, Kaz knew that Lord Oswal was weak and faltering. With each passing second, the moment drew nearer when he would collapse—this time for good. For now, though, he was still the one who must be obeyed, and for those who served him, only just emerging from the madness they had lived with for these past few years, he was a beacon of trust.

"Everyone out of the keep! Everyone out!"

The citadel of the Grand Master began to collapse. Columns cracked and tumbled down the steps. The outer walls of the building caved in. The roof, unsupported, came crashing down on the rest. In mere seconds, the stronghold was in ruins. Yet parts of the structure continued to shift, and those who had been in the vault knew that something massive was digging its way out.

Lord Oswal glanced at his men and noted their consternation. "We can do nothing at the moment! It's nothing we can fight for now! When our strength is greater, then we shall hunt it down, but not before! No questions now! To the gates! Go!"

The shattered roof of the Grand Master's devastated citadel shifted position and slid determinedly into the side of another building, caving in the wall.

"Kaz," a muffled voice peeped. "I promise I'll stay with you if you just let me down, even though it's fun, but it's kind of hard to breathe like this, and I know you must be tired."

"All right, Delbin, but if you run off, you'll wish you'd stayed down in the vaults!"

"Actually, they might still be kind of interesting, if they haven't caved in com—"

"Come on!"

From the ruins of the collapsed building, a huge form arose. Some of the knights glanced back, then froze and stared in dismay. Worn to the point of breaking, a few even fell to their knees in resignation. The Grand Master paused in his own flight and returned to them.

"What are you doing?" he shouted in his most commanding voice. It was a strain to continue on as he did, but Lord Oswal refused to give in. He waved a fist at them. "Get up *now!* Whatever destruction that beast causes, it cannot destroy the knighthood so long as one of us believes! Do you understand?"

Chagrined, they began to move again. The light of the one moon visible was suddenly augmented by an unholy glow. Now it was Kaz who paused and gazed back at the center of the keep and the leviathan that was lit up by that horrible glow. The outline of the huge, winged form couldn't be missed. Beneath the dragon, held tightly in its forepaws, was the shadow box containing the malevolent power of the emerald sphere.

Riding on the back of the stone creature, Argaen Ravenshadow laughed insanely. The elf's unliving servant spread its wings. Kaz began to move again, but ponderously, his attention fixed with fascination on the great monster as it rose into the air. He marveled that such a creature, even magical, could lift its stone weight into the air.

The stone dragon lurched as its wings beat, causing it to lose altitude and crash into the roof of yet another building. The weight was too much. The roof caved in, and then the floor below it. The beast didn't struggle, but instead seemed confused. Kaz wondered if Argaen Ravenshadow had lost control.

"The libraries," Lord Oswal muttered. Kaz nearly stumbled, not realizing that the Grand Master had come up behind him. "It's destroyed the libraries as well. We will have much rebuilding to do. Come, Kaz. Odd as it sounds, we have to abandon the keep for the safety of the wastelands of Solamnia."

The Grand Master had as yet truly not seen what lay outside, and Kaz hoped his mind would be able to stand the shock. The elder knight was a veteran campaigner who had faced some of the deadliest threats the Dragonqueen's warlord had sent against him, but he was older now, and the past few years had taken an exceptional toll on him.

Behind them, they could hear the beating of the dragon's wings as it forced itself up into the air again.

A rush of wind and a brief shower of emerald light told them that Ravenshadow and his pet had flown over them. The gates, wide open, stood just before them.

Kaz and the Grand Master found a small jumble of figures, including the minotaur's companions, near the gates, where uncertainty reigned. Already the stone dragon was little more than a black blot framed in the moonlight of Solinari. Below the blot, like a dim beacon, the sphere continued to glow. Kaz stepped through the milling group and out of the keep, his eyes on the receding form until it left the brilliance of the moon and was swallowed up by the darkness of night.

Somehow his battle-axe was still in his hands. He raised it high in a brief but futile gesture at the magic thief.

"This isn't over, Argaen Ravenshadow!" Kaz muttered darkly in the direction the elf had flown off. "Not at all. Somehow I'll track you down. We've business left unfinished, you and I."

Brave words, he thought bitterly as he returned his battle-axe to its harness. *But where do you plan to start, Kaz? You have only all of Ansalon to search!*

"It doesn't matter," he muttered aloud. "All of Ansalon won't be able to hide that elf." The minotaur smiled grimly at the night. "This is *personal* now."

Chapter 16

Kaz sat brooding on the ground near the front gates, his eyes closed in contemplation of what he would do when—not if—he and Argaen Ravenshadow met again.

The flicker of a torch warned him of the knight's approach.

"You are the minotaur called Kaz?" the knight asked. He was a middle-aged human whose most distinctive feature was his rapidly receding hairline.

"How many other minotaurs are there in Vingaard Keep, human?"

The man ignored the jibe. "We found two horses that apparently belong to your party."

"Did you?"

"They are being kept in the east end of the keep until the stables can be cleared."

Kaz looked up at the man. "The Grand Master didn't send you here just to tell me about our animals, did he?"

The silence that followed spoke volumes. Like many humans, this knight had difficulty dealing with a minotaur. Here was a monster, an enemy, despite what had happened this very night, despite the part Kaz had played in the final days of the war—if that was even remembered anymore by more than a few.

"The Grand Master wishes to speak to you." A tone of menace crept into the human's voice. "He is very nearly exhausted. Do nothing to further the strain."

The minotaur rose, allowing him to look down on the knight when he answered. "Lord Oswal is a comrade and a friend, human. I'll do my best to ease his problems. You might help by being more respectful to those whom the knighthood and your Grand Master in particular have in the past called an ally."

Kaz marched off to where he knew he would find the Grand Master. A bit more respectful now, the knight hurried after him with the torch. They had not made it more than a few dozen paces when a shout from the watch at the gates broke the silence of the keep.

"Riders approaching!"

"Paladine! What now?" Kaz whirled on the knight accompanying him. "Tell your lord that I'll be with him shortly . . . I hope."

"I'll come with you, minotaur. If there is a danger to Vingaard, I may serve my liege best by—"

"Fine." Kaz left the human in midspeech and, utilizing his long stride and powerful legs, raced toward the front gates, approaching so fast that he startled one of the guards. The knight jumped up and pulled his sword free, actually taking a slash at the minotaur before Kaz was able to convince him that he was a friend. He had forgotten momentarily that he was dealing with men whose minds had suffered for quite some time.

"Who called out?" Kaz asked the sentry.

"Ferril. Ferril called out."

Kaz called out to the indicated sentry. "You! How many riders?"

It may be that, in the darkness, the one called Ferril could not tell it was a minotaur he spoke with. Certainly he was respectful enough. "Difficult to say from here, sir. A small army. More than a hundred."

More than a hundred! They might be in for a full-scale assault! "Can you identify them?"

"Not yet."

The knight who had followed Kaz joined him again. "What news?"

"More than a hundred riders. You'd best tell the Grand Master."

"He's in no condition! He couldn't possibly take command."

The minotaur's eyes narrowed, and even by torchlight they glowed blood-red. "Do you mean you *won't* inform your lord of a possible attack?"

The human opened his mouth, then clamped it tightly shut. Stiffly he replied, "I'll inform him at once!"

"Good for you," Kaz muttered under his breath as he watched the man practically vanish before his eyes. A horn sounded from somewhere out in the countryside. He looked up at where Ferril stood watch. "What was that?"

"Signal horn." The man was anxious. "I think—the Triumvirate be praised!—I think they are brothers!"

"Knights of Solamnia?"

"Yes!" The other knight on the wall and the one near Kaz began to cheer. The minotaur shouted them down.

"Quiet! They may not be what they seem! They might be some of the Dark Lady's servants, or if they are your fellows, they might not be in their right minds!"

The knight next to Kaz looked up at him with an uneasy expression. "You think we should keep the gates closed?"

"If only until we are certain. It follows common sense, don't you think?" He glanced upward. "If the Grand Master should come, I'll be up on the battlements watching."

Surprisingly, the knight saluted him.

When Kaz reached the top of the wall, Ferril was waiting for him. Judging by the expression on the human's face, Ferril had only just discovered that he had been conversing with a minotaur.

Kaz gave him a casual look. "Something wrong?"

"No . . . sir." Ferril, a Knight of the Sword, was uncertain how to address someone like Kaz.

"Good." Leaning forward on the wall, Kaz peered out over the countryside of Solamnia. He had some difficulty making out the oncoming force. They looked like a black tide on a gray surface. Still, at the rate they were riding, they would be at the gates of Vingaard in an hour's time. He suspected there were well over a hundred riders, likely closer to two hundred. Indistinct as they were, the group's size as a whole gave some idea of the numbers.

"Could we hold them if they don't turn out to be your brethren?" Kaz asked the knight.

"For a time . . . until they succeed in finding some way over the wall."

"What's happening, Kaz?" a familiar voice piped.

Both minotaur and human jumped. Kaz turned and snorted angrily at the figure who had somehow managed to sneak up next to them. "What're *you* doing up here, Delbin?"

The kender smiled. "I heard people running around, and someone said that someone was coming with lots of horses, so when I heard the horn, I knew they were nearby, and I—"

"Take a breath, Delbin!" Just then the horn sounded again. "Why're they doing that?"

"They want us to respond," Ferril said excitedly. "They must be comrades."

"Maybe you should respond."

Shaking his head, the man replied, "I cannot. The horn that usually stands by the gates has vanished. No one is able to locate it."

Delbin, meanwhile, was doing his best to peer over the wall, a difficult thing considering his height.

"Do you think they'll attack?" he asked eagerly. "I've never seen an actual siege, though maybe it won't be a very long one, since there are so few—"

"You up there! Kaz, is that you?"

"The Grand Master!" Ferril whispered reverently.

"Yes, Lord Oswal." Kaz shushed the kender, who had been about to speak again.

"Can you see the riders?"

"They'll be with us before long."

"How many?"

Kaz looked at Ferril. "Somewhere between a hundred and two hundred. We can't make them out any better."

There was a pause as the Grand Master evidently digested this information. He was determined to be in command.

"You four will have to protect the gates alone, I'm afraid," the elder knight decided.

"I'll help real good, Grand Master," Delbin began.

Instead of the consternation that the minotaur expected, the Grand Master chuckled. After a moment, Oswal said, "I'm sorry. I shouldn't laugh. Three knights, a minotaur, and a kender guarding the front gates of Vingaard Keep! A *kender* guarding Vingaard Keep from possible invasion! No offense is meant, Delbin, but I never thought to see the day!"

"I'll be a good fighter, honest!"

"I'm certain you will." To the defenders as a whole, he added, "Call out the moment you know whether they are friend or foe. May Paladine and his sons watch over you." Lord Oswal turned and departed, undoubtedly to rally his few other stalwarts.

"How does he keep going?" muttered Kaz.

"He is the Grand Master," Ferril answered simply, as if that explained everything.

* * * * *

Before very long, the newcomers were near enough to make out. The men were obviously armored well, but in the dim moonlight, it was still impossible to tell anything specific about their appearance. Kaz glanced up at Solinari. Over a third of the moon was gone, as if eaten up. Slowly it dawned on Kaz that another body was overwhelming Solinari. It was a moon that represented the darkness within men and other races—Nuitari, the black moon, whose presence, overshadowing its bright rival, could not be a good omen.

"There are sure a lot of them, Kaz."

"I know, Delbin."

"They've got banners and lances and everything."

"We'd better pray they're friends, then."

The riders slowed a few hundred yards from Vingaard. A small group, maybe five or six, started forward.

"They're Solamnic Knights, Kaz."

"Let's let them talk first."

"Who guards the gates up there? I see someone!" the apparent leader shouted.

Kaz stiffened. Relief that these were true Solamnic Knights and not marauders in disguise washed over him, tempered a bit, however, by his personal feelings concerning the knight who had spoken.

Ferril responded to the call. "I am in charge of the gates!"

"Why did you not respond to our horn?"

"Ours cannot be located, milord, and the situation here has not warranted time for a thorough look."

The company leader's voice softened. "The Grand Master . . . how fares he?"

"All things considered, well, milord." Ferril continued.

"Forgive me, but I must ask you to identify yourselves before we dare open the gates."

"Understandable. Know that I am Bennett, Lord of the Order of the Rose, nephew to Oswal, Grand Master of the knighthood. I have with me some two hundred fellow knights. How—how fares Vingaard Keep, man? Are there still enemies that must be rooted out?"

Kaz chose to call out before the sentry could respond. "Vingaard Keep struggles back to normality, Bennett, which does not mean that all of its enemies were mere figments."

Bennett stood in his saddle and peered up. Kaz was standing too far away from the nearest torch to be made out clearly. "Who is that? Your voice sounds familiar! What order do you belong to?"

"The order of survival, human. I'm not one of you, but you know me just the same." Kaz shifted over so he was visible.

"A minotaur!" the man next to Bennett shouted. More than one man unsheathed his sword. "Vingaard is in the hands of the enemy!"

"Be still!" Bennett commanded sharply. To Kaz, he said, "I do not think you are part of an enemy force. I think you are a minotaur with definite suicidal tendencies, else why would you have come where you were supposedly wanted for crimes—eh, Kaz?"

The minotaur laughed grimly. "Call me an optimist."

This time, it was Bennett who chuckled. "You have nothing to fear, Kaz, not from me or anyone here."

"Milord!" Ferril saluted and leaned back to call down to the knight standing by the gates. "Open the gates for the Lord of the Order of the Rose!"

While the gates were unbolted and opened, Oswal's nephew signaled back to his men. The column slowly began to move forward. There were scattered, tired cheers from some of the returning band.

Kaz glanced at Delbin, who was watching the parade of armored figures with delight. While the kender was thus occupied, the minotaur descended from the wall to meet Bennett.

Some of the men were milling around on their horses, staring at the long-neglected interior of the keep with mild shock.

"A word with you, human," Kaz called.

A look of annoyance briefly flashed across Bennett's face before he succeeded in controlling himself. "There will be time to speak later, Kaz. Right now, I would speak to my uncle. We have much to discuss."

"Then I'll come with you. I can fill you in on some of it."

"As you please."

Bennett dismounted and handed the reins of his horse to another knight. Kaz began almost immediately to relate what he knew, going through the madness and illusions, the meeting with Argaen Ravenshadow and the subsequent betrayal of his party, Lord Oswal's struggle, and the destruction of the vaults and much of the keep as the dark elf made good his escape. By the time he was through, Bennett was shaking his head.

"Paladine preserve us! I cannot fathom all you have said, minotaur, and I know there must be much more that my uncle can tell me."

"I'd hoped that you'd sighted his pet on your way here, since he headed in the general direction of south."

"Leave this to the knighthood, minotaur. We owe Argaen Ravenshadow for these past few years of manipulation and deceit."

"I owe him, too. He made a fool of me and nearly succeeded in poisoning me. Through me, he gained access to his prize. I want that elf!"

Bennett turned to face him. "The knighthood will deal with him! He owes us for lives! He owes for disgracing us—"

"I see no reason why you two cannot pursue him together," a voice called out. "I think that might be best for all concerned."

"Uncle . . . milord!" Bennett immediately knelt before the elder knight. "Glad I am to see that you are fit!"

"A sham, nephew. I am in fact ready to teeter over, but no one will give me time. Praise be that Paladine chose to make me a cleric as well as a knight, for I doubt I would still be standing if not for his power."

"You are the foundation of the orders, uncle."

"And you are still the eager young squire, Bennett." Lord Oswal bade his nephew to rise. "The two of you should not argue. Kaz, you will need the might of Solamnia behind you. I do not doubt that the dark elf will be found in some dire region. As for you, nephew, respect the knowledge and honor of this minotaur. Huma called him friend. I do now. Learn from his experience. In many ways, Kaz knows more than I."

"I find that impossible to believe, milord, but I shall do as you say."

"Fine. What about you, Kaz?"

"You have my word. Argaen Ravenshadow is my goal. I've sworn that I'll hunt him down if I have to travel beyond the ice in the south."

The Grand Master smiled sourly. "Let us hope it does not come to that."

"This is all a bit pointless," Bennett remarked in exasperation. He looked from his uncle to the minotaur. "I have been told that the magic thief flew south. But where in the south? Surely not Silvanesti or Qualinesti! Ergoth? Kharolis? Where?"

Kaz gritted his teeth. He took a deep breath and was about to launch into another tirade when the Grand Master spoke. "We will solve nothing with bickering," Lord Oswal said wearily. "I suggest we try to get some rest. Bennett, walk with me for a bit, please. I wish to hear what you have seen since your departure. I wish to discover what else the knighthood must make amends for."

Bennett grimaced. "As you wish, milord."

"Get some sleep, Kaz."

"A good suggestion, Grand Master."

Kaz watched the two depart and felt exhaustion suddenly take control of his body. Arguing, however briefly, with the Grand Master's nephew had just about used up his own reserves. He looked around. The sky would be his roof tonight, as it had been for so many nights in his life. He looked for a secluded spot.

The place he finally chose had only one drawback, and that was the sudden appearance of a particular kender, even before Kaz had a chance to lie down.

"Where've you been, Kaz? I've been looking all over for you since you vanished back at the gate while I was watching the knights arrive. How come you're sleeping here when there are so many other places? Though I guess we can't sleep at the library anymore, because the building isn't in too good shape anymore, is it?"

"Delbin, unless you have something important to say, why don't you go to sleep, too?" Kaz removed his battle-axe and harness and lay down. He put his hands under his head and stared up at the sky. Until tonight, the only things really visible had been the moons. Now, however, the stars were apparent. Kaz started to pick out the constellations he knew.

"Are we gonna stay here for a while, Kaz?"

"In Vingaard? Not if I can help it!" the minotaur grunted. "One can only take so much of the knighthood. I start searching for Argaen Ravenshadow tomorrow. The colder his trail becomes, the harder it'll be to find him."

"At least we won't have to go far."

"What's that supposed to mean?"

Delbin shrugged innocently. "Well, I mean, he probably headed for the mountains east of Qualinesti or for the southern part near Thorbardin. Don't dwarves live down there? You wouldn't go that way when I asked last time. Did you have trouble—"

The minotaur sat up. "Delbin, do you know where the elf is?"

"I do now. I was going to write about everything that happened and how big and powerful the knights looked when they arrived a few minutes ago, but when I reached for the book, I found this little crystal that I knew had to be Argaen's, and when I thought about him real hard, all of a sudden I could see him landing someplace in the mountains just north of Qualinesti. I think they're partly in Ergoth and partly in Solamnia, but I could be wrong."

"Let me see what you found."

Delbin pulled something out of his pouch. "I thought you might want to see it, but you looked pretty busy. I bet maybe Argaen put it into my pouch while he had me imagining I was helping you by opening the vaults."

A look of wonder passed over Kaz's bullish visage as he eyed Delbin's prize. It was the same trinket that Ravenshadow had used to find the kender the first time he had disappeared, searching in the library. Kaz snatched the magical device from his companion's diminutive hands.

"You saw where the elf was going just by thinking about him?" Ravenshadow's image was burned into his own mind now.

The artifact in his hands began to glow a little, and something murky appeared within it.

"That's how it did it last time," Delbin offered helpfully.

"Quiet!" Kaz continued. A dragon, even a stone one, could cover astonishing distances in a short period of time. The mountains Delbin had described, however, were fairly near, several days' ride at the very most. It amazed Kaz that the dark elf would position himself so close to the land of his people.

The murky image began to waver. Argaen Ravenshadow. His home. The emerald sphere of Galan Dracos.

With a flicker, he was suddenly flying high above a mountain range. Had he not flown on the backs of dragons in the past, the angle would have sent him reeling. As it was, he was able to study the range.

He knew these mountains, had seen them from a distance several times. The northernmost tip of Qualinesti was only a day to the south. How could Argaen hope to keep out of sight of his kin?

Slowly the image focused on one mountain in particular. The peak began to grow larger and larger—or rather, Kaz, through the crystal, was descending. Within seconds, he was below the tip of the mountain and still descending.

The ruins sprang from nowhere.

One minute he was gazing at yet more mountainside, and the next he was hurtling toward the roof of some long-abandoned structure. Kaz allowed himself a smile. He not only knew his prey was in a particular set of mountains, but he also knew where in those mountains.

Who?

The voice echoed through his mind, and Kaz nearly fell back. Only barely did he succeed in keeping his grip on the crystal.

"Kaz?"

Who? the voice demanded. There was an ethereal quality to it.

The crystal began to grow hotter. Kaz no longer had any desire to hold on to it, but now it appeared to be holding on to *him*. The image in its center had faded, but the voice remained in the minotaur's head, growing increasingly powerful and demanding.

Where? Who?

Gritting his teeth, Kaz called out. "Delbin! Knock . . . knock it from my hand. Hurry!"

The kender reached into his pouch and pulled out, of all things, his ever-absent book. Taking it in both hands, Delbin struck the minotaur's hand with all his might. Smoke arose from the book as the tiny artifact burned the edge of it before being sent flying away.

Clutching his hand where it had been burned, Kaz watched the crystal strike the ground and crack into several pieces. In that same instant, it ceased to glow. The voice that had been demanding the minotaur's identity vanished as well.

Both Kaz and Delbin stared at the shattered remnants for several seconds before the kender dared to ask, "Kaz, what happened?"

"Someone was trying to locate *me* while I was locating the elf."

"Someone?"

Kaz nodded, eyeing his injured hand. He hoped Tesela had the strength left to heal it. He had a feeling he was going to need to be at his best. The voice had not been Argaen Ravenshadow's—of that, at least, he was sure.

Then, who?

Chapter 17

The group selected to hunt Argaen Ravenshadow would, by necessity, be a small one. Of the two hundred or so knights the Grand Master now had under his command, a good quarter of them would not be fit for very much activity for at least a few days. Still more were needed back at the keep to guard the walls of Vingaard and start clearing the debris left over from the stone dragon's departure. All in all, the Grand Master was stretching his resources to the limits when he assigned fifty knights to his nephew.

Darius, Tesela, and Delbin, of course, all insisted on coming along as well. To the knight, it was a sense of duty, of honor. The cleric insisted that they were likely to need her healing skills where they were going. Kaz suspected her real reason was Darius himself. Adversity had thrown them together.

As for Delbin, he did not need a reason, and Lord Oswal was more than accommodating when it came to the kender. If he stayed behind, without Kaz to watch over him, the knights rightly feared that he would pilfer everything in sight, plus, no doubt, some things that were not.

Those riding with the party were personally chosen by the Grand Master, and the entire expedition was supplied with whatever could be spared in the way of food and materials.

Just before noon, they started out the front gates. There was no cheering, for those riding forth might be heading to their deaths, and nearly every knight remaining behind manned the walls against equally uncertain destiny. When Kaz looked back, just before Vingaard Keep became too distant, he saw that the men on the walls were still there, silently watching.

The shortened day passed without incident. There were signs of occasional goblin activity, but not one of the creatures was sighted. The column avoided villages and other settlements. Until people could be brought to understand what had happened, it was best to give civilization a wide berth.

The most promising sign of the day was the presence of the bright sun. It was encouraging. Certainly it raised spirits.

Just before nightfall, a scout reported signs that a relatively large band of men, some riding and some on foot, had been in the area earlier that morning. They, too, were headed in a southerly direction. No evidence indicated that they were heading toward the same destination as the column, but the thought nagged at Kaz. Who could they be?

When night came at last, there was some debate as to whether or not they should press on. Common sense won out. Everyone needed rest.

A perimeter and watches were established. Kaz felt as if time had slipped back several years and he was once again in the great war. He wondered what they would do if Argaen's unliving servant returned under cover of darkness.

He felt the twin edges of the blade, admiring the workmanship of the metal axe head. His face reflected back at him, crystal clear despite the dim light of the night sky. Kaz studied the image for a minute wonderingly, when something registered. The minotaur stared at the axe head, at the handle, and then at the sharp edges. . . .

That was it! The area where the axe had been chipped after it had struck the rocky hide of Argaen's monster was whole and unbroken once more! Sharp as ever again! He also recalled a moment in the vault, when the unliving beast had shied away from the minotaur's seemingly futile attack with the battle-axe. Could the stone dragon actually fear the axe? Granted, the weapon was somehow magical, but why would a creature that size, magical itself, fear Sardal's gift?

How powerful was the battle-axe? Could it do anything else besides mend itself? Kaz grunted, recalling how, before, he had found himself carrying the axe after leaving it behind. A one-time fluke, or would it come to him again if the need arose?

"Kaz?"

Kaz looked up at Bennett, who seemed disturbed about something. "What, human?"

"We may have trouble—trouble that you might be familiar with. Would you follow me?"

Kaz arose and followed Bennett.

They moved toward the eastern side of the camp. One or two knights stood guard in the camp; the rest, along with the minotaur's companions, were asleep. The only other knights awake were those on sentry duty on the edges of camp.

The countryside consisted of small hills covered with wild grass and ugly, twisted trees. It was not a region Kaz would have voluntarily traveled through, but dire circumstances seemed to delight in forcing him to cross it again and again.

"What is it you want me to see?"

"Nothing, perhaps, but the knight ahead of us reported something I felt you would appreciate being told about."

The knight on guard duty saluted Bennett and looked uneasily at the minotaur. Bennett cleared his throat and told the man, "Describe what you thought you saw."

"Milord." He was a Knight of the Crown, such as Huma had been, but much older, a veteran who perhaps had decided to stay with that particular order rather than move on to the Order of the Sword. "I would not have even mentioned it, milord, but I was told that all strange things, no matter whether they seemed like a trick of the eyes or not, should be reported."

"What did you see?" encouraged Kaz.

"It was only for just a moment, mind you, but I thought I saw an animal. Just a glimpse of one, but it did seem real. The odd thing was, it looked to be completely white, only not like some of our horses. More like that of a corpse."

"White like a corpse?" Kaz grimaced. "What sort of animal did it appear to be, knight?"

"I cannot say for certain, for I only caught a glimpse. A large cat, possibly, or—or—"

"A wolf?" the minotaur finished for him.

The knight nodded. "A wolf. Yes, it could have been a wolf."

Bennett glanced at Kaz. "That cannot be possible. You know that, minotaur."

"You came for me, which means you've enough doubt to think it possible. It may be that Argaen knows a few more tricks than we thought. He keeps surprising me with his Sargas-be-damned ingenuity!"

"Dreadwolves!" Bennett shook his head. "I'd thought never to hear about them again. I thought everything concerning Galan Dracos could be buried from sight and mind forever."

"For a dead man, the renegade mage does seem to pop up in one way or another, doesn't he?" Kaz considered. "With your permission, Bennett, I think we should talk to some of the other men on guard duty."

"Very well."

The first man they spoke to reported nothing. The second man proved no more informative than the first, and they spent even less time with him.

Bennett seemed to think the whole thing pointless. "Perhaps there is an albino wolf out there. I have seen albinos in other species from time to time, and they do tend to be nocturnal."

"Perhaps." Nevertheless, Kaz continued on.

It took them a moment or two to locate the next nearest sentry, for the man was standing on the other side of a small rise. It was a good place to keep watch, for the knight avoided the light of the moon and anyone approaching would have to be right on top of him before noticing him.

"You there," Bennett called out softly. While he spoke to the guard, Kaz, his axe resting lightly against his shoulder, peered around. Something was making him uneasy.

"Milord?" The man turned but did not abandon his post, as was proper.

"Have you seen anything tonight that you have not reported . . . anything at all?"

The other knight peered at them, trying to make out who stood next to his commander. In this place, each of them was little more than an outline. "Nothing, milord, unless you count a couple of carrion crows. They seemed to be going nowhere in particular."

"Hopefully they'll keep right on going," Kaz muttered, his back almost to the man. The light of Solinari caught the mirrorlike finish of the metal axe head and glittered in the minotaur's eye.

Beside him, Bennett turned and sighed. "I think we should cease this. There's nothing to be gained. If anything should arise, we will be forewarned by those on watch."

"I suppose so." Kaz lifted the axe head from his shoulder. As he did, both his reflection and that of Bennett caught his eye momentarily.

"Is that all, milord?" the guard called out.

Kaz froze, then carefully glanced back to see where the knight was standing. The guard was directly behind them.

"That is all. Return to your duties," Bennett replied.

Turning away, Kaz lifted the axe so that once again the side of the head would reflect everything behind him. He saw the same odd, distinct reflection of his own visage and Bennett's shoulder. Of the other knight, there was not even a shadowy outline.

Yet, when he turned back again, Kaz could see the dark form of the man, still there.

The knight on guard duty was casting *no reflection* in the mirrorlike surface of the axe head!

Kaz hesitated. The sentry, his attention fixed on the surrounding countryside, paid him no attention. *What does it mean?*

Noticing the minotaur's strange behavior, Bennett, too, had stopped. "Is there something—"

"Quiet. Wait a moment," Kaz whispered. The minotaur, axe ready in one hand, stalked over to the other knight. "You!"

The man turned around slowly. "What is it you wish, minotaur?"

"Your name."

"Alec, Knight of the Sword."

"Alec"—Kaz tightened his grip on the battle-axe—"do you know what the phrase *Est Sularis oth Mithas* means?"

There was a short pause. "I cannot recall at the moment."

Every muscle in the minotaur's body tensed. "I didn't think so."

The battle-axe came up in a vicious arc that should have ended with the flat side striking the unsuspecting Alec. There was only one problem. Alec was neither unsuspecting nor a knight. Kaz's swing sailed a foot above the false knight's head even as the man ducked and his longsword flashed out.

"Kaz! What are you doing?" demanded Bennett.

The minotaur parried a powerful thrust and growled, "We may be under attack at any moment, commander!" Another swing of the axe proved as futile as the first. "In—in case you haven't figured it out by now, this isn't a knight!"

"Paladine!" Bennett unsheathed his own sword and started forward, but Kaz yelled. "Forget me! Warn the camp! Go!"

Bennett paused for a second, then nodded his head and ran. He withheld a shout, for fear of giving away their discovery to anyone waiting beyond the camp. Quiet and caution were important now.

As soon as Bennett vanished, Kaz began to regret sending him away. He was finding the imposter quite a deadly swordsman. The man was tall and, between his arm and longsword, had a lengthy reach.

They traded blows for several seconds, but something seemed to be eating away at his opponent's determination. The knight imposter was hesitant in his movements.

Of course! "Your friends seem to have abandoned you, human!"

Kaz had struck the right nerve. "Unlike you, minotaur, we are faithful to our mistress. They—they would not abandon me!"

In the background, Kaz could hear the shouts of men in the camp. His opponent began to fight with renewed vigor. It seemed, the human was correct; the camp was now under attack.

"We will overrun your Solamnic friends, beast, but don't worry. You won't be alive to see it!"

"I'd wager you wore a black suit of armor five or six years ago," Kaz snarled. "You're dead wrong on two counts, though, guardsman! First, the knights defending the camp will prevail, and second, I plan to be very much alive!" He gave the human a grim, toothy smile. "Yes, you look to be one of the Black Guard. By the way, I saw your warlord, Crynus, die. He had become quite a madman by then."

The guardsman's sword wavered.

The battle-axe caught him in the chest and across the neck. It sliced through the breastplate without slowing. Slowly he toppled to the ground, his head only loosely attached to his neck.

Cursing, Kaz stood his ground and waited for some sign of a new foe. Nothing.

Moments later, several knights, Bennett's aide Grissom among them, came running in his direction. Kaz turned toward them with relief, only to find half a dozen swords pointed in his direction.

"What's this?" he growled.

"What have you done to the man on watch here, minotaur?"

It was obvious that neither Grissom nor the others knew exactly what had transpired here. Kaz knew that some of the knights distrusted him, but not to this extreme.

"Talk to your commander, human! I was the one who *discovered* our danger!"

Grissom hesitated. "Why would you betray them? You once fought for the same side."

Kaz sighed. How many times would he have to explain this?

"Have those weapons lowered, Sir Grissom! The minotaur is an ally, a valuable one!"

At the sound of Bennett's voice, the other knights stood aside. Grissom saluted his superior. "My apologies, milord! All we knew was that you had come into the camp warning of danger!"

"Do not apologize to me, Grissom. Apologize to Kaz; it was his honor you impugned."

"Milord?"

Bennett looked at his aide critically. "Is that so difficult to understand? Must I apologize for you? I certainly will, because he deserves it. After all, he may have saved all our lives."

Grissom exhaled sharply and turned back to Kaz. "I apologize for my quick judgment, minotaur. I assumed that there was only one person who could be responsible for this."

"They killed the man who stood guard here," Kaz explained to the man, "and one of their own took his place so that no one suspected. We're fortunate we caught them before they could really get organized."

"They tried to attack the camp only seconds after I was able to warn the men," Bennett interjected. "They were hardly expecting the entire camp to be awake and ready. One wave came in. We killed perhaps six or seven and wounded a few more. We lost only one man besides this one. They fled almost immediately afterward. The cowards!"

"I don't think we've seen the last of them. This man was one of the warlord's Black Guard, Bennett."

"There seemed to be quite a few of them roaming around in central and southern Solamnia. Kharolis, too. Raiding runs have increased noticeably." To Grissom, Bennett said, "See if you can find the body of our brother who gave his life here. Before we leave tomorrow morning, he and the other man will be given rites. Double the guard for the rest of the night."

"As you command, milord. What of this one?" Grissom tapped the body with the tip of his blade.

"Have someone gather the enemy dead. We'll have a separate pyre for them—and wish them ill on their way to their mistress. If we leave them as is, they might become breeding ground for some plague, and that's the last thing we need."

Two knights were left to stand guard while all but Grissom went in search of their dead comrade. The aide saluted and returned to camp to take care of the other orders Bennett had given him. The Grand Master's nephew stayed with Kaz.

"How did you know he wasn't one of us? I don't know half the men in my command. Too many of them are from outside the Order of the Rose."

"*Est Sularis oth Mithas.*"

" 'My Honor is my Life.' It's the code by which we live. What about it?"

"He couldn't tell me what it meant if his life depended on it—which it did."

Kaz had a theory about the dwarven axe's name, Honor's Face. What had the dwarf been like who had forged such a unique weapon? Had he been aided by some mage, or visited, perhaps, by the god Reorx himself? Kaz now believed that the mirrorlike flat side of the axe head apparently reflected the faces and forms of only those with honor, those who could be trusted. Enemies, beings without honor, cast no reflection—a handy tool that the minotaur wished he had known about earlier. He wondered if Sardal Crystalthorn had known of it.

Sardal Crystalthorn. He had almost forgotten about the other elf. Was Sardal in league with Argaen? Kaz decided it was doubtful, or else the elf never would have given him the dwarven battle-axe. Giving such a fine weapon to Kaz, in addition to saving his life, was not the act of a dark elf.

"Minotaur?"

Kaz blinked. "What, Bennett?"

"It might be good if you got some rest. You look nearly asleep on your feet."

It was true. Buried in his thoughts, Kaz had been drifting further and further from consciousness. Elves and magic battle-axes could wait until morning. Sleep was a luxury that Kaz had been unable to afford of late. He needed to catch up now, before they came upon Argaen Ravenshadow.

*   *   *   *   *

They were not bothered again that night, though the watch remained fully alert. The dawn came with Kaz and the others feeling only slightly refreshed. A full day of rest was really in order, but no one was willing to sacrifice that much time. There was a sense of urgency where this mission was concerned.

As they drew ever nearer their destination, Kaz began to worry about the human, Darius. The young knight rode close to Tesela and often talked to her, but Kaz, glancing back now and then, also knew the man was looking up into the heavens more and more, with a fatal stare. He knew what Darius was looking for: the stone dragon that had left him for dead.

Kaz had seen that look before, during the war. Darius was waiting for the beast to come and try to finish the task. It was almost as if he felt that it was unfair he should have survived when the others had perished. Such beliefs led to foolish, even suicidal, actions. The Knights of Solamnia, Kaz thought, were too eager to die. What bothered the minotaur more was that he knew his own race was susceptible to such compulsions.

Even Kaz was becoming too pessimistic. In an effort to ease his mind, he reached into one of his pouches for one of the dry biscuits the knighthood had provided. They had little in the way of taste, but they were solid and filling. Long used to such fare, Kaz discovered that his fondness for them was actually growing—another sign, he was sure, that his mind was rattled.

What he touched in the pouch was not one of the biscuits, however, but rather a scrap of parchment. He grasped it by one end and pulled it out. It was a rolled parchment that someone had sealed with amber. Where,

Kaz wondered, had he— Of course! With all that had happened to him, he had forgotten completely about this little item. This was the parchment that Sardal Crystalthorn had asked him to deliver to Argaen Ravenshadow. All this time . . . He wondered what message the dark elf had sent along. Again the minotaur wondered: *Could Sardal be in league with the magic thief?*

Kaz decided to break the seal and see what Sardal had written.

The amber proved to be more of a problem than he would have expected. A flick of his thumb should have broken it off, but his nail kept sliding away. In exasperation, he pulled out a dagger and worked on it. The dagger, too, slipped from the seal.

Cutting around the amber turned out to be a tricky maneuver, what with trying to hold on to the reins and the bouncing of his horse. Nonetheless, he managed to trace a circle, and the seal fell to the earth. Kaz put away his dagger and started to unroll the parchment.

A golden void opened up before him.

"Kaz!" someone cried, possibly Delbin.

"Pala—" The minotaur had no chance to complete his oath before his horse rode blissfully *into the void.* The search party, everything, vanished.

The void was beautiful, inspiring, but Kaz had no time for such contemplation. It was all he could do to hang on as the horse fell and fell and fell and fell . . . until it seemed they were destined to keep falling until the Final Day. Not once did his steed give any indication of panic. It still tried to gallop, apparently ignorant of its predicament.

At last their descent began to slow. The minotaur felt his own movements begin to decelerate. In a matter of seconds, it became nearly impossible to do anything but breathe, and even that was becoming increasingly difficult.

Like a fly trapped in honey, he thought helplessly. A fury was building within him, one that in combat made him a terror. Now, though, it did nothing but further frustrate him. For all his strength, he was unable to move, to defend himself.

As he and his mount came to a complete stop, so, too, did his capacity, even to breathe. Kaz was certain he was going to die now. He waited for suffocation to wash over him. It did not. He almost wished for it, for now came the fear that he was meant to be trapped in this void forever, ever staring off into the beautiful golden nothing.

"Aaahh, minotaur!" a voice boomed all around him. "What have you done to yourself now?"

He knew the voice. It was Sardal Crystalthorn who had snared him.

*   *   *   *   *

"Kaz!" Delbin shouted.

Several of the knights were forced to restrain their horses. Bennett stood in the saddle and looked around in vain for the minotaur. Darius cursed, and Tesela prayed to her goddess for some clue as to what had happened to the minotaur.

Bennett sat down. "The Abyss take that dark elf! This must be his doing! He's been watching all along, waiting for the proper moment!"

"Do you—do you think Kaz is dead?" Darius finally ventured.

"No, but I think the thief must have captured him somehow." Bennett turned to look at the others. "We have to move on. Kaz's only chance—*our* only chance— is to find the elf before he grows any stronger! With any luck, we will be able to save the minotaur. Wherever he is, if he lives, Argaen Ravenshadow will know."

Tesela removed her hands from her medallion. "I can feel nothing where Kaz is concerned, but that may mean very little. There's no trace of him in this area. That much I can say with confidence."

Bennett nodded, as if that were the confirmation he

had been waiting for. As far as he was concerned, there was no more time to waste. "It's settled, then. We move on."

As the knight turned to signal the others, Tesela and Darius exchanged looks of uncertainty. If Kaz was a prisoner, spirited away by their enemies, what chance did this small force of knights have against such formidable power?

Nonetheless, no one even suggested turning back.

Chapter 18

It was two days after the column had departed in search of Argaen Ravenshadow. The Grand Master was trying to discover everything that had been done in his name over the years his mind had not been his own. What he had discovered shamed him. All this time, he had imagined he had fended off the evil, the madness. Staring longer and longer at proclamations that bore his name, proclamations that he remembered vaguely as having started out as something else, he knew why the general populace had turned on the Knights of Solamnia. After finally having the courage to hope for a brighter future, they had been seemingly betrayed by those sworn to watch over them. It was like the great war all over again, when the knighthood had fought on and on while it was the ordinary citizens who paid the price for decades of stalemate.

Lord Oswal was stirred from his work by the sudden intrusion of one of his guards. "Milord?" the man whispered urgently again.

"What is it?"

"We have a party of travelers at the gates, demanding justice."

"Justice?" Were the people revolting already?

"It—it might be best if you saw for yourself."

Oswal pushed his chair back and stood, wishing at that moment that his brother Trake had not succumbed to the poisons of the traitor Rennard, for then he would still be head of the knighthood.

"Give me a few moments. Tell them I am coming."

"Milord."

The Grand Master looked around for his boots. His boots discovered—how they had gotten underneath the bed was something he would never understand—the Grand Master readied himself and started for the gates. Knights of his royal guard saluted and fell into line behind him. With all that had happened, the knights remaining in the keep had become virtually paranoid about the safety of their lord. Whether he wanted them to or not, his guards were now determined to be with him during any matter that hinted of trouble.

The captain of the watch saluted him as he reached the gates. "Well, where are they?"

"Outside, milord."

"Outside? Have you forgotten your manners? Just because someone has a grievance, there is no reason to leave them barred from Vingaard."

The watch captain paled. "With all due respect, Grand Master, I think you should see for yourself!"

Lord Oswal had found that his patience was short these days. "Nonsense! Not another word! Have they given their word that they come in peace?"

"Yes, but—"

"How many are there?"

"A dozen or so, mi—"

"*A dozen?* Let this fearsome army in, captain. *Now!*"

"As the Grand Master desires." It was obvious that the other knight still had qualms, but he would obey his lord.

The order to open the gates was given and obeyed with great speed. The Grand Master, with his guards standing at the ready, stared in amazement at the newcomers. Small wonder that his men had been hesitant! They were minotaurs!

Other than Kaz, Lord Oswal had seen precious few minotaurs this close up. And the few he had seen were either prisoners or had died by his sword. In all honesty, a band of minotaurs was probably the last thing he had expected.

"Who is in charge here?" a nasty-looking, disfigured giant snarled.

The Grand Master folded his arms and, in a voice that had more than once silenced his rivals in midsentence, replied, "I am in charge here, minotaur. I am Oswal, Grand Master of the Knights of Solamnia! For what reason do you leave your lands in the east?"

"We are here on a mission of honor and justice. Such things, I have heard, are held in great esteem by the Knights of Solamnia. As for my name, I am Scurn." The minotaur gave a perfunctory bow. Lord Oswal took an instant dislike of him.

Studying the others, Oswal, for the first time, saw the ogre standing in the rear of the group. "What is *that* doing with you? Is that one your prisoner?"

"Molok is one of us. It is he who first brought forth the news of the disgrace one of our own has brought down upon us."

"One of your own?"

"His name, noble lord, is Kaziganthi De-Orilg, as listed in the formal charges. A son of the clan of Orilg, of which we are all distant relations. Orilg was one of the mightiest of our early champions, and Kaz has brought such dishonor to the clan that we were sent to bring him back for justice."

An insight into the family structure of minotaurs would have interested the elderly knight at any other time. It was known that family was foremost, but to hunt down a fellow clan member for staining the honor of the clan . . . perhaps there was not so much difference between the minotaurs and humans, after all. Lord Oswal yearned to learn more, but there was the more urgent matter of the charges.

"You still have not mentioned what it is that your kinsman is supposed to have done." Judging from the look in Scurn's eyes, the Grand Master doubted that this one needed any excuse to go hunting down Kaz. That look of hate was mirrored in the ogre's eyes, Oswal noted.

A strange pair, the Grand Master thought.

Impatiently Scurn explained. "In the war, Kaz was sworn to the service of one of the armies sent into Hylo."

"A slave-soldier." Oswal was interested to see that some of the minotaurs—he realized that certain of them were female!—cringed a bit at that word.

"Nevertheless," the disfigured leader growled, "he was sworn to the service of that army, and an ogre captain in particular. Kaz served ably"—Scurn seemed reluctant to admit as much—"until the taking of a human settlement. He disagreed with the decisions of his captain."

Not surprising, the elder knight thought. Ogres were notorious for their sadistic streaks.

A memory began to surface. Huma and Kaz had told him of this time. As the Grand Master recalled, the ogre captain had been in the process of amusing himself privately with the slaughter of old folk and children, something horribly dishonorable by minotaur standards. Did the group here know that? He doubted they would take his word for it.

Lord Oswal found his eyes drifting to the ogre in the back. What was his part in all of this? Was he a blood relation to the one who had died? A comrade? The knight's experiences with ogres had always led him to believe they worried little about anything except their own lives. That this ogre had sought out the minotaurs for a crime against one of his own kind, even murder, was unusual. If the minotaurs were not so caught up in their beliefs of honor—as, regrettably, many knights were—they would have seen the incongruity of the situation. No, this ogre had to have some other motive besides justice. Most ogres would have settled for revenge, if they even remembered the incident at all after a few months.

"As further proof of Kaz's guilt," Scurn was saying, "we have this. . . ."

Scurn held up a small spherical object in his hands. The Grand Master recognized it immediately as a truthcrystal, a minor magical artifact that reenacted some historical scene over and over again. Lord Oswal watched the magical image as Kaz struck the ogre from behind, murdering him again and again. The Grand Master remained unmoved. The trouble with truthcrystals was that they did not live up to their name. Any decent mage could create distortions. To the minotaurs, however, who shunned sorcery and yet were too ready to believe it, it was all too real.

Lastly, a written proclamation from those who served as elders among the minotaurs was produced, dictating that, by the laws of that race, this posse was performing a deed of honor in seeking out one who was a disgrace, a coward, and a murderer. The proclamation emphasized Kaz's fleeing from the scene, a dishonorable act, more than the death of the ogre. According to minotaur code, that was enough to have him executed—or, at the least, sentenced to a battle of impossible odds.

Lord Oswal read the proclamation over. He greatly trusted Kaz, but he was, in the end, an avid proponent of justice and law. The minotaurs who ruled their race were, until their own kind removed them, legitimate masters, and their word was lawful.

"Why come here? Why show me this?"

"We believed the minotaur would come here. Is such the case?" The look in Scurn's eyes dared the Grand Master to lie.

He would not. "Kaz was here two days ago. He has gone south with a small force of my own men."

Oddly, there were some looks of relief and murmured comments among the crowd of minotaurs. A male and female who, as far as a human could discern, resembled one another, seemed most pleased. The leader was not.

"South! We missed him by two days? Where does the coward go in the south?"

"The 'coward' rides to the mountains just north of Qualinesti. He and my nephew ride to face a magic thief who threatens not just Solamnia but also all of Ansalon with his actions!"

"Kaz rides into danger?" asked the female minotaur.

Scurn snorted in disdain. "With a force of knights at his back, he can afford to be brave!" To Lord Oswal, he asked, "You claim this as truth?"

The elder knight straightened. "My honor is my life, minotaur! You have my word!"

The disfigured minotaur smiled cruelly and, replacing the proclamation and the magical sphere, pulled out what appeared to be a crude map. "In that case, my lord, I would ask you to show me exactly where they travel . . . all in the interest of honor and justice, which we also hold dear."

* * * * *

How long? Has the Final Day come and gone while I remained frozen here, helpless?

Kaz had heard nothing more from Sardal Crystalthorn. Perhaps the elf, satisfied with the results of his trap, had no more need to speak to him. And Kaz would have to remain where he was, forever staring out at the golden void.

No more had the melancholy thought escaped his mind when he found the opposite was true, for motion began to return to him. He could breathe, turn his head, flex his arm, blink! It was astonishing to think how wonderful it was to blink his eyes! Below him, the horse, too, began to move, neighing and shaking its head as it realized that it could run once more—or fall.

For with the return of motion came a return to falling! Kaz frantically tightened his grip as best as possible, hoping, selfishly, that the horse would somehow soften the minotaur's own landing.

Then, as abruptly as it had first appeared, the golden void gave way to green grass and trees—a forest, in fact. The moment the horse's hooves touched solid ground, Kaz was tempted to ride as if demons were after him. One important thing prevented him, though. That was the figure of Sardal standing before him, a wizard's staff held high.

The elf was smiling and his robe was of the purest white. Kaz did not trust him for a moment.

"I thought for a while there I'd never get you out of that trap! I thought minotaurs were competent enough to follow simple instructions like giving parchments to unsuspecting, deceitful dark elves!"

Kaz looked around. The trees told him nothing. He could be in any forest, though he had a suspicion that he knew this one. "Where am I? How long—how long was I trapped in—in whatever that was?"

"You are fairly near your destination. A bit south, in Qualinesti, if you really want to know. It is now three days since you apparently departed Vingaard Keep."

"I was only trapped for a day or so?" *Not an eternity?*

"I imagine that it would seem a lot longer, considering that you would have no need to eat, drink, or sleep. It was meant as a punishment."

"*Punishment?*" Kaz's eyes burned red. His hand went to his battle-axe, the same battle-axe that none other than Sardal Crystalthorn had given him.

"Not for you, but for Argaen."

"Argaen?"

"I knew he had gone beyond all limits. Always, with his lack of ability, he has turned to the younger races for inspiration. He studied the traits of each race, especially the humans, for several years. He even lived among them. Yet, while the humans have many worthy traits, it was the worst of them that attracted Argaen. Argaen was always one who, lacking all but the least magical prowess, felt he had somehow been deprived of a birthright. So, secretly, he began to steal magic. By that I mean he stole items of power from those around him."

"Why didn't you stop him?"

"The truth, sadly, was only discovered recently, when he sent me what he obviously believed was an innocent note asking for information about the mad human mage, Galan Dracos! It became very clear that he wanted the treasures of Dracos that the knights had gathered. Until recently, he had been singularly unsuccessful in gaining entrance to the secret vaults. What happened, Kaz? How did he slip past the safeguards of the vaults? Argaen was never much of a thief when it came to physical traps."

Kaz told the elf all about what had transpired, starting with the party's first glimpse of Vingaard Keep and leading up to the moment when he had opened up the parchment. Sardal shook his head wonderingly.

"All that work gone to naught! Do you know, minotaur, that I invested much power in that prison I was forced to free you from? It's not something I can do again too soon, you know. What was it that Argaen stole from Vingaard?"

Kaz described the emerald sphere and its chaotic power, drawing on memories of what Huma had told him as well as more recent information. When he had finished, he asked, "The knights, Sardal, and my friends—what has become of them?"

"They moved on. Bennett gave you up for dead or a prisoner of Argaen. Either way, it was his assumption that the best course of action would be to continue on despite your loss. Such a loyal companion."

"Bennett is a Knight of Solamnia. I would've done no less."

"I fear, however, that they are going to run into some difficulties. You see, what remains of the Dragonqueen's armies has slowly been gathering near here. In secret, so they think. But such as they cannot hide from the eyes of elves. Your friends are riding into great danger, minotaur."

"Then I'm wasting my time here!" growled Kaz. He started to turn his mount around. "Which way?"

"Time is never wasted if you plan well," uttered the elf philosophically.

Kaz pulled up short, craning his head so that he could look back at Sardal. "What's that supposed to mean?"

"It means I have a quicker way of getting *us* to *our* destination . . . and he should be arriving just about now."

The minotaur's mount suddenly shied as it scented something off in the woods. Kaz readied his dwarven axe. Whatever the horse had scented was moving slowly, taking its own pace.

Out of the woods behind Sardal Crystalthorn came a huge beast. It was at least as large as the horse Kaz rode. Huge paws touched the ground lightly and silently. A red tongue hung from a maw large enough to swallow Kaz's arm. The fur was sleek and silver.

It was the biggest wolf that Kaz had ever seen. From his past experiences with those mockeries of this magnificent creature, the dreadwolves, the minotaur had gained a certain distrust of anything that resembled them.

"I discern the reason for your distrust, warrior, and I mourn the fact that so many cubs have become the playthings of twisted beings like Galan Dracos and Argaen Ravenshadow. You may place your trust in me, however, for your cause is Habbakuk's as well as Paladine's, and my lord Habbakuk's cause is ever mine."

"What *is* it, Sardal?"

Sardal did not deign to answer, for the subject of Kaz's question was more than capable of speaking for himself.

"I am Greymir, who runs with Habbakuk, lord of the animals, and serves him in the mortal world. My liege has commanded, at this elf's request, that I give you both safe transport to that place of darkness where the scavenger called Ravenshadow even now moves ever closer to his greatest folly and a resurrection of Krynn's greatest threat."

As pale as a minotaur could be, Kaz continued to gape at the magnificent beast. With the banishing of Takhisis, he had thought his existence might turn forever to more mundane business. He had tried to do his best to shun the likes of sorcerers and magical quests, but obviously not with much success. It was as if time were reversing itself. Once more Kaz was one of those caught in a game involving the gods. Greymir's presence was all that Kaz needed to convince himself that this had gone beyond some elf's petty ambitions—but how far beyond?

"What—" he began.

"As you said," Sardal interrupted, "time is wasting. Dismount and take only what things you truly need."

"We're—we're going to ride *that*?"

"You who've ridden dragons should certainly not fear me," Greymir commented smoothly.

The minotaur's horse, after its initial fear, was now eager to rub noses with the huge wolf. Kaz trusted animals' instincts only so far. He held up Honor's Face so that Greymir's reflection, if any, would be clear.

"A noble weapon, that," Habbakuk's emissary remarked. "And you are more or less correct about the reflections—or lack of them." Greymir's visage was plain to see in the battle-axe. So, then. The dwarven weapon had not failed Kaz so far. He would trust in it.

"I trust you are satisfied," Sardal said, a little petulantly.

"I am." Kaz dismounted. The battle-axe was returned to his shoulder harness as he reluctantly stepped over to the great wolf. Greymir lay down so as to allow the minotaur to climb onto his back. So huge was the animal that there still remained room on his back for the elf, who immediately joined Kaz. The weight of two full-grown figures seemed to make no difference to Greymir, for he rose to his feet with ease. The wolf stared at Kaz's horse, and the steed trotted off, as if given orders. Greymir pawed the ground.

"Hold tight!"

Greymir raced with a speed only a dragon could match. Trees whirred full speed in the opposite direction. Birds flew in place. Kaz knew that Greymir's paws did not even touch the earth. This was the stuff of legend, the stuff of wonder. This was the stuff that one breathless minotaur would have preferred never to have experienced.

Daylight was losing its battle with the night. Kaz knew his companions must have reached the mountains nearby now. Fifty against how many?

"They will have aid," came a voice that he recognized as the wolf's. The magnificent creature could listen to his thoughts. . . . "You are the most worrisome minotaur I have ever observed." This last was followed by a chuckle from Greymir.

Kaz concentrated on maintaining his grip.

The mountains swallowed them up. Entering those mountains was like entering a new and fearsome world. It was too reminiscent of the evil that had hung over Vingaard Keep so long. It was the renewed presence of the emerald sphere of Galan Dracos.

"Not long now," came Greymir's voice.

A mocking howl suddenly echoed through the mountains. Kaz snarled, recognizing the sound. No living animal howled like that.

"Dreadwolves," Greymir commented sadly. "My twisted young," the wolf continued, his anger swelling. "And there is nothing I can do for them. They are only shells with vague, tortured memories."

241

The howls echoed from everywhere. Argaen knew they were coming and was trying to slow their progress with his illusions. This time, however, no one would be fooled.

"The elf is ignorant of us—and *they* are not illusions," Greymir growled, pulling to an abrupt stop, gazing at the horrid scene unfolding before them.

"Habbakuk and Branchala!" Sardal whispered.

Suddenly dreadwolves were everywhere, surrounding them. Kaz ceased counting after fifty or so. The sight was sickening, as if the burial ground of all wolves were suddenly upturned by evil Chemosh, lord of the undead. Countless red orbs stared sightlessly at them. Rotted tongues hung out of maws filled with yellowed teeth. Bones showed through.

"Hold tight. Prepare to defend yourselves!"

A dreadwolf atop a high ledge laughed. It was a very human, very maniacal laugh. Kaz had no time to think about it, however, for Greymir was already moving again.

The dreadwolves attacked as one.

Hampered in his movement, Kaz could only make a partial defense as dozens of bloodthirsty horrors swarmed about the swiftly striding wolf. Even his partial blows, however, were enough to dismember several dreadwolves, although the monstrosities immediately rose up again, as their body parts drew back together. It was difficult to kill something that was already dead and could pull its body parts back to one complete form. Still, time was bought.

Greymir never paused in his flight, but somehow managed always to have a dreadwolf in his jaws or trampled under his feet. Monster after monster was tossed aside. But Kaz and Sardal had cuts all over their legs and sides. Greymir had scores of minor wounds. Given time, the dreadwolves might have brought them down.

With a few amazing strides, the gigantic wolf broke free of his unliving counterparts, striking one last foe with his hind paws as he passed by. The dreadwolves gave chase, but they were soon left far behind.

"Thank the gods *that* is over," Sardal muttered.

Kaz, happening to gaze skyward, saw something he had hoped never to see again. "We're far from safe, though, Sardal. Look up there!"

Circling menacingly above a mountain a short distance to the north was the stone dragon.

Greymir began slowing. "I have brought you as far as I can. You will have to go by foot the rest of the way, but it is not far. Perhaps it is even too close."

"Where will you go?"

"I asked one boon when my lord Habbakuk sent me forth, and he did grant it." Greymir came to a halt. "Please dismount."

The two did. The great wolf turned to face toward the direction they had just come from, back where the dreadwolves still roamed.

"We thank you sincerely for your aid, emissary of Habbakuk."

"Your request gave me an opportunity of my own. I could not come to this land without a reason. If anyone should be thanked, it is you and the minotaur for enabling me to complete a task that has long been overdue, a curse upon my kind."

In the distance, they could hear the howling of a dreadwolf or two.

Greymir's burning eyes narrowed at the sound. "I could do nothing before, what with you two on my back. Now I shall deal with them properly. May you gain success in your own quest."

With that, the huge wolf raced off.

"It has pained him for the past few years that such as the dreadwolves exist," Sardal said. "He goes to destroy those twisted forms so that the souls of the pack members who once fostered them may rest in peace."

"I thought they'd all died with their original master, Galan Dracos. Where did Argaen Ravenshadow learn such foul sorcery? I wouldn't have thought him capable of it."

Sardal looked at him grimly. "Argaen is not capable of it, although he may have come to believe that he is responsible. Argaen, you see, is only a tool. No, minotaur, the dreadwolves still obey their first and only master."

"The emerald sphere! I felt it!"

"Yes, my friend. Galan Dracos lives!"

Chapter 19

"Those mountains in the midst of the range, I think," Bennett commented calmly to Sir Grissom. The other knight nodded obediently. Behind them, Darius, Tesela, and Delbin listened with various combinations of impatience, anxiety, and anger. Kaz was gone, swallowed up by some fiendish trap. It was not the column moving too slowly that bothered them, but that Bennett seemed to accept the disappearance of Kaz so easily.

"This is *war*," he had replied to Tesela's angry questions. "As much a war as the one fought more than five years ago. Kaz knows, if he is indeed alive."

There were traces of recent activity, men on horseback and on foot. The tracks went toward the mountains, away from them, parallel to their own path—essentially everywhere. A few times, men had thought they had seen the stone dragon.

"Ready arms," Bennett ordered.

The men in front had lances, should the foe block the mountain paths. The men in the ranks were divided between those with bows ready for any enemy hiding in the rocks and mountainsides, and others who had swords in case they were set upon from low ground. It was the unspoken duty of Darius that he would watch over the cleric and the kender. He was more than willing to test his blade in their defense. Tesela, meanwhile, was composing herself. In defense of the column, she would utilize her powers as best as she could.

Even Delbin was ready. He had succeeded in finding a sling and ammunition. The sling was a lucky find; he had been looking for his book, in order to record the coming battle. The sling seemed as though it might be useful, so he kept it at the ready.

The column moved into the mountains.

Perched atop one peak, the stone dragon, momentarily unnoticed, continued to watch them. It had not been given orders to attack. Not yet.

That was quite fortunate, for soon it was apparent that the knights had other concerns—concerns wearing armor and sporting a nasty variety of weapons.

Their first mistake was in believing that the knights would even think of retreating. Their second was assuming that fifty men were just fifty men, when they were actually dealing with the best-trained fighters in all of Ansalon. The first wave of attackers, both on the ground and on the slopes of the mountain, died nearly to a man as each knight did his part. Only one knight died, an arrow through his neck, and only two others were injured. Some twenty or thirty of the enemy perished, however. The fierce battle lasted several minutes.

As the disorganized figures scurried back into the safety of the mountains, Bennett ordered those who would prefer to give chase to maintain their positions.

The column would move as a whole or not at all.

The next clash came only five minutes later.

* * * * *

"How much longer can we afford to stay here, minotaur?"

Kaz gazed down to where another patrol was scouring the nearby area. It was all too obvious what—or rather, *whom*—the patrol was looking for.

"As long as it takes our friends down there to tire themselves out."

They were slowly inching their way toward the keep that Argaen Ravenshadow had made his own. Finding it had been fairly simple; the two of them had moved steadily and stealthily in the direction of the peak where the stone dragon now perched. As they had assumed, the keep lay below that particular mountain.

Getting there . . . now, *that* was a nasty problem.

The region was a kendertown of activity. Patrols scurried everywhere. Kaz was truly astonished at the number of hardened fighters; this was the bulk of what remained of the once-terrible force of the Dragonqueen. The dark elf was indeed building himself an army! How long had he planned such a thing? When had he first contacted the various raider commanders? What had he offered them?

Ravenshadow's keep had been built long ago, probably by someone dreaming of a new life. It was old but solid. A high, serviceable wall surrounded it, save at the back of the keep, where a mountain provided a natural barrier to outsiders. There were several taller buildings toward the back end of the keep, one a squat tower that had probably served as the lord's residence. It was in that tower that Kaz suspected he would find Argaen Ravenshadow himself. Despite the damage the elements had done to the keep as a whole, the dark elf had apparently seen no reason to have it repaired. What had happened to the original inhabitants, neither Sardal nor Kaz could even guess, but at one time, the minotaur estimated that the place could have held almost four hundred souls. Certainly the size of the keep indicated that. The size also hinted at how massive Argaen's army had become; the keep was fairly overwhelmed by men and horses. There were groups of ogres and other races that had forged alliances with Takhisis.

Time was rapidly running out. So much activity meant only one thing to Kaz: His friends were under attack. Every moment he delayed brought them closer to death—if it was not already too late.

The going was too slow. Dodging patrols and riders. Being forced, at one point, to wait and quietly kill a trio of searchers who had gotten too close in their search. Still the keep was far away.

"They are moving on," Sardal whispered.

The patrol had decided to continue down the path before them. No one would find the three men Kaz had been forced to dispatch, but if they went far enough, they might find traces of one very large wolf.

Thinking of Greymir, Kaz wondered how the emissary of Habbakuk was faring. The dreadwolves were nothing if not maddeningly persistent, and they were nearly impossible to kill. Kaz could not help wondering whether Greymir had fallen to them, and if the others were now closing in on the elf and him.

"We waste valuable time," Sardal reminded him.

Kaz replied in a manner that left it quite clear what he thought about the elf's comment. While Sardal suppressed a smile, the minotaur scanned the area quickly and, deciding it was safe, stepped out into the open.

"We are fortunate," Kaz's companion added, "that Argaen does not dare trust another mage."

"Why can't he?"

"Very simply, what Black Robe would not be tempted by the power channeled by the emerald sphere? Argaen is not strong enough to match a true magic-user."

"Which makes him perfect for Galan Dracos."

"Yes." Sardal looked saddened. "Poor Argaen. I wonder if he knows yet what role he may be playing."

Kaz grunted.

A warning shout came from behind them. Both turned at the noise. For whatever reason, two of the men in the last patrol had backtracked just in time to see the minotaur step out into the open. They had only one viable option, and the minotaur put it into action with but a single word.

"Run!"

Horns sounded. Kaz heard more shouts, an indication that the rest of the patrol was nearby. It wouldn't be long before the alarm alerted others.

"We cannot . . . cannot run mindlessly!" Sardal gasped as he ran.

"Save your breath!"

Kaz's footing became unstable. He immediately discovered that he was not alone in his predicament. Sardal was falling forward, and startled cries alerted him to the fact that their pursuers were having problems of their own.

An earthquake? Kaz wondered.

"M-Minotaur!" the elf bellowed. Sardal was rolling helplessly down the incline. As much as Kaz would have liked to aid him, he was having enough trouble preventing himself from toppling after him. The tremors continued to toss loose objects about.

Barely on his feet, Kaz stared wide-eyed as the side of one peak seemed to melt downward. He blinked, but the astonishing sight remained. The emerald sphere had to be the cause of this. Argaen Ravenshadow must be trying to harness its abilities. And he was not succeeding.

Chaos. Huma had said that Galan Dracos called the sphere his channel into the power of chaos, or something along those lines.

Something bumped him from behind. Kaz lashed out, only to find his arm snared by the powerful grip of a human almost as tall and broad as himself. The man had to be part ogre. He had to try to fight off this foe before he lost his footing entirely.

The human was trying to twist the battle-axe out of Kaz's grip. As he fought back, his left foot slid downward. Minotaur and human compensated, but Kaz found himself at a definite disadvantage. His adversary had the higher ground. Kaz's grip was loosening, and worse, the soldier was now drawing a dagger. Kaz couldn't gain more than a temporary foothold.

Kaz fell into a sitting position. His opponent followed him down facefirst, striking the earth hard. His grip all but vanished, and the two of them separated. The soldier began to tumble over and over uncontrollably. By the time Kaz reached more level ground, his adversary lay absolutely motionless.

The earth finally ceased rippling, but the games were not over. The formerly solid ground, though no longer rising and falling, was now like mud. Kaz rose and immediately sank to his knees. Beyond him, Sardal cautiously made his way toward the minotaur. He was up to his ankles in the mudlike earth, but each step sank him a little deeper.

A horrible slurping sound caught Kaz's attention, and he turned just in time to see the boots of his opponent, the only portion of the man still visible, sink into the earth. The minotaur glanced down at the muck surrounding his own legs and froze in trepidation.

He began to sink even faster.

"Don't stand still!" Sardal shouted. "Spread your mass! It will slow the sinking!"

The logic was questionable, but the results were evident. Kaz actually succeeded in raising himself up a bit. There was still one problem. "How do we get out of here?"

A shadow loomed overhead. Kaz didn't have to look up to know what it was.

Ravenshadow's stone dragon.

The creature circled above them, seeming to debate

what it should do. Kaz readied his battle-axe, knowing that even if the unliving creature feared it, it wouldn't do the minotaur much good if the dragon simply dropped on top of him. At least, however, he would try to get in one blow.

Several tons of solid stone came hurtling down, blotting out the sun. Kaz closed his eyes, awaiting the final moment, but the moment never came. There was a heavy thud, as if something massive, such as a dragon made of stone, had struck a hard surface and bounced off.

"Branchala be praised!" whispered Sardal from nearby.

Kaz dared to open his eyes. Apparently the stone dragon, much to its annoyance, had bounced off something, for it was now careening madly about, trying to regain control. Sardal was smiling wearily. The minotaur looked from elf to dragon to elf again.

"What'd you do?"

"I devised a spell that I thought just might be strong enough to repel Argaen's pet. It worked, I am happy to say." The elf looked very relieved.

"*Might?* You weren't certain?"

The dragon had not yet given up. It tried once more to regain control, but with similar results. Still, it was keeping them effectively pinned down. Worse yet, the survivors of the patrol that had been chasing the two were slowly wading their way toward the duo. Kaz counted perhaps seven men, five with swords, one with an axe, the last with a pike.

Enemies behind him, a monster above him, and his maneuverability nearly nil. Things *had* been better, even during the war.

Paladine knows, I've tried to live up to your memory, Huma, Kaz thought darkly, *but the gods have frowned on this minotaur and I think my luck's finally run out.*

The sounds of horses running and men in armor jolted him from his somber thoughts. His first inclination was to expect the worst: that the patrol had been joined by reinforcements. Kaz and Sardal looked back.

A force of knights was cutting its way through the meager resistance. Kaz imagined he saw two or three mages, all elves, riding in the rear of the group.

Sardal laughed lightly. "I had given up all hope that they would come in time!"

Kaz turned on his companion, eyes wide. "You knew they were coming?"

"While you were ensnared in my trap, I spoke briefly with my people and also sent a message off to the nearest of the Solamnic forces. The southern keeps have been pursuing the remnants of the Dragonqueen's army since the war ended."

The minotaur nodded.

"As for my own people—" Sardal broke off. Kaz looked up, saw nothing but one massive set of stone claws, and realized, even as he was torn from the boggy earth with a *schlupp!*, that Sardal's spell had been exceeded. The stone dragon rose high in the air, its prey held tightly. Kaz was greatly surprised to find that he was still breathing. Indeed, he was not dead, and the stone dragon apparently had no intention of killing him. The animated horror turned up into the sky and fled from the danger of the elven mages, directly toward the keep of its master.

The stone claws squeezed Kaz's arms tight against his body, and the intense pressure made him loosen his grip on Honor's Face. Before he could react, the battle-axe slipped free and plummeted into the muck below, vanishing beneath the surface of the liquefied earth. He tried picturing the dwarven weapon, tried to call it back to him, but nothing happened. How he had done it before was beyond him. Now he was unarmed and alone.

The claws squeezed ever tighter. The minotaur could no longer breathe. Perhaps, he thought as things turned to darkness, the stone dragon was going to crush him to death.

A moment later, he no longer cared. Unable to breathe, he passed out completely, cursing only the fact that he would not go down fighting.

*   *   *   *   *

A part of him knew that this was yet another dream and memory mixed together, but that part was buried in the back of his mind. He only cared that this was the day of oath-taking, a day of both pride and shame, of honor and indignity.

With the rest, Kaz took his place before those the ogre and human lords had made elders of the minotaur race. There was the one bearing the title of emperor, who had never been defeated in arena challenges, though some said that was due to trickery. There were the elders, supposedly the strongest and smartest of the minotaurs. Some of them were true minotaur champions, like Kaz. Most were suspected of the same treachery as the emperor. It mattered not, for they were as much slaves to the overlords as the rest of their people.

Long ago, when they had first been conquered, the minotaurs, in order to save their race, had taken oaths of utter obedience. Bound by their own strict code of honor, they trapped themselves in an endless cycle of slavery. The few malcontents were quickly and quietly dealt with by the masters. Oath-breakers were very rare, however.

Now, in the interminable war between Paladine and Takhisis, the minotaurs were an important part in the efforts of the warlord, Crynus. A minotaur was worth any two fighters from the other races—generally more than two. They fought and won battles others would have given up as lost. Parceled out so that the temptation to rebel would never be concentrated in too great a number—the warlord did not care to take chances—the minotaurs strengthened every army tremendously. All that was needed was to insure their loyalty with the oath.

Crynus was here himself, and he seemed to gaze at Kaz in particular. The minotaur felt both proud and disturbed. Someone signaled for the oath to begin. A horn sounded, yet now it was a Solamnic battle horn, and the man who had been the warlord became Grand Master Oswal. The other figures seated before the assembled throng became knights. Bennett sat on his uncle's right, and Rennard, smiling merrily—something Kaz had not seen him do in the brief time they had known each other—sat on the elder's left.

This is a dream! one part of the minotaur's mind shouted. This is not right.

"An oath is only as good as the man," muttered someone to his right, "and a minotaur is no man."

Kaz whirled about and found himself among a legion of young knights waiting to take their own Solamnic oath. The one who had spoken was Huma, who looked at Kaz with contempt.

"How long will this oath last?" Huma asked with a smirk. "The one you gave your masters lasted only until you tired of it. How long before you turn on me? I'm disappointed in you, Kaz. You have no honor. None whatsoever. You tried to be like me only in order to convince yourself you aren't a dishonorable coward and a murderer!"

The minotaur's eyes grew crimson, and he longed to hold the dwarven battle-axe again, to show the human the truth of it with the blade of the axe. Even as he longed for it, Kaz realized that the axe was in his hands. Matching Huma's smirk, Kaz raised the weapon up—and found himself staring into the side of the axe head, at his own reflection, which was slowly fading away.

"How did—?" Huma uttered, but it was no longer Huma's voice. Instead, it was that of Argaen Ravenshadow, or perhaps Galan Dracos. It was impossible to say.

With the sudden manifestation of that voice, or those voices, Kaz gained some measure of control of his own dream. He hefted the axe, but he knew the figure *he stalked toward could not be Huma. Instead, he imagined it was Ravenshadow. Ravenshadow he was more than willing to deliver to the Abyss.*

"Wake him up, curse you! No more games!" a voice that seemed to come from all around him commanded.

*   *   *   *   *

Kaz was jarred back into reality. That was the only way to describe it. From dream to waking, with no transition in between. It was enough to make his head spin. He started to slump, only to discover that something held him up by the wrists.

"Open your eyes, *old friend!*"

The minotaur did.

Argaen Ravenshadow lay seated before the malevolent emerald sphere in the center of what seemed to be a makeshift wizard's laboratory in the keep. He seemed in good health, free of his wounds, although he leaned to one side in an odd manner. He also seemed annoyed, at something other than Kaz's presence. There was, barring the stone dragon, one other presence of import in what passed for Argaen's home. It was *he*, of course, who had welcomed the minotaur. It was *he* who now floated above the emerald sphere itself, as much a part of it as it was of him.

He was Galan Dracos, of course.

Chapter 20

The raiders attacked again. The second time, the
enemy did nothing so foolish as to charge the knights. Instead, they kept to the ridges and mountainsides and
rained death down upon the band. Two knights were
struck down in the first volley, despite raised shields.
There were just too many archers above and around
them. One or two knights answered with strikes from
their own bows, and though each attempt put them in
jeopardy, they did not shy away from the task. One man
fell across Tesela's horse, and the cleric, despite herself,
could not help gasping in horror. Darius helped her remove the unfortunate knight. There was no time to stop.
Indeed, it would have been certain death to do so.

From the left of the column, rocks came bounding

earthward as someone sought to start an avalanche. A Solamnic archer cut down one man, but others remained hidden. One knight's horse was toppled as several large stones crushed its hind leg. With amazing speed, the knight brought his sword down across the animal's neck, relieving it permanently of the terrible pain. Under the protection of his fellows, the man claimed the mount of a fallen comrade.

While the knights had no intention of retreating, Darius feared for his two companions, especially Tesela. He looked back toward the rear of the column, hoping that his comrades might be able to cut a path for the two, but the attackers were already swarming over the rocks. Sending Tesela and Delbin back now would be tantamount to condemning them to death, though what sort of future they had if they remained was also questionable.

It was then that Darius first noticed that the kender was gone.

He whirled around and almost caught an arrow because of his foolish hesitancy. Delbin was nowhere in sight, but the knight was certain he would have remembered if the kender had been killed. Rather, Darius was nearly positive that his kender companion had somehow, in the middle of combat yet, sneaked away.

"Damn you, Delbin!" Darius muttered as he moved forward with the rest of the column.

Had he known where the kender presently was, the knight would undoubtedly have withdrawn the statement. Delbin was not heading toward safety, which Darius assumed. He was, in actuality, scurrying through the myriad paths in the range, making his way ever deeper into the mountains. Intent on the knights below, the enemy did not notice the small figure stealthily threading his way through the oncoming forces. If the truth be known, the kender was making better time than the column. Delbin felt some uncharacteristic kender guilt at seeming to abandon the others, but that was outweighed by his determination to reach the stronghold of the magic thief, Argaeñ Ravenshadow. A trait that many other races overlooked in the kender was their intense loyalty to their friends. Delbin's best friend, someone who was as close to him as his own family, was probably a prisoner of the dark elf. Nothing would make the kender turn back.

Not once did Delbin imagine that Kaz might be dead.

A figure moved in the rocks ahead of him. Delbin, his sling ready, quietly moved closer, as only one of his kind could. The figure sharpened into the backside of an archer. The man had a good supply of arrows and looked ready to use them all. Delbin glanced around and saw other ambushers spread around the area, but only this one blocked his path. The kender chose a proper bullet for his sling, loaded the weapon, and with no hesitation, swung the sling around and around above his head. It seemed a bit unfair to strike the man without his knowledge, but Delbin considered the fact that the human had no such compunction where the knights below were concerned.

On the next swing, he released the bullet. It soared swiftly through the air and struck the archer soundly in the back of the head. A river of red briefly washed over the man's backside before the archer fell forward—and over the edge where he had been kneeling. Delbin sincerely hoped he would not hit somebody when he landed.

Scurrying past the spot where the archer had stationed himself, Delbin saw the keep. It really did not seem that far away.

Suddenly Delbin felt the shock of the earth itself rippling wildly. There were screams as some of the attackers fell to their deaths, and curses from above and below the kender's position. Delbin enjoyed the movement of the earth—it seemed like one of the most enjoyable things he had ever experienced—but the liquefying earth that materialized around his feet fast became an annoyance.

Kender liked to move, and mud was strictly for gully dwarves. It was difficult to find solid ground, for despite its new traits, the ground he moved upon looked no different from unaffected patches nearby. The only way to tell the difference was to actually step on the surface and hope one didn't sink.

That concern died when Delbin noticed the stone dragon rise from behind some smaller peaks. Sharp kender eyes saw the shape clutched tightly in its claws. Delbin had seen the creature up close and knew how big those claws were. To him, there could only be one person as big as the helpless figure he saw in the distance, and that was Kaz. Kaz, his friend, needed rescuing, and the only one who would be able to rescue him was the kender himself.

A mask of stern resolution on his face, or the nearest facsimile he could muster, not knowing how stern resolution was supposed to look, Delbin picked up his pace. He would not let Kaz down.

* * * * *

After his initial shock, Kaz fell back into the dark realm of unconsciousness and did not revive for quite some time. When he did, he discovered himself chained up in a chamber. This was hardly the way he had wanted to enter the keep. He scanned his surroundings. There was actually very little to see. He could make out a single entrance, where the door stood tantalizingly open—either through great carelessness or overconfidence. The walls of the room were cracked with age but still quite sturdy. Cobwebs decorated the ceiling. The chains that held Kaz looked to be formidable, and whoever had secured them to the wall behind him had known his business.

He wondered what the situation was like outside. He suspected it was a full-scale battle, something he had hardly expected. Delbin and the others were out there, possibly injured or worse. Nothing was going right. Nothing had ever gone right. Kaz snorted in self-pity. Did the gods have nothing better to do than pick on a lone minotaur who wanted only to live the rest of his life quietly with an occasional trial of blood to keep him from becoming too bored?

He was still sitting there feeling sorry for himself for all the troubles the world had dumped on him when a guard suddenly materialized. He was not alone, however. There was one very familiar figure with him.

Argaen Ravenshadow walked in, and Kaz saw immediately that his previous brief encounter with the dark elf had been no figment. Ravenshadow did indeed lean to one side as he walked, and it was obvious he did not feel well enough to actually straighten up. This seemed to annoy the elf only slightly, but it gave the minotaur great satisfaction.

The gifts of the emerald sphere are tainted.

The dark elf stopped before Kaz and stared at him for quite some time. Argaen started to speak, seemed to think better of it, and turned to the guard.

"You are dismissed for now. I will call you if I need you."

Oddly, the guard hesitated. Kaz was rather surprised by the open defiance, but Argaen appeared to expect it. He stared the man down, and the guard finally thought better of his insubordination and reluctantly obeyed, closing the door behind him. The elf waited until he was certain they were quite alone before speaking.

"You saw *him*, did you not, minotaur?"

Kaz shivered involuntarily, but he kept a calm appearance. "I saw. Even expecting something like that, it was surprising."

Ravenshadow smiled, but his smile had a peculiar quality, almost as if the elf were mocking himself. "A great prize, yes? Not only is the most powerful artifact of Galan Dracos under my control, but I have made contact with the master sorcerer himself!"

"How did he survive, Argaen? Sardal thought he had, somehow . . ."

"Sardal? Is that whom you are with? I should have recognized his presence sooner. I'm sure I would have, but there is so much to do and so little time to do it, as they say. Still, I feel that you are the one person I should take time out to talk to, if only because of the role you are destined to play."

Kaz stiffened.

Ravenshadow waved off any comment. "You ask how Dracos survived? He did not. Your comrade, Huma of the Lance . . . he saw what truly happened. Dracos knew he had failed in his bid to be a god and also knew that he could only expect the most imaginative of the Dragonqueen's tortures as reward for his folly. Better, I would agree myself, to destroy both body and spirit, to cease to exist."

"I know all that."

"Do you know, then, that it did not go as Dracos planned? Even *he* is not infallible, evidently. Instead of death, he discovered himself in a sort of unlife, a specter floating helplessly in the chaos of his own shattered creation." The smile on Argaen's face altered subtly. The thought of Galan Dracos condemned to everlasting emptiness pleased him.

Kaz wondered what the elf would have said if he had known a similar fate had been planned for him at Sardal's hands. *Another failure on my part*, the minotaur bitterly recalled. Had Huma ever failed so often and so greatly? Likely not.

"It was all he could do to slowly pull the emerald sphere back together. He thought it would enable him to free himself, but in that he was wrong, and so he patiently waited, seeking one with the skill and cunning he needed.

"I know all too well now that some of the things I thought I was responsible for were his doing. For some reason, he could not draw sufficient power from the crystal itself, but he could extract it from those other objects that the knighthood so foolishly piled with the fragments of the sphere. I daresay that they will find most of those items worthless and powerless now, if they investigate. Dracos is living on borrowed time, though. He was fortunate; if not for my intervention and the timely appearance of you and your little kender friend, he would have failed. Vingaard Keep would have returned to normal. For our success, I thank you, minotaur."

Kaz, however, was not paying attention to the elf's sarcastic remark. Instead, at the mention of Delbin, his thoughts had turned fleetingly to his companion and the rest of his friends. Were they still alive?

"You seem pretty calm for someone whose stronghold is under attack by a large force of Solamnic Knights—or don't you know about them yet? Has anyone bothered to inform you, or do they just alert their true master, Dracos?"

Argaen flinched ever so slightly, a sure sign that Kaz's remark had struck home.

"The attack goes on, if that is what you were seeking to discover, minotaur," Ravenshadow replied. He was trying to once more assume the bland mask that Kaz had originally mistaken for the typical elven posturing when dealing with outsiders. Even now, the mask was failing to stay in place. Ravenshadow did have reason to worry about the battle. The elf added, "We will not be disturbed in here, however."

"You don't seem completely confident about that." Kaz smiled back for effect.

With a speed unnatural for any human or minotaur, Argaen struck Kaz across the jaw. A minotaur's jaw is a bit harder than a human's or an elf's, and Kaz had the slight satisfaction—slight because his mouth throbbed with pain—of seeing Ravenshadow wince at the impact.

"If I didn't *need* you, minotaur . . ."

Kaz glared back. "For what? What do you need me for?"

Argaen seemed a bit taken aback. Finally he replied, "To assuage him."

It was said with such uncertainty that it took Kaz several seconds to actually comprehend what the elf had said. When he did understand, he grew grim.

"He—he wants me to work on freeing him from the wraithlike state he now is forced to endure. Only revenge against the knighthood vies with his desire to be whole again. He was the one who demanded that I send the stone dragon after you. I would have preferred you dead, of course."

"No doubt."

"Do not mock me, beast. You are in a disagreeable situation. When he succeeds in teaching me how to give him a true form, when at last he walks the land of Krynn again, Galan Dracos will exact his revenge on the knighthood. First you. The others will follow."

Kaz had no ready reply. He could only imagine the fate awaiting him at the hands of Dracos. Dracos had cheated death, had even cheated Takhisis! If he became a threat once more, what would happen to Krynn? There was no Huma this time, and Kaz knew his own limits quite well.

Kaz glanced at the elf, who was watching the minotaur's visage with interest.

"Now that I have impressed upon you your own future, or lack of it, I want you to consider this. Once Galan Dracos becomes a living, breathing creature again, there is, however remotely, the reality that he can die. Very quickly, if necessary." Argaen gave his prisoner a knowing look.

So that was it! Ravenshadow wanted an assassin to perform the task that he himself did not have the nerve to attempt. The elf was offering Kaz a chance to strike down the master mage before Dracos gained full control of his powers and the emerald sphere. Did the elf think he was that stupid?

No. That desperate.

"Make no mistake about this, minotaur. I will control

the emerald sphere, or Dracos will. You have a choice in the matter. I will leave you to decide. It may be that if you take too long, I will find that I do not need you, so I recommend haste."

Argaen gave his false smile and turned to leave. Kaz waited until the elf was nearly at the door before calling out, "Argaen, where did you learn to create and control the dreadwolves? I thought only Galan Dracos could do that."

The figure before him stood frozen for an instant, his face turned from the minotaur. Then, with a haste that gave Kaz the answer he had expected, Ravenshadow flung open the door and barged out of the room. His rapid retreat was punctuated with harsh footfalls. After a moment, the guard peered into the room. He gave the minotaur a singularly passive look and then closed the door, leaving Kaz alone with his thoughts.

So it was Galan Dracos, indeed, who controlled the dreadwolves. Imprisoned as he was with no true form, Dracos had still been able to reach out and perform his dastardly spells.

Several more precious minutes passed. Kaz could hear nothing from outside. He tested the chains again. Very sturdy and very constraining. Even with his strength, escape by sheer force seemed next to impossible, yet Kaz did not relish waiting politely for his execution.

Futilely, he tried once more to struggle against his bonds. Kaz thought of his companions—Delbin, Tesela, Darius, and Sardal—and others he knew, like Bennett, Grand Master Oswal, and Lord Guy Avondale, who might die. The minotaur thought of Huma and how, before this had all begun, he had tried to live up to the ideal that his Solamnic companion represented. But he was a minotaur, not a knight—a minotaur and a rebel among his own kind, besides.

The chains strained but held.

Kaz slumped back against the wall and took a deep breath. He did not let up. Though his body was still screaming from his first attempt, he tried again without hesitation. What other choice did he really have?

He fell back against the wall and readied himself for a third attempt. His wrists and ankles were already raw. His only hope was that whoever had installed these chains had thought in human terms. Even for a minotaur, Kaz was strong.

On the next attempt, he felt some part of his bonds loosen. The chain that held his right wrist seemed to give just a little. Encouraged, Kaz put his full effort into that one side and felt it give a bit more. Gritting his teeth and breathing heavily, he again threw the full force of his body into it.

The chain tore loose with a loud clatter.

The scrape of metal breaking free from solid stone reverberated throughout the chamber. Two feet of solid chain dangled noisily from his wrist.

The door burst open even as he flung his arm back into place. The guard glared at him.

"What's that noise? What're ya up to, cow?"

From the doorway, it was impossible for the human to make out the fact that Kaz now had one free arm. When the minotaur refused to answer and even turned away from his interrogator, the guard stepped closer. His sword was out, and the tip was on a level with Kaz's throat.

He repeated his question. "I heard a noise, cow! Ya make that?"

In reply, Kaz brought his right arm around and, utilizing the two feet of chain, caught the guard's leg. The human had only a moment to realize that a minotaur's reach far exceeded that of a man, especially when the minotaur held a length of hard chain as well. The guard fell backward, losing his sword and striking the stone floor with a harsh crack. Kaz quickly dragged his prize over to him, his eyes flickering back and forth to the open door where the appearance of just one more guard would doom his escape attempt.

Hope crumbled to frustration when he discovered that the guard had no key. It was probably in the hands of Ravenshadow, who didn't trust anyone but himself. Kaz spat out several colorful minotaur epithets. Not only did he lack keys, but the guard's sword was also out of reach, which meant that he could not use it to defend himself if someone came upon him before he succeeded in freeing his other arm and his legs.

If only he had his twibil. The double-edged, dwarven battle-axe had come to him magically before—why not now? What made it decide when to come or not to come? How desperate a situation did Kaz have to be in? Was it lost forever in the muck the stone dragon had torn him from?

He had no more than thought the latter question when he realized that Honor's Face was there in his left hand.

Now Kaz had a weapon, a weapon of power. Whether it was up to facing a master sorcerer like Galan Dracos or even a cunning magic thief like Argaen was unknown, but Kaz felt certain that the dwarven craftsman who had fashioned it had forged it strong enough to take on something as simple as chains.

Honor's Face sliced through the metal chains as it might have sliced through the very air. Both the wrist and ankle cuffs proved impossible to remove without keys, however. So be it; at least they would not interfere with his movements.

Still no one had come, a fact that puzzled Kaz as much as the fact that it was so silent outside the chamber. Slowly making his way to the doorway, he discovered that the outer corridor was windowless. A few torches lit the dim hall. Kaz had begun to suspect that one of the reasons it was so silent was that he was underground now, most likely under the tower. Certainly that would explain the lack of windows.

The shadow of someone carefully moving down a side corridor in his direction made Kaz flatten against the wall. There was nowhere to hide save his former cell, and he had no intention of retreating into it.

With little other choice, he raised the battle-axe high. One adversary or more, his best bet would be to charge the moment the owner of the shadow came into sight. Surprise was on his side.

There was still only one shadow. A lone guard who had heard the noise? Why not summon help, then?

A hand and boot slipped around the corridor. Kaz stiffened in anticipation. A head peeked out.

"Sardal!"

Kaz almost let the battle-axe drop to the floor as he exhaled sharply in relief. The elf looked up at the minotaur in surprise, saw the massive blades, and blanched.

Kaz was the first to recover. "How did you find me? Where did you come from?"

"Lower your voice or speak not at all, friend! Branchala be praised that we have found one another! I pray that together we may find some way to turn that monstrous evil back before it is too late!"

"Too late?" Kaz eyed the elf fiercely. "What's happened, Sardal? I've been chained up until a moment ago. *What's happened?*"

"You do not know?" Sardal seemed stunned. It took a few seconds for the elf to collect himself. "No, you would not know, trapped as you were in the lower chambers of this keep."

"Something's happened to the others? Delbin? The humans?"

Sardal looked as grim as an elf could, which was very grim indeed. "Only a barrier surrounding this keep, one of incredible magnitude, hardly the work of one such as Argaen. I was barely within its boundaries when it was cast. A second or two more and I would have been trapped in it."

"And the others?"

"The Knights of Solamnia and those of my people who aid them are the better force, but the Dragonqueen's former servants hold the more advantageous positions.

Even if there was no barrier, your companions and the knights would not be able to reach the keep's outer walls before darkness, and in the night we are at a further disadvantage."

"Why?"

"Nuitari rules among the moons now, my friend. Tonight the black moon will devour all but a trace of Solinari. I fear the sorcerers without will not be able to break the spell of the shield, which leaves it up to you and me, minotaur. And since I am hampered by the same difficulties as my brethren, I fear that my aid will be somewhat limited."

"Which leaves most of it up to me," Kaz muttered.

There were times, he reflected, when it would have been better to have been born a simplistic gully dwarf. At least no one expected *them* to save the world—or die trying.

Chapter 21

Argaen Ravenshadow raged at the object of his desire, the gleaming emerald sphere wrought by Galan Dracos.

"No more tricks! I know your power! I know what you can do! The minotaur did not lie, did he? Why else have I come up short each time I sought to bind the sphere to my bidding? Is it because it still follows the dictates of another master?"

Above the crystalline artifact, an indistinct form wavered almost haughtily. At the moment, it little resembled any human form. It was a mere misty outline, a gauzy shroud. There had been times when it had worn a more definite form, when Ravenshadow had found himself staring into the unsettling eyes of the renegade mage Ga-

Ian Dracos. Argaen found he was more than happy to deal with the wraith in this less disturbing form.

There was no response. Sometimes there was; sometimes there was not. The magic thief could never be certain when he was going to receive an answer, and sometimes he even wondered if he had imagined the others, for when Dracos spoke, his voice was little more than a drawn-out breath.

When it became apparent that this time he was wasting his energy, the elf finally whirled away from the silent specter and turned his concerns to other matters. It had seemed as if everything was going his way for a change. The mostly human raiding bands in the south had answered his call with surprising speed, almost as if they had expected his summons. To the north, the ogre tribes were amassing again after lying low for most of the past five years. The elf had promised them a tool of great power in their seemingly hopeless struggle, for without the dragons of darkness the servants of Takhisis had no edge. Now they had Argaen Ravenshadow.

Through a stroke of astonishing luck, he had secured the artifact he needed to make him first and foremost among the Dark Queen's servants, only to discover that there was more to the emerald sphere than even he had surmised.

Ravenshadow stalked to a window and stared out at the eerie tableau before him, the shimmering that represented the barrier keeping both his enemies and his allies from him.

There was a question he had asked himself more than once in the past day, even before the minotaur had made his unnerving remarks. The dreadwolves were further testimony that Dracos *did* need him—but for what? The wraith had more power than it would admit to, but it still needed him. Why? And how could the dark elf turn that need to his advantage?

A bitter smile briefly played over his lips as he watched the tiny figures in the distance waver like unstable puffs of smoke. Ravenshadow, at present, was only able to command the least of the object's abilities, yet that had already given him a taste of incredible power. If he could only bind himself to the core, truly control the flow of magical power that the sphere only acted as a conduit for, he would be like a god. . . .

Or dead. A pawn of the creator of this amazing tool.

He needed to know more. He needed to know what his place was in the schemes of the vague figure floating above that which rightfully belonged to the elf. Then— *then* Ravenshadow would deal with the fool. Dead was dead, and Galan Dracos had had his chance. The future now belonged to Argaen Ravenshadow.

Turning from the window, Argaen glanced at the hourglass on one of the tables he used for his studies. The books and manuscripts he had stolen over the years were forgotten now and were piled to one side, for the time-piece now held precedence. It held roughly three hours' worth of sand, approximately half of which had already fallen to the bottom. Three hours of safety. That was the barrier's limit. It would cease to exist then. The sand in the hourglass fell too readily, he thought. By nightfall, his protection would be gone. Before then, he had to master the sphere. He had no more shadow boxes; the one he had used to carry the sphere had been nearly burned out by the time they had arrived here.

Without thinking, he tried to straighten up. Cursing suddenly, Argaen thought of his pain. Everything he had gained was a half-measure. By rights, the emerald sphere should have granted him sufficient power and control to heal himself. Yet he still couldn't even stand straight without tremendous agony. . . .

He put his hands in his robe pockets and turned to once more face the emerald sphere and that other who floated vaguely above it. Briefly the fingertips of his right hands touched what he sought. Argaen did not smile, though he felt the urge to. Instead, he spoke to his "partner" of circumstance.

"Let us begin afresh. . . ."

The dark elf stepped toward the gleaming artifact, his eyes never leaving the specter.

So caught up was he in his new machinations that Argaen Ravenshadow failed to take notice of a small form watching from the alcoves.

Delbin, like Sardal, had gotten within the boundaries of the barrier spell at nearly the last moment. The kender had only become aware of what was happening when he turned around and saw a hapless human, one of the enemy, trapped in the essence of the barrier itself, frozen like a statue. While the idea of such a spell tickled his imagination, Delbin knew that it could only mean trouble for Kaz and the others. The kender had immediately picked up his pace.

Getting inside had turned out to be remarkably easy. Delbin was very proud of himself. As far as he knew, during his search through the upper floors of the main building, he had done none of the things that, for some reason, irked his minotaur companion. His only problem now was not knowing where to look next. Kaz was in this place somewhere, and Delbin had the feeling that something was going to happen very soon, and there might be no one to prevent it except *him*.

Looking down at the dark elf and the indistinct phantasm that Argaen insisted on addressing as Galan Dracos, a name Delbin knew from Kaz, the kender felt an odd, unfamiliar emotion stir within him. A member of any other race would have recognized it immediately, but not a kender. It was a rarity among his own kind, but Delbin had spent enough time among the other races so that he was finally able to put a name to it.

Fear.

* * * * *

Sardal had wanted to say more, and Kaz had certainly wanted to hear more, but such was not to be, for something chose that moment to come prowling through the corridors.

This was no dreadwolf. They had no inkling exactly what it was, save that it was a guardian, a watchdog of sorts. A watchdog on two feet, which was how they first became aware of it. Kaz heard the footfalls.

Whatever it was breathed heavily, so that they could hear it at all times. Sardal, with a shake of his head, indicated that it had not yet picked up their presence. That was a hopeful sign. A dreadwolf would have been hot on their trail by now. Nonetheless, it was heading in their direction.

With the unknown danger wandering toward them, Kaz and the elf had no choice but to retreat down the hall. Speed was of the essence, but so was stealth.

For Sardal, moving silently was no problem. For a being of Kaz's stature, built for strength and not for subtlety, it was next to impossible. His feet seemed to find every uneven portion of the floor, causing him to stumble several times. Naturally the battle-axe bounced against the wall more than once because of this. Each time, he expected creatures to come boiling out of the stone walls.

Their unseen pursuer moved ever closer, but it didn't seem as if it had taken real notice of them. Kaz began to wonder if the thing was deaf. Even he would have known by now there were some intruders.

Sardal paused at one point, looking back in the direction they had come from. The footfalls of the creature behind them had finally faded to nothing. Kaz thought the elf looked rather pale.

"What's wrong?" the minotaur asked.

"I scarcely can believe it, but I think I have been leading us in circles."

A shriek caught them both by surprise. Something huge, furry, and two-legged threw itself on Sardal, who went down with a muffled cry. Kaz readied a strike at the rampaging attacker, but there was too much risk of hitting the elf instead. Abandoning his battle-axe, the minotaur took hold of the creature from the back and tried to pull it off the elf.

They struggled at a stalemate for several seconds. Then the head of the creature slowly bent back as Kaz pulled at it. He slipped one arm around its neck, further strengthening his hold. The head swiveled to look at him, and the minotaur caught a glimpse of the only face he had ever seen that would make an ogre or a goblin look handsome by comparison—not to mention the face of the biggest vermin he could possibly imagine.

The ratman released its hold on Sardal and twisted around, trying to get its sharp teeth and claws on the minotaur's bare skin. Kaz would have none of that, however. Strong though it was, the monstrosity was at a disadvantageous angle, and Kaz slowly tightened his grip on his adversary's larynx. Jaws snapped a few inches from his face and claws scratched his chest and arms. He refused to budge.

With a gurgle, the creature suddenly convulsed in his arms and went limp. Kaz saw blood running down its back. Sardal had stabbed it from behind.

"I would recommend haste, minotaur. I sincerely doubt that this poor misfit is alone."

Kaz found himself scanning each dark corner thoroughly, as if ratmen were about to come leaping out of every corner now. "Agreed. I just have to retrieve my—"

After a moment of waiting for Kaz to finish his sentence, Sardal finally asked, "Your what?"

The minotaur did not reply at first, instead gazing around the hallway. In frustration, he kicked the dead ratman.

Sardal watched him impatiently. "Is there something amiss?"

"Honor's Face! I can't find the battle-axe you gave me!"

"Perhaps it was thrown during battle. . . ."

"I put it down here." Kaz pointed at a spot no more

274

than a couple yards from the site of the struggle. "I was afraid I might chop *your* head off instead of his."

"Then it is lost, minotaur, and we had best depart before those who took it return. They might be some of *his* brethren." The elf indicated the corpse and shivered slightly. There was something disgusting about such a creature. He doubted whether the beast had been born like that. More likely, it was something that Argaen had stolen from some Black Robe. Sardal hoped it had never been human.

"Let me try something first." Kaz, now smiling, closed his eyes. Whoever had stolen his battle-axe was in for a surprise. How could they know that he could summon it back to him? He pictured the weapon, the mirrorlike axe head gleaming, and called it to him as he had done before.

"What is it you are doing?" Sardal asked, his tone hinting of annoyance.

Kaz opened his eyes and stared at his hands—an empty pair of hands. "It's not here!"

The elf looked at him worriedly.

"The axe! It comes to me when I call it, when we're separated!"

"It does?"

Leaning toward the elf, Kaz looked into his eyes. "You didn't *know* that?"

"No . . . but it might explain things a bit. I always thought there was some secret about that axe. The dwarf would never explain. Said I should just keep it ready. He wanted it kept away from those who would misuse it, but he saw that someone would eventually have need of it. I think he was almost as confused as I am now. It is quite possible that Reorx worked through him. I often wondered about that. The battle-axe sounds like a product of his mischievous mind. Anyone who would forge a thing like the Graystone of Gargath . . ."

Kaz was completely ignoring the elf. He stared grimly at his empty hands. With the battle-axe, he had stood some chance, however little, against Argaen and Dracos. He had even come to believe that the twibil was the key to destroying the emerald sphere—didn't Magius's wizard's staff shatter it the last time?

"We have to move on," Sardal was concluding, "with or without your axe."

The minotaur nodded. "We must be on guard for traps."

"Those are aptly timed words, minotaur! They will make an appropriate epitaph for you!"

Argaen Ravenshadow was suddenly there before them, his left hand stretched back as he prepared to hurl something at the two stunned figures.

* * * * *

Only moments before, Delbin had watched wide-eyed as the dark elf, face alight with obsession, seemed about to achieve what he had failed to do before. Ravenshadow had one arm raised high and the other pointed toward the emerald sphere. His outstretched hand barely skimmed the surface of the artifact. The elf's body trembled.

Above the sphere, the misty form of Galan Dracos seemed to intensify. Delbin got the odd impression that the wraith was waiting for something, something that had as yet not manifested itself. The form shifted and twitched in what the kender guessed was growing impatience.

Suddenly the phantom straightened, solidifying to the point where its features became truly distinct. The almost reptilian visage twisted into a look of savage madness. Dead eyes stared off into space, and a soundless cry issued from the specter's lips. At the same time, Argaen Ravenshadow fell back from the crystalline sphere with a scream of both pain and astonishment.

"Free! The minotaur free! And Sardal here as well!" the dark elf snarled at the air. His words made only partial sense to the eavesdropping kender. Ravenshadow locked eyes with the ghostly Dracos. "Show me where they are!"

The wraith faded, turning almost nonexistent. Some silent communication passed between mage and elf. Ravenshadow nodded, then suddenly vanished. One second he was there, reaching into his robe pockets, and the next second he had disappeared. There was no puff of smoke, like the magic of illusionists. Ravenshadow simply ceased to be there.

The kender marveled at this for quite some time before realizing that this was his chance to do something—but what? Galan Dracos no longer floated half-seen above the emerald sphere, either having decided to follow the elf or to return to some otherworldly domain. Either way, it meant that Delbin was completely alone. His only excuse for not attempting something was his own bewilderment. Perhaps if he climbed down and got a better view of the place, he might be able to think of something.

Delbin waited three or four dozen breaths before he decided it was safe to climb out of his hiding place. No human could have fit into the space he had watched from. With ease, he stretched out, got a hold on the wall beneath him, and scurried down like a spider, jumping the last three feet. Where a human would have made noise, he landed as silently as an autumn leaf falling from a tree. Delbin turned around. There were all sorts of neat things that he would have been eager to look over if the situation had been different, but concern for Kaz was paramount.

His eyes focused on the scarred surface of the sphere. Were there eyes there looking back at him? Delbin waited, but no figment of Galan Dracos rose to crush him. It was only a trick of his own mind. During their months together, Kaz had more than once chided the kender for letting his overactive imagination get the best of him. Delbin had never been able to make him understand that an overactive imagination was a normal kender trait.

His eyes trailed back to the emerald sphere. It was the cause of everything, he decided suddenly. Argaen had used it to drive the knights mad—or had the emerald sphere used the elf? Delbin shook his head. That didn't matter. He knew only that Argaen was planning to use it again, and that Kaz thought a lot more people would get hurt if that happened.

It was what Delbin had to deal with. If he could destroy it—the sphere was too large to fit into his pouch, so he couldn't just wander off with it—then everything would be wonderful again. People would be happy once more, which was the proper way to be.

How to shatter it, though, was the question. Delbin looked around the room. There were lots of shelves and tables with all sorts of interesting stuff on them. He looked at the spellbooks that Ravenshadow had shoved aside on one table, massive tomes, possibly centuries old. They looked pretty heavy. Maybe one of them would do the trick. There was also the hourglass.

While the kender pondered what would work best, a mist slowly rose from the emerald sphere.

"Why . . . not . . . try . . . the . . . battle-axe?" a voice like a drawn-out breath whispered mockingly in his ear.

The battle-axe—Kaz's battle-axe, he realized—was suddenly there next to the table. Delbin caught only a glimpse of the weapon, for he was already turning toward the origin of the voice.

The wraith that was Galan Dracos looked down at him with eyes that made the kender shiver and turn away.

"There is . . . nowhere . . . to go . . . and I have *need* . . . of you!"

An invisible hand took hold of Delbin and began to drag him back toward the emerald sphere. He struggled in vain.

"No," continued Dracos. "I think . . . I need . . . you . . . a little more . . . pliable."

A great shock surged through every inch of Delbin's body and he slumped, but his body was moved by a force other than its own ever nearer to the sphere and its creator.

"Soon . . . I will be . . . alive again," the wraith said to the limp form, "and my mistress . . . my forgiving . . . mistress . . . will at last . . . rule Krynn!"

Chapter 22

Several dozen tiny black objects went flying toward Kaz and Sardal.

Even as Kaz realized that he was going to take the brunt of the magic thief's attack, the projectiles faded harmlessly less than two feet from his face.

"You have become what you always thought of our race, Argaen! Much too predictable. Is that the only spell you can perform consistently? Creating those little baubles is a toddler's trick!"

As Sardal spoke, Kaz noticed a smile creeping onto Ravenshadow's visage.

The ceiling above the minotaur and his companion collapsed.

Sardal raised his hands in defense, but he was too slow

to effectively protect them both. To Kaz's horror, the elf's hurried spell stabilized the ceiling above the minotaur, but not above Sardal himself. Great chunks of cut stone rained down upon the elf. Kaz could see that some of the stones were glancing off harmlessly, but enough were still hitting his companion, who had saved his life at least twice now.

All the while, Argaen Ravenshadow laughed insanely. Sardal had underestimated the dark elf. He had always been a magic thief, with little power to call his own. That had changed now, and it looked as if his old friend had become Argaen's first victim.

Snarling in anger, Kaz turned his gaze on Ravenshadow and charged him. He never made it. Argaen stopped laughing and stared down at the floor before the minotaur's feet. A gap began to spread across the floor. Kaz leaped over the treacherous chasm, fully intending to land on his adversary.

Stone claws sprouting from both walls caught both his legs and one arm. The sudden stop nearly wrenched one leg out of its socket. Kaz bit back a bitter, painful scream.

Argaen Ravenshadow had decoyed him.

Like a child with a new toy, the dark elf was experimenting with his newfound powers. He twirled one hand before Kaz, remaining just out of reach of the minotaur. Tiny winged serpents fluttered out of the circle he sketched in the air, flitting around Kaz's face. With his free hand, Kaz tried to swat them away. He was bitten several times in the process and succeeded only in crushing one. They were astonishingly quick, like hummingbirds.

After a minute or two, Ravenshadow tired of this and waved his hand. The winged serpents faded away.

"Once I would have only been able to dream of doing something so extraordinary. My masters said I lacked the aptitude. What they inferred was that there was weakness in my bloodline, that perhaps one of my progenitors had been a human."

Kaz, who understood what elves could be like, knew what sort of life Argaen must have had. Pure bloodlines were more important to them than to even the Knights of Solamnia.

"Being part human doesn't necessarily weaken the blood. I've met many powerful human sorcerers."

That produced a smile—a chilling one, but a smile nonetheless. "That is what I believed as well. The rumor was never confirmed, but I chose to study humans anyway and discovered within them a vitality that the elven race lacks."

"You chose to admire . . . the wrong aspects of humanity, Argaen," a familiar voice called out from behind Kaz.

"You still live, Sardal?" the magic thief commented blandly. He took a step closer to Kaz, but his eyes were on the elf behind the minotaur. Kaz eyed the distance separating him from the dark elf. Another two steps and Ravenshadow would be within his reach.

"You still live, Sardal," Argaen repeated in that same bland tone, "but not for long."

"More true than . . . you think, friend."

Argaen started to take a step forward, but froze in midstep and looked the minotaur square in the eye. Kaz found himself suddenly swung toward one of the walls, one leg temporarily loose. He was slapped against the wall with bone-jarring force. While the minotaur fought to stabilize himself, Ravenshadow walked past him toward the other elf.

"You *are* dying, aren't you?" he said at last, his tone odd. Kaz thought he almost detected a slight trace of guilt in the magic thief's voice.

Ravenshadow stood over Sardal, who lay pinned under several large portions of the ceiling. A gaping hole above indicated just how much stone—more than enough to crush him to pulp—had actually fallen on the elf. Only quick thinking on Sardal's part had prevented that, but one especially large chunk of stone had slammed into Sardal's rib cage. It was a wonder he could speak, let alone breathe.

"Argaen . . . it is still . . . not too late! No one is . . . safe around . . . the forces that Dracos . . . sought to tap! Even the Dragonqueen . . . was hesitant!"

"You think that I cannot control such power?" All guilt was gone from the renegade's voice. He spat down on the dying figure at his feet. "Even *you!* Elderly fools! I know more about the workings of magic than all of them combined, including you! While they have been content to play with their powers, I have studied and learned—and now I have access to more power than any of you can imagine!"

"All that power . . . requires skill." It was obvious now that Sardal was struggling to stay alive. "You have . . . have . . . " He could not finish the sentence.

"Nonsense. I have studied everything I could get my hands on. I know what to do. It is only a matter of proportion."

"Argaen . . ." Sardal gasped, his eyes staring.

It took some time before either the dark elf or Kaz realized that Sardal Crystalthorn was dead. The eyes of the battered elf still stared. Ravenshadow muttered something under his breath and bent down beside the body, obscuring it from the minotaur's eyesight. When he rose and stepped away, Kaz saw that Sardal was no longer there!

The minotaur struggled against the magical hands that held him fast. "What've you done with his body? Saving it for another one of your spells?"

The dark elf turned around and gave him a stony stare. "Sardal Crystalthorn will have a proper burial. We might have been adversaries in the end, but I will honor him still."

Kaz was tempted to say something about his captor's twisted code of honor, but held back when he looked closer at Ravenshadow's face. Killing Sardal had taken more out of the dark elf than Argaen might admit.

"At one time, I meant to share what I found with him," Argaen said quietly. He seemed only marginally aware of the presence of the minotaur. "Sardal was the only one who really tried to help me. I thought he would understand at first." Ravenshadow looked up at his captive, and his face was abruptly bland once more. "That is neither here nor there, however. Time is extremely precious now, and I cannot afford to deal with you properly. I underestimated your amazing strength, Kaz—my experience with your race is very limited. As it stands, I think I must ask you to accompany me. An old friend has been dying to see you." The attempt at sardonic humor sounded flat, even to the dark elf. He turned, glanced at the pile of rubble that had killed Sardal, and then stared at the hole in the ceiling.

Without a word and barely a thought, Argaen Ravenshadow gestured toward Kaz.

The minotaur found himself lifted toward the stone ceiling with frightful speed. Just before the tip of his horns hit the ceiling, the ceiling opened. The opening didn't appear to be like a trapdoor, but rather like a mouth. As he was pushed through to the next floor, Kaz couldn't help but imagine that he was about to be eaten. The feeling was enhanced by the total darkness into which he was thrust. Something caught him around the waist and legs, and he had a nightmarish thought that these were teeth. The mouth closed, but another one opened above him. Kaz saw that what held him were more stone hands.

He was being passed up through the levels of the keep like some unwanted trinket. Kaz was passed through four more levels, each time with the same horrifying rush to the ceiling.

Eventually Kaz's journey came to a halt. His relief at having to face no more oncoming ceilings quickly died when he realized where he was. He was now a prisoner in the chamber of the emerald sphere.

"Here he is, wraith!" shouted Argaen Ravenshadow,

whom Kaz had not seen materialize in the chamber. He was simply there, next to the minotaur, calling out to the creator of the artifact. "Shall I allow him a quick death? I know how much that would madden you!"

The emerald sphere flared violently. Ravenshadow laughed mockingly. "You cannot harm me, even though I know you would like to try! I have a piece of you, so to speak!"

While Kaz watched, puzzled, the dark elf shoved a hand into one of his robe pockets and removed a curved object. In the odd light of the room, it glinted a brilliant green . . . an emerald green. Kaz knew what it was instantly.

Argaen had a chunk of the emerald sphere.

He doubted that the elf could have taken the piece from Galan Dracos directly, and that could only mean that the magic thief had, at some point, scoured the ruins of the renegade mage's stronghold up in the mountains between Hylo and Solamnia. Kaz knew that the knights had not found all of the shattered remnants of the sphere, even with the aid of sorcerers and clerics. It was just too impossible a task. Argaen must have been lucky enough to locate this particular piece.

"To think"—Ravenshadow turned to his prisoner and smiled briefly—"that I originally carried this as some sort of good-luck charm. How true that turned out to be! While I hold this, minotaur, I am shielded from him!"

Shoving the shard back into his pocket, the dark elf stalked up to the emerald sphere. As he neared it, mist began to rise above it, slowly congealing into the vague form of Galan Dracos. The wraith looked from Argaen to Kaz, silent all the while.

It was Ravenshadow who finally spoke. "He is yours! The companion, the friend, of your enemy! The closest you will come to revenge against the Solamnic Knight! Whatever you wish to do with him is up to you, but our bargain stands! First you will show me how to bind the sphere to my will!"

"Come . . . then." The voice made the minotaur's hair stand on end. That voice had haunted his dreams. This was no longer a creature strictly human. When Galan Dracos spoke, his voice was like the wind, seemingly drifting toward the listeners from all around.

The elf took another step toward his prize.

"No! I won't let you do it!" A figure leaped from one of the shadowy corners nearby and landed on Argaen. Kaz struggled, feeling the stone hands loosen as Argaen's concentration broke under the surprising assault. First the minotaur's arms, and then his legs, were free. He started toward the two fighters. The newcomer was Delbin, and Kaz knew that, against Ravenshadow, the kender stood little chance.

No sooner did he think that than the dark elf managed to pull Delbin from him and toss him aside like a rag doll. Somehow Delbin landed on his feet, but that was the only good fortune they had, for immediately Ravenshadow whirled on both of them.

All strength fled from the minotaur's massive frame, and he collapsed without taking another step. Frantically Kaz tried to rise, but it proved too much effort. Oddly, he felt as alert as before. It was only his body that lacked all strength. Delbin was likewise hampered.

Argaen looked them over coldly, then whirled back to face the emerald sphere. "How did that kender get in here?"

"I . . . was not . . . expecting . . . a kender. Neither apparently . . . were you." Dracos sounded annoyed with both Ravenshadow and himself.

Glancing back at the hourglass on the table, the dark elf snarled, "Time is running out! Tell me what I must do, and this time nothing must go wrong!"

"You . . . will not . . . be disappointed."

Kaz blinked, the only physical act he was still capable of. Dracos seemed anxious . . . very anxious.

Raising his hands high in the air, Ravenshadow stared at the emerald sphere. It started to pulsate, slowly at first, then faster and faster as the seconds went by. The elf became enraptured by his work. Slowly Galan Dracos began to dissipate.

Kaz had failed. There was no denying it. He could only watch helplessly as the emerald sphere grew brighter and brighter—so bright, in fact, that the minotaur had to shut his eyes. Thus it was that he did not see exactly what happened next.

In the last seconds, Argaen Ravenshadow faltered. The burning brilliance of the artifact did not bother his eyes, but for some reason he began to blink uncontrollably, regardless.

Outside, Nuitari, the black moon, had only just eclipsed Solinari.

A ghostly laugh reverberated throughout the chamber. The misty form of Galan Dracos no longer hung above the sphere.

With a roar of agony, the dark elf collapsed against the crystalline artifact. The glare died, and Kaz felt life returning to his limbs, all too slowly. Somewhere Delbin groaned.

Ravenshadow pulled away from his prize and looked up to the heavens with a face contorted by numerous vying emotions. He laughed, but that laugh held both pleasure and sorrow. That laugh also held insanity.

His eyes were blood-red.

"I told you, elf, that only through you could I live again!"

The voice was that of Argaen Ravenshadow, but Kaz knew that the eyes, the mind, belonged to Galan Dracos.

This was what the wraith had been waiting for. This was why Dracos had needed the dark elf. The renegade mage had been unable to create more than an insubstantial form for himself, a form ever tied to the emerald sphere.

Argaen, however, had boasted that he was protected against the specter's power thanks to the shard he carried. Kaz believed him, for he doubted that Dracos would have tolerated the magic thief all along if he had had the power to take over his body. What had happened to change things? Ravenshadow had put the shard into his robe pocket; had it slipped out somehow during the struggle with Delbin?

That was it, of course. Galan Dracos had been able to manipulate Argaen toward this moment and then let the kender do his bidding.

Kaz found that he could now raise himself to a sitting position. Dracos, enthralled by the success of his plot, was laughing and laughing. He clutched his newfound body tightly.

"Mistress, mistress, I thank you for your benevolence and this second chance!" roared Galan Dracos.

The minotaur shivered. There was no question as to who the sorcerer's mistress was. Kaz was almost to his feet when the mage remembered him and turned.

"Kaz! Minotaur, I hope you did not think I was going to neglect you!"

"The thought had crossed my mind. Feel free to, human."

Dracos laughed again. That laugh was getting on Kaz's nerves. "I hope you appreciate how precious these last few moments of your life are; I can promise you, from personal experience, that death is not always a relief!"

The minotaur straightened. If the reborn mage was going to kill him, Kaz would die with honor and dignity. "So I gathered. You didn't escape the Dragonqueen after all."

"Not quite. I was trapped in my own creation, but the claws of my mistress reach very far. Though she could not remove me from my selfmade prison, she spoke to me. I still could aid her with her conquest of Krynn, even after her defeat and temporary exile by your belated comrade."

"Temporary?"

"Temporary." Galan Dracos smiled through Ravenshadow's visage. More and more, the elf's body seemed

288

gaunt, and the skin, though it might only have been the minotaur's imagination, appeared a bit scaly. "Tonight, Kaz, you will watch the world welcome Takhisis back to Krynn! Tonight!" He laughed again in that same mocking tone.

The laugh broke off in midstream as two things happened simultaneously. The first was the hourglass, which, without warning, exploded, sending glass shards and bits of sand flying about the room. The other was what at first seemed to be an attack of some illness so virulent that all of a sudden Dracos pitched forward and fell to one knee, screaming.

"Cease . . . your . . . struggling! This is . . . my body now!"

Kaz scanned the room hurriedly, seeking something he could use against Dracos, or Ravenshadow, or whoever was controlling the body.

"Kaz!" Delbin rushed to his side.

"Get out of here, Delbin! Go and find the others! I've got to stop him if I can!"

"He's got your battle-axe, Kaz! I saw it! That one called Dracos has it, only it's invisible now, so you can't see it—"

"Where? Just point!"

"I don't know. He hid it!"

Eyeing the agonizing figure of the elf, Kaz held his breath and concentrated on the axe. Maybe, just maybe, with both Dracos and Ravenshadow fighting for control of the body, the spell on the battle-axe would be weakening. If so . . .

Delbin whistled. "How'd you do that? Can you do it again? That's a neat trick!"

As Kaz gazed down at the dwarven axe, new sounds reached the minotaur's ears. The sounds of battle had returned. The barrier that Ravenshadow had formed with the guidance of Dracos was no more.

*   *   *   *   *

Thrusting a sword through an overanxious opponent, Darius looked up and saw a strange dull haze surround the keep. At first he thought it was some new addition to the spell that Argaen Ravenshadow had evidently cast, but then he spotted several figures in the distance. At least three of them had their arms raised and were staring intently at the keep.

Another man came at him with an axe, and he put up his sword to block the blow as best he could. Something bright flashed in his adversary's eyes, and the man faltered.

"Do something!" Tesela shouted from behind him.

Darius realized that she had saved his life. While his opponent tried to move back out of range until his eyes cleared, the knight urged his mount forward, reached under the other's frantic swings, and ran the man through at the neck.

"Darius! Look at the keep!"

He did—and covered his eyes as the spell of the other mages reacted with the barrier spell and the entire region was lit up brightly.

When he dared look again, the barrier was gone. The keep was open to attack.

"Stay close to me!" he shouted at Tesela. "This is our chance to rescue Kaz!"

With renewed morale, the knights surged forward.

* * * * *

"You have . . . your god-spawned battle-axe . . . again! No matter! That will not . . . help you now!"

Dracos had recovered somewhat, and now pointed a finger at his adversary. Kaz was thrown back, but he managed to keep a grip on his weapon. He landed on a table, crushing several tomes and breaking the table itself in two. The minotaur was only slightly stunned; he had suffered worse blows in tavern brawls with drunken, hateful humans.

Dracos swore bitterly and swerved toward the emerald sphere.

Kaz looked at his battle-axe, momentarily debating whether to throw it or not. He might succeed in striking the sphere, but there was no guarantee that it would shatter.

Galan Dracos made it to the artifact, but he paused there, oddly indecisive. He seemed to be of two minds, and Kaz sourly reminded himself that he *was* indeed of two minds. What Argaen Ravenshadow lacked in sorcerous ability, he more than made up for in willpower, and he was not about to surrender his existence to Dracos. Ravenshadow was an elf, and he had centuries of training behind him, something the human mage had evidently not taken into account.

Kaz took one look at the sphere and then at the struggling sorcerer. The minotaur hefted his battle-axe. Perhaps he could get two targets with one blow.

The doorways were suddenly brimming with onrushing soldiers.

Cursing, Kaz turned to meet them. He should have realized that it was only a matter of time before guards were summoned to investigate the commotion.

The first man came at him, a spear thrust barely missing Kaz's shoulder. This man, too, underestimated the reach of the minotaur, and Kaz brought the axe around, ripping a great gap in the human's chest. The man tumbled to the floor as two others moved closer. They were armed with longswords. Behind them, a third man, clad in the dark armor of one of the Black Guard, saw the crazed mage and shouted Dracos's name.

Another guard went down under the minotaur's onslaught, only now two more joined in. Against four, Kaz was hard pressed. These were not goblins; these were veteran warriors.

Kaz couldn't see what was happening, but the guardsman who had called out the mage's name now gave a shout and ran toward his master, sword at the ready.

That relieved the minotaur of one opponent, but the other three still kept him at bay.

"Give me that, you little vermin!" a voice shouted from the other part of the room. Kaz could spare no time to glance back, but he could think of only one person the guardsman could be shouting at. In his present danger, he had forgotten that Delbin was still in the chamber. The kender was quick and armed with both a knife and a sling, but Kaz thought less of Delbin's chances than he did of his own.

"Stop him!" Ravenshadow—*Dracos*, Kaz corrected himself—shouted.

The minotaur had no time to wonder what his companion was doing, for in the next instant, a huge form broke through the roof, sending massive sections of stone tumbling down on everyone. A guard in the corridor outside screamed as he was crushed by the stone. Kaz and his opponents leaped away from one another as a particularly large chunk fell between them, collapsing the floor and falling through to the next level.

Above him, the stone dragon opened its mouth in a silent roar.

One of the guards sought to take advantage of the moment and jumped across the gap. Kaz turned and caught him as he was landing. Before the man could secure his footing, Kaz shoved him backward with the top of his battle-axe. Cursing, the guard fell into the hole.

Temporarily free, Kaz located Delbin. The kender was backed into a corner by the ebony-armored guardsman. In Delbin's hands was a barely visible item, Ravenshadow's shard. Off to one side and still near the emerald sphere, the two minds within the dark elf's body continued their struggle. Occasionally words would bubble forth.

The stone dragon finally worked its way into the chamber, leaving a gaping hole in its wake, and proceeded to go wild. The one opponent still left to the minotaur screamed as a massive paw crushed him into the floor. The beast's tail swished back and forth madly. Whichever of the battling mages had summoned the beast barely controlled it now; it was possible that no one really did anymore.

That left fighting it up to Kaz—and Delbin.

The kender cried out. Kaz saw the guardsman strike the small figure down, but the dragon chose that moment to swipe at him with a huge rocky paw. The minotaur was buffeted and fell to one knee. The battle-axe almost slipped from his grip.

Rage washed over Kaz. He saw the black figure lean over the still form of the kender, take the shard, and give it quickly to Dracos-Ravenshadow. He saw the elven body straighten and knew that, with that shard, one of them had finally triumphed.

The stone dragon swiped at Kaz again, and this time the minotaur, still on one knee, defended himself with the dwarven axe.

Honor's Face cleaved through half the paw without even slowing.

Kaz gaped, momentarily at a loss. The unliving leviathan reared back and mouthed a silent roar of anguish. It could not perish, not in the sense that a living creature could, but even this creature had a sense of self-preservation.

Small wonder, then, that the beast feared the axe. If it were used properly, Kaz could fight the stone dragon. He should have realized before, especially after his first attempt at chopping his chains off. He remembered how easily the axe had cut into the wall.

The massive creature stumbled backward, in the process creating more destruction. What remained of the ceiling was weakened even further. The wings of the beast flapped madly as it tried to rise from the chamber. One lucky blow caught the guardsman who had struck down Delbin. The hapless warrior went flying against—nearly *through*—one of the far walls, and Kaz knew he was dead.

"Kill him! I command you!" Crouched over the emerald sphere like a protective mother, Dracos-Ravenshadow screamed at the stone leviathan. Kaz could see that he was slowly accumulating power with the aid of the magical device.

Reluctant but unable to defy the command, the false dragon snapped at the valiant figure before it. Kaz held his ground and defended himself again, this time swinging the axe in a downward arc. The beast tried to halt the descent of its massive head, but its momentum worked against it. Kaz struck it squarely on the muzzle, the axe not stopping until it had split both the upper and lower portion of the jaws in two. A fault, beginning at the cut, now ran back through much of the creature's head. The stone dragon staggered drunkenly. Its movements became stiffer, and Kaz realized that the magic was weakening.

Encouraged, Kaz made a move toward the robed figure, his true adversary, regardless of whether the human or magic thief now inhabited that mortal shell.

As Kaz moved, an entire section of the floor gave way. Into the chamber beneath went one of the dead guards, several tons of stone, a table and the artifacts spread on top of it—and Honor's Face. Kaz himself barely succeeded in catching hold of what remained of the floor. With a tremendous effort, he tried to pull himself up.

"I wish I could take the time to kill you slowly," someone with Ravenshadow's voice uttered madly, "but I fear time is precious right now."

The floor crumbled a bit more, and Kaz frantically changed his hold. The stone dragon loomed over him.

Dangling by one hand, he looked down at the jagged rubble below, knowing that the fall would surely kill him. His eyes darted to the beast above him and at the robed form stepping around the emerald sphere. His eyes burned green.

"I have the power now to form yet another shield. By the time they break that one, I will have the strength to deal with them permanently! You can die knowing that you have failed! I'm only sorry that I will not be able to witness your death!"

To the stone dragon, Dracos-Ravenshadow shouted, "For the last time, kill him and be done!"

The broken but still deadly jaws of the stone dragon opened wide and the beast lunged. As its head came down, Kaz used every bit of his will to summon Honor's Face.

Instantly the axe was in his hand. Kaz looked up at on-rushing death and muttered, "Paladine, guide my hand, or we're both in for it!"

It may be that Paladine did guide his hand. It may have just been the desperate strength of the minotaur, who knew that this was the end, one way or another. It may have been pure luck.

His swing was timed perfectly; it caught the stone leviathan directly in the head near the fault. The battle-axe sank deep into hard rock, and Kaz was nearly flung across the room as the huge beast shook prodigiously. The minotaur landed soundly on the rubble-strewn floor, screaming as his left arm and leg were twisted grotesquely beneath him.

The axe was wedged in the stone dragon's head, which was now nearly split in two. The leviathan made one feeble attempt to knock the weapon free, but its movements were jerky. The spell could no longer hold together. As Kaz watched through dazed eyes, the stone dragon stiffened completely, teetered momentarily, and then fell over.

If there had been any poetic justice, Kaz decided, Dracos-Ravenshadow would have turned at that very moment and seen the portent of his doom. His eyes would have widened, and he would have had time only to mouth a scream.

Instead, the dragon toppled over onto both mage and sphere. The robed figure never saw death coming.

In the end, Kaz could still not say who it was he had

fought—Dracos, Ravenshadow, or some unholy combination of the two. What mattered was that the unholy threat was dead. Kaz blinked his vision clear and looked again. A single twisted arm was all that remained visible of his enemy. He smiled.

Oceans of relief washed over him, and in their wake came the blissful nothingness of unconsciousness.

Chapter 23

At times his life seemed little more than collapsing and waking, and never more so than now. Kaz had visions of elegant, somber-looking elves surrounding his body. He dreamed of being carried through the mountains by a huge furred creature that might have been Greymir. Bennett and Darius were standing near him while Tesela prayed for his recovery. He, in turn, insisted they find Delbin, who, Kaz thought, might be dead. Each vision was punctuated by timeless intervals of darkness in which the minotaur heard voices, some real, some not. Briefly he dreamed of the overwhelming presence of the Dragonqueen.

The Dragonqueen's presence faded abruptly as another voice overwhelmed it. Kaz's confused mind knew that it could only be Paladine, but the voice sounded very much like that of Huma. After that dream, he found he was able to sleep better.

At last voices, actual voices, brought him back to the world of the living. Kaz opened his eyes and found himself lying on a mat in a large tent, surrounded by several arguing figures.

"They have no right to him, milord!" Darius was shouting.

"It would be a stain on our honor if we did not allow them to present their cause!" Bennett replied. "Besides, it is Kaz who must decide!"

Tesela was also in the room, but at the moment, she was saying nothing. Watching the others with mild amusement was an elf. Kaz had to look hard, for the elf reminded him greatly of Sardal Crystalthorn. The newcomer noticed that the minotaur was awake and inclined his head slightly in greeting. He was one of the elves from Kaz's memory.

The cleric turned abruptly, and her eyes grew wide as she saw that her charge was awake. She rushed over to his side and put her arms around him. "Kaz! Thank Mishakal you're going to be all right!"

"Unnh! I'll need your goddess's services again if you don't ease up!"

The two knights broke off their argument and greeted him profusely. They were acting as if he had almost died. He was about to question them when a fifth figure entered the tent.

Delbin's face lit up, and the kender went bounding over to his friend. "Kaz! You're alive! They said you might die because you lost so much blood, but I knew you were strong, and did you see what they did with the big green thing in the chamber? How come it didn't shatter? I mean, Argaen shattered pretty good when the dragon fell on him, but the sphere was okay—"

"That accursed thing is still in one piece?"

The elf spoke. He stood with arms crossed and seemed

298

to be leaning back, though there was nothing to support him. He wore a robe of white. "The abomination created by the renegade Galan Dracos has been removed from Argaen Ravenshadow's stronghold. We cannot allow it to be returned to Vingaard, not after what happened the first time."

"Speaking for my uncle, the Grand Master," Bennett added, "I have agreed to turn it over to the elves. They intend to bury it in a secret place far, far below the surface of Krynn. Farther than even the dwarves would ever dare dig."

"Why bury it? It should be destroyed!"

"We have tried." For the first time, the elf seemed annoyed. "We have failed, though I cannot say what still holds it together now that Galan Dracos is truly dead. Should we find a way to destroy it in the future, we will do so. The emerald sphere by itself is not dangerous. It is only, as you know, a means of drawing power from other sources, especially chaos."

"No one will ever use it again," Bennett finished.

Kaz nodded, but he was not completely satisfied. He fervently hoped the emerald sphere would stay where the elves buried it, at least until Kaz had gone to join his ancestors.

"The enemy's morale failed when they saw that no one defended inside the keep anymore," Darius offered. "Many are dead or captured, and the rest are scattered loosely about the mountain chain. They will never be a coherent force again. That leaves the ogres in the north with no allies."

"When Solamnia is stronger, we will deal with them," Bennett commented.

Greatly relieved, Kaz turned his attention to Delbin. "What about you? I thought you were dead! I saw the guardsman strike you!"

Tesela, who moved to stand beside Darius, explained, "He only had a large bump on his head. Delbin must've been struck with the flat of the blade. Judging by what was going on, I'd say that his attacker didn't have time to be bothered with killing a kender."

"How fortunate." Kaz patted his companion's back. "I want to thank you for coming after me, although you shouldn't have. It was a very brave, very heroic thing to do."

"The kender has explained as well as possible what happened to Galan Dracos and Argaen Ravenshadow," the unknown elf interrupted. "An astounding and horrible conclusion. Branchala be praised that you were able to bring about his—*their*—death before it was too late. There is much I must discuss with my people when I return." A strained look passed across the elf's otherwise bland features. "Tell me, minotaur. Sardal Crystalthorn . . . did he die well?"

"He did."

"We have recovered the body. I shall leave you now. I know you have many pressing matters to deal with." The elf nodded to each of them and departed without another word.

Kaz rose haltingly. "What does that mean?"

The humans hesitated, but Delbin, in a sudden reversal of mood, worriedly replied, "They're out there, Kaz! All of them! There's a real ugly one—I guess he must be the leader—and there's even an ogre! You've got to get away before—"

From without, a deep voice bellowed, "Come out, coward! Come out and face your people! Face justice! Face honor!"

Kaz stiffened. "When did *they* get here?"

Bennett turned grim. "About an hour ago. They have already been to Vingaard, Kaz, and my uncle deemed their quest honorable enough to tell them where we were heading."

"He should never have—" Tesela began, but Kaz quieted her with a wave of his hand.

"The Grand Master did what I'd do, human. I've run from them too long. I can't keep doing that forever. Just once, I'd like to have a little peace and know that no one is trying to track me down."

"If you need someone to back you up, Kaz"—Darius gripped the handle of his sword—"I owe you my life, and I consider you a friend."

"No, this is something I've got to do alone. It's a matter of honor." Kaz looked around for the dwarven battle-axe and then ruefully looked in his left hand, where he was already holding it. The others looked at it in surprise; none of them had noticed it before.

Bennett eyed it with professional interest. "Where did you get *that*?"

"From a friend." Kaz hefted the axe and took a deep breath.

"Before you step out there," Bennett added, "I think you might like to know that they have spent much of the time arguing about you. There seems to be a difference of opinion."

"I'll keep that in mind." The minotaur departed from the tent.

Silence reigned as Kaz stepped out of the tent into the open. Several knights paused in their duties to watch the confrontation.

About a dozen minotaurs stood before him, gathered in a half-circle. Two he recognized for certain—the brother and sister, Hecar and Helati, respectively. Kaz allowed himself a moment to admire Helati, who was easily the most attractive of the handful of females in the party, then turned to face a scarred menace who was the apparent leader.

"I am Scurn. I am leader."

A movement by Hecar indicated a difference of opinion, but Scurn deigned not to notice it. Kaz concentrated on the disfigured minotaur who stood before him, knowing that if he was the leader, it was because he was the most powerful fighter.

Scurn seemed to require a reply.

"You know who I am."

Scurn's eyes burned. There would be no dealing reasonably with this one, Kaz realized sourly. The scarred minotaur could barely contain himself.

Someone moved behind the line of minotaurs. It was the ogre. Kaz tried to make out the ugly visage, but the ogre kept himself at least partly obscured.

Eyes sweeping over Kaz, Scurn said, "You are accused of murder, the murder of the ogre captain you served under. Struck down from behind during the confusion of battle, he had no chance to defend himself. Our dislike for their kind is no secret, but such an act was a dishonor to your clan and to your people, and a crime in any civilized part of the world." The scarred minotaur gave him a nasty smile. "That murder also required the breaking of an honor-binding oath of loyalty sworn before the elders and your emperor, a terrible deed unheard of, and was compounded by your cowardice when you fled rather than face proper punishment. When your crimes became known to the elders and the emperor, a proclamation for your capture and judgment was issued, and we were sent out to bring you to justice. Will you admit your guilt? Will you save what honor you have left?"

"He deserved to die," Kaz said quite bluntly. He was only now remembering how long-winded his people could be when speaking of matters of honor.

"You broke your oath and brought dishonor on your clan—our clan. The dishonor was greater because of who you were, a champion of the arena, one who might have brought the crown of emperor back to our clan. You ran, shaming all of our ancestors who gave their lives in combat. You did not even face your victim in fair combat, but instead slew him from *behind!*"

"Untrue," Kaz replied coldly.

"You have no honor!" Scurn intoned.

"Life without honor is not worth living," the other minotaurs chanted automatically in unison. It seemed to Kaz that some of them, however, spoke the words with little conviction.

"You are a proven coward."

"A coward weakens the race." This time, more than one hesitated in the recital.

Hecar threw down his axe. "This is a travesty! I will not take part in it! It would be a stain on our own honor!"

Scurn turned his murderous glare from Kaz to the other minotaur. "Know your place, Hecar!"

"I know you could easily defeat me, Scurn, but I would consider myself a coward if I did not speak the truth! You know what Kaz has done this time!"

"It changes nothing!"

Helati stepped up and joined her brother. "It means *everything!* I find it difficult to condemn one who has proven his courage and strength as Kaz has done! The Grand Master's own nephew calls him one of the most honorable comrades he has fought with. I question more the myriad tangles in our code of honor that make us slave-soldiers to *his* kind!"

The ogre stiffened, knowing that Helati was speaking of him, but he stayed in the background nonetheless. It was surprising, Kaz thought, that his accuser was even here.

"Present deeds do not make up for past crimes, Helati! You would also do well to remember your place!" Scurn waved a huge, clawed hand, as if wiping the conversation away. "We waste enough time! Either accept your fate, Kaz, and return with us, or we will settle things now!"

"Then let's settle it now." Kaz threw his battle-axe to the earth. "I've no time to make a weapon with my own hands, as custom dictates, so I'll make do with my hands alone."

Kaz heard footfalls behind him and knew that the others had followed him out of the tent. The humans wouldn't understand what was going on. Kaz had chosen to face his fate, and that meant a trial by combat, with the odds greatly slanted against him. Under other circumstances, he would have been allowed a few days to prepare himself and to fashion a weapon from the land around him; only a self-made weapon was allowed to the condemned. Although technically Kaz was not sentenced to death, the odds were so great that few facing such a trial ever survived. It was intended that way. Dying in a battle against incredible odds was one of few accepted ways for a minotaur to regain his honor in the eyes of his people.

After five years, Kaz was only now understanding the extent of his race's madness and hypocrisy. Little good it would do him.

"He's going to fight all of them?" Tesela asked someone unbelievingly. "He'll be slaughtered!"

"This is minotaur law, cleric," Bennett replied, though it was evident from his tone that he liked the situation as little as she did. "I cannot interfere. His honor is at stake."

"His *life* is at stake!" she muttered, but quieted after that.

Kaz was relieved. He was afraid that someone would try to interfere. Vastly outnumbered as they were, the minotaurs would cut a bloody swath through his companions if they were forced to defend themselves. He wanted no one else to be injured, much less killed. This was his battle alone.

By rights, the minotaurs should have spread out, encircling Kaz. One at a time or in groups, they were then to attack until either he was dead or triumphant.

Scurn looked at the others in open frustration. "Take your places!"

Hecar, who had still not recovered his weapon, stepped away. "I withdraw from this group. I find the murder of which Kaz stands accused questionable despite the evidence. I came because honor was at stake, but I see nothing here to make me believe that Kaz has shamed our clan and our race. He is no coward, and after the trials he has faced—whose outcome has undoubtedly affected the future of our people as well as the lesser races—I believe he has redeemed himself, if he ever truly needed to."

Helati joined her brother. "I will not take part in this travesty, either. Kaz broke a sacred oath of loyalty, yes, but I question whether those he swore it to were ever worthy of that oath in the first place. Honor has many faces, but I never saw one that resembled an ogre."

With mounting rage, Scurn looked left and right as others of his companions abandoned him. Of the entire party, only two minotaurs stayed with the disfigured leader. He looked at them and roared, "Get back with the rest of them! I'll fight him alone! You heard me!"

Hesitantly, the two stepped back. Scurn, smiling nastily, moved within an arm's length of Kaz. The scarred minotaur was an inch or two taller than he and carried a battle-axe, a monstrous weapon far larger than Honor's Face, a true minotaur's axe. Still staring at Kaz, Scurn threw the axe aside.

"I've no need of weapons to defeat you!"

Kaz snorted in wry amusement. "This is what you want, is it?"

"Pray to the ancestors while you still have time."

"I'll give thanks to them that any blood they shared between our lines is so far in the past that I don't even have to consider you one of my kin."

Scurn bared his teeth. "Whenever you are ready . . ."

There was no signal to begin. The two combatants merely tensed and, in unspoken agreement, threw themselves at each other. Scurn caught hold of Kaz's left arm with his right and tried to drive a stiff hand below Kaz's rib cage. Kaz caught the hand just in time and forced it to one side. With his free hand, Kaz shoved his opponent back.

The two minotaurs separated. Again they came together. Kaz tried to put a foot around the back of one of Scurn's legs, but the other minotaur would have none of it. Instead of catching his opponent's leg and tripping him backward to the ground, Kaz suddenly found himself balancing on one foot as Scurn caught the other with his hand and pulled it up. Only a quick twist by Kaz prevented him from falling, but the scarred minotaur now had an advantage in balance and took it, charging into Kaz's side headfirst.

Kaz grunted in pain as the tip of one of Scurn's horns caught him in his midsection. He put a restraining hand against the other's head and kept him at bay. Blood trickled down his legs.

While Scurn sought to impale him, Kaz reached up with his other hand and chopped downward as hard as possible. His first blow hit Scurn on the head, a fairly hard spot on a minotaur. His second blow, however, landed on the softest part of the back of his opponent's neck.

Scurn cursed and pulled himself away with amazing strength. Kaz refused to let up and charged, one hand held high in front of him. He took hold of one of Scurn's horns while the other minotaur was still backing away, and he turned. The motion pulled his adversary forward to the ground, muzzle first.

Kaz leapt down, but Scurn was already rolling away, and all the former got for his efforts was a faceful of dirt and a sharp rattle through every bone in his body. Both minotaurs moved away, quickly rising to their feet. Scurn was breathing heavily, but not because of exhaustion. He was caught up in the feverish excitement of the fight. He was one of those who lived for battle. Kaz, an older veteran, eyed him with distaste and a little shame; he, too, had once been like the disfigured minotaur.

Again and again they struggled, neither gaining much advantage. After ten long minutes of constant engagement, both were battered and bleeding, but ready for the next round. The other minotaurs and several of the knights cheered them on.

One who did not share the mood of those around him was the ogre, Molok. In the beginning, he had watched eagerly, hoping for a quick humiliation and death for

Kaz. That no longer appeared possible. Scurn might even lose, and then Kaz would see Molok and know him for who he was.

The ogre rubbed the side of his head, thinking of where Kaz had struck his brother down all those years ago. Most races believed ogres had almost as little love for one another as they did for outsiders, but such was not true. Like the minotaurs, ogres had some belief in clan, and Molok's brother had been all he had in the way of blood family. With the dragons gone and Takhisis exiled from Krynn, it was all the ogres could do to keep from being overrun by their enemies and former slaves. They had no time for a single ogre's vengeance. But vengeance was an ogre trait, and Molok, devious and determined even for one of his kind, at last hit upon a plan that would not only end in the death of Kaz, but also reveal the minotaur's complete dishonor in the eyes of the minotaur race. Honor meant little to Molok, but he knew that Kaz's people lived and died for it. To kill *and* shame his brother's murderer was the best revenge he could ask. The mage he had paid to create a false truthcrystal had done his work well. The minotaurs, both condescending and ignorant concerning magic, had taken the bait.

All that work would be for naught, however, if Kaz lived.

Of course the minotaurs had expropriated the ogre's weapons. Now there were other choices, however, for some of the horned ones, in their rebellion against Scurn, had laid aside their own weapons. Molok simply had to lay his hands on the proper one. . . .

As strong and skilled as Scurn was, he had not faced nearly as many challenges in his life as Kaz had. Experience finally began to show as the latter struck more and more telling blows. The scarred minotaur backed away, shaking his head, but Kaz would not let up. He caught Scurn's arm while it was still raised in defense and twisted it inward, forcing his opponent to turn with it or have it broken. As the other minotaur turned, he came in line with Kaz's knee.

Kaz bent his leg and swung the knee upward. He did not strike Scurn in the face, as some would have, but rather on the unprotected neck. His kneecap caught Scurn directly in the throat, and the younger minotaur choked. While his adversary fell to his knees and tried desperately to breathe, Kaz put both hands together and hit him squarely in the lower jaw. The first blow, combined with his other injuries, stunned Scurn. He sat back and tried to focus on Kaz, his breathing labored.

Everyone waited for the final blow. It was all Kaz needed to vindicate himself in the eyes of his fellows. He raised his clenched hands high . . . and then lowered them, unclenching them as he did.

He stared at the other minotaurs. "No more! To continue would be dishonorable. I will not strike down a defenseless opponent."

"No!" Scurn croaked, but he could do no more than shake a fist. Kaz's knee kick to his throat had been the deciding blow; he could barely breathe. "Kill me! I'm shamed!"

Kaz snorted in disgust. "That's your problem." He turned his attention back to the rest of his people. "Is there anyone else who wishes to challenge me? Have I proven myself? If so, I—"

There was a commotion to his right, and Kaz whirled to see Helati standing there, a grim but satisfied look on her face. In her hand, she held a knife. Little more than the handle was visible, for the entire length of the blade—and minotaurs use extremely long blades—was buried in the chest of the ogre, who stood gaping at Kaz with hateful but dying eyes. A short sword, hidden between the ogre's massive arm and chest, slipped to the ground.

The ogre, gasping uselessly, collapsed.

Minotaurs and humans turned, stunned and uncomfortable. Bennett swore as Kaz had never heard him swear, surprising many. In the excitement of the ritual combat, no one had paid attention to the ogre. No one had expected a lone ogre to attempt anything, surrounded as he was by countless armed humans and more than a few minotaurs.

Helati wiped her blade off on the ogre's corpse. "I thought he was moving around to get a better view. I didn't think even an ogre could be so suicidal. He really wanted you dead."

"I should have known not to give an ogre the benefit of honor," Bennett interjected. "Their kind could never know anything but killing."

"Less than six years ago, Bennett, you would've said the same thing of me." Kaz studied the face of the ogre, still twisted in hate despite death. His eyes widened in rueful surprise. "In the case of this one, however, I think you're justified. Their ugly faces are all pretty much the same, but I think this ogre and the one I'm supposed to have murdered are blood kin. There are clan markings that look familiar even after all this time." He grunted ruefully. "I'd no idea that ogres had such loyalty to one another."

"The truthcrystal—" one of the minotaurs started to mutter.

Kaz shook his head at the simpleness of a race that prides itself on its supposed superiority. "If the rest of you had seen as much sorcery as I have, you'd have long ago realized that any good mage could create one with a false image."

No one replied, but Hecar nodded. Kaz was glad to see that there was at least one reasonable mind among them. He looked down at Scurn, who was still kneeling in the dirt. Now that he had fought Kaz and lost, he seemed not to have any purpose anymore.

"I take it I'm free to go," Kaz finally said. No one contradicted him. Kaz looked down at Scurn one last time. "Someone see to him. He fought a good battle. His death would've been a waste."

Without another word, he turned and walked back to the tent, stopping only to retrieve his battle-axe.

His friends, seeing the set expression on his face, said nothing. Even Delbin remained quiet.

Only when he was back in the tent, alone, did Kaz relax. Exhaling sharply, he threw his battle-axe on top of the mat where he had slept and, smiling tiredly, whispered to himself, "At last!"

Chapter 24

BENNETT WAS STAYING IN THE SOUTH TO COORDINATE
things with the keeps in that general region, cleaning up
what little resistance remained and resupplying Vingaard with both men and materials. He had chosen Darius as his liaison. Tesela remained with the knights as
well. There were injuries to heal, she explained to Kaz,
but he knew that she and Darius shared a mutual interest
in one another.

Bennett wanted to provide Kaz with an escort to Vingaard Keep, where he swore that his uncle would honor
the minotaur with the highest decorations an outsider
could receive. Kaz thanked him, but declined that offer
and others, except Bennett's offer of strong horses for
each of the minotaurs.

As for his own people, Kaz saw them off the very next morning. Scurn was in no condition to lead the party; he was one of those who had lived believing in his invincibility, and with that illusion shattered, he seemed to have nothing left. The others were surprised when Kaz refused to return with them. They had grown accustomed to thinking that the only reason he roamed throughout Ansalon was to escape his shame. Only two of them could understand his desire to travel and live among the "lesser" races.

Hecar and his sister Helati were staying behind as well. Kaz was pleased to have them, especially Helati, who attracted his eye. The smiles she returned gave him hope for the future.

At the moment, Kaz walked with Bennett toward where the other two minotaurs were preparing the mounts. Kaz and Bennett had talked much during the morning, and there was a deeper respect, a deeper friendship between the knight and the minotaur, than there had ever been before.

"Where will you go next?" Bennett asked.

"I don't really know. I think I'll let them decide," Kaz replied, indicating the other two. "As long as it's peaceful, that's all I ask."

Bennett smiled slightly. "You would get bored in a matter of days. You live for challenge."

Kaz grunted. "Maybe, but not as much as I used to. I've had enough to last me for some time."

Helati looked up, saw Kaz, and smiled. He could not help but smile back.

"Is she . . . pretty?" the knight asked quietly, almost reluctant to broach such a personal matter.

"One of the most beautiful females I've ever seen."

"Beauty is truly in the eye of the beholder, then."

"We're ready," Helati called out to them.

"Mount up. I'll be with you in a moment." He reached out and shook hands with Bennett. Kaz gave him a toothy smile. "May Paladine watch your backside."

"Yours as well, Kaz."

"Kaz! Wait up! I think I've got everything, but people keep asking me to return things that don't belong to me even though I don't know how they got into my pockets and where they—"

"Take a breath, Delbin." The kender, leading his pony by its reins, hurried over to the others.

"You're taking him with you?" Bennett's expression showed relief at the prospect of the kender leaving his camp, but puzzlement that anyone would want to travel with one of Delbin's race.

"Someone has to watch over him." There was genuine affection for the kender in Kaz's eyes.

"Do you think that three minotaurs are enough?" Bennett asked.

Kaz shook his head in a display of mock sorrow. "I doubt it."

The minotaur mounted, and as he did, Bennett had a good look at the dwarven battle-axe that Kaz had hooked securely into his back harness. It seemed to glisten.

Assuring himself that the others, especially Delbin, were ready, Kaz looked down at the human one more time. His mood grew serious.

"Keep the knighthood vigilant, Bennett. Takhisis is out there, far beyond Krynn, but she has her eye on our home. Someday she might find a way to return to Krynn without the likes of demons such as Galan Dracos or fools such as Argaen Ravenshadow. That's who we really fought—her, not a mad mage or a magic thief."

"We have learned, Kaz. We will be more careful."

"I hope so." With an abrupt change of emotion, he turned with a smile to Helati and asked, "Well, where would you like to go first?"

She looked at her brother, then returned her gaze to Kaz. "You mentioned something about the icy regions to the south. . . ."

"South it is, then!" Kaz saluted Bennett and winked.

"It should be fairly quiet down there this time of year!"

The human chuckled and watched as the minotaur led his companions away. Kaz looked back once and waved. Bennett silently wished him luck. With a kender riding alongside him, and with Kaz's own propensity for getting into trouble, the knight was certain he would need it.

Bennett almost wished he were going along.

The Minotaur Wars

Richard A. Knaak

A new trilogy featuring the minotaur race that
continues the story from the *New York Times*
best-selling War of Souls trilogy!

Now available in paperback!
NIGHT OF BLOOD
Volume One

As the War of Souls spreads, a terrible, bloody
coup led by the ambitious General Hotak and
his wife, the High Priestess Nephera, overtakes
the minotaur empire. With legions of soldiers
and the unearthly magic of the Forerunners
at his command, the new emperor turns
his sights towards Ansalon. But not all his
enemies lie dead...

February 2004

New in hardcover!
TIDES OF BLOOD
Volume Two

Making a bold pact with the ogres, and with the
assurances of the mysterious warrior-woman
Mina sweetly ringing in his ears, the minotaur
emperor Hotak decides to invade Ansalon. But
betrayal comes from the least expected quarters,
and an escaped slave called Faros, the last of
the blood of the lawful emperor, stirs up a fresh,
vengeance-driven rebellion.

April 2004

The Ergoth Trilogy

Paul B. Thompson & Tonya C. Cook

Explore the history of the ancient **Dragonlance**® world!

THE WIZARD'S FATE
Volume Two

The old Emperor is dead, sending shock
waves throughout the Ergoth Empire. Dark
forces gather as two brothers vie bitterly for the
throne. Key to the struggle for succession are
the rogue sorcerer Mandes and peasant general
Lord Tolandruth—sworn enemies of one
another—and the noble lady Tol loves, whose
first loyalty is to her husband, the Crown Prince.

February 2004

A HERO'S JUSTICE
Volume Three

The Ergoth Empire has been invaded on two
fronts, and the teeming horde streaming across
the plain is no human army. As the warriors
of Ergoth reel back, defeated and broken, the
cry goes up far and wide, "Where is Lord
Tolandruth?!" Banished by Emperor Ackal V, no
one had seen Tol in more than six years. To save
Ergoth, Egrin Raemel's son rides forth to find Tol
and forge an alliance between a kender queen,
an aging beauty, and a lost and brilliant general.

December 2004

A WARRIOR'S JOURNEY
Volume One
Available Now